D1079085

Madame Serpent

JEAN PLAIDY

arrow books

Published by Arrow Books in 2006

5 7 9 10 8 6 4

Copyright © Jean Plaidy, 1951

Initial lettering copyright © Stephen Raw, 2005

The Estate of Eleanor Hibbert has asserted its right
to have Jean Plaidy identified as the author of this work.

This book is sold subject to the condition that it shall not, by way of trade or otherwise,
be lent, resold, hired out, or otherwise circulated without the publisher's prior consent
in any form of binding or cover other than that in which it is published and
without a similar condition including this condition being imposed
on the subsequent purchaser.

First published in Great Britain in 1952 by
Robert Hale Ltd.
Random House, 20 Vauxhall Bridge Road,
London SW1V 2SA

www.rbooks.co.uk

Addresses for companies within The Random House Group Limited
can be found at: www.randomhouse.co.uk/offices.htm

The Random House Group Limited Reg. No. 954009

A CIP catalogue record for this book
is available from the British Library

ISBN 9780099493174

The Random House Group Limited supports The Forest Stewardship
Council (FSC), the leading international forest certification organisation.
All our titles that are printed on Greenpeace approved FSC certified paper
carry the FSC logo. Our paper procurement policy can be found at:
www.rbooks.co.uk/environment

Typeset by SX Composing DTP, Rayleigh, Essex
Printed and bound in Great Britain by
CPI Cox & Wyman, Reading, RG1 8EX

✢ Contents ✢

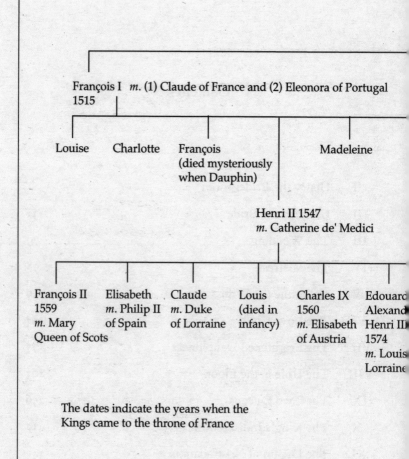

François I   *m.* (1) Claude of France and (2) Eleonora of Portugal
1515

Louise   Charlotte   François   Madeleine
                                   (died mysteriously
                                   when Dauphin)

Henri II 1547
m. Catherine de' Medici

François II   Elisabeth   Claude   Louis   Charles IX   Edouard
1559   *m.* Philip II *m.* Duke   (died in   1560   Alexand
m. Mary   of Spain   of Lorraine   infancy)   *m.* Elisabeth Henri II
Queen of Scots   of Austria   1574
                                                                         m. Louis
                                                                         Lorraine

The dates indicate the years when the
Kings came to the throne of France

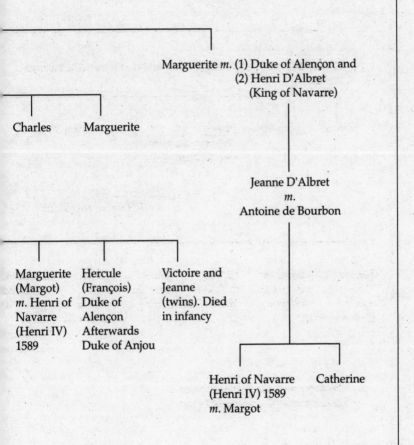

Marguerite *m.* (1) Duke of Alençon and
(2) Henri D'Albret
(King of Navarre)

Charles   Marguerite

Jeanne D'Albret
m.
Antoine de Bourbon

Marguerite   Hercule   Victoire and
(Margot)   (François)   Jeanne
m. Henri of Duke of   (twins). Died
Navarre   Alençon   in infancy
(Henri IV)   Afterwards
1589   Duke of Anjou

Henri of Navarre   Catherine
(Henri IV) 1589
m. Margot

❧ Chapter I ❧

HENRY THE BRIDEGROOM

At Amboise the French court was *en fête*. It usually was, for the King himself had said that if he would live peacefully with the French, and have them love him, he must keep them amused for two days in each week or they would find some more dangerous employment.

The Château of Amboise was a favourite of the King's. From its rocky eminence, imperiously and cautiously it seemed to watch the undulating country and the silver stream of the Loire which watered it. Its thick embattled walls, its great buttresses and its round towers and tall windows made of it a fortress rather than a castle. Strong and formidable indeed it was outside; but inside, with its libraries, its great banqueting halls, its ceilings decorated with the *fleur-de-lys* or the salamander in the midst of flames, it was a magnificent setting for the most magnificent King in Europe.

The court had feasted, and in the great hall, which was hung with the finest tapestry and cloth of gold, the King's sister and his favourite mistress had an entertainment to offer him. It would be witty, for these two were the wittiest women in a witty court; it would perhaps divert him from his thoughtful mood.

He lay back in his ornamental chair, a gorgeous figure in his padded clothes, that were studded with pearls and diamonds; his sables were magnificent; on his breast and fingers sparkled diamonds and rubies; and about him hung the scent of the Russian leather cases in which his fine Flanders linen was stored.

He had been at Amboise only four days and already he was thinking of the next move. He could rarely stay in one place for more than a week or two at a time – even his beloved Fontainebleau could not hold him for more than a month; and then must begin the great upheaval of moving court, the carrying to another palace of his bed and all the artistic and carefully selected furnishing of his apartments which he could not bear to be without. He took a malicious delight in watching these removals – so uncomfortable for everyone but himself. He would sit in his chair, legs crossed, throwing an amorous smile at a pretty girl, making a witty observation, giving a friendly admonition. He was usually gracious, ever demanding, often sardonic; he was the most distinguished, charming man in France, born to admiration and flattery and taking them as a right; he was intellectual, ready to do a kindness provided the effort demanded was not too great; he was always ready to undertake an adventure, whether of love or war; amusing, seeking to be amused, loving artists as he loved women, he was the adored, the Sybarite, the pampered King of France.

He was too clever not to know what was wrong with him now. He was leaving behind that glorious period of youth when everything he had desired – until that great disaster of his life had overtaken him – had seemed ready to fall into his hands. He had never been the same since that humiliating defeat had befallen him; until then, it had seemed that Fortune, as well as the women of France, had chosen him for her darling. He would never forget the Battle of Pavia, when he had been made the prisoner of Spain; only his sister Marguerite, his pearl of pearls, facing death and danger on a hazardous journey across France to Spain, with her tender nursing had saved his life.

Now in this brilliant hall of his beloved Amboise, instead of the sparkling eyes of his own countrywomen, he was seeing those of the Spanish women who had lined the streets of Madrid to catch a glimpse of the prisoner their King had brought home from the wars. They had come to jeer, and instead they had wept. His charm was such that, sick at heart, defeated and humiliated as he was, those foreign women had looked upon him and loved him.

That was past, but he had a Spanish wife as a result. He glanced now with some distaste at the heavy face of Eleonora. She was too pious to please him. Moreover, he had been in love with Anne d'Heilly for nearly ten years. There were hundreds of women who aroused his interest fleetingly, but to Anne he remained faithful – in his way. He liked to see them bathing in his pool; he had had mirrors fixed about it that he might catch views of them at all angles. He was an artist. 'The little one with red hair,' he would say. 'She pleases us. She is charming, that one. I remember such another when I was campaigning in Provence.' Then he would try to catch at the days of his youth in Provence with the little red-haired one. What was the use? He was getting old. He was a man who could laugh at himself as readily as he laughed at others; so he must laugh now. Once he had been like a faun, so gay, so handsome; now perhaps he resembled more a satyr. Age should not come to kings. Kings should be eternally youthful. Then he remembered an impatient young man who had yearned for death to overtake an old king. So it has come to this! he thought. I, Francis, shall soon be such another as old Louis – panting after young women, buying their favours with this bit of jewellery, that work of art. No wonder a gay king grows sad.

They had started the play. Yes, it was amusing. He laughed; and the court waited on his laughs. But he was not fully attending. The dark one was charming, draped as she was with the flimsiest of stuff; she would look more charming on sheets of black satin. Come, come! He was not really interested. He was trying to force himself to amorous intent. In the old days, what a man he had been! The greatest lover in a country that idealised love. The greatest lover – and, did they whisper behind his back, the worst soldier?

Now he began to wonder whether he would not have some new improvements designed for this palace. He had a passion for architecture, and it was his pleasure to invite artists to his court to delight his ears and eyes as he lured women to delight his other senses. He thought of old friends – a sure sign of creeping age! Leonardo da Vinci! Poor Leonardo! I honoured him with my friendship, thought Francis, but perhaps posterity will say he honoured me with his. I loved that man. *I* could make a king. There is my son Francis, who will be King one day. But only God can make an artist.

He realised that. So he treasured these artists. Writers, painters, sculptors, designers in stone – he would have them know that there was patronage, even friendship, for them from the King of France. Many of these courtiers about him now had writhed at the writings of Francis Rabelais, and they could not understand why their King was so pleased with the quick-witted monk, for in truth the fellow showed no more respect for the King than he did for the courtiers. But, was the King's retort, how amusing it is to see others satirised, even if one must pay for the pleasure by enduring a little slyness at one's own expense.

And now, because he saw old age at hand, he wished to dwell on the glories of his youth. Not yet forty, he reminded himself, but not the same wild boy who had set a bull and three lions to fight here in the moat at Amboise; no longer was he the young man who had tackled a boar single-handed and refused the aid of his attendants while his mother wrung her hands in fear, though she glowed with pride for her beloved, her King, her 'Caesar'.

Well, he was still the King, and when he was not moody as now he was the gayest man in the court. He wished that he was more like his old friend and enemy, the King of England. There was a man endowed with the precious gift of seeing himself as he wished to see himself. A great and glorious gift! sighed Francis. A stimulus in youth, a comfort in age.

And he laughed down his long nose, thinking of Henry and his charming new wife, Anne, and wicked old Clement righteously excommunicating the pair of them.

Thinking of Henry and Clement brought his mind back to an irritation which had been disturbing him a good deal of late. There was the boy – the object of his dissatisfaction – as one might expect, sitting moody and alone in a corner. What an oaf! What a graceless boor! Francis thought about offering a groomship of the Chamber and a pension to anyone who could make young Henry laugh out loud. How did I get me such a one? he asked himself. But I will endure his scowls and boorish ways no longer.

He looked up and beckoned to him the two people whom he

5

loved and admired more than any in the court – Anne, his mistress, and Marguerite, Queen of Navarre, his sister and beloved friend of his childhood. What a distinguished pair! One could look at them and be proud that France had produced them both. Indeed, what other country could have produced them? They were both beautiful in different ways, Marguerite *spirituelle*, Anne voluptuous; they were both in possession of that other gift which Francis looked for, in addition to beauty of face and form, in all the women with whom it delighted him to surround himself. They were of an intelligence which equalled, and he was not sure did not excel, his own; with them he could discuss his political cares; they had intelligence with which to advise and wit with which to amuse him. Mistresses he had in plenty, but Anne remained his love; as for Marguerite, there had been a passionate devotion between them since he had been old enough to talk. Mistresses could come and go, but the bond between the brother and sister could only be broken by death. 'I loved you before you were born,' Marguerite had said. 'Husband and child were as nothing compared with the love I have for you.' She meant that. She had hated her husband for deserting her brother at Pavia; she had left her home and tempted death in order to go to him in Madrid. Now she sensed his mood more quickly than did Anne, for he and she were like twins – never completely content unless they were near each other, quick to sense a sorrow, ever ready to share a joy.

She said, smiling at him: 'My dearest, you are sad today?'

He signed to them to sit one on either side of him, and leaning towards Marguerite, took her hand and lifted it to his lips. All his movements were graceful and full of charm. 'Sad? No!' he said. 'But thinking of this Italian marriage.'

'I like it not,' said Anne. 'What *is* this family? Who are these Medici tradesmen to marry with the reigning house of France?'

'My love,' said the King, 'you echo the words of my counsellors. Repetition, alas! can be tedious, even from your sweet lips.' He signed to the musicians. 'Play! Play!' he commanded, for he did not wish too much of this conversation to be overheard.

'The Pope is a rogue, Sire,' persisted Anne. 'And if truth be tedium, then tedium must be endured.'

'A rogue!' cried Marguerite. 'He is worse than a rogue; he is a fool.'

'My dear ladies, I would tell you of the advice I have had from the boy's godsire. He thinks that it is a sorry matter when the son of a royal house should mate with the daughter of tradesmen. He adds, with Tudor ingenuousness, that there would have to be some great profit for a King to consider such a marriage; but he feels that if the profit were great enough, then God would bless the match.'

They laughed. 'Had you not mentioned that was the opinion of young Henry's godsire,' said Marguerite, 'I should have known those were the sentiments of Henry VIII of England.'

'The saints preserve him!' said Francis mockingly. 'And may he get all his deserts with his charming new wife. I have written to him and told him that is what I wish him.'

'He will thank you from the bottom of his heart,' said Marguerite. '"Now what *are* my deserts?" he will say. "What but riches, power, success and content for such a godly man as I! For if ever a man deserved these things, that man is Henry of England!" He will think you had naught else in mind.'

7

'I would poor Francis could offer the King of France one-tenth of that devotion which Henry Tudor lays at the feet of the King of England!' sighed Francis. 'Mind you well, I love the King of France – none better – but for his faults, whereas Henry Tudor loves the King of England for his virtues. True love is blind.'

'But he is right when he says there should be profit,' said Anne. 'Is the profit great enough?'

'They are rich, these Medici. They will fill our coffers which alas! my Anne, you have helped to deplete. Therefore rejoice with me. Also, there are three very bright jewels which the little Medici will bring us. Genoa, Milan, Naples.'

'Set in the promises of a Pope!' said Marguerite.

'My beloved, speak not with disrespect of the Holy Father.'

'A Holy Father with an unholy habit of cheating his too trusting children!'

'Leave Clement to me, my love. And enough of politics. I am disturbed and wish to unburden myself to you two wise women. It is the boy himself. By my faith, had his mother not been the most virtuous woman in France, I would say he were no son of mine.'

'You are perhaps hard on the little Duke, my King,' said Anne. 'He is but a boy yet.'

'He is fourteen years old. When I was his age . . .'

'One does not compare a candle with the sun, my beloved,' said Marguerite.

'My love, should not the children of the sun show some lustre? I hate sullen, stupid children, and it would seem that I have got me in that one the most sullen, the most stupid I ever clapped eyes on.'

'It is because he is the son of your dazzling self, Sire, that you look for too much. Give him a chance, for as your gracious sister says, he is young yet.'

'You women are over-soft with him. Would to God I knew how to put some sparkle of intelligence into that dull head.'

'Methinks, Francis,' said Marguerite, 'that the boy is less stupid when you are not present. What think you, Anne?'

'I agree. Speak to him of the chase, my love, and one sees in his face your very vivacious self.'

'The chase! He is healthy enough. Would to God the Dauphin were the same.'

'Don't blame your boys, Francis. Blame the King of Spain.'

'Or,' said Anne lightly, 'blame yourself.'

His eyes smouldered for a moment as he looked at her, but she met his gaze challengingly. She was provocative, very sure of herself, alluring; and he was still in love with her after nearly ten years. She took liberties, but he liked a woman to take liberties. He was not her god, as he was Marguerite's. But he laughed, for he could not escape that ability to see himself too clearly. She was right. He had been a bad soldier, too reckless: and the result – Pavia! He was to blame, and the fact that young Henry and his elder brother the Dauphin had had to take their father's place in the Spanish prison as hostages for his good faith, was not their fault but his.

'You take liberties, my dear,' he said with an attempt at coolness.

'Alas! my love, I fear 'tis true,' she answered pertly. 'But I love you for your virtues as well as your faults. That is why I tremble not when I speak truth to you.'

Marguerite said quickly: ''Twas an evil fate. The King had to return and the Princes to take his place. But let us face the real issue. The boys came back from Spain . . .'

9

'Where young Henry had forgotten his native tongue!' cried Francis. 'Would I, a Frenchman, however long exiled from France, come back gibbering a heathen tongue?'

'It was Spanish he spoke when he returned, Sire,' said Anne. 'And spoke it fluently, I understand.'

'Indeed he spoke it fluently. He looks and thinks and acts like a Spaniard. More like the son of my enemy than mine own.'

''Tis true he is a sullen boy,' said Anne. 'What will the Italian child think of her bridegroom, I wonder.'

'She will take him most thankfully,' said Marguerite. 'Is he not the son of the King of France?'

'I wonder,' said Anne mischievously, 'if she will think the sullen boy worth those three glittering jewels – Genoa, Milan and Naples.'

'She will,' said Marguerite. 'For we do not bargain too hotly when we buy with other people's money.'

'Particularly when the bills may never be paid!'

'Enough!' said Francis with a hint of asperity. 'Clement is a slippery rogue, but I can hold him to his promises.'

'How will the child arrive?' asked Anne.

'Not without much pomp and many rich gifts as well as the Holy Pope himself. Not only will he bring her, but he will stay for the marriage.'

'What!' cried Anne. 'Does he not trust us to make an honest woman of her?'

'Doubtless,' put in Marguerite, 'he thinks our Henry will rob her of her virginity and send her back.'

'After filching her jewels and her dowry!'

Francis laughed. 'He does not know our Henry. He can rob a banquet of its gaiety, but never a maiden of her virginity.

Holy Mother! I wish the boy had a bit more fire in him. I could wish he resembled his godsire across the water, for all that fellow's pomp and perfidy.'

'I hear,' said Anne, 'that his Grace of England was a fine figure of a man. And still is, though mounting fast to middle age.'

'We are of an age,' growled Francis.

'But,' mocked Anne, 'you are a god, my love. Gods do not grow old.'

'I am thinking of the boy,' said Marguerite. 'Now that he is to become a bridegroom something should be done. He should have a friend, a good friend, who will show him how to lose his fear of us all and, most of all, his father; someone who can explain that he is awkward largely because he lacks confidence in himself, someone to explain that the only way to overcome the effects of those unhappy years in Spain is to banish them from his thoughts instead of brooding on them.'

'As usual you are right, my darling,' said Francis. 'A friend – a dashing young man of charm and beauty, a gay young man with many fair friends.'

'Dearest, it was not exactly what I had in mind. There is no man at court who would have that subtle touch which is necessary. Spain is branded on the boy's brain – how deeply, none of us know; but I fear very deeply. It needs a gentle hand to erase such evil memories. He must recover his dignity through a subtle, gentle influence.'

'A woman, in very fact!' said Anne.

'A clever woman,' said Marguerite. 'Not a young and flighty creature of his own age. A woman – wise, beautiful, and above all, sympathetic.'

'Yourself!' said Francis.

Marguerite shook her head. 'Gladly would I perform this miracle . . .'

'Miracle it would have to be!' put in Francis grimly. 'Transform that oaf, ingrained with Spanish solemnity, into a gay courtier of France! Yes – a miracle!'

'I could not do it,' said Marguerite. 'He would not allow it for I have witnessed his humiliations. I have been present, Francis, when you have upbraided him. I have seen the sullen red blood in his face and the angry glitter in his eyes; I have seen that tight little mouth of his trying to say words which would equal your own in brilliance. He does not realise, poor boy, that wit comes from the brain before the lips. No! He would never respond to my treatment. I can but make the plan; some other must carry it out.'

'Then Anne here . . .'

'My well-loved lord, your demands upon me are so great that I could serve none other; and my zeal in serving you is so intense that I should have nothing but languid indifference for the affairs of others.'

They laughed, and Marguerite said quickly: 'Leave it to me. I will find the woman.'

Francis put an arm about each of them. 'My darlings,' he said, and kissed first Marguerite, then Anne, 'what should I do without you? That son of mine is like a hair in my shirt – a continual irritation . . . passing and recurring. The Virgin bless you both. Now let us dance. Let us be gay. Musicians! Give us some of your best.'

The King led Anne in the dance, and was delighted that his mistress and his sister had at length succeeded in lightening his mood; the courtiers and ladies fell in behind him and Anne. But in a corner, trying to hide among the tapestry hangings, the young Prince Henry slouched, wondering how soon he might be able to slip away to the peace of his apartments – loathing it all, the laughter, the gaiety, the courtiers and the women; but hating his father most of all.

* * *

The King dismissed his attendants, for he wished to be quite alone with Diane, the handsome widow of the Sénéchal of Normandy. As they went out, they would be smiling among themselves. Ha! So it is *La Grande Sénéchale* now, is it? What a King! What a man! But what will the charming Anne d'Heilly have to say to this? What a game it is, this love! And how delightfully, how inexhaustibly our sovereign lord can play it!

The King bade the widow rise. His narrowed eyes took in each detail of her appearance with the appreciation of a connoisseur. He was proud of women like Diane de Poitiers. By the Virgin, we know how to breed women in France, he thought.

She was afraid of him, but she did not show it. She was flushed and her eyes were brilliant. Understandable! She would be excited by a summons from the King. He told himself that she had scarcely changed since that other encounter of theirs. When was it? It must be nearly ten years ago! Her skin was still as beautiful as a young girl's. It was difficult to believe that she was quite thirty-three. Her features were regular, her raven black hair abundant, her dark eyes lustrous, her figure perfect! She delighted him, and not less so because of that coldness, that lack of response to his admiration and immense physical charm.

She was clever too. It amused him to keep her guessing the reason for this summons, or, rather, to let her draw conclusions which must be making her heart flutter uncomfortably beneath that perfect but so prim bosom.

The King of France looked like a satyr as he regarded the woman standing before him.

He had seen her with the Queen and had thought: Ah, there is the woman. She could make a man of my Henry. She will teach him all the arts and graces which she has at her own pretty fingertips. She will teach him all that it is good for him to know, and nothing that is bad for him. She will teach him to love her own virtues, and to hate his father's vices; and then I will put my head close to that charming one, and together we will find a mistress for him, a young, delightful girl, unless, of course – and this may well be, for I could suspect my Henry of any mediocrity – he wishes to remain faithful to his Italian bride.

'There is a favour I would ask of you,' he said, his warm eyes caressing her.

She had risen. She held her head high, and protest was written in every line of her beautiful head and shoulders.

He would not have been himself if he could have resisted teasing her.

'I beg of you be seated. We would not have you stand on ceremony. Come here . . . beside me.'

'Sire, you are very gracious to me.'

'And willing to be more so, dear lady, could I but get your kind consent. I often think on that long ago encounter of ours. Can it be ten years ago, Diane? Why, you are the same young girl. They say it is a magic you have. They say you have discovered eternal youth, and by the faith of a nobleman, I would say, as I look at you, that they are right.'

'I have no magic, Sire,' she said. 'And if you have sent for me that I may tell you of magic, I can only say that I am desolate because they have not spoken truly. There *is* no magic, Sire. If I had it, it should be yours.'

'Ah! But you have magic in your beauty, fair Diane. And it is that magic which I would ask you to give.'

'Sire, there are many beautiful women at your court who sigh for your attentions . . .'

'The charms of Venus will not do. It is chaste Diane whom I seek.'

No, he thought; she has hardly changed at all. She had not been a widow ten years ago. A twenty-three-year-old beauty married to one of the richest and ugliest men in France. Shame! To give a lovely young girl of fifteen to a middle-aged widower! But Jean de Poitiers, with three daughters to marry, had thought the Grand Sénéchal of Normandy a good match for young Diane. She had been docile and borne the old fellow – two girls, was it? He thought so. He had been interested in her at the time. He had been interested then in every beautiful woman in his kingdom – duchess, grande sénéchale, or wine-keeper's daughter, it mattered not! He was ready to welcome all to his bed – and hardly one of them able to refuse him! But Diane was one who had refused.

As he watched the calm face and sensed her hidden alarm at what she believed to be his renewed attack upon her virtue, he saw her again, a frightened woman kneeling before him, begging him to spare her father's life. The old fool had been in the Constable of Bourbon's conspiracy, and was at the time in a dungeon at Loches awaiting execution. And Diane had come to plead for his life with a monarch who was ever susceptible to the pleas of beautiful women. She had wept, but had kept her wits sharp; and he guessed that she had understood that bit of badinage which had passed between them. Inconsequently, as was his wont, the King had fallen in love with the pleader; he had said that as she would become his very good friend he must grant her request, for there was nothing he enjoyed better than bestowing favours on his very good friends.

And afterwards, when the old man's life was spared, and he had looked for appreciation of his generosity, those big dark eyes had been opened wide in horror, those damask cheeks had flushed scarlet; worse still, she had wept. She feared she had been foolish; she had not understood the King, she declared. Was he suggesting that he had spared the father's life in exchange for the daughter's honour?

Those bitter tears! That respectful distaste! She was very clever, of course; and next to beauty in a woman he admired cleverness. What could he do? She had won. She had fooled him. He bade her depart. 'Your beauty enchanted me, my dear Diane,' he had said, 'but your wit has outstripped me. Go back to your husband. I hope he appreciates your worth.'

He bore no malice; there was little malice in his nature; he saw her now and then, for she was one of his Queen's women; she was so demure in the black-and-white mourning she always wore for her departed husband.

But how could he resist the joy of teasing her! He would lead her to expect the worst – or the best. The rape of chaste Diane by the satyr King of France! And then he would let her down suddenly, so that she would be angry even though she would pretend to be relieved.

'I have thought of you since that day you went to tell your father that his life was saved. Do you remember?'

'Yes, Sire. I remember.'

'How gaily you went! Did you tell your noble father how you bought his life with . . . counterfeit coin?'

She said clearly: 'My father would not have understood had I told him. He was half crazed after his imprisonment in that dark dungeon of Loches. Four stone walls and only a small window, through which his food was passed, to give him light. And then . . . on the scaffold . . . to be told that his life was saved, but must be lived in a dungeon. I had thought you had said, "A pardon". I did not understand it was to be imprisonment.'

'There was much we did not understand – you of me, I of you, my chaste Diane.'

'And there he remained, Sire, a prematurely old man.'

'Traitors may not live like loyal men,' said Francis coolly, 'even though they possess beautiful daughters. And alack, if the daughters are virtuous as well as beautiful, that can indeed be a sorry thing for traitors.'

She was silent, but he knew that she was very much afraid.

'And your father now?' he asked.

'You will graciously remember that he was released a little while ago, Sire.'

'I rejoice. I would have lessened your anxiety had you let me. I may be the ruler of France, but I am the slave of beauty.'

'Sire, your goodness is known throughout France.'

'Now we understand each other. I need your services.'

She drew back, but he was already tired of the banter. He went on quickly: 'It is the Duke of Orléans of whom I wish to speak to you.'

'The little Duke!'

'Oh, not so little, not so little! He is soon to be a husband. What think you of the boy?'

'Why, Sire, I know not. I have seen him but once or twice.'

'Speak freely. Say he is an oaf and a boor, and more like a Spanish peasant than a King's son. I shall not gainsay you.'

'He is a handsome boy, I think.'

The King laughed. 'Can it be, Sénéchale, that those bright eyes of yours do not see as surely as they enchant? I tell you there is no need to choose your words so delicately.'

She smiled. 'Well then, Sire, when I think of the little Duke, it is of a shy boy, awkward in his manners.'

'An oaf, in other words.'

'Well, he is young yet.'

'The eternal cry of women! He is young . . . yet. And because he is young . . . yet, the women must feel tender towards him. He is fast putting on the years of manhood, and none of a man's manners with them.'

'I have heard he has often led the chase.'

'So have the dogs! Now, I have been considering how best to nurture this son of mine, and I have chosen you as his nurse.'

'Sire!'

The King's smile was mocking. 'Nothing is asked that could offend chaste Diane. It is simply this: my sister and Mademoiselle d'Heilly feel that the boy is to be pitied rather than blamed. They think the gentle hand of a woman could do much to help him shed his ugly Spanish mail and don the armour of a Frenchman. I have chosen that your hand shall assist the change. Neither my sister nor Mademoiselle d'Heilly know yet of my choice. You are clever enough to guess why. You, Sénéchale, are *my* choice.' He lifted his shoulders expressively. 'Mademoiselle d'Heilly may be a little jealous, you understand? The voluptuous rose can sigh now and then for the grace of the lily; Venus may envy Diana. She knows

18

how my eyes will light up at the sound of your name, and how I adore a lady's virtue, while now and then I am given cause to lament it. Then . . . my sister. You are a devout Catholic, and my pearl of pearls flirts with the new faith. But I, your King, choose you. I choose you for your virtue, for your honesty and your dignity and wit; and because you are a Frenchwoman of whom France can be proud. Therefore, I choose you to tutor my son. I would have you teach him the graces of the court. Beg him to emulate his father's virtues – if in your clear-sighted eyes he has any virtues – and above all, teach him not to imitate his father's vices.'

Diane was smiling now. 'I think I understand, Sire. I will be his friend. Poor boy! He needs friends. I will make a great gentleman of him. I am honoured that my gracious King should think me worthy of this task. I never had a son. I longed for one.'

'Ah!' said the King. 'We long for sons, little dreaming that when they come they may resemble Henry of Orléans. I trust you to do your work well.'

The interview was over. She bowed and left a faintly regretful King who continued to think of her after she had gone.

✻ ✻ ✻

Young Henry lay in one of the enclosed gardens watching clouds chase one another across the summer sky. He felt safe here. If he heard anyone coming he would get up quickly and run away. He wanted to be alone; he always wanted to be alone.

He would rather be at Amboise than in Paris. He hated Les Tournelles, that old palace near the Bastille, since for Henry it was overshadowed by the prison and therefore a constant reminder of his dark childhood days. His father would not live in the Louvre; it was too dark and gloomy and old-fashioned; he had grand schemes for altering it. There were always grand schemes for altering buildings. He was building Fontaine-bleau, and that would be really beautiful; but there was no peace to be had there. His father was always discussing what should be done and who should do it; and showing how clever he was, while everyone worshipped him because he was the King.

Henry hated the brilliant man who was his father; and the hatred went deeper because, if Henry could have chosen to be like anyone on Earth, he would instantly have selected the King of France, his father.

How he talked! How did he think of all those clever things to say? How did he know as much as he did and still have time to hunt and write and sing and go to bed with women? Henry did not understand it. He only knew that this dazzling man was a cheat and a liar, and that the most wretched time that he, Henry, and his brother Francis the Dauphin had ever spent, had been brought about by their father.

They were to have gone to Spain – oh, only for a little while, they had been told. They were to be hostages because their father had been beaten in battle by the King of Spain and had had to promise to marry the King of Spain's sister Eleonora, and to do many other things besides. And to make sure that these things were done, the little Princes must take their father's place as prisoners in Spain. Only for a little while! But as soon as their father was free, he had forgotten his promises, forgotten his sons.

They had crossed the Pyrenees into Spain, and for four

years they had remained in that hateful land – prisoners of their father's enemy.

Young Henry pulled up a blade of grass and bit it angrily. His eyes clouded with tears. He had hated it. At first it had not been so bad, for Eleonora had looked after them; she had loved them and told them she was to be their new mother. How kind she had been, determined on making them good Catholics, wanting them to love her as if they were truly her own little boys.

But then the King of Spain had begun to understand that the King of France was a liar; and the two little boys were taken from the kindly lady who was to be their stepmother and put in the charge of low ruffians who jeered at them because their father was a cheat.

Henry was deeply humiliated and his brother Francis was sick often; Henry suffered terribly wondering if his brother was going to die and he be left all alone in Spain.

Their clothes, as they grew out of them, had been replaced by shabby, dusty velvet. 'Look at the little Princes!' the guards had jeered. 'Sons of the lying King of France!' And in Spanish too! Nor would they answer a single question unless the boys asked it in Spanish. Henry never learned quickly, but he did pick up Spanish. He had to. And that was one of the things which made his father despise him so utterly. When he came home he had forgotten his native French.

How overjoyed he and Francis had been to know they were going home at last. Home . . . after four years! Henry had been five when he left France; he was nine when he returned. He had thought life was going to be wonderful then. But the big, dazzling man in jewel-studded clothes, whom everyone adored, and who made everyone laugh and be happy to be near

COUNTY LIBRARY

F/2154293

him, looked in dismay at his two sons, said something to them which Henry did not understand at all and Francis not fully; and then he had called them sober Spanish dons. Everyone had laughed. Henry hated laughter. He himself never laughed; but his tragedy was that he wanted to.

It was easier for young Francis. After all, he was the Dauphin, and people tried to please him because he would one day be the King. Young, morose Henry, they left to himself. His father shrugged his shoulders and hardly looked his way. Henry had no friends at all.

And as he lay on the grass absorbed in his miseries, someone came into the garden. It was a lady dressed in black and white. He scrambled to his feet. He hated her because he had to bow to her, and he could never manage the bow. People laughed at the way he did it – not the French way, not the graceful way! Clumsy, Spanish, oafish – more like a peasant than a Duke!

She smiled and he realised that she was beautiful. It was a true smile, he saw at once; it seemed to imply friendship, not superior contempt. But on second thoughts he could not believe that, and he was suspicious.

'I hope you will forgive my intrusion into your privacy,' she said.

'I . . . I will go and leave the garden to you.'

'Oh, please do not.'

He was moving away from her; if he could reach the opening in the hedge, he would run.

'Please sit down,' she begged. 'Just as you were . . . on the grass. Otherwise I shall be convinced that I have driven you away, and that will make me very unhappy. You would not wish to make me unhappy, would you?'

'I . . . I . . . cannot see that my presence here . . .'

'I will explain. I saw you from the palace. I said to myself, "Ah! There is Monsieur le Duc d'Orléans, whose advice I wish to ask. Now is my opportunity!"'

The hot blood rushed into his face. 'My advice?' he said.

She sat on the grass beside him, surely an undignified thing for a great lady to do. 'I want to buy some horses, and I know that your knowledge concerning them is great. Would you, I was wondering, be kind enough to give me a little advice.'

He was staring at her, still suspicious, but his heart had begun to pound. He felt ecstatically happy one moment, suspicious the next. Was she taunting him, teasing him? Was she going to show him shortly that he did not know anything about the one subject he really believed he understood?

'I am sure that you could find . . . people to . . . to . . .' He was preparing to rise to his feet. He would make some attempt to bow and dash out of the gardens.

But she had laid a hand on his sleeve. 'I could find people to talk and look wise, I doubt not; but what I want is someone whose judgement I can trust.'

His mouth grew sullen; she was making fun of him.

She went on quickly: 'I have watched you come riding in from the chase. I saw you on a chestnut mare . . . a lovely animal.'

His mouth turned up at the corners very slightly. Nobody could make fun of his mare, for she *was* perfect.

'I should like to have a mare like that, if, of course, it is possible to get one. I doubt if I could match her perfections.'

'It would be difficult,' he said; and he began to speak, without a stammer, of the delightful animal – of her age, of her exploits, of her habits.

The lady listened entranced. He had never had such a long

conversation with anyone before, but as soon as he realised how much he was talking, he became tongue-tied again and longed to escape.

'Do tell me more,' she said. 'I see I was wise when I decided to ask your help.'

So he found himself telling her of the merits of others of his horses.

In turn, she told him of her home, the château of Anet in the lovely valley of the Eure, and of the forests which surrounded it. It was wonderful hunting country; but there again, she said, she felt that a little of the right sort of knowledge would make it even better. There was so much that should be done.

There was the cutting down of trees, he added; and the planting of fresh ones. He could tell her quite a lot about hunting country.

She wished that he could see it. 'I confess I should enjoy escaping from the court for a while,' she said.

Then he asked who she was. 'I do not think I have seen you before.' He was sure he had not, for if he had, he could not have failed to remember her.

'I am in attendance on the Queen. I love her dearly, but sometimes I am lonely. You see, I am a widow. It is two years since my husband died, but if one has been happy, one cannot forget.' She smoothed the rich black and white of her gown with delicate white hands. She was like a statue, thought the boy; the statue of some beautiful saint. 'I fear I do not fit in with this gay court,' she added.

'Nor I!' he said bitterly. And now he did not wish to run away; in fact, he wanted to go on sitting here, talking to her; he was afraid that someone else would come into the garden and claim her attention, so that he would have to remember he was a shy boy, awkward and uninteresting.

'You do!' she told him. 'You are the son of the King. I am just a lonely widow.'

'My father . . . hates me!' He spoke vehemently. He dared not say he hated his father, but his tone implied it.

'Oh no! Nobody could hate you. Your father least of all. I have two little girls. I know. Parents cannot hate their own children.'

'My father can. He loves my little brother, Charles. He loves my sisters Madeleine and Marguerite. I think too – though he is often angry with him – that he loves the Dauphin. But myself . . . never. I am the one who angers him most.'

'No, no!'

'But I assure you that it is so. His looks, his words tell me so. One can be mistaken in looks, but not in words. Francis is the Dauphin, and one day he will be King, and my father does not forget that. But he sneers at him. He says he is too solemn and dresses like a Spaniard and likes water better than wine. Francis is cleverer than I; he can learn French ways more quickly. But little Charles is the one my father loves best. Lucky Charles! He was too young to be sent to Spain.'

'You could win your father's favour as easily as Francis.'

'How?' The boy was pathetic in his eagerness.

'It would take time. Your father has always surrounded himself with people who joke and laugh. He does not mind if the joke goes against himself even, as long as it makes him laugh. If you can make your father laugh, you are halfway to his heart.'

'He laughs at me . . . but in derision.'

'He wants to laugh for amusement. Mind you, his wit is of a high order, and it is not easy.'

'My young brother can make him laugh.'

'Oh, Monsieur Charles will be the King all over again. My lord Duke, if you were less afraid of offending your father, you would offend him less.'

'Yes,' said the boy eagerly; 'that is it. I am always wondering what I must answer him, even before he has spoken to me.'

'This is the first thing to learn, then: there is nothing to fear. And when you bow or kiss a lady's hand, you should not wonder whether you are doing so with a lack of grace. You should not care. You should stand up straight and hold your head high. If you do not try very hard to please people, often you can please them more. You must forgive me. I talk too much.'

'Indeed, no! No one has ever spoken so kindly to me before.'

'I am glad I have not bored you, for I was going to take a great liberty. I was going to ask you if you would be so good as to pay a visit to my home and look at those stables of mine . . . and perhaps ride out and advise about my land.'

His face lighted up. 'I can think of nothing I should like better.' The light died out of his face. 'I should not be allowed to leave the court.' He scowled, visualising the scene with his father. 'So you wish to visit a lady! My dear Henry, the affairs of the heart must be conducted with some decorum . . . even here in France.' Something like that, he would say, and with that coarseness always so gracefully expressed, would smirch the honour of this beautiful lady. Henry knew he could not bear that to happen.

'You could come accompanied by a few attendants. Why not?'

'My father would never allow it, I fear.'

'Monsieur le Duc, have I your permission to ask your noble father if I might take a small party, including yourself, for a brief visit to my home?'

She had a way of putting it that made it seem less unattainable. That was the way with some people. They were able to say with ease what they meant; he was so clumsy.

'That would give me great pleasure,' he said. 'But I fear you will soon wish to send me back.'

She laughed. 'Forgive me if I say you must dispense with such modesty. Always remember that you are the Duke of Orléans, the son of the King himself. Forget those unhappy years in Spain. They are gone and cannot return. I hope *you* will not be bored at my château. I shall do my best to give you the hospitality worthy of a king's son. Now, have I your permission, my dear friend, to make my request to the King? Please say yes.'

'I shall be desolate if I may not come, for I long to see your château and your horses and your land.'

She held out her hand and he took it, blushing hotly.

She put her head close to his. 'Never forget,' she said, 'that you are the son of the King of France.'

She was right. He was the King's son. He had never felt his importance so keenly before.

He stared after her as she left the garden. She gave him a smile over her shoulder as she went.

So beautiful, he thought, like a goddess, and yet so kind withal!

The summer months were the happiest Henry had ever known. Miraculously, his lady had gained the King's consent to the wonderful visit. He was not the same boy when he supped and talked and rode with Madame La Grande Sénéchale of Normandy.

'I will call you Henry,' she said, 'and you shall call me Diane, for we are friends, are we not – friends for as long as we both shall live?'

He stammered something about hoping he would always be worthy of her friendship. They rode together, though not as much as he would ride in the ordinary course of events. Diane was not so fond of the chase as he was, and she had no intention of risking an accident to her beautiful body. She was making an excellent job of the task which the King had set her. In her company the boy seemed to shed all his awkwardness; it was a pity that it returned as soon as others were with him.

She was getting fond of him. He was not without charm; and the devotion he was beginning to feel for her was flattering. It was so disinterested; she was accustomed to admiration, but that of the boy was different from anything she had before experienced. She was filled with pity for him. He had been so badly treated that it was small wonder that he responded as he did to a little kindness.

In a very short time after their first meeting, it seemed to Henry that there was no happiness to be found away from Diane. To him she was perfect, a goddess in truth; and he asked nothing from her but to be allowed to serve her. He looked about for what he could do, but there seemed nothing. He longed to wear her colours and enter the jousts; but so many men wore a lady's colours, and that just to win her favours. Henry wanted none to mistake his devotion. He did not wish for favours as ordinary people understood them. It was favour enough for him to be able to sit near her, to watch her beautiful face, and to listen to the wisdom that came from her perfectly moulded lips, to bask in the kindness she alone offered him.

She had given him a horse when she bought those which he had chosen. She had asked which in his opinion was the finest of the lot, and when he had told her – little guessing what was in her mind – she said that one should be his. He had protested with tears in his eyes. He wanted no gifts; he wanted only to be allowed to serve her. But she had laughed and said: 'What are gifts among friends?'

'It shall be my dearest possession,' he had told her earnestly.

Everything she did was exalted; nothing was ordinary. Even when she discussed his clothes and told him what to wear, how to bow, how to greet men and women, she did it with such grace and charm that it did not seem like a lesson. One thing she could not teach him, and that was to smile for others; he kept his smiles for her alone.

When he heard that he was to be married to an Italian girl, he was much alarmed; he went to Diane at once and told her of it.

Then was she her most sweetly sympathetic. She held his hands just as though he were in truth her own son; and she told him how she, a little girl of fifteen, about the age that he was now, had been given into marriage with an old man. She told him of her own fears. 'But, Henry, I quickly learned that there was nothing to fear. He was an old man; and this little Italian is your own age. It is not for you to be afraid of a little girl.'

'No, Diane,' he said, 'I should not be afraid, should I? But I wish I need not marry. I have no wish to marry.'

'But, my dear little friend, those of high birth must marry.'

'I would have wished to choose a bride, then.' He lifted his eyes to her face. 'But she whom I would choose would be too far above me.'

Diane was startled. What had happened to the boy?

She laughed lightly. 'Oh come, my lord, who is too exalted for the Duke of Orléans?'

He was about to stammer something when she turned the subject quickly.

It was well, she thought, that he was about to be married. She hoped the little Italian girl would be pretty enough to charm him.

It was with great delight that Henry heard Diane was to be of the party who would accompany him down to Marseilles where he was to meet and marry the little Medici.

❦ Chapter II ❦

CATERINA THE BRIDE

*I*n the valley lay the noblest city in all Europe. Its domes and spires that glittered in the smokeless air seemed to challenge the quiet hills which stopped only at its gates. The river gleamed silvery grey in the distance as it twisted westwards through the valley of the Arno, through Tuscany to Pisa and to the sea. The country was fertile, rich with its vineyards and plantations of olives. The town was richer; its bankers and wool merchants had made it prosperous, but it possessed a greater richness than they could give, to share with the world. Leonardo da Vinci and Botticelli, Dante and Donatello had beautified it; and Michelangelo, still a comparatively young man, was on this summer's day, at work within its walls. Its palaces and churches were storehouses of treasures; but in this city there was one possession which was more highly valued than art and learning. This was freedom. And the townsfolk looked to their ruling family to remember Florentine pride and Florentine independence.

The sun burned hotly in the Via Larga, scorching the thick stone walls of the Medici Palace. The first of the renaissance palaces of Florence, it looked strong enough to withstand any attack, for it was not only a palace, but a fortress; constructed to face the glare of an Italian sun, delightful in the contrast of light and shadow it presented, it was arresting, with its grim, almost prison-like lower structure and the decorative designs of the upper storeys. It was one of the most impressive buildings in a city of beauty.

In one of the upper rooms of this palace, little Caterina sat at her lessons. Her head ached, for her eyes were tired, but she must give no sign of this; she must never mention physical disability; she must never forget her dignity; she must, in fact, always remember that she was a member of the ruling house of Florence. Cardinal Passerini, who, by orders of the Pope, ruled the city under his master and at the same time supervised her learning, and her Aunt Clarissa, who supervised her manners, together with the Holy Father himself, who she saw less frequently, all impressed this upon her. She was important, because on her their hopes were fixed.

'Do not forget, Caterina Maria Romola de' Medici,' Clarissa Strozzi would say – for Aunt Clarissa always used her full names to stress the need of preserving dignity – 'do not forget that you are a daughter of the house of Medici. It is for you to show dignity, courage, and learning always – passion and folly never.'

When these lessons were done, there would be more lessons to follow – deportment, dancing, riding, and conversation with the Cardinal, Aunt Clarissa, and perhaps Filippo Strozzi, Aunt Clarissa's banker husband. Besides the study of languages, she must learn the history of her own family and that of the ruling houses of other countries. Aunt Clarissa insisted that she know each glorious incident in the life of her great-grandfather, Lorenzo the Magnificent; he was Aunt

Clarissa's hero and she often compared him with Giulio de' Medici, who now, as Pope Clement VII, was head of the family. Caterina had been shocked to hear the Holy Father spoken of with disrespect, but the greatest lesson she had had to learn was that of hiding her feelings; so Caterina listened and showed no sign of her surprise.

Now she pushed her long fair hair back from her thin little face, and as she was about to return to her books she heard a scratching at the door, and, forgetting her dignity for a moment, she leaped up and let in Guido, a spaniel with adoring brown eyes. She had two of them — Fedo and Guido — and only these two living beings knew her as a little girl who sometimes liked to romp and laugh more loudly than would have been seemly if any but they had heard it.

Guido was frightened. He cowered against her and licked her hand. He had the air of a dog who has escaped some terrible fate, but who knows his escape to be temporary. She guessed at once that the pursuer was Alessandro — the boy who called himself her brother and whom she called The Moor. He loved nothing better than to maltreat dogs and young serving boys and girls, any of whom he could torture without bringing trouble on himself. One day he would, she guessed, try to have similar fun with grown-up people.

She put a hand down to the dog and fondled his silky coat. She would have liked to have knelt on the floor and flung her arms about him. But the idea of Caterina of the house of Medici stooping to caress a dog in a room where she might be discovered must be immediately dismissed.

She had been right. It was Alessandro who had been chasing the dog, for he now pushed open the door and came into the room. He shut the door and leaned against it, looking at

33

Caterina while the dog tried to hide behind his mistress' feet; and Caterina, giving no sign of the violent beating of her heart, lifted her eyes to look at Alessandro.

They called him a Medici! Why, why, Caterina asked herself passionately, had her noble father gone about the world, planting his seed in such ignoble ground! How could he have loved the low Barbary slave who must have been Alessandro's mother? But evidently he had, if only for a short while, since Alessandro was here in the palace with her – her half-brother. The Pope insisted that he should live here, although Aunt Clarissa would have gladly turned him into the streets. A bastard, by good fortune; for what if he had been her legitimate brother! But no! Noble blood could never produce that low brow with the dark hair growing down almost to the eyebrows, that short, broad nose, that vicious mouth, those lecherous, protruding eyes. Caterina would have been terrified of Alessandro if she had not known herself safe from his vicious ways. He dared not hurt her; but he hated her all the same. She was the legitimate daughter; he was the illegitimate son; but the Holy Father, loving the boy though he did, would not allow harm to come, through Alessandro, to the little girl who was the hope of his house.

Alessandro came slowly into the room. He was fourteen at this time – eight years older than Caterina, and already showing many signs of the man he would become.

The dog whimpered.

'Be silent, Guido,' said Caterina, and kept her eyes fixed on her half-brother's face.

'The brute escaped me!' said Alessandro.

'I rejoice to hear it,' retorted Caterina.

'He knows not what is good for him, that dog. I was going

to feed him.' Alessandro laughed and showed teeth like those of a rat. 'I had prepared a delicacy for him . . . all for him.'

'You shall not harm my dog,' said Caterina.

'Harm him? I tell you I would have fed the brute.'

'You would only give him food that would harm him!' Her eyes flashed, for alone with Alessandro she would not consider her dignity; she would not smile when she was being hurt; she would answer his taunts with taunts of her own. 'You call killing things sport,' she said. 'And the more cruel the killing, the greater is the sport to you.'

He did not answer her. Instead, he bared his teeth at the dog and murmured: 'Come, little Guido, dear little Guido. I would feed you, little Guido.'

Caterina dropped to her knees; her usually sallow cheeks were flushed; she was frightened that she was going to lose her spaniel, one of the best friends she had. 'Guido,' she whispered frantically, 'you must not go near him. If he catches you, you must bite.'

'If he were to bite me,' said Alessandro, 'I would cut him into little pieces. Or perhaps I should put him into a cauldron and bring him slowly to the boil. I do not allow dogs to bite Alessandro de' Medici, Duchessina.'

'You shall leave my dogs alone,' she said with dignity, rising and looking at him. 'Go and have your sport with others if you must, but leave my dogs alone.'

'When I see the Holy Father,' said Alessandro, 'I shall tell him that the Duchessina has become a hoyden who wastes her time frolicking with dogs. Then they will be taken from you. Perhaps I shall ask that they may become mine.'

She was trembling. The Holy Father would believe Alessandro! How strange it was that the great man, who cared so much for power and hardly anything for his six-year-old cousin whom he courteously called his niece, should be so affectionately disposed towards her ugly bastard half-brother.

'Then,' she retorted, '*I* shall tell that I heard one of the serving girls screaming in your apartments, and I shall see that she holds nothing back when she is questioned.'

'You forget I have a way of enforcing silence. That girl will not relish losing her tongue.'

'I hate you!' said Caterina vehemently. 'I shall tell Aunt Clarissa.'

'Even if she believed you, she would not consider me worthy of punishment.'

'Then I shall tell the Cardinal.'

'He will not believe ill of one whom his master loves as the Holy Father loves me.'

In spite of her training, an impulse to run to him, to kick him, scratch him and bite him came to Caterina. She might have done so, for her mounting fears for her dog were fast destroying her control, had not the door opened that moment and Ippolito come into the room.

What a contrast he made to evil-looking Alessandro! Ippolito was the handsomest young man in Florence; he had inherited all that was best in the Medici family, and none of its shifty weakness and sly cruelty. He was only sixteen, but he was loved by the Florentines, who looked upon him, in spite of his illegitimacy, as their future ruler. They saw in him his illustrious ancestor, Lorenzo the Magnificent, as well as his noble father, the Duke of Nemours; already the boy had shown himself to be by nature bold and courageous, yet kindly, a lover of the arts. He possessed those qualities for which the Florentines looked in a leader; and it was hoped that the time would soon come when this young man would take the reins from the hands of Passerini, who ruled the city under Clement, that Pope whose vacillating European policy had brought unrest to Italy.

Caterina rejoiced to see Ippolito. She admired him; he had never been unkind to her, although it was true he had not much time to bestow upon such a very little girl. She knew that Alessandro was afraid of Ippolito and that Ippolito had nothing but contempt for The Moor.

Caterina said quickly: 'Ippolito, Alessandro threatens to hurt my dog.'

'Surely not!' said Ippolito, advancing and glancing contemptuously at Alessandro. 'Has he not dogs of his own on whom to play his vile tricks?'

'I will thank you to remember to whom you speak!' cried Alessandro.

'I do not forget it,' answered Ippolito.

Now that Caterina's control had broken down, she could not restrain herself, and, emboldened by the presence of Ippolito, who would always take the side of the weak against the strong, she cried out: 'No, Alessandro. Ippolito does not forget that he speaks to the son of a Barbary slave!'

Alessandro's face darkened and he stepped towards the little girl. He would have struck her if Ippolito had not quickly stood between them.

'Stand aside!' growled Alessandro, his dark brows coming down over his flashing eyes. His voice rose to a scream: 'Stand aside, or I'll kill you. I'll put out your eyes. I'll tear your tongue from your mouth. I'll . . .'

'You forget,' said Ippolito, 'that you are not speaking to those unfortunate slaves of yours.'

'I shall tell His Holiness of this when I am next summoned to his presence.'

'Yes, tell him you tried to strike a little girl. Tell him you teased her and frightened her about her dog.'

'I will kill you!' yelled Alessandro.

He turned away suddenly, because he was afraid of his rage and what he might be tempted to do either to Ippolito or Caterina; and there would be serious trouble if he harmed one of his family. He would do the wise thing. He would see blood flow for this; but it must not be Medici blood. He would have some of his servants whipped. He would think up new tortures for them to endure. He ran from the room.

Ippolito laughed aloud; Caterina laughed with him; then she lifted her eyes shyly to the boy's face. Never had he seemed so attractive as he did now when he had, with his clever words, driven Alessandro from the room. He was very handsome in that rich mulberry velvet that suited his olive skin, his blue-black hair and those flashing dark Medici eyes which were not unlike her own. She felt that she could have worshipped Ippolito as though he were one of the saints.

He smiled at her very gently. 'You must not let him frighten you, Caterina.'

'I hate him!' she cried. 'The Moorish bastard! I wish he need not be here. I do not believe he is my half-brother.' She touched the velvet of his sleeve. 'Ippolito, do not go yet. Stay and talk a little while. I am afraid Alessandro will come back.'

'Not he! He is watching one of his slaves being whipped by now. He can never leave a spectacle of bloodshed.'

'Do you hate him, Ippolito?'

'I despise him.'

She felt warmed by their common feeling for Alessandro. 'I

would give much,' she said, 'to hear that he were not my half-brother. Alas! I have many brothers and sisters in Florence, in Rome, in every town in Italy where my father sojourned. In France also, I have heard.'

Ippolito looked at her and smiled mischievously. She was quite a charming little girl when she was not prim and silent; he had not thought, until he had seen her exasperated by The Moor, that she could be so angry and so delightfully friendly. He wanted to please her, to make those lovely eyes shine with joy. 'There are some, Caterina,' he said quietly and confidentially, 'who say Alessandro is not your half-brother.'

'But if he were not, why should he be living here?'

'Caterina, can you keep a secret?'

'Why, yes.' She was overjoyed at the prospect of sharing something with this handsome young man.

'The Pope cares more for Alessandro than for you or for me. It is for that reason that people say he is not your brother, Caterina.'

Her eyes were big with excitement. 'But . . . *why*, Ippolito?'

'The Pope calls you niece, but the relationship is not as close as that. People say that the relationship of the Pope and Alessandro is very close indeed.'

'You cannot mean . . .?'

Ippolito laughed and placed his hands on her shoulders; their faces were close and he whispered: 'The blackamoor is the son of the Holy Father!'

'And his mother?' whispered Caterina.

'Some low serving-girl.'

'But the Pope himself!'

'Popes are human.'

'But they are said to be holy.'

39

Ippolito laughed gaily. 'But you and I know differently, eh?'

Caterina was so happy that she threw off completely the restraint of years. This was wonderful news brought to her by the most wonderful person in the world. She danced round the room; then collapsed on to her stool. Guido jumped on to her lap and started licking her face.

Ippolito laughed aloud to see them. So this was the little cousin whom, until now, he had thought so plain and solemn. He was delighted that his bit of gossip had been able to bring about this transformation.

❖ ❖ ❖

Caterina made her way down to that chamber of mysteries where Bartolo, the astrologer, spent most of his nights and days. She ran swiftly and silently down the great staircase; she was afraid that she would meet someone and be called upon to explain her presence in this part of the palace.

At this hour of the day, Bartolo took his exercise in the palace grounds; solitary he walked, in his flowing black robes, his white hair flying from beneath the round cap he wore. Embroidered on the cap were the signs of the zodiac; the magician's person carried with it that odour of his magic room – the scent of herbs and blood of animals, musk, verdigris, civet, and the ingredients from which he made perfumes and lotions, potions and poisons. Few dared approach Bartolo. If any of the serving-men and women saw him walking in the grounds, they would look away quickly, and try to forget that they had seen him.

But at this hour, Caterina felt she must be safe. Bartolo was not in the magic chamber, but others were. These were the two young brothers, Cosmo and Lorenzo Ruggieri, whom Bartolo was training to become seers and astrologers as he was himself. The boys would be there among the charts, the cauldrons, the skeletons of various animals, the perfumes, the bottles and the powders. They would be awaiting the coming of their little Duchess, and they would have ready for her that which she had asked them to prepare for her.

The staircase narrowed and turned. Now she was in a stone corridor, and she could already smell the sickly sweet odour of the magician's rooms. She reached a door which led to a passage at the end of which was another door that would open into the room itself. She knocked.

'Enter!' said the high-pitched voice of Cosmo Ruggieri.

She went into the vaulted room on the walls of which hung parchments decorated with mysterious characters. She glanced at the big chart of the heavens, at the cauldrons standing among the rushes on the floor, and the skeleton of a cat on the bench.

The Ruggieri boys bowed low. They were faithful servants of their little Duchess. Often they had given her charms to protect her from the wrath of her aunt and the sorrow of the Cardinal – and all unknown to old Bartolo. Caterina, whose respect for the occult was one of the greatest emotions in her life, admired these two boys who were learning to be magicians.

'You have it?' she asked.

Cosmo said: 'We have. Get it, Lorenzo.'

'Yes, give it to me quickly,' said Caterina. 'It would not do for me to be caught here.'

Lorenzo took a waxen figure from the pocket of his flowing gown. There was no mistaking whom it was meant to represent. The brothers had cunningly reproduced the ugly face and squat figure of Alessandro.

'And he will die within three days?' asked Caterina.

'Yes, Duchessina, if you pierce the heart at midnight and say, "Die, Alessandro! Die!"'

The lovely dark eyes were opened wide in horror. 'Cosmo . . . Lorenzo . . . it is a bad thing to do. I am afraid.'

'There are many in this palace, Lady Duchess,' said Cosmo, 'who would say it is a good thing to do.'

'He is going to kill my dog. I know he will . . . if I do not kill him first.'

'He will surely die if you pierce the heart of this waxen image,' said Lorenzo.

'It is not wrong for me to do this?' She looked from one to the other.

'It would not be wrong,' they chanted simultaneously.

'Then I will do it.' She took the figure and, wrapping it in a kerchief, put it into her pocket.

'Duchessina,' said Lorenzo, 'if any should discover the figure, I beg of you, do not tell whence it came.'

Poor Lorenzo! He could not hide his thoughts. He was terrified of the ugly Moor. He was picturing what would happen to him and his brother if Alessandro discovered that they had supplied the figure.

But Cosmo was bolder. 'It will not be discovered,' he said.

'I swear I would tell none where I found it,' Caterina assured them. 'I must go,' she went on. 'I shall never forget what I owe you both.'

Hurriedly she made her way to the upper regions of the palace.

In her own apartments she took the image from her pocket

and studied it. But for its size it might have been Alessandro himself that she held in the palm of her hand.

She must do this thing. If she did not, poor Guido would surely die – die agonisingly of poison. Ippolito was her dear friend, but he could not always be at her side to protect her from the cruel Moor, any more than she could always be with Guido. It seemed to her that the only way to save the dog – and at the same time to make life happier for those poor slaves of Alessandro's – was to remove him from this world altogether.

There was no harm in this, only good.

Caterina was frightened. At midnight, when she had gone to that drawer where she had carefully hidden the figure, it was no longer there. Alessandro had his spies everywhere. They obeyed him because not to obey him meant they would suffer those hideous tortures which he was always inventing.

She was waiting now for Alessandro's revenge. She knew that it would be terrible, for the Moor would know why she had acquired that figure; he would know exactly what her intentions had been.

She was startled when a serving-girl came to her room to tell her that her cousin Ippolito wished to see her.

Caterina was surprised, for she had thought Ippolito was out hunting. He must have returned sooner than usual. She was glad. Now she could tell her cousin what she had done; she could ask for his advice and his protection.

When she knocked on his door, there was no answer, so she went in. There were some books on the table, but no sign of Ippolito. He would come soon, she was sure; and she felt at peace. She need not be afraid of Alessandro while Ippolito was in the palace.

And then suddenly she heard the swish of a curtain; she turned, a joyful smile of welcome on her lips, and there, peeping between the curtains which he grasped with his ugly hands, grinning at her, was the hideous face of Alessandro.

She jumped up and gave a little cry of horror; but Alessandro did not look angry; he was smiling; he put a finger to his lips. 'It is a surprise I have for you, Duchessina.'

She stammered: 'I . . . I had not thought to see you here.'

'No? You thought to find handsome Ippolito. But there are some, Caterina, in this palace, who think me as handsome as Ippolito.'

She gripped the table. She wanted to run, but her legs seemed to have lost their power. Yet she could not control her tongue. She had not really learned those lessons which the Cardinal and her aunt had taken such pains to teach her. She cried out: 'Then they say so because they dare say nothing else. You force them to lie . . .'

He advanced slowly towards her. 'You are not pleased to see me, Caterina,' he said mockingly. 'It was to be a surprise. A most happy surprise. I have something to show you.' He took the figure from his pocket and held it up. 'Where did you get this, Caterina?'

She kept her lips tightly shut.

'Answer me,' he said slowly. 'Where did you get it?'

'I shall never tell you,' she said, and she smiled suddenly. He was afraid of the magicians, so he would not dare try his tricks on Bartolo or the boys.

'I know,' he said. 'You are so fond of me that you wanted an image of me, that you might look at it when I was absent.

44

Never mind now. Come with me, and see what else I have to show you.'

She knew now that she was about to suffer Alessandro's revenge; she had known it must come because Alessandro never failed to take revenge. He drew aside the curtain and as she approached, he pointed to the floor. There lay the body of Fedo. It was stiffening, but the legs were contorted and she knew that Alessandro had poisoned the dog in a way calculated to give the maximum of suffering to the poor animal.

Caterina sank on to her knees and touched Fedo's body. Tears came to her eyes and ran down her cheeks. She sobbed bitterly. Alessandro stood very still, smiling at her.

'Most unseemly!' he murmured. 'What would Aunt Clarissa say if she could see Caterina now?'

Caterina lifted her reddened eyes to his jeering face; and then suddenly she lost control as she never had before. She forgot everything but that her beloved dog had been cruelly done to death by this wicked boy.

She flew at him; she did what she had often longed to do. She kicked him; she bit him; she pulled at that stiff, ugly black hair. She screamed: 'I hate you! I hate you! I hate you!'

That Alessandro stood calmly laughing at her she did not notice; she was blinded by her rage.

A woman came running in. Alessandro said: 'Bring the Cardinal or my lady. The Duchessina has gone mad.'

And still he stood there calmly, though it was not his nature to be calm; and he smiled at the blood which was flowing from the wound her teeth had made in his hand.

'She has sharp teeth, this savage Duchessina!' he murmured as though to himself.

And then, suddenly, Caterina was aware of the tall figure of the Cardinal and with him her aunt, Clarissa Strozzi. Caterina turned from Alessandro and looked at them in horror. The Cardinal's tired eyes in his cadaverous face expressed disbelief of what those eyes had witnessed; but Clarissa Strozzi was never at a loss for words.

'Caterina Maria Romola de' Medici!' she said. 'I would not have believed, after all our care, that you could behave thus.'

Caterina saw that on Alessandro's face was the same shocked expression as was on those of her aunt and the Cardinal. She burst out angrily: 'But . . . he poisoned my dog . . . my dear little Fedo. He poisoned Fedo . . . most cruelly. He is too much of a coward to hurt me, so he hurts my little dog . . .' Her voice broke and she began to cry miserably.

'Be silent!' commanded Clarissa. 'Let us hear no more of this. Go to your room at once. There you will stay until summoned.'

Caterina, only too glad to escape, ran from the room. Miserable and bewildered, she did not stop running until she reached her own apartment. Guido greeted her and she fell upon him weeping bitterly. He licked her face; the loss of Fedo was his as well as hers.

❖ ❖ ❖

Caterina was summoned to the apartments of the Cardinal, and taken to that room which was like a cell in its austerity. Not that the Cardinal made much personal use of this room; it was kept for occasions such as this; the rest of the Cardinal's apartments were sumptuously furnished, as fit for a man of his rank. On chairs that were like thrones sat the Cardinal, Clarissa Strozzi, and Caterina. Caterina's feet did not touch the floor, but her face was solemn and expressionless. She dared show no emotion, for Aunt Clarissa's eyes would be upon her until this ordeal was over. On the floor Guido lay stretched out. He had just eaten what had been given to him, and he was there that his mistress might watch his death agonies. This was her punishment. She had loved her dogs; she had loved them so much that she had been trapped into a lowbred display of violent emotion. So now, she must watch, unmoved, the terrible suffering of a beloved friend.

Caterina knew what was in Aunt Clarissa's mind. This was the necessary lesson. All emotion must be suppressed, for emotion was childish. Caterina must be made to realise that there was only one thing that really mattered in her life – the advancement of a great and noble house. Alessandro was responsible for this trouble, but, in Aunt Clarissa's mind, Alessandro, the bastard of very uncertain parentage, was of no importance whatever. He could be ignored, while Caterina must learn her lessons.

Poor Guido! He was beginning to suffer cruelly now. Caterina wanted to scream: 'Stop! Stop! Kill him quickly. Do not let him suffer like this. Hurt me . . . but not Guido. What has Guido done?'

Be still! she admonished herself. She pressed her lips tightly together. Show nothing. Oh, foolish little Caterina, if you had not shown Alessandro that you cared for your dogs he would not have thought of hurting you through them; if you had hidden your feelings about Fedo's murder, Guido would now be in your arms, not lying there in agony. Silly Caterina! At least learn your lesson now.

They watch you now: Aunt Clarissa, who has no feeling but determination that a great house shall continue great; the

Cardinal, who cares for nothing but that he keeps the goodwill of the Medici.

If she showed emotion now it would be her favourite horse next. She must not cry. She must watch this horror; she might be wretched, heartbroken, but she must show nothing.

She sat clenching her hands; she was white and her lips trembled a little; but the eyes that were lifted to Aunt Clarissa's face were dry and devoid of expression. Aunt Clarissa was satisfied.

✤ ✤ ✤

With their attendants, Caterina, Alessandro, and Ippolito made the long and tedious journey through Tuscany to Rome. Florence and Venice might be the most beautiful of Italian cities, but Rome was the proudest. The Eternal City! How grand it seemed, how noble set upon the seven hills, surrounded by the purple slopes, the rocky Apennines on one side, and on the other the sparkling Mediterranean Sea.

The Holy Father wished to receive the younger members of his family in audience; he had been having ill reports of their conduct from stern Clarissa Strozzi, who complained that the Cardinal Passerini was too indulgent. A word from the Holy Father was needed; and Clement could never resist an opportunity of seeing Alessandro. So there must be this visit to Rome, to the Vatican itself; and Caterina was pleased, for she loved to travel, and a change from the monotonous daily routine of life in Florence was desirable.

Now she noticed, as they came into the city and people stood about to watch their ceremonial entry, that there were sullen looks instead of smiles, murmuring instead of cheering. But the overpowering beauty of the city made her forget the people. There rose St Peter's itself, though not yet completed, grand, eloquent almost, with its lesson to offer. The great church was built on that spot, in one of the gardens surrounding Nero's circus, where, after his martyrdom, St Peter had been buried. He would have suffered, but a great church bore his name, and he would never be forgotten. The Emperor Nero, at whose command St Peter had been tortured, had committed suicide. Whose was the triumph – the saint's or the tyrant's?

The day after their arrival the Pope would give them audience, and they would be led through the halls and rooms, peopled by Papal lackeys dressed in red damask, to the audience chamber, where the Holy Father would receive them. Caterina had never seen her kinsman except when he was surrounded by the pomp of his office. Now they would go in procession to the Vatican City; they would mount the hill – the centre of a group of three that overlooked the Tiber – and they would pass from palace to palace catching glimpses of the river and the Sistine Chapel, and the old fortress of the Castle St Angelo.

Clement was glad that the children were in Rome. He would like to keep them there, but conditions were uneasy. Not that that worried him greatly. He had too high an opinion of his power to doubt for a moment his ability to quell a grumbling populace. The people distrusted him, he knew; and they considered the state of unrest in Italy due to the policy he had pursued with those monarchs who stood astride Europe – the three most powerful men of a turbulent age – Francis of France, Charles of Spain, and Henry of England. But there was one, Clement believed – for his vanity was not the least of his faults – who was greater than any of them, and that man was the Holy Father himself, Giulio de' Medici, called Pope Clement VII.

He decided now to see the children alone and separately, so that he might embrace Alessandro unseen and none might wonder at his affection for the boy. He said to his Master of the Household, whose duty it was to be with him wherever he was: 'Excellency, I would be alone with the young people. Have them brought in separately.'

The dignified figure in the black-and-purple cassock bowed low and went into Monsignor's apartment to tell him the wishes of His Holiness the Pope.

Caterina came first. Etiquette demanded it. She walked reverently to the portal chair on which Clement sat with his white robes spread about him. Caterina knelt and the Pope held out his hand that she might kiss the fisherman's ring.

She lightly touched it with her lips, but she could feel little reverence for the ring. The teaching they were giving her was robbing her of all real emotion. She looked at the seal through half-closed eyes while she received the sacred blessing; she saw her kinsman's name on the seal and the image of St Peter sitting in a boat as he cast his nets.

He kept her on her knees.

'My daughter, I have heard sad reports of you. You have been guilty of many sins, and this grieves me . . .'

He went on and on, yet he was not thinking of her sins, but of her marriage. His mind was flitting from one noble house to another. He wanted the son of a king for Caterina.

Yes, thought the Holy Father, rounding off his homily, I shall try for a king's son for Caterina.

'You may leave me now, daughter. Work harder. Give yourself to your studies. Remember a brilliant future awaits you. It is for you to preserve and glorify the honour of the house of Medici. Be worthy of that trust.'

'I will, Father.'

She kissed the ring and departed.

Ippolito next. Alessandro should be saved until he had done with this bastard sprig of their family tree. He disliked the boy. How dared he wear that arrogant air, that look which was going to remind others as well as the Holy Father of their famous ancestor, Lorenzo the Magnificent. Still, he was a boy, and boys were precious; lacking legitimate offspring, one must welcome the illegitimate, particularly if they were male. The Holy Father could picture this boy, swaying the populace. It was often so with a charm of manner, a handsome face and a plausible tongue. Ippolito would have to learn modesty.

He told him so as the handsome head was bent and the boy knelt before him.

He was dismissed with alacrity, and now, thought the Holy Father, Alessandro!

The Moor came in, his long arms swinging, depravity already written on his face, for all to see except one blinded by love, as was the Holy Father. He rose and held out his hands; he embraced the boy.

'My son, it is a pleasure to see you looking so well.'

Then Alessandro knelt as the others had knelt, and the Pope caressed the wiry black hair, and the fisherman's ring was lost in the thickness of it.

Clement thought of the boy's mother and that sudden passion which she had aroused in him. A slave girl, picked up on the Barbary coast, working in the kitchens – a girl with Alessandro's hair and Alessandro's eyes, warm-natured, loving – the great man's mistress for several months of a year she had made memorable.

My son! thought the Pope. My son! And was angered that he could not say to all the world, This is my son! That could not be, and he must pass the boy off as a bastard of Caterina's father, who had so many bastards that one more credited to him made little difference.

He was an earthly father now. 'My son, how like you Rome? You would like to rest here awhile?'

Alessandro would like to stay in Rome. He told of the viciousness of Caterina and showed the wound in his hand where she had bitten him.

'My son, you shall not live under the same roof with such a savage.'

'I am treated badly there, Father. I am made to feel of no importance.'

'My son, my son!'

'I would I had my own palace, Father.'

'You shall, my son. A palace of your own, where you shall no longer be ignored, where you shall not have to submit to such treatment from . . . your sister.'

Alessandro was delighted. Master in his own house where all should tremble before him! Here on Vatican Hill had once stood Nero's Circus. *There* was a man who had known how to amuse himself . . . and others. One day Alessandro would be such a one . . . a wise Nero. He would make sport and know how to enjoy it.

'I thank you, Father.'

'My son, come close to me. One day Florence shall be yours. I will make you ruler of all Florence. That is what I plan for you. But for the moment this plan is a secret, my son, yours and mine. For the time being you shall have your own establishment – a palace of your own in Florence.'

And so, after that visit to the Holy Father, Caterina was spared the indignity of living under the same roof as Alessandro.

✤ ✤ ✤

It was three years after that visit to Rome; they had been three happy, peaceful years, with the friendship between Caterina and Ippolito growing stronger as the months passed. Alessandro had been given a fine villa about half a day's ride from the city. It was comforting to see very little of him and to see more and more of Ippolito. Caterina had begun to dream, and her dreams included her handsome cousin. She could think of nothing more delightful than spending her life with him in this city which they both loved so dearly. Ippolito, it was believed, would one day rule the city; what could be happier than that Caterina, legitimate daughter of the house, should rule it with him? The more Caterina thought of this, the more likely it seemed to her that this could come about.

Happy days they were, sharing confidences, riding, and always with Ippolito. She did not know whether he was aware of what was in her mind. Perhaps to him she was just the agreeable little cousin. She was only nine years old. Perhaps young men of nineteen did not think of marrying nine-year-old girls. But in a few years she would be marriageable, and then . . . her wedding would be arranged.

She would long for Ippolito to speak to her of this, but he never did. She was glad that cruel Alessandro was not here in the Medici palace that he might guess her secret and find some way of torturing her.

And so the happy, sunny days passed by – three whole years of them – until that day when disaster came upon the house. The Eternal City sacked, its palaces and churches looted, its citizens torn limb from limb, its virgins raped along with its matrons! The Holy Father, thanks to the magnificent rear-guard action fought by his brave Swiss guards, had escaped to the Castle of St Angelo, but remained there a prisoner. Florence was in revolt against the Medici. Alessandro and Ippolito were driven from the city; but the little Caterina – the only legitimate child of the house – was held by the new Government of Florence as a hostage and sent, for safe keeping, to the Convent of Santa Lucia.

Here in the convent her life must be devoted to fasting and prayers; her room was a narrow cell with nothing bright in it except the silver crucifix which hung upon the wall; she must live the rough, hard life of the nuns. But it was not that which hurt her; it was not for the cold of stone walls and the hardness of her bed that she wept bitterly into her coarse sheets at night. It was for Ippolito – her beloved, handsome Ippolito, who was . . . she knew not where. They might have killed him, as they would have killed the Holy Father if they had caught him. He might be living as a beggar, roaming the countryside beyond the city. All her prayers, all her tears were for Ippolito.

Six months passed in the gloom of Santa Lucia. She hated the sombre nuns in their stale-odoured garments; she hated the interminable hours of prayer.

'Ippolito!' she would cry. 'Where are you?' She would whisper to the figures of the saints: 'Tell me, where is Ippolito? Only let him be safe and I will never sin again.'

Outside the walls of the convent the plague had come to

Florence. In the streets, men, women, and children were dying in their hundreds. Was Ippolito one of these?

Then, like a sinister fog, the plague crept into Santa Lucia.

Caterina de' Medici was too valuable a hostage to be allowed to run the risk of being taken by the plague. There was one thing left for the Government of Florence to do with this valuable little girl. On the other side of the city stood the Convent of Santa Annunziate delle Murate – the only spot in the whole of Florence that had escaped the plague. So one night three men called at the Santa Lucia and Caterina was summoned from her cell to learn of her departure; and without ceremony, a concealing cloak wrapped about her, Caterina, in the company of these men, set out to cross the plague-stricken city.

She saw terrible sights on that night. She saw bodies of men and women stretched out on the cobbles, some dead, some dying; she saw doctors in masks and tarred coats bravely doing all they could for the stricken people; the black-clad Misericordia passed along the streets carrying a litter in which was a victim of the dreadful disease; she heard the jangling of the dead-cart, and the voice of the priest saying prayers for the departed as he walked ahead of the cart. She heard people carousing in the taverns; she saw women and men making love in a frenzy of impatience, as though they wished to snatch at every enjoyment they could find, since tomorrow they might have their place in the dead-cart.

It was fantastic, that journey; it seemed unreal to little Caterina; she felt numbed by the suddenness of change that touched her life and shattered it. She felt she could only wait for horror to overtake her. She tried to see the faces of those muffled in their cloaks. She was in the streets of Florence. What if she came face to face with Ippolito?

But they had crossed the piazza and made their quick way through narrow streets towards the Santa Croce, and there, rising before her, were the grey walls of her new prison.

The door was opened to them. She saw the black-clad figures, so like those she had lived with in the Santa Lucia, and she was taken into the presence of the Reverend Mother of the Santa Annunziate delle Murate. Cool hands were placed on her head while she received the blessing; she was aware of quiet nuns who watched her.

But when the men had been shown out and she was alone with the Reverend Mother and the nuns, she sensed a change all about her.

One of the nuns so far forgot the presence of the Reverend Mother as to come forward and kiss Caterina, first on one cheek, then on the other.

'Dear little Duchessina, welcome!' said this nun.

Another smiled at her. 'We heard you were coming and could scarce wait to see you.'

Then the Reverend Mother herself came to Caterina. Her eyes were bright, her cheeks rosy; and Caterina wondered how she could have thought her like the Reverend Mother of Santa Lucia.

'Our little Duchess will be tired and hungry. Let us give her food; then she may go to her cell and rest. In the morning, Duchessina, we will have a talk.'

It was confusing, and she was bewildered. So many strange things had happened to her that she could no longer be surprised. She was given a place of honour at the long refectory table; she noticed that the soup had meat in it, and she remembered that this day was a Friday; the fish was served with sauces; it was more like a meal in the Medici palace than in a convent. There was conversation, whereas at Santa Lucia there had been a rule of silence during meals. But she was too tired to think very much about these matters, and as soon as the meal was over and prayers had been said, the two nuns who had greeted her on her arrival took her to her cell. She felt that the bed was soft, and that reminded her that they had eaten meat. The nuns were very friendly, respectful even; she could ask them why they ate meat on Fridays. She did.

'Here in the Murate, Duchessina, we may eat meat on Fridays. It was a special dispensation from the Holy Father many years ago.'

They were shocked by the coarseness of the shirt she wore, and brought her one of fine linen. 'This will be better for your delicate skin, Duchessina.'

'At Santa Lucia,' she told them, 'all wore coarse shirts next the skin.'

'That is well enough for Santa Lucia, but here in the Murate we are not of lowly birth, as many are in Santa Lucia. Here we temper godliness with reason. For the glory of God, we wear our sombre robes, but for sweet reason's sake we wear fine linen next our skins. Now sleep, dear little Duchess. You are among friends here.'

First one bent down to kiss her. 'My brother is a member of the Medici party,' she whispered. 'He will rejoice to know you are safe with friends.'

The second nun bent over her. 'My family await deliverance from the republicans.'

Caterina stared up at them and they laughed.

'Tomorrow we will show you who are the supporters of your noble family. There are many here in the Murate.'

'And are there some for the republicans?' asked Caterina.

'Some. But that makes life exciting!' said the nun who had first kissed her.

Caterina could not sleep when they had left her. She realised at once that life was going to be very different from what it had been in Santa Lucia.

✦ ✦ ✦

'Pray be seated,' said the Reverend Mother.

How small the child looked in the big chair, her feet scarcely touching the ground. But what poise, what dignity! So rare in one so young. This child was going to be quick to learn and a joy to teach. For that very reason and because she was doubtless observant, it was imperative for the Reverend Mother to have a talk with her.

Yesterday Caterina had witnessed the entry of a young novice into the convent. There was a significant ceremony which always took place on such occasions, and from this ceremony the convent took its name. The novice arrived outside the convent walls accompanied by high dignitaries of the Church, who, with their own hands, broke down a section of the wall, and through the hole they made the novice passed. When she had done this the wall was built up again. It was solemn and significant; the novice had passed behind the grey walls for ever; she was built in and could not leave the Murate.

And little Caterina was puzzled. She had been for six months with the nuns of Santa Lucia, and Santa Lucia, with its fastings and strict observances, would seem what a convent should be. Here in the Murate there were amusement and laughter; the nuns were highly-born ladies, gay rather than earnest. It might seem to that logical little mind that, for all its ceremonies and outward show of piety, the Convent of the Murate was less holy than that of Santa Lucia; and it was very important what this little girl thought of the Murate, for one day she was to make a grand marriage and hold a very high position in the world. She must be made to understand that the Murate's way of life was, in its comfort, as godly as that of the Santa Lucia in its austerity.

'You are a little puzzled by our ways here, Duchessina?' asked the Reverend Mother.

'I am very happy here, my Mother.'

She was a little diplomat already. It was certainly very important that she should be made to see the Murate point of view.

'You never saw such ceremonies as you witnessed yesterday when you were at Santa Lucia. Yet, in that convent, the strictest rules of Holy Church were adhered to. Here, you think, we eat meat on Fridays; our services are beautiful; our church full of colour; we do not wear coarse linen; you think we are not so forgetful of the vanities of the world as our sisters of Santa Lucia.'

'Oh no, Reverend Mother.'

But the Reverend Mother continued: 'We wash our bodies, and that the nuns of Santa Lucia would tell you is a sin.'

Caterina was silent.

'And yet,' said the Reverend Mother, 'it is the Santa Lucia that has been visited with the plague, and the Murate is the only unpolluted spot in Florence. That is a miracle, my little one. Let us pray now. Let us give our thanks to the saints for showing us that our way of life is the one which has given them most pleasure.'

The Reverend Mother watched the grave little face while Caterina murmured her prayers. The child was learning the first of the lessons the Murate had to teach her.

✤ ✤ ✤

Caterina loved to sit stitching at the tapestry with those who were her friends. There were hardly any in the convent who were not her friends; but those nuns whose families supported the Government felt it their duty to treat the little Medici with some reserve.

As they stitched at the altar cloth which they were making, they talked. Caterina loved to speak of Ippolito, to tell the nuns of his charm and his gaiety and his chivalry; she even confided in one or two of them the hope that she would one day marry him. She knew that he was alive. She could not say how she knew, but she was certain of it. 'It is something inside me that tells me this is so,' she tried to explain.

She was happy in the Murate – as happy as she could be without Ippolito. And with that peaceful feeling within which told her she would see Ippolito again one day she felt that she might enjoy these pleasant hours. There was one summer's day as she sat at work with the others on this altar cloth that a conversation took place which she was to remember all her life.

Lucia, a garrulous young nun, was talking of miracles which had been performed in the convent.

'Once,' said Lucia, 'the Murate was very poor indeed, and there was great trouble throughout Florence. The city was as poor as the Murate, and the citizens thought to beg relief from the Impruneta Virgin. So they brought the statue into the city and every convent was expected to make some offering to the Virgin. Now, here in the Murate, we had nothing at all, and we did not know what to do.'

'Ah!' said Sister Margaretta. 'You are going to tell the story of the Black Virgin's Cloak. I have heard it many times.'

'Doubtless you have, and doubtless our Duchessina has never heard it.'

'I have not,' said Caterina. 'Nor has little Maria.' Little Maria was the novice whose ceremonial entrance Caterina had recently witnessed. 'We should like to hear, should we not, Maria?'

Maria said she would like to hear the story of the Black Virgin's Cloak.

'Well,' went on Lucia, 'the Reverend Mother summoned all the sisterhood to her and she said, "Do not despair. We will give the Impruneta Virgin a cloak. It will be a cloak such as has never been seen before in Florence, a cloak of rich brocade, lined with ermine and embroidered with gold."

'The nuns were aghast, for how could they in their poverty give such a mantle? But there was about the Reverend Mother a look of such holiness that there were some, as they declared afterwards, who knew a miracle was about to be performed. "Listen to me," said the Reverend Mother. "This mantle shall be made through prayer. For six yards of brocade three psalters in honour of the Holy Trinity shall be sung; fifty psalms for each yard with *Gloria tibi Domine*, and meditations on the great favours Mary received from the Father, Son, and Holy Ghost. For the ermine skins seven thousand times the *Ave Maria*; for the embroidered crowns sixty-three times the Rosary; for a golden clasp seven hundred times the *O Gloriosa Domina*; for a golden button seven hundred times the *Alma*

Redemptoris Mater; for embroidered roses seven hundred times the *Ave Santissima Maria.*" Well, there were many prayers to be said for each item that went into the making of the cloak; and so, in addition to other duties, the nuns of the Murate must say these thousands of prayers. It meant hours and hours of devotions.'

Caterina leaned forward. 'But even then,' she said, 'they would have no mantle to lay at the feet of the Virgin, for you need brocade and ermine and silver and gold for such a mantle, and these were only prayers.'

'But you have not heard all, Duchessina. On the day when the gifts were to be given, many people were gathered in the *piazza* before the municipal palace. The great figure of the Virgin was placed there, waiting to receive the gifts; and gifts there were in plenty – beautiful gold and silver and precious stones. And there stood the Reverend Mother and sisters of the Murate empty-handed, but faces shining, for in their minds they saw the beautiful mantle that was made of prayers. And then . . . what do you think? Two men came forward, and at the feet of the Virgin, on behalf of the Murate, they said, they laid a mantle of brocade lined with ermine, embroidered with roses in exactly the detail the Reverend Mother had described to her nuns. The two men were angels, and that was the miracle of the Virgin's Cloak. There, Duchessina. What do you think of that? I might say that from that time the Murate passed into prosperity, for the tale spread and many rich ladies came to share the life of the convent, and many donations were given. It was a great miracle.'

'Oh, it was wonderful!' cried Maria; but Caterina said nothing.

'Well, Duchessina?' asked Lucia.

'I think,' said Caterina, 'that it was a very good miracle, and I think that the two angels were two men.'

'Two men! You mean it was no miracle?'

Caterina's solemn dark eyes surveyed the nuns. She felt old and wise in spite of her youth. 'It *was* a miracle,' she said, and as she spoke she felt that this was how the present Reverend Mother would have explained it to her, 'because the Holy Virgin would have put the idea of the cloak into that Reverend Mother's head. "Make a mantle of prayers," she would have been told, "but at the same time have one made embroidered with jewels. Let two men appear as angels and lay it at my feet. For if you made such a mantle yourself, rich as it is, it would not please the people so much as one made of prayers and presented by two whom they could think of as angels."'

'You mean you believe it to have been a trick?'

'It was a miracle,' insisted Caterina. 'It brought prosperity to the convent. The object of miracles is to do good. Miracles come from Heaven, but they are sometimes made on Earth.'

Lucia put an arm about Caterina and kissed her. 'You are too clever for us,' she said.

Knots of people stood outside the convent walls. They murmured amongst themselves.

'She is but a child.'

'A child of serpents.'

'We could not harm a child.'

'She will be eleven or twelve . . . old enough for mischief, if she be a Medici.'

'The nuns will keep her from doing harm.'

'She will lure the nuns into mischief. You know not these

crafty Medici. They are born cunning. The city is in a state of siege. A Medici is sending those shots into Florence. A Medici is preventing our food reaching us, and here we stand starved, ragged, and wounded, and there are those among us who say, "Spare the Medici child!" Shall we spare the spawn of tyrants?'

From inside the convent walls, Caterina heard the shouts of the people. She knew there was no longer safety for her at the Murate. Trouble had risen in Florence and was creeping close to the sanctuary of the walled-in-ones. Even her friends who loved her, even the Reverend Mother, could not save her now.

The whole of Florence was rising in hatred against the Pope. Some time ago, dressed as a pedlar, he had escaped from St Angelo, and when the plague had driven its ravishers from Rome, he had returned to the Vatican. Now he was determined to subdue Florence, but Florence was not easily subdued. The Florentines had relentlessly cleared a space one mile wide all round the city, burning beautiful villas and destroying rich lands so as to give the enemy no cover. Every one of them had given himself up to the task of defence – even artists like Michelangelo had left their work to join in the fight. For months the struggle had gone on, and Caterina knew that the citizens of Florence had not forgotten that the Convent of the Murate sheltered her, a daughter of that house which was bringing death and disaster to Florence.

She knew that another happy period of her life was fast coming to an end. She had grown to love the convent, her lessons, the sensuously stirring chants for which, at one time, the convent had been censured by Savonarola; she had loved the spice of intrigue, the sending out of baskets of pastry by certain nuns of the convent to members of their families, baskets which would be embroidered with the Medici sign of seven balls, and were meant to indicate that, shut away from the world though the nuns were, they retained their interest in politics.

Notes were sent into the convent in the baskets. It was thus that she had heard that Ippolito was safe in Rome. She had felt lightheaded with joy when she had heard that; but it was not such good news that Alessandro was also in Rome. In all the years that Caterina had been away from Ippolito, she had never forgotten him.

And now, outside the convent walls, an angry mob was shouting for her.

'Give us the Medici girl! Give us the witch! We are going to hang her in a basket on the wall of the city so that Clement's men may have her for their target.'

'Hang her in a basket! That's too good for her. Give her to the soldiers! Let them have their sport with her. Then we can decide how she shall die.'

Night came and the city was quieter. Another day of siege had been lived through.

There was a sudden knocking on the outer door of the convent, a knocking that echoed through those great corridors and seemed to be answered by the violent beating of Caterina's heart.

The Reverend Mother took her lantern and, going to the door, found there three senators from the Government of the city. They had come for Caterina de' Medici.

Caterina knew this could mean only one thing. It was the sequel to that obscene shouting which had been going on all day outside the convent walls. Death for Caterina! Death? Such horror, indeed, that death seemed preferable.

In their cells the nuns were praying – praying to the Virgin for a miracle that would save their Duchessina. But Caterina had no time for prayers. She ran to her cell, and there, in a frenzy of terror, she cut off all her lovely fair hair. When she had done this, she ran from cell to cell until she found a dress of the Order, and this she put on. After that, she felt composed and ready to face what might be awaiting her.

She went down to the men who had come for her. The Reverend Mother and the nuns, as well as the men, stared at her in astonishment.

'I am Caterina Maria Romola de' Medici,' she said haughtily. 'What do you want of me?'

'I am Salvestro Aldobrandini,' said the leader of the men, 'a senator of the Florentine Government. It has been decided that you shall leave the Convent of the Murate, where you are suspected of carrying on intrigues against the Government. You are to be transferred to the Convent of Santa Lucia, and we order you to leave with us at once.'

'I shall not go,' she said.

'Then we must take you by force.'

'You would not dare walk through the streets with me in these clothes.'

'You have no right to wear those clothes. Take them off.'

'I refuse. Will you take a nun, a bride of Christ, through the streets of Florence?'

That was a clever stroke. They all knew it. Nuns were sacred, vowed to Christ; and it would not be easy to carry a struggling female, her head shorn and her dress proclaiming her to be a nun, through the streets of Florence.

'We do not wish harm to befall you,' said Aldobrandini. 'We have men to defend you as we pass through the streets.'

Caterina, alert of mind, was quick to sum up the character of this Aldobrandini; he did not like the task which had been allotted to him. He was wavering.

'I refuse to take off these clothes,' said Caterina.

The Reverend Mother said: 'Good sir, leave her with me until morning. I will pray with her. She will then find in her heart the courage she needs.'

To the astonishment of all, Aldobrandini agreed to wait until morning; and all that night the nuns of the Murate prayed for Caterina.

✣ ✣ ✣

The little procession rode silently through the city. Aldobrandini had chosen the quiet streets, but it did not take long for the news to spread. 'They are taking the little Medici out of Florence. They seek to protect her.'

Rough jests passed from lip to lip; obscene threats were murmured, then shouted.

Aldobrandini wanted no violence. If anything happened to the girl now, he would be held responsible at a later date. Already Clement's brief humiliation was over. He had made peace with the mighty Charles of Spain, who, for a considera-tion, was now his ally; and Florence was realising her mistake in siding with France and England instead of with Spain.

'Give us the Medici!' shouted a voice. 'Give to us the daughter of tyrants. Let her learn to suffer . . . as we have.'

The hoarse cry was taken up. 'Give us the Medici!'

Caterina had need of all her courage, but her long training helped her to hide her fear, and she was glad of it now. She looked neither to right nor left; she sat her horse with haughty grace and seeming indifference to the snarling cry of the mob.

Suddenly there was a rush, a flurry of blows and cries, and

the ranks of her guards were broken. The little Medici was seen clearly for the first time.

'It's a nun!' shouted a voice. 'A holy nun!'

'They've tricked us. They are not bringing the Medici this way. They have tricked us with a nun while she makes her escape.'

Even now Caterina looked straight before her and continued to ride on as though what was happening about her was no concern of hers.

There was a pause in the rush of the rabble, which gave her guards a chance to close around her again. The crowd fell back.

'They're tricking us!' shouted a voice. 'They've dressed her up as a nun! Come! Shall we allow them to trick us?'

But the people were unsure; they were afraid to harm a bride of Christ.

The fear in Caterina's heart was replaced by triumph. She had performed a miracle no less than that Reverend Mother had with her cloak. She had saved herself from she knew not what – perhaps death itself. How wise, she told herself, to rely, not upon prayers, but on her own Medici wits.

✤ ✤ ✤

A few months after that terrifying ride through Florence Caterina was in Rome. Florence had surrendered; Clement was in command, so he sent for his young kinswoman to join him; she was getting very near a marriageable age.

How wonderful it was to meet Ippolito after all these years! How exciting to find him more handsome than ever, and that there was a change in his attitude towards her! She was no longer the little girl whose company he had enjoyed at the

Medici Palace; she was nearly fourteen; she had lost that angularity of form and was budding into womanhood.

Life had become miraculously pleasant once more. She had grown fond of her friends at the Murate, but how she enjoyed the gaiety of Rome! There was another reason for pleasure: Alessandro was not in Rome; he had been installed in the Medici Palace in Florence, for Clement had kept his promise to the boy and had, to the horror of all Italy and the terror of Florence, made the monster ruler of that great city. Ippolito had been stunned when he had heard that Alessandro was to have what had been promised to him; he was still bewildered; he could not believe that the Holy Father could treat him so shabbily; he was angry for himself and afraid for Florence. It was Caterina's chief concern to try to lift him from the frustration and melancholy which enveloped him.

They were both lodged in one of the palaces of Vatican City, and life there, with the coming and going of ambassadors and the ceremony which surrounded the Papal Court, was varied and full of interest for the girl who had lived so long behind convent walls. But she must make Ippolito happy; she must prove to him that there was greater joy in life than ruling Florence. She saw that she delighted him with her quick retorts, her plump little body, her rich fair hair and those fine, flashing eyes of hers. He had been happier since her return.

They rode together. Caterina was an excellent horse-woman. With a few attendants, they would spend the whole day on horseback whenever they could manage it.

It was to Caterina that Ippolito unburdened himself of his unhappiness; he could speak of little else during their first weeks together, for not only had he been robbed of his inheritance, but he was being thwarted in his choice of a career.

'Caterina, the Holy Father has sent for me. He dismissed Excellency and said he would speak with me privately. Then he told me of the future he has planned for me.'

She saw her dream of happiness threatened. 'Ippolito! You are not going away from here?'

'It is not that. He wishes me to go into the Church.'

'You . . . into the Church! But you are not a churchman!'

'So I told him. I said, "Holiness, I consider myself unfit for the honour you would bestow upon me. I am not a man of God. I have been brought up to believe that Florence would be mine." Then he grew angry. "Enough!" he cried. "Florence has been provided with a ruler." He was angry; but I was angry too. I forgot I was in the presence of the Holy Father. "I marvel, Holiness," I said, "that one of such uncertain parentage should be put above me." He clenched his fist and all but shouted at me, "You are so certain of *your* parentage then?" I said proudly that my father was the honoured Duke of Nemours and my mother was a Florentine lady, whereas, though it was known who was Alessandro's father, his mother was said to be a Barbary slave. Then was he truly angry. "It is no concern of yours," he said. "I am determined you shall go into the Church."'

'Oh, Ippolito, can you not hold out against his wishes?'

'Our lives are in his hands, Caterina. And there are times when I forget that he is our Pope. There are times when I hate him. He cares nothing for us; little for the Church. Power is his god. He has made Alessandro, his secret bastard, ruler of Florence; and Florence under Alessandro, Caterina, resembles Rome under Nero. No one is safe from his lust and his cruelty. People are flying from the city when they can. Do you remember the two Ruggieri brothers?'

'Cosmo and Lorenzo!' she cried.

'They have escaped from Florence. They bring sad tales with them. You knew Alessandro as a vicious boy; he has become a monster. I hear His Holiness has arranged a marriage for his bastard with none other than the daughter of Emperor Charles.'

'Poor Emperor's daughter!' said Caterina.

Ippolito turned his eyes upon her. 'Caterina, I thank the saints that His Holiness let the monster masquerade as your brother. If he had not, it might have been you who would have been married to Alessandro.'

Caterina could not speak. There were no words to express the horror such an idea brought to them both.

It was so great that it made Ippolito forget his troubles; Caterina, lifting her eyes to his, thought she saw a response to her own delight.

Ippolito took her hand and kissed it.

'Life has consolations to offer, Caterina,' he said. And they laughed and whipped up their horses.

Never had Caterina been so happy. She sent for the brothers Ruggieri. She gave them orders for perfumes and lotions. She begged them to look into her future. It was exciting to wrap herself in a cloak and slip quickly through the streets of Rome to the room these brothers shared. She begged them to let her look into the magic mirror. She would see the face of the man who was to be her husband. The brothers had fled from Florence; they had not, here in Rome, the necessary articles for their study. They would do their best for their little Duchess. Soon they would find some means of showing her the face of her future husband.

But Caterina believed she saw it; it was noble and dark, a handsome face with eyes that flashed and sparkled – Medici eyes very like her own.

This was to be in love. To sing for happiness, to see the river sparkling as it had never sparkled before, the grand and imposing buildings softened, more lovely, the faces of those about her more gentle, the sun more warming; in this new emotion was the dread that she might not see Ippolito this day, then the overwhelming delight when she did.

Ippolito could not remain ignorant of this joy which had seized her. He must see it in the shine of her eyes, in the inflexion of her voice when she spoke to him.

They spoke of their love when they rode out together. This is the happiest day of my life, thought Caterina, looking back at that most gracious of cities glittering in sunshine that had never been so bright as it was on this day of Caterina's happiness.

Ippolito said: 'I pray the saints that you are as happy as I am, Caterina. I bless them because the Pope cannot marry you to Alessandro.'

'Do not speak of him on such a day as this.'

'No,' agreed Ippolito. 'Let us speak of ourselves instead.'

'Oh yes . . . of ourselves, Ippolito.'

'I love you, Caterina. I loved you when you were a little girl and we were together in the palace in our beloved Florence.'

'I loved you also, Ippolito. I have never ceased to think of you during the years of our separation. I knew that we should be together again.'

They had stopped. The attendants kept some distance behind; they had known, before the young people were aware of it, of this state of love between them.

Ippolito took her hand and kissed it.

'The Holy Father means us for each other,' he said. 'Depend upon it. He would not allow us to be together if that were not so.'

'You are right, Ippolito. Oh, how happy I am!'

'I too. Caterina, since you love me, it does not seem to matter that I have lost Florence.'

'I understand. I have been unhappy; I have suffered . . . loneliness and horror. But I do not care now, Ippolito, because life has brought me this.'

They longed to kiss, to embrace, but how could they, here in the open country with their attendants behind them? They could talk of their future, though; they could promise love and passion with their eyes.

'Caterina, I do not believe the people of Florence will long submit to Alessandro's tyranny.'

'No, Ippolito. I am sure they will not.'

'And then, my love, I shall rule Florence . . . and you with me. We shall be together in the palace where we spent our childhood.'

She said: 'Ippolito, can one die of happiness, for if one can, I fear you will lose me.'

He answered: 'I cannot bear to look at you and not kiss you. Let us ride.'

Later there were embraces; there were kisses; it was not possible to keep such a charming love affair secret. And why should it be secret? Ippolito, Caterina, cousins and both Medici. Why should their union be denied the Papal blessing?

The happy days marched quickly past.

Such a matter could not be kept long from the Pontifical ears. The news was whispered among the Swiss Guards and the Palatine Guards and the palace lackeys until it came to the ears of the bishops and cardinals, and through them it reached Monsignor, who in his turn passed it on to the Master of the Household, his Excellency, whose duty it was to live close to the Holy Father himself.

His Holiness was furious. He hated Ippolito – hated him for his handsome face, his charming manners and his popularity. He knew that, if he were not very careful, he was going to have trouble with Ippolito. The stubborn youth had tried to turn his back on a brilliant career in the Church, and all because Alessandro had been made ruler of Florence. Ippolito would be another such as his father and Lorenzo the Magnificent. Ippolito did not fit into the papal schemes.

Now, Caterina did. Great wealth and power were to come to Clement through this girl. Her marriage was his first consideration now, and great plans were afoot.

The Pope looked at his long hands and seemed to see pictures of men as on playing cards that he would hold fan-shape and wonder which to play. There was the Duke of Albany – not a good choice, for he was Caterina's uncle by marriage; there was the Duke of Milan, ailing and old enough to be her grandfather, though his declining fortunes went against him rather than his age. The Duke of Mantua? The life this man had led was similar to that led by Caterina's own father and that which Alessandro was now leading in Florence. Such a marriage was not desirable. Caterina's father had made a grand marriage with a lady related to the royal family of France, and what had happened? Death for the parents, after the birth of one child – a girl, Caterina – who had by a miracle escaped the result of her father's sins. No! He wanted a husband who was rich and powerful, though power and birth came before riches, as it was with Medici wealth that he should be drawn into the net. There was the King of Scotland. But that was a remote and poor country. 'It would cost me more than her dowry to bring me news of such a place!' he said to himself. There were others. The Count of Vaudemont, and even the Duke of Richmond, illegitimate son of Henry VIII of England. The Pope frowned on illegitimacy, although he himself was illegitimate and had risen to power in spite of it.

But now into the marriage market had stepped a dazzling bargain. A bride was wanted for Henry of Orléans, second son of none other than the King of France.

When His Holiness had heard of this, he had kissed his fisherman's ring and asked the Virgin's blessing. The house of Medici allied to the mighty house of France!

First sons had a way of dying; some were hurried to their deaths. The wives of second sons could become queens. Queen of France! Breeding children that were half Medici, and ready to be very kind to their mother's family! If this marriage could be arranged, it would be the brightest event that had ever taken place in the Medici family. The marriage of Caterina's father to a connexion of the Bourbons would be nothing compared with Caterina's marriage with the house of Valois.

He must go carefully. He had spoken of the proposed French marriage to Emperor Charles, who, laughing slyly up his sleeve, had suggested the Pope try to bring it about. He was thinking that a sharp rebuff from France would do Clement good. Does a royal house mate with such as the Medici? They were rulers of Florence, it was true, but they had their roots in trade. No, thought Charles. Francis would laugh down his long nose at the effrontery of the Pope, and make some witty remark at his expense. But there was something Charles had forgotten which the Pope remembered. There were always ways of tempting the French King. He had ever cast covetous eyes on Italy, and if Clement promised the Duchy of Milan as part of a fabulous dowry, he might bring this about. Tentative negotiations were already going forward, and the Pope was optimistic.

And now this news. This crass stupidity. These absurd young people! It seemed that the whole of Rome was talking about 'the Medici lovers'. And Ippolito – the eternal thorn in his side – was the cause of it.

The Pope sent for Caterina.

Through the long series of halls and rooms, past the papal lackeys and the guards, she came. She was in that dream of soft happiness which was always with her now; her thoughts dwelt constantly on Ippolito. She and Ippolito together, all through their lives; and if Alessandro did not die or was not displaced, well then it would still be Caterina and Ippolito, happy, in love for ever. Being together was all that mattered. Where they were was unimportant.

Monsignor was waiting for her in one of the outer chambers. He looked so sombre in his purple cassock that she felt sorry for him; indeed she felt sorry for all who were not Caterina and Ippolito.

'His Holiness awaits you,' said Monsignor; and he led her into the presence.

She knelt and kissed the fisherman's ring, and felt relieved that it was not to be a private audience, for Excellency did not leave them.

'My dearly beloved daughter,' said His Holiness, 'I am

making arrangements for you to leave Rome immediately.'

'Leave Rome!' she cried out before she could stop herself. Leave Rome! Leave Ippolito?

The Pope expressed silent surprise at such bad manners.

'To leave Rome immediately,' he went on.

She was silent. Tears were in her eyes. She was afraid His Holiness would see them. Why was he sending her away? She sensed in this some threat to her love. She could not help it; she must speak.

'Holy Father, I . . . I do not want to leave Rome now.'

Excellency was standing very still. Even the Holy Father was silent. They could not understand her. Could she have forgotten that it was not for any to argue with the Pope of Rome?

The Holy Father's lips were tight. 'There is a threat of plague in Rome. We cannot allow our dearly beloved daughter to take the risk of remaining here.'

It was untrue. There was no plague in Rome. She knew, instinctively, that this was a plot to separate her from her beloved Ippolito.

She forgot decorum, forgot the dignity due to the Holy Father. 'Where . . . where shall I go, Father?'

'To Florence,' he said.

'Oh, Father, is . . . my cousin Ippolito to come with me?'

There was a horrified silence. Excellency's face was a blank mask that hid surprise. The Holy Father looked down into the anguished eyes of his young relative, and found himself answering her question instead of reprimanding her.

'Your cousin Ippolito is to go on a mission to Turkey.'

She did not speak; her lips trembled. She knew that she had been living in a dream. There was to be no happiness with

Ippolito. It was not the wish of this all-powerful man that they should marry. They had been together through carelessness, through indifference to the torture separation must mean to them both.

Perhaps the Holy Father had some pity in him. He looked down at the misery in that pale young face.

'My daughter,' he said, 'you should rejoice. A great future awaits you.'

She did not mean to speak but the words escaped her: 'There is no future for me without Ippolito; without Ippolito I do not wish to live.'

The Pope was not so angry as he should have been at this affront to ceremonial dignity. He remembered his heated passion for a Barbary slave who had given him Alessandro.

'My daughter,' he said, and the gentleness of his voice startled Caterina out of her misery temporarily, 'my well beloved daughter, you know not what you say. I am arranging a great marriage for you. I hope to send for you in Florence. You will go to France, if all is as I plan; to France, my daughter, to marry the second son of the King.' He laid his hands on her head to bless her. 'To France, daughter. The second son of the King! Who knows, one day, you may be Queen of France. Miracles can happen, daughter. It may be that our family has been chosen to rule great countries. Sigh not. Weep no more. Your future is bright.'

Dazed with wretchedness, she allowed herself to be dismissed and led away. This was the end of rapture. This was goodbye to love. Clement's ambition, in the shape of the second son of the King of France, had come between her and her lover.

Chapter III

THE WEDDING

Riding on horseback from Florence down to the Tuscany coast, surrounded by all the noblest people of Florence, was a broken-hearted little girl. She was still dazed, bewildered by this horror which had overtaken her; she was supposed to rejoice at what they were pleased to call her great good fortune, and she could only weep.

Her uncle, Filippo Strozzi – a widower, for Aunt Clarissa had died before she was able to see what she would have called 'this great and happy event' – was in charge of the concourse until it should be joined by the Pope; after each day's journey he would summon his niece and talk to her, implore her to show some interest in her good fortune, to hide her melancholy, to suppress her folly, and with her family rejoice. But every member of her family did not rejoice, she pointed out.

Indeed, it was so. And Filippo Strozzi was inclined to think His Holiness had erred in making Ippolito of the party which was to conduct Caterina into France. 'It will put an end to rumour,' Clement had said. 'There must be no more of this talk of the Medici lovers.' Filippo shrugged his shoulders. All very well for His Holiness. Perhaps the life he had led did not give him great understanding of young and passionate lovers. Not that Clement had pursued unswervingly the life of a celibate. There was that depraved monster, Alessandro, to prove that. But His Holiness would never allow passion to interfere with ambition, and, being a man of little imagination, no doubt believed his young relatives would behave in similar fashion. Filippo was a man of the world, and, looking from the sad, smouldering eyes of Ippolito to the rebellious ones of Caterina, he knew it had been a mistake to include the young man in the party.

Ippolito was handsome enough, romantic enough to turn any girl's head; he had made a success of the mission in Turkey and had returned much earlier than had been expected – the lover, eager to see his love again. As for the girl, she was, even at fourteen, an adept at hiding her feelings, but the softness of those lovely eyes of hers when they rested on the young man betrayed her. Filippo would feel most uneasy until they boarded the French galleys which would take them across to Nice.

While Filippo longed for a sight of the Tuscany coast, Caterina dreaded it. She knew that once she left the soil of Italy she was doomed. There would be no escape then; but while she sat her horse and Ippolito was close to her, it was possible to dream, with the hope that out of the dream reality would come.

Why should they not ride away together?

Sometimes, during that journey, it was possible to exchange a few words with her cousin that would not be overheard by those surrounding them. Then in desperation she would throw aside reserve and plead for the fulfilment of their love.

'Ippolito, let us break away. Let us ride fast . . . anywhere, what does it matter? Let us be together.'

Ippolito looked at her sadly. She was only a child. She knew nothing of the world. Where would they go? How would they live? Escape was impossible. They would be brought back to the Pope.

'I would not care, Ippolito. We should have had some months, weeks, days together.'

'Caterina, do you think I have not brooded on this? I have made plans. But each one ends in wretchedness. I could not take you to that. Where would we live? Among beggars? Among robbers? There would be a price on our heads. There would be no safety. Caterina, you have been carefully nurtured. Oh, I know, you have faced dangers, but you have never known starvation, my love. Believe me, I have pondered this. I have looked for a way out for us as I have never looked for anything else, but I can find none, for there is none.'

'There is always a way, Ippolito,' she protested tearfully. 'There is always a way.'

But he shook his head. 'No, dearest cousin. We are as nothing — you and I. Your feelings? My feelings? Of what import are they? We are not meant to love. We are meant to marry and beget children . . . or to become celibates of the Church. For you, my love, life is not so cruel as it is for me. You are but a child and, say what you will, a glorious future awaits you. But for me . . . a life which I do not want.'

'Do you think I want a life away from you?'

'Oh, Caterina my love, you are so young. Perhaps you will love your husband. He is your own age. Why should you not? There will be happiness for you, Caterina, when you have forgotten me.'

'I shall never forget you!' she cried stormily; and she was hurt and more bewildered than ever. I would not have cared what happened to us as long as we could remain together, she thought. He does not love me as I love him. I think of him, and he thinks of comfort, safety, the future.

But the dream persisted. She believed that one day he would come to her and whisper his plan for their escape. But he did not, and it was with great relief that Filippo saw them all embark and leave the coast of Tuscany behind them, while Caterina, with despair in her heart stood, straining her eyes for the last look at the land she had hoped never to leave.

As they sailed towards Nice Filippo was constantly in the company of Caterina.

'My child,' he implored her, 'what will these French think if you go to them, a sullen-eyed bride? What will your young bridegroom think? Calm yourself. Be reasonable.'

'Reasonable!' she stormed. 'I am leaving all that I love, to live among strangers. Is that cause for rejoicing?'

'You are going among those who will cherish you. It is true that I, His Holiness, and Ippolito – those of your blood – cannot stay with you; but you will have your own countrymen and women about you. Why, you have the boy astrologers, the young Ruggieri, whom His Holiness allowed you to take with you; there is Madalenna, of whom you are fond; and there are others, such as young Sebastiano di Montecuculi. I could name dozens. You could not be alone in a strange land with so many friends from Italy about you.'

She did not say to him, 'I care not who is with me if Ippolito is absent.' But he understood; and he was kind and gentle to her as he never had been before.

She watched the pomp which the arrival of the Pope must create, and she knew now that, though Ippolito remained with her, he was already lost. It was a thrilling spectacle – sixty vessels hoisting their flags, saluting the Holy Father as he stepped aboard his own galley, which was sumptuously draped in gold brocade, sailing with the fleet towards Marseilles in a grand procession behind the leading vessel, which bore the Holy Sacrament. But there was no thrill for Caterina; there was only a sense of loss.

❀ ❀ ❀

During the second week of October in the year 1533, watchers at the Château d'If and the great fortress of Notre Dame de la Garde saw the first of the convoy, and signalled to the impatient people of Marseilles that the long-awaited fleet, which was bringing with it a bride for the son of their King, was on the last stage of its journey.

Outside the town was encamped the little bridegroom with his father and the courtiers; they were awaiting the arrival of the bridal party, since etiquette asked that the King should not enter his town until after the Holy Pope had made his entry.

The bells were ringing out; and the thunder of hundreds of cannon echoed in the streets. The people were impatient for a glimpse of the little Italian bride.

In the boat which had brought her to the shores of France, Caterina waited for what would happen next. Apprehension had subdued her misery. She was beginning to realise the significance of all this pomp and ceremony. Perhaps in the excitement of coming events she could forget some of her unhappiness.

She was told that the Constable of France would shortly come aboard to have a word with her. She waited expectant while the great man was rowed out to her boat. The sight of him, surrounded by attendants, alarmed her. He had a fierce mouth and cruel eyes.

He bore the feminine name of Anne de Montmorency, and he told her that great efforts had been made for her comfort while she stayed in Marseilles. He personally had supervised arrangements. It made her feel very important such a man should take such trouble on her account. There would be, he told her, one of the finest houses in the town at the disposal of her and her retinue. A similar house had been found for His Holiness and all the bishops and cardinals and Church dignitaries who had accompanied the Holy Father. There was another house for the French party. Anne de Montmorency would have the little Duchess know that France was honoured to receive her and her distinguished relative. Caterina, in perfect French, made the reply which was expected of her and was rewarded by the grim man's look of approval.

He took his leave and left her to await the time when she would land on French soil and make her way into Marseilles. But before this could take place there must be the entry of the Pope in his ceremonial procession, followed by the King in his; after that it would be her turn.

At length it came. Seated on a roan horse that was covered with brocade, Caterina rode into France. Behind her and before her rode the nobility of Italy. It mattered not that among them was Ippolito, for Ippolito was lost to her for ever. She dared no longer look his way; she dared not ride, a weeping bride, to meet her bridegroom.

And as she rode she became aware that all eyes in that vast crowd which lined the streets were fixed upon her; and those eyes were unsmiling. Did they dislike her, then? Had she disappointed them?

She was frightened, realising afresh that it was not only her lover whom she had lost; she had also said goodbye to home.

She held her head high. These foreigners should not know that they had frightened her. She would have courage – the same sort of courage which had carried her through the Florentine mob. She would have need of it.

Ippolito, she thought, oh, Ippolito, is it then too late? Could we not run away even now?

But Ippolito, riding ahead, so handsome that eyes followed him, was resigned to his loss. She must be resigned to hers also.

She began to think about her young husband and wonder what he was like.

The Pope himself performed the ceremony. Side by side, Caterina and Henry stood before him, repeating the solemn words. All about them were the dazzling nobility of France and Italy.

Caterina scarcely heard the service; she was only vaguely aware of the crowded church; all her interest was for the boy beside her.

He was tall, she saw, and well-built; his muscles hardened, she was to discover, by fencing, tilting and, of course, the chase. He was dark; and because, in her thoughts he had been an ogre, a monster not unlike Alessandro, she thought him handsome in his gorgeous, bejewelled clothes. He seemed to brood, though, to be sullen, and she feared he was not pleased with her. She wondered that, in view of her love for Ippolito, she could have cared; yet she did care. It hurt her pride that she should have disappointed him. He kept his eyes averted; she wanted to smile at him, to imply that it was frightening for her as well as for him; she wanted to tell him that she had dreaded this marriage; that she had suffered the torments of misery; but that now she had seen him she felt a little happier. She had loved and lost, and happiness was dead as far as she was concerned; but she did not dislike her bridegroom; she could even fancy he bore a slight resemblance to Ippolito, for he was dark and tall and handsome. But the boy did not give her a glance.

When the ceremony was over, Caterina forgot her bridegroom, for the most dazzling, brilliant personage she had ever seen in the whole of her life came forward and took her hand. She lifted her eyes and looked into the twinkling ones that smiled down at her. They were kind eyes, though they looked tired and had dark bags beneath them; they were debauched eyes, but not depraved; they were amused, but not sardonic; they seemed to say, 'This seems an ordeal, does it not? But it will pass, and you will find that it contained much to laugh at. That is life.'

'I will lead the bride back to my own residence,' he declared, 'where a banquet is awaiting her.'

This kind and charming man was none other, she knew, than Francis himself, the King of France. She flushed as she murmured her thanks. She could not but be charmed; she could not help the flutter of excitement that his presence brought to her. Such grace, such kindness, such brilliance must inevitably dim even the image of Ippolito.

She had seen him before. He had kissed her when he had welcomed her to France; he had called her 'daughter', and had given her rich gifts. She had known that richer gifts had gone from Italy to France – and there was the promise of many more – but never had gifts seemed so precious as those given with the charm of the King. He had not forgotten, either, to whisper a compliment on her appearance, which had not been necessary to the ceremonial etiquette, but had been given out of kindness, to make her feel happy and at home. She realised now, as he took her hand, that if her wretchedness had lifted a little, if a life that must be lived without Ippolito had in the last few days seemed a little less grey, it was due to this man.

Now, for the wedding ceremony, he looked more dazzling than he had at their first meeting. He wore white satin, and his mantle, studded with pearls and precious stones, was of cloth of gold. She herself was magnificent with her corsage of ermine and her white satin gown, studded with pearls and diamonds, but she felt insignificant beside him.

How the people cheered him! How they loved him! Who would not? He was a King who looked like a King.

'Well, little daughter,' he murmured to her, 'the ceremony is over. Now you shall be our daughter in very truth.'

'Sire,' she answered, 'you have made me feel that I already am. I shall always remember that the biggest welcome I had in France was from her King.'

He looked at her with a smile, and thought that it was a shame that she should be married to his tongue-tied son, since evidently she would know how to make the remarks which would be expected of her.

'My sweet Catherine,' he said, 'you are now a French-woman. You are no longer Italian Caterina, but French Catherine. This is a christening ceremony as well as a wedding. How do you like the change?'

'It sounds very pleasant . . . as you say it.'

'I see you are well schooled in diplomacy. A necessary art, I do assure you, for ladies and gentlemen of the court.'

'A necessary art for all, Sire.'

'Ah, you are a wise little girl. Tell me . . . in confidence if you like. What do you think of your husband?'

'I like his looks.'

'And what of his quiet ways?'

'I have scarcely had time to know them.'

'Well, well, little Catherine. Marriages are made in Heaven, you know.'

'Some are,' she said quickly, 'but mine, Sire, was made in Rome.'

He laughed. 'And in France, my dear. We studied your picture and I said, "What a charming child!" And I thought then that I should love my new daughter.'

'And now that you have seen her in the flesh, Sire?'

'And now, I no longer say, "I think", but "I know".'

'You are quick to love, Sire.'

He looked at her sharply. She looked demure. He wondered what tales had reached her of the amorous King of France.

'Love,' he said lyrically, 'is the most beautiful of all the gifts the gods have given us. I have been falling in love since I was your age, my child. And the result is that I do it easily and naturally. It is second nature to me.'

It was making her almost happy to be on such merry terms with this enchanting man. She found herself laughing as she had never thought to laugh again.

'Oh yes,' went on the King, sincerely now, 'we are going to be friends, my little Catherine. Now tell me. You have seen very little of our country yet, but what do you like best about it?'

She answered him immediately with a candid glance. 'Its King, Sire.'

He was delighted, for after all was it not delightful to be in the company of a charming little diplomat of – what was it? - fourteen? He was pleasantly surprised with his daughter-in-law. She was more French than Italian already, he was willing to swear.

The King would have his little Catherine sit next to him at the banquet. Oh yes, he knew her place was beside her new husband, but *Foy de gentilhomme*, the boy should have her beside him for a lifetime. Would he grudge his father her company at her first French banquet? When the King talked, all stopped to hang on his words. They noticed his tenderness towards the little girl; she was his dearest little daughter Catherine – Caterina no longer, he declared. She was his Catherine, his little French Catherine; he had had her gracious permission to make the change.

'The little Catherine has made a conquest of the King!' Some said it; some thought it. Well, of course, it was not difficult for a young woman to please the King, but there had been some speculation about this one, for the King seemed to despise the boy they had brought her to marry.

At the first of the three great tables, with the King, her new husband, the Princes her brothers-in-law and the Cardinals, sat Catherine – she was even thinking of herself as Catherine now. Caterina was the girl who had thought life would be drab and dreary for evermore because she had lost her lover; Catherine was not sure of that. She still loved her cousin; she still believed that she would love no other as long as she lived; but this charming King had made her realise that she could laugh again, that she could be happy, if only for a moment or two.

She was glad that the Pope was not at this table; he held the place of honour next to the Queen at the second. It was exhilarating, she found, to be among these people who, until now, had been names in the lessons she had to learn concerning them. That Queen was the lady the King had been forced to marry after his humiliating defeat and imprisonment. No wonder he hardly looked at her. She had a sweet and kindly face, but she looked prim compared with some of the ladies. Catherine studied them now. They were at the third table, and among them was the dashing and fascinating Mademoiselle d'Heilly, the King's mistress, who remained his favourite whilst others came and went. Catherine could understand why. She was lovely with her bright, fair, curly hair and her intelligent face; she was speaking now, and all those about her were laughing gaily.

There was one other whom Catherine noticed at the ladies' table. This was a tall and beautiful woman as dark as Mademoiselle d'Heilly was fair, and almost as lovely. She was noticeable because, in that array of sparkling colours and flashing jewels, she wore the black and white of mourning. How striking she looked! She was conspicuous among them all; she caught the eye by her very austerity.

Catherine decided that she would take an early opportunity of learning the identity of the tall dark lady who wore black-and-white mourning.

But of all the people around her there was one whom she must regard with the most interest and apprehension. Her husband! Her heart fluttered as she appraised him. She was astonished at her feelings. She had expected to view him with distaste and horror; but how could she feel those emotions for a shy boy only a month or so older than herself? She could see in him a likeness to his father, and she felt that she already loved the King. The boy naturally seemed insignificant when compared with his father, but that likeness was more than reassuring; it was – and she did not understand this – strangely exciting.

I wish he would smile at me! she thought. I wish he would give some sign that he is a little interested.

Once he looked up and caught her eye upon him. He was trying to take a peep at her when he thought himself unobserved. She smiled shyly, but he looked down on his plate and blushed.

She felt wounded and therefore angry with him. Why had she thought him like his father, that man whose manners were the most courtly, the most charming she had ever known!

But suddenly, she saw his expression change. He was very handsome now; and she was angry that he could smile for someone and not for her. Who was it?

Why, it was none other than the lady in black and white!

✤ ✤ ✤

During the merry-making the King had taken the Pope into a small antechamber for a little private talk.

The King was saying: 'They are young yet, Holiness. Here in France we let them be together . . . as friends, you understand? The idea being, your Holiness will see, that they should understand each other before the marriage is consummated.'

The Holy Father shook his head. 'Nay, Sire. They are both of marriageable age. I see no reason for delaying the consummation of the marriage.'

The King lifted his shoulders with elegance. 'Our little Catherine barely fourteen and my son a few months older!

Marriage, yes, Holiness. But give them time to fall in love. In France we hold love of great importance.'

Francis smiled his most charming smile, while he thought: why not say what is in your mind, crafty one? You want our children to provide successors without delay. You want to make sure there are Medici hands stretching greedily for the crown of France.

'Young people,' declared the Pontiff, 'need to marry young if they are to lead godly lives. Let them get their childbearing started early. It keeps the Devil behind them. I say the marriage should be consummated at once.'

Francis smiled whimsically, trying to imagine them together. Poor little Catherine! Worthy of a more gallant husband! The young oaf had scarcely looked at her all day; instead, he had stared at the Poitiers woman with calf-love in his eyes. Who would have believed she would have that effect upon him! A woman old enough to be his mother!

'Then let it be,' said Francis. 'Poor child, she will, I fear, find him an inadequate lover.'

The Pope was alarmed. 'Sire, what mean you?'

Francis, realising how his light remark had been mis-construed, could not resist the desire to tease. 'Alas! Holiness, I have my fears regarding the boy . . . in that respect.'

Little beads of sweat stood out on the pontifical brow. 'You cannot mean . . . you surely do not mean? . . .'

'Alas! alas! I do, I fear, Holiness.'

'I did not understand. You mean . . . an inability to procreate children?'

Francis burst out laughing. 'Oh, that?' He shrugged his shoulders. 'For that we must wait and see. I mean, Holiness, that I fear he will give a poor account of himself as a lover. So young! So inexperienced! He has never had a mistress.'

The Pope was so relieved that he joined in the King's laughter. 'You must forgive me, Sire. You French think continually of love. One forgets that.'

'You Italians, what do you think of . . . trade?'

The Pope would have liked to slap the dark and smiling face.

'Making trade,' he said shortly, 'can at times be more profitable than making love.'

'In Italy, perhaps,' said the King. 'But here in France it has often proved that love is not only more delightful but more profitable than trade. So, who are right – we French, or you Italians?'

The Holy Father had no intention of getting involved in a battle of words with the French King. He said: 'Then, Sire, you agree that the marriage should be consummated this night?'

'Not a night shall be lost!' cried Francis ironically. 'And how long will my poor country be honoured by your noble presence, Father?'

'I shall stay the month.'

Francis smiled slyly. 'They are young and healthy, both of them. A month . . . yes, I should say a month.'

The Pope tried to emulate the soft voice and smiling irony of the French King. It was not easy. The King merely despised the Pope, while the Pope hated the King.

The boy and girl lay in the costly bed. They were both afraid.

The wedding day was over; they had been undressed by their attendants and ceremoniously conducted to the marriage bed. And now they were left together.

Each sensed the other's fear.

Catherine thought, Oh, Ippolito, it should have been you. Everything would have been different then . . . different and wonderful.

Cautiously she touched her eyes and found them wet.

The boy was sweating. He felt that of all the ordeals he had been forced to face in his miserable life, this was the worst.

She could feel his trembling. Could he hear the beating of her heart? She knew and he knew that their duty must be done.

She waited for him to speak. It seemed that she waited a long time.

Then: 'You . . . you must not blame me. I . . . I did not want this. But . . . since they have married us . . .'

His voice was lost in the darkness.

She answered quickly: 'I did not want it either.'

But now she knew that, great though her fear was, she was less afraid than the boy. That moved her suddenly, and she felt a longing to comfort him.

Why, though he was older than she was – only by a few months, it was true – hers was the greater knowledge of life. She had loved Ippolito and lost him; she had lived and suffered as a woman, whereas he had never been anything but a boy.

It was her place, therefore, to comfort, to lead.

'Henry,' she said gently, and she moved towards him.

❖ ❖ ❖

These two lay still and silent in the state bed until the early hours of the morning, when they fell into deep sleep.

When Catherine awoke it was broad daylight. She thought for the moment that she was in her bedroom in Florence; but almost immediately she was aware of her young husband beside her, and, remembering her wedding day and the night that followed it, she felt herself flush hotly.

Her flush deepened, for she saw now what had awakened her. On one side of the bed stood Clement, on the other the King of France.

'Charming! So charming!' murmured the King. 'As sweet as buds in Maytime.'

The Holy Father said nothing; his dark, crafty face was set in lines of concentration.

'My little Catherine is awake!' said the King, and he stooped to kiss her. He whispered: 'How fared you, Catherine? What have you to say for the honour of France?'

Catherine bade good morning to these two illustrious personages. She murmured something about it being unseemly that she should lie while they stood.

'No ceremony, my little one, on such an occasion,' said the King. And, turning to the Pope, he said: 'I think your Holiness may set his mind at rest. Let us pray to the saints that you may return to Rome in a month's time, rejoicing.'

Henry had opened his eyes; he immediately grasped the significance of the papal and paternal visits. He flushed hotly, hating his father, hating the Pope, and hating his young wife.

✤ ✤ ✤

A month later, papal duties necessitated the return of Clement to the Vatican; but before he left, with his cardinals and bishops, he gave audience to his young relative.

He told Excellency that he wished to speak in private with the young Duchess of Orléans.

Catherine knelt and kissed the fisherman's ring, thinking, I shall not do this again for a long time. And this thought gave her pleasure.

After the blessing, the Pope asked: 'My daughter, have you news for me?'

'No, Holy Father.'

'No news!' The Pope was angry. In spite of hopes and prayers it had failed to happen, and he must return to the Vatican an anxious man. He blamed the young people. They had not been assiduous in their efforts, or the Holy Virgin would not have failed the Pope himself.

'I fear not, Holiness.'

'Daughter,' said the Pope. 'The Dauphin of France does not enjoy the best of health. Have you forgotten what your position would be were he to die?'

'No, Father.'

'The Duke of Orléans would become the Dauphin of France, and you the Dauphiness. And with the death of the King . . .' The Pope's voice took on a hint of malice as a picture of the handsome sensualist, who delighted in the lusts of the flesh, lying dead, rose before his eyes. 'With the death of the King,' he repeated, and added quickly, 'for death is something to which, my daughter, we all must come, and with the death of that delicate boy, you would be the Queen of France. Have you thought what this would mean?'

'I have, Father.'

'One frail life between you and the throne of France. And should this circumstance – shall I say happy or unfortunate circumstance? – come about, I trust you would be ready to do your duty by your family.'

'I would pray that that should be so, Father.'

'Never forget the need for prayer, and remember this may

well happen for the good of France . . . and Italy. It may be the will of God that this should be. Have you prayed regularly that your union should be fruitful?'

'Regularly, Father.'

'That is well. Rise, my daughter.'

She stood up, and the Holy Father rose with her. He laid his hands on her shoulders and kissed her forehead. The Pope was puzzled, unsure of the King of France. What had he meant by the boy's being an inadequate lover? Had there been some subtlety behind that remark after all?

The Holy Father said very quietly: 'My daughter, a clever woman can always get herself children.'

✤ Chapter IV ✤

THE MISTRESS

At the French court it was thought that the little Italian was colourless; she was too quiet, too eager to please. They did not know, they could not guess, what emotions were hidden from them. Catherine rejoiced in the hard training which had taught her to smile when she was most unhappy.

During the first year, she mourned Ippolito. It seemed to her that the memory of her handsome cousin would be with her for ever. I am the most wretched person in the whole of this country, she assured herself.

But at the same time, she was finding it difficult to recall very clearly what Ippolito looked like; the tones of his voice had become blurred; and, odd though it was, when she tried to conjure up images of her cousin they would become merged in that of her young husband.

She could not hate Henry, although she wanted to. She wanted to feel towards him as he did towards her. She embarrassed him; she wanted to tell him that he embarrassed her. 'Do you think I want to be with you!' she longed to shout at him. 'Why, when we are together, and you think it is you I wish to love, it is not. It is Ippolito! If you think that I desire you, then you are mistaken. It is Ippolito whom I want, whom I have always wanted and always shall.' There was in her a passion, a desire which frightened him. He was so cold; he wanted to keep aloof. Love between them – but that was the wrong word for it – was to him a duty which he undertook as he might a penance. Love! There was no love. Only the need to get children.

He avoided her as much as possible. Whenever he could, he would escape to the Château d'Anet, where his great friend would entertain him. Catherine could not understand that friendship between the beautiful widow and her husband. What could two such people have in common? Why was it that he sought the company of such a dignified, such a worldly woman, when his wife, his own age, was ready to be his friend even if she could never love him.

Catherine felt shut in by youth and inexperience. She was lonely often, frightened sometimes. She was indeed a stranger in a strange land.

But for the friendship of the King, she would have been desperately unhappy. When he talked to her she would be conscious of an exhilaration; she would be actually glad that she had come to France. He enchanted her; he fascinated her. She felt that, in a strange way which was incomprehensible to her, she was in love with the King. It was her delight to think over his conversation with her and those about him; to try to read what was in his mind. Sometimes she would say to herself: if only Henry were like his father! And then, again, she would be glad that he was not, for although Henry avoided her, he avoided other women as well. It was only that attachment to a woman old enough to be his mother that persisted. Catherine thought she understood. Henry had no mother, and he felt the need of one. Henry was only a boy. She wondered — not without excitement — when he would become a man.

Life seemed to be made of pleasure. There was always a masque about to begin, or a banquet to prepare for, balls, jousts, and journeys. The meeting of Francis and Clement had not been solely the occasion of the marriage of their young people; they had made plans for campaigns against Spain and England. The King, loving pleasure so much that it was never easy to tear himself away from it, yet yearned for military successes to wipe out the defeat of Pavia. As for the Pope, he was always ready for a new ally, providing that ally kept his plot secret. And who could be a better ally than the King of France, now tied to him by the bonds of relationship?

So, while awaiting the fruition of his schemes, Francis, being impatient, must be kept amused. There was Marguerite to soothe him with her sisterly devotion; Anne d'Heilly to respond to the love he gave her; many lovely women to divert him.

He kept close to him some twenty or thirty young women, all renowned for their beauty and their wit. Wherever he went, they rode with him, and he would listen to their counsels rather than to those of his masculine advisers. It was not sufficient to be beautiful enough to charm his senses; they must be clever enough to please his lively mind. Theirs was the task of providing erotic and intellectual pleasure for their master. If his appetite was jaded, they must serve up old dishes garnished to taste like new. No sultan ever had a more solicitous harem. They must be skilled in the arts of lust and politics; they must be strong enough to endure hours in the saddle without fatigue; perfectly formed that they might sport with grace in a mirrored chamber; sharp-witted enough to converse with foreign ambassadors. Entry into this esoteric band was reserved for the very talented, and was considered the highest honour which could befall a lady of the court. Catherine longed to join the Little Band. She could not, of course, be one of those to whom the King made love, but she fervently wished that on those days when they rode off together and would be away for the whole of the day, that she might be with them. Anne, the King's favourite mistress, was head of the Little Band, and she had shown preference for the little Italian.

If only I could join, Catherine would think. Not only would it show Henry that his father, who despises him, is fond of me, but I should have many happy days in which to forget my melancholy.

She realised that she was becoming increasingly anxious to show Henry that she was not dull and stupid, that she was worthy of some notice. Indeed, she was piqued by this young husband of hers. Not that she should have cared. He was of no account. The King had nothing but contempt for him, and Catherine was not surprised, considering the way he would blush and stammer when spoken to and had hardly a smile for anyone.

Why should she care? She kept telling herself that it was not his regard she sought. Let him escape to Anet whenever he could; she did not care.

In such contempt did the King hold his son that he would not give him a separate establishment even now that he was married. Catherine did not mind that. It meant that they must share household with the other young Princes and Princesses. And a grand household it was – far grander than anything Catherine had ever known before – with its hosts of officials, chamberlain's equerries, pages, doctors, surgeons, ladies and gentlemen, stewards, and pages. Still, it was expected that Henry should have an establishment of his own.

Catherine was much less lonely living with the other young people than she would have been in a household of their own. She was growing quite fond of them all. Young Francis, a delicate boy, was gentle in his manners and kind to the little stranger; his clothes were very sober in cut and colour, and he preferred drinking water to wine. The two Princesses, Madeleine and Marguerite, were quiet little girls, but eager enough to be friends with her. As for young Charles – his father's favourite – she secretly disliked him. He was too boisterous and found it immensely funny to play rather unpleasant practical jokes on the members of the household. Catherine had found a dead rat in her bed on one occasion; and on another a pail of icy water had fallen on her head when she entered a room. She bore these tricks with good humour; she did not wish to offend one so beloved of the King, and she gathered that she had not fared badly at the hands of young Charles. She had heard that one of the women of the household – a pious creature – had, on going to her bed at dusk, found a man there, naked and dead. Catherine's quiet acceptance of the tricks played on her was such as to make the young Duc d'Angoulême feel that she was not a worthy subject for his fun, and she was very quickly left in peace.

She wondered how quiet, sensitive Henry could be the brother of such a one. She was, even more than she realised, bringing Henry increasingly into her life, by continual comparisons with others. She made up her mind, time and time again, to tell her husband of the love she had had for her cousin in Italy; but she never did.

Three important events took place in that first year. The first of these was her election to the Little Band. An excellent horsewoman, she knew she could qualify in that respect, and she decided to tell Francis of her desire.

Most humbly she begged for an audience in private, and when she stood before him she became overcome with fear and wanted to run away. Francis watched her with amusement.

'You must forgive me, Sire,' she blurted out. 'I am afraid I came here to you thoughtlessly. Please give me leave to retire.'

'Indeed you shall have no such leave until I hear what is on your mind.'

'I dare not.'

'I know. It is that husband of yours. *Foy de gentilhomme!* It is no use coming to me, little Catherine. It is true that I sired him. Yes, my dear, I am responsible for that dark deed! But do not ask me to make a man of him, for it would grieve me to deny you anything, and in asking that you would ask the impossible!'

'Sire,' she said, 'it was not of Henry I wished to speak, but of myself.'

'Ah! A happier subject, my little one!'

'I am a good horsewoman, I believe, Sire. You yourself have complimented me. It was this that gave me the temerity . . .'

'Well, well?'

'On occasions, with a light remark, I have had the great honour of seeing a smile appear on your face. I . . . I think I may have pleased you . . .'

She felt now as though she were outside the scene, as though she were watching a play in which the actors were the King of France and his little daughter-in-law. She had made the play, had written the dialogue; because she understood the character of the King and the character that the King believed his daughter-in-law to possess, she had written some very good dialogue.

She knew, she said, that she was not beautiful; but in view of her relationship to him, he would not look for beauty in her. In short, she was asking a great favour, while all the time she knew that it was to be refused her.

'But, Sire, when I watch you ride off with *La Petite Bande* I so yearn to be with you that I am heartbroken until I see you return.'

She knelt and buried her face in her hands, begging the King to give her leave to depart. She had been over-bold. He must forgive her, for if he did not her life would be wretched. It was only his smiles that she lived for. She longed to win them so much that she had been tempted into this indiscretion.

Though she kept her face hidden, she knew exactly how he would be looking. This was new – this platonic love, this admiration which amounted almost to worship and adoration. Francis was always attracted by novelty. He had experienced the complete devotion of a mother; he still enjoyed the adoration of a sister; women, women everywhere to count it an honour when his lustful eyes rested upon them – Anne among the others; but he knew enough of these mistresses of his to realise that he could never be certain of their devotion. No! If he died this night he could say with certainty, 'Two women loved me. One was my mother; one was my sister.' He felt that he might add to that, 'My little daughter-in-law was also fond of me.'

He lifted her and kissed her on both cheeks.

'My darling,' he said, 'it was good of you to open your heart to me thus. Why, you shall have a special place in my *Petite*

Bande. It shall be your task to ride beside me, to amuse me with your talk and tell me your secrets. How like you that?'

She kissed his hands, and she laughed with him because she was so happy. This was a piquant situation such as he loved. So original, so amusing – to have his little daughter, for whom he was indulging in a platonic love affair, among his courtesans!

So Catherine rode in the *Petite Bande*. But this did nothing to endear her to her husband. Her friendship with his father seemed to make him more suspicious of her than ever.

But Catherine seemed to grow up quickly among the King's ladies. She heard chatter of the private parties that were enjoyed in the King's apartments; she heard of things which she had never known existed; and her thoughts, as she listened, would go unaccountably to Henry; and she could not stop imagining Henry and herself at these parties.

The second upheaval of that eventful year caused a deep alarm in Catherine's heart. Suddenly and mysteriously, Pope Clement died. For the man she cared nothing. How could she care? She looked upon him as the destroyer of her happiness. But for his ambitions, she would have been Ippolito's wife; and together she and her cousin would have ruled the city of Florence. But she was diplomat enough to know that Clement was her only powerful relative, and that the King of France had agreed that she should marry his son because of the benefits such a marriage would bring to France. But, alas! The dowry was not yet paid in its entirety; and what about those tempting jewels – Naples, Milan, Genoa? A new Pope would snap his fingers at the ambitions of the Medici.

People whispered about her. It angered her that they did not think it necessary to keep their voices low when she was near. 'Here is a fine matter!' it was said. 'Our King has been fooled.

Where is the fine dowry, where the Italian provinces which alone made possible this marriage between a Medici girl and a Valois Prince? Here is our King's son saddled with a marriage which can only demean himself and France.'

Catherine's thoughts were muddled. Was she truly alarmed? She hardly knew. It was fortunate that she could show a calm front. What would happen to her now? Would the marriage be dissolved? Would she be sent back to Italy?

'If you are,' said a voice within her, 'and if your marriage is dissolved, you will be free. You can return to Rome. And Ippolito will be there.'

Oh, joy! To be with Ippolito once more, to be free to love. She would not have to live with a husband whom she did not love. No more of that furtive intimacy that he made so clear was solely for the begetting of children. 'How happy,' she murmured, 'should I be to say goodbye to *you*, Henry!'

But, alas! Ippolito was a Cardinal. He could not take a wife. Nonsense! Ippolito could break away from the Church if he wished.

She waited, uncertain of her desires, while fresh news came from Rome. There was rejoicing throughout the Eternal City – throughout all Italy – at the death of one who had made himself despised and hated. Each night, it was said, the grave of Clement was raided by the mob, who desecrated his body, and in their hatred of him did all manner of vile things which they had longed to do to him while he lived. Only the intervention of Cardinal Ippolito de' Medici had prevented an enraged populace from dragging Clement's body on a hook through the city.

Oh, Ippolito, dearest Ippolito, thought Catherine. How like you to protect, in death, the man who, in life, made you unhappy, who wrecked our lives, when he kicked aside our love for his ambition!

And thinking thus, she grew angry with Ippolito. He was not strong enough, she thought. He allowed us to be parted.

The third incident of importance did not seem such at the time it took place. She had no great liking for the Dauphin, but she had always sought to please him, and he had grown to like her mildly. One day he sought to honour her, and being in need of a new cupbearer he thought to please her by selecting a young Italian whom she had brought with her in her suite. Count Sebastiano di Montecuculi was a handsome and very patriotic young man whose earnestness had pleased Catherine, so that she was glad now to hear that he had been selected for favour.

'I am deeply grateful for the honour you do my country-man,' she told the Dauphin.

Then she dismissed the matter from her mind.

A lovelier spot than that on which Diane's castle of Anet stood could not be found in the whole of Europe. Past its high stone walls flowed the Eure, and beyond it stretched out the gently sloping vineyards. Diane, under Henry's guidance, was doing everything humanly possible to make the place all that huntsmen could desire; she had enclosed a small but thick forest in which wild beasts were preserved; her stables were acknowledged to contain some of the best horses in the country; the castle itself combined luxury with comfort, and to Henry it was Home.

He was growing up. He was past sixteen, and out of this idyllic friendship that had begun on the day of his first encounter with his beautiful benefactress, passion was beginning to grow.

As for Diane herself, she was fond of the boy. She looked upon him as she might have looked upon a delicate plant which, after a doubtful start, had blossomed into unexpected beauty. He was her creation. She had pruned away the awkwardness until dignity had developed in its place; quiet he was, for she could not cultivate wit where there was no root; but she had taught him self-confidence; she had made him conscious of his royal standing. He was deeply grateful to her.

She had been quick to sense the change in his attitude towards herself. Once she had been a goddess, a saint in a stained-glass window; now she was the perfect woman. He had become a husband since the first days of their friendship, but nearly two years of married life, while doubtless it had made him aware of love and passion, had not taught him to love his wife.

Diane had known for some time that this was a problem she would have to face.

She was expecting him to arrive at Anet on this day. Soon she would hear the horns of the huntsmen who would ride with him. She would see him, at the head of his attendants, come clattering into the courtyard, colour in his usually pale cheeks, his eyes bright with eagerness at the thought of seeing her.

She was fresh and perfumed from her bath. This odd habit of taking frequent baths alarmed her women. They thought that the baths contained some magic which kept her young; it amused Diane to see the fearful way in which they poured out the asses' milk and emptied it away when the bath was over. They asked themselves how any woman could, without the aid of magic, preserve a perfect figure such as Diane possessed, after the birth of two children. It was no use telling them that exercise did that for her. They would not believe it. Diane was up with the dawn, when she rode for two hours in the fresh morning air; after that she returned to her couch, where she read until midday, thus preserving not only an elasticity of body, but of mind. Diane said she lived by regular habits which she had proved to be good; those about her said she lived by magic.

As a practical Frenchwoman, she now knew that the time had come for her to make a decision. Henry was yearning to be her lover, but the suggestion that he should become so, must, as all suggestions between them, come from her. She was by no means a sensual woman, and she did not feel the desire for a lover; she had been a faithful wife to her middle-aged husband, and she felt it no great hardship to live without him. Her horror at the King's advances had been genuine; but now she could calmly consider those of his son.

She was more fond of Henry than she was of anyone else, even her own daughters. He was so dependent upon her; he adored her so naïvely. Would, she wondered, physical contact lessen or strengthen the bond between them? This step from the stained-glass window to the bedchamber needed a good deal of consideration. One thing was certain: Henry was in need of love, physical love. If Diane did not give it, would he look elsewhere? If he did, and if he found it, Diane's rule would necessarily decline. There were many people who thought the Italian girl colourless; Diane was not so sure. It might be that the girl preferred to keep in the background than make blunders. It was not folly which would lead her to act thus, but wisdom.

What was she to do? She was fond of the boy; she had come to regard him as important in her life. Was she to lose him to his wife or a possible mistress? Moreover, for all his modesty, he was the King's son – a person of some consequence in the court. Diane needed influential friends at court. Mademoiselle d'Heilly was growing in importance – she had now been married to the Duke of Etampes to give her standing and respectability at court – and she had always hated Diane. The woman was loved devotedly by the King; Diane must be loved in the same devoted manner by the King's son. No! She could not risk losing Henry; he was too important to her both practically and emotionally.

She said to her woman: 'Madeleine, do I hear the sound of horses' hoofs?'

'I think you may, Madame. I heard the horn full five minutes ago.'

Diane was smiling as she went to the window. She saw him ride into the courtyard at the head of his party. Yes, he was indeed a noble youth. He leaped from the saddle and called to his grooms with that air of authority which had grown from her coaching, and which he seemed to put on when he came to Anet.

A page came in. 'Monsieur d'Orléans is here, Madame.'

'Tell him he may come to me here.'

She was lying on the couch when he came in. She dismissed her attendants. He knelt and kissed her left hand, and with her right she touched his hair. It was thick and dark. She caressed it lightly, and he lifted his head and looked at her, so that she saw he was filled with emotion.

'I had thought you would be here earlier,' she said. 'It seems long since you came.'

'I rode hot-foot,' he answered. 'Never have miles seemed so long.'

'You look at me oddly, Henry.'

'You are so beautiful.'

She laughed lightly. 'I am glad I find favour with you, my dearest friend.'

He kissed her hand again; his lips were hot and he was quivering with his passionate desire for her.

Marriage had indeed changed him. She thought: how is he with the little Italian? She was faintly jealous of the child, envying her her youth and her status as his wife.

She said: 'I think of you often, my dearest. Henry, I think I am a little jealous.'

He lifted his head to stare at her, not understanding; he was always slow of understanding.

'Jealous,' she said, 'of Catherine.'

He flushed and looked quickly away from her. She liked his shyness. How much more appealing it was than his father's practised ways!

She went on: 'I am an old woman, Henry, compared with you. It makes me sad that I should be so old and you so young.'

He stammered: 'You . . . you could never be old. You are perfect. Age? . . . What is age? How I wish I were of an age with you! I would gladly throw away those years which separate us.'

She took his face between her hands and kissed him. 'How adorable you are, my Henry. You see, I think of you as mine. But I must not.'

'Why?' he asked. 'Why . . . should you not?'

'You must not come to Anet as you have been doing, my dearest. You see . . . we are friends; that is all. Always I shall think of you as my dearest friend. But now you are no longer a boy. You have a wife . . .'

'But what has she to do with our friendship?'

'Everything, Henry. You have a wife . . . and you visit me. How can we expect the rest of the world to understand this friendship of ours? They laugh. They sneer. Mademoiselle d'Heilly – I should say Madame d'Etampes – has slandered us, Henry.'

'How dare she!'

'My darling, she dares much. Her position enables her to do so with impunity.'

'I have always hated her. Oh, how dare she breathe a word against *you*! Were she a man, I should challenge her.'

'My chivalrous darling! A king's son may not challenge another, you know. You never do yourself justice. You are ever ready to forget your rank. I had to show you with my love and admiration that you were worthy of the world's regard. I did. My God, I am glad that the task was mine. Every moment has been a joy to me. But now it is over. You have a wife. You must have children. You are no longer a boy who can visit a woman, if you wish to avoid gossip.'

'Diane, I care not for that. I care for no one but you. Let them say what they will. I must come to you. I love you . . . you only. Nothing else in my life is of the slightest importance to me. I was miserable, and you changed my life so that I cannot live it without you. If they say I love you, then they are right.'

She said quietly: 'It is not wise, is it, this friendship of ours?'

He stood up and turned his back to her. She knew that he was greatly excited, and that he was going to say that which he dared not say while he looked at her.

He stammered: 'If . . . they . . . say that I am . . . your lover and you are my . . . mistress . . . then I am honoured. They could not shame *me* by such talk. They could only make me long that this were so.'

She did not speak, and suddenly he turned, and running to her, threw himself at her feet, burying his face in her black-and-white satin gown.

❖ ❖ ❖

He stayed a week at Anet. He did not hunt. He spent the days with her as well as the nights. He was in a state of ecstasy; he was overwhelmed, shy and masterful in turns.

She thought: it is delightful to be loved like this.

He talked a good deal, and it was unusual for him to talk very much, even to her; he sat at her feet, kissing her hands, as he poured out his heart to her. He explained his hatred for his father's way of life, and how he had always longed for one love – one love alone; he had little dreamed that such a blessing could come to him. He wished he were not a King's son. Then he might not be married to a wife whom he could not love; he could have married Diane. He would have been completely happy if their union could have had the blessing of the Church. He wanted no other than Diane; he never would as long as he lived. She must not talk to him of age, for what did age matter to lovers? He wanted her to know that she was enshrined in his heart for ever.

'There will be your duty to your wife,' she reminded him.

'That is impossible now. It would be more distasteful even than before. I could never banish your image from my mind for one moment. I have not done so since I have known you.'

'My darling,' she said, 'you are so wonderful.'

'*I?*' He was genuinely astonished. 'But I am so unworthy.'

'No, no. You are young and delightful and you mean everything you say. You enchant me. I could not bear to lose you now. Henry, never let anyone part us.'

'Never!' he swore.

They exchanged rings. 'I shall wear yours always,' he told her.

They kissed solemnly.

'These are our marriage vows,' he told her.

❖ ❖ ❖

His father sent word for him to return to Paris at once.

He laughed. 'I refuse to go.'

'Henry, you must be wise. You dare not enflame his anger.'

'I have no wish to go to Paris. There is only one place where I wish to be. Here . . . with you . . . at Anet. This is our home, Diane – yours and mine.'

'Do not let this wonderful love of ours bring harm on either of us,' she begged. 'Remember the ruthless power of your father. He is quick to anger. He knows that you are with me. If you will not protect yourself from his anger, you must protect me.'

She knew that would be enough to send him riding back to Paris.

The court was at Fontainebleau, Francis's favourite spot in the whole of France; he had not completed it to his satisfaction, and at this time was absorbed by the artistic work of Il Rosso on his, Francis's, own gallery. Fontainebleau had a hundred delights to offer – a mixture of wild country and cultivated gardens, with the little Seine close by, pushing its way through the vineyards.

Francis was weary. He was trying to whip up his old

enthusiasm for the new war he was proposing to carry into Italy. He could never stop thinking of Italy, and longed to add it to his possessions. It was a bitter blow that Clement should have died when he did, before he was able to pay Catherine's dowry.

And then there must be petty matters at home to worry him. He was not well, and his sickness was manifested by an ugly abscess which made him feel weak and ill until it burst and healed. It was not the first time this troublous thing had worried him, and his physicians said that it was a good sign that it did appear, for if it did not, his condition would be serious. Francis, like Henry of England and Charles of Spain, was suffering from the results of excesses.

Anne, who heartily disliked Diane, had pointed out to him that Catherine had, as yet, no children. How, demanded Anne, could the poor child hope for them, when her husband spent most of his time with the old woman of Anet? The King should talk to his son and point out where his duty lay.

While Francis could smile at his mistress's jealousy of a woman who was almost as beautiful as herself, though some ten years older, he conceded that there was some truth in what she said.

Nearly two years of marriage and no child born to the young pair! It was far from satisfactory with the Dauphin still unmarried. The Dauphin himself presented yet another problem. A wife for young Francis was needed quickly. The King was tired and his abscess was throbbing; and Italy was as far out of his reach as ever, in spite of his second son's undignified marriage.

When Henry stood before him, Francis saw the difference in his son at once. The conquering lover! So Diane had scorned the father and taken the son. Was the Grande Sénéchale of Normandy really quite sane?

The King dismissed his attendants with a wave of the hand.

'So,' he said, 'without permission you absent yourself from court. You were always a boor. You came home smelling of a Spanish prison. *Foy de gentilhomme!* You shall not play your peasants' tricks at my court.'

Henry was silent, though there was hatred in those dark eyes of his.

'Where have you been?' demanded the King.

'You know. Did you not send for me at Anet?'

'At Anet! Carousing with your aged mistress!'

Hot colour burned in the Prince's face. His hand went to his sword.

Francis laughed. *'Pasques Dieu!* She has put some fire into you, then! She has taught you that a sword is to be used and not merely to impede the gait.'

This reference to his awkwardness stung Henry to speech. 'The example you have set us does not . . . er . . . does not . . .'

Francis cut in: 'Come along! Come along!' He mimicked Henry's voice: '". . . is not one which my brothers and I, in the interest of virtue, should follow!" That is what you are stammering about, is it not? But do not, my son, have the effrontery to place yourself with the Dauphin and the Duc d'Angoulême. These are men. They take their pleasure, but they are not ruled by one woman, so making themselves the laughing-stock of the court.'

Again that quick movement to the sword-hilt, that sharp pace forward. My God, thought the King. I am liking this boorish son of mine the better when he shows anger.

'It . . . is easy to see people laughing at others,' said Henry, 'but we do not always see them laughing at ourselves.'

'Ah! There's subtlety here. Pray explain your meaning.'

'I care not if people laugh at me. Who are these people to laugh at a pure love? The morals of this court – set by yourself – are a matter to make the angels weep.'

Diane, thought the King. You have done your work well.

'You are insolent, Monsieur,' he said. 'Take care that you do not arouse my anger as well as my contempt.'

'I care not for your anger, Sire.'

'What!' cried the King in mock anger. 'I will put you in a dungeon . . . and there your mistress cannot visit you.'

'You are amusing yourself at my expense.'

The King went to his son and laid a hand on his shoulder. 'Listen to me, my son. Do what you will. Have twenty mistresses. Why not? It is sometimes safer to have twenty than to be faithful to one. I no longer doubt that if any dare laugh in your face you would know how to deal with him. But there is a serious outcome of all this flitting back and forth to Anet. What of the little Duchess, your wife?'

'What of her?'

'She is young; she is not without charm; get her with child, and then think of the months you might, with a free conscience, happily spend at Anet or wherever the fancy took you. None drank more freely of the fountain of love than I; yet however sparkling the drink, never did I forget my duty to my house and country.'

Henry was silent.

'Think of these matters,' said Francis more gently. 'I would not keep you from your pleasure. The good God knows I am glad to see you growing up at last, for in faith I thought you never would. Women are a complement to the life of a man.

Do they not give us birth, pleasure, children? I rejoice to see your inclinations take a natural turn, and I leave you to deal with any that should mock you. But I do ask this of you: remember your duty to your wife and to your line.'

Francis smiled at the sullen face before him and gave the boy's shoulder a not unkindly slap. Let us be friends, Francis was saying. After all, you are my son.

The long, bright eyes were even a little wistful. He was rather proud of the big, strong-looking boy.

But Henry looked away from his father, back into his childhood, and there he saw the gloomy shadow of a Spanish prison.

It was Francis's nature to forget what was unpleasant; but Henry never forgot his friends . . . nor his enemies. He turned from the affection his father was offering him. There was one person in the world – and only one – whom he could love and trust.

At the jousts next day, he rode into combat, defiantly and proudly displaying the black-and-white colours of Diane de Poitiers.

❧ Chapter V ❧

CATHERINE THE WIFE

The entire court was laughing at Henry's passion for Diane. He, with a wife of his own delectable age, to fly from her to the bed of a woman more than twenty years his senior! It was like the opening of one of Boccaccio's tales or something from the Queen of Navarre's Heptameron.

When Catherine heard it, she was so moved that it was necessary for her to shut herself into her own apartments. She felt furiously angry. The humiliation of it! The whole court laughing at Henry, his mistress, and his poor, neglected wife!

When she looked at herself in the mirror she scarcely recognised herself. Her face was the colour of a tallow candle, and the only brightness was the blood where her sharp teeth had bitten the flesh of her lips. Her eyes were cruel with hatred. She was an older Catherine now.

She walked up and down her room, murmuring angry words to Henry, to Diane. She was imploring the King to send her back to Italy. 'Sire, I will not stay here to suffer this humiliation.'

Then she laughed aloud at her folly, laughing bitterly until she flung herself on to her bed weeping.

It is the humiliation of it, she told herself.

She kept repeating that with a vehemence which shook her. I should not otherwise care.

And why should she care? Many a *Queen* had suffered similar humiliation before her. Why should she care?

It is because she is so old. That is what makes it so humiliating.

There was a voice within her that mocked her. But, Catherine, why should you care? You have no children. Perhaps now you will have none. There will surely be a divorce and you will be sent back to Rome. Ippolito is in Rome, Catherine.

Ippolito is a Cardinal.

But the voice within was mocking her. Think of it, Catherine. Think of the joy of it. Reunion with handsome Ippolito!

I will not think of it. It is wrong to think of it.

She was pacing up and down again; she was at her mirror; she was laughing; she was weeping.

Courage, said her lips. You must go among the people of this court; you must smile at Diane; you must never show by a look or a gesture how much you hate her, how easy it would be to take a dagger and plunge it into her heart, to drop a poisoned draught into her cup.

She hardly knew the sad and cruel face which looked back at her. They thought her cold, these fools. She . . . cold! She was white-hot with hatred, maddened by jealousy.

She was a fool to shut her eyes to the truth.

'What do I care for Ippolito?' she asked of her reflection. 'What was my love for him? A pleasant girl-and-boy affair, without passion, without jealousy; while in me these two now burn. No, not Ippolito. It is not he whom I love.'

She laughed suddenly and loudly.

'I could kill her,' she murmured. 'She has taken him from me.'

How many jealous women had said those words, she wondered; and looking into those passionate Italian eyes, she answered herself. 'Many. But few have really meant them. I love Henry. He is mine. I did not ask to marry him. I was forced to it. And now I love him. Many women have felt this jealousy, and many have said: "I could kill her". But they have said it idly. I am different. I mean it. I *would* kill her.'

Her mouth twisted grimly. 'If she were dead,' she whispered close to the mirror so that her breath made a mist on the glass, 'I would make him wholly mine. I would show him love and passion such as he never dreamed of, for in me a furnace of desire is smouldering. If she were dead, he would be with *me*. We should have children to the honour of the land . . . his land . . . and mine.'

She pressed the palms of her hands together, and in the mirror she saw a woman with murder in her eyes and a prayer on her lips.

It had needed this tragic sorrow to awaken her, to bring to life the real Catherine. In this moment of revelation, she knew herself as she never had before. How pale the face, how set the features! Only the blazing eyes spoke of murder. The world should see those eyes as mild, expressionless. The true Catherine should hide behind shutters, while the false smiled on the world.

How easy it was to make resolutions; how difficult to keep them! Often she must shut herself away, feigning a headache so that she might be alone with her tears. People were saying: 'Poor little Italian! She is not strong. Perhaps this accounts – with Diane – for her inability to get children.'

One day, having heard some light remark concerning her husband and his mistress, she felt her emotions too strong for her. She made her way to her apartments, told her women to leave her as she wished to rest, and when she was alone, she lay on her bed and sobbed quietly like a child.

What could she do? Good Cosmo and Lorenzo Ruggieri had given her perfumes and cosmetics; she had taken a love potion.

They were no use. Diane had more potent magic. And when Henry did come to her he was awkward and apologetic. 'My father insists that we should get a child,' he had said, as though it were necessary to make excuses for his presence.

Why did she love him? He was slow-witted and by no means amusing. It was incomprehensible that he should be in her thoughts all day and haunt her dreams by night. He was certainly courteous and kind, so anxious that she should not know their intercourse was distasteful to him that he could not help showing quite clearly that it was. By all the laws of human nature she ought to have hated him.

What could she, who was young and untutored in the ways of love, do to win him from the experienced woman who had taken him? She had no friends whose advice she could ask. What if, as she rode out with the *Petite Bande*, she told her troubles to the King? How sympathetic he would be! How gracious! How angry with his son for his lack of courtesy! And then, doubtless, he would, with embellishments, tell the story to Madame d'Etampes; and the two of them would be very witty at her expense.

There was no one to look after Catherine's welfare but Catherine herself. She must never forget that. That was why she must hide these bitter tears, and no one must ever know how passionately, how possessively she loved the shy young boy who was her husband.

Alarmed she sat up on her bed, for she could hear footsteps approaching the room. There was a timid knock on the door.

She said in a cold and steady voice: 'Did I not say I was not to be disturbed?'

'Yes, Madame la Duchesse, but there is a young man here – Count Sebastiano di Montecuculi – who begs to be allowed to see you. He is very distressed.'

'Tell him he may wait,' she said. 'I am busy for a while.'

She leaped from the bed, dried her eyes, and dusted her face with powder. She looked at her reflection anxiously. It was impossible to eliminate all signs of her passionate weeping. How stupid it was to give way to the feelings! One should never, in any circumstances, be so weak. Sorrow and anger were emotions to be locked away in the heart.

Ten minutes had passed before she had the Count brought to her. He bowed low over her hand; then he lifted his sad eyes to her face,

'Duchessina,' he said, 'I see that this evil news has already reached you.'

She was silent, annoyed that he should have noticed the traces of grief on her face, and, having noticed them, been tactless enough to refer to them. But what evil tidings did he speak of?

As she continued silent, the young man went on: 'I thought it my duty, Duchessina, to carry the news to you. I know your strong feelings for your noble cousin.'

Her feelings were under control. Was it only where her husband was involved that they got the better of training and her natural craft?

She had no idea to what the Count referred but she said with the utmost calm: 'You had better tell it to me, Count, as you heard it.'

'Oh, Duchessina, you know the condition of our beloved city, how its sufferings are almost unendurable under the tyrant. Many have been driven into exile, and these, with others, met together in secret. They decided to send a petition to Emperor Charles begging him to free Florence from Alessandro. Duchessina, they selected your noble cousin, Cardinal Ippolito de' Medici as their ambassador.'

'And Alessandro's secret spies discovered this. I know. I know.'

'He got as far as Itri. He would have embarked there for Tunis.'

'And they killed him.' Catherine covered her swollen eyes with her hands. 'My poor noble cousin. My dearest Ippolito.'

'It was in his wine, Duchessina. His death was terrible, but quick. He did not suffer long.'

For a few seconds she was silent; then she said: 'Would there were some to avenge him.'

'His servants were mad with grief, Duchessina. Italy mourns the great Cardinal. Florence is desolate.'

'Oh, our poor country, Sebastiano! Our poor suffering country! I know how you feel. You and I would *die* for our country.'

'And count it an honour to do so,' said the young man earnestly.

She held out her hand and he took it. She was excited by a

sudden thought which had come to her, conscious of that strange force which warned her of great events. Standing before her was a man whose eyes glowed fanatically when he spoke of his country.

'Yes, Sebastiano,' she said, 'for the sake of your country you would gladly die a thousand deaths. There are men like that. Not many – but I think that you are one of them. If you were, your name would be remembered throughout Italy for ever, with honour, my dear Count, with reverence.' Her eyes glowed, and the Count, looking at her, wondered how he could ever have accepted the general opinion that she was insignificant. 'There have been times,' she went on, 'when I have been privileged to see into the future. I fancy I see something now. One day, Sebastiano, you will be called upon to do great deeds for our country.'

She spoke with such conviction, her eyes glowing almost unnaturally, that it seemed to the young man as if some mysterious power spoke through her. He stammered: 'My lady Duchess, if that should be, I should die happy.'

Catherine withdrew her hand, sighing.

'Ah well,' she said, 'you and I must live our lives as wisely as we can. But we will never forget the land of our birth.'

'Never!' he declared fervently.

She walked away from him, speaking quietly, as though to herself. 'I am married to the son of a King . . . but the second son. The Dauphin is not strong, and I have wondered – as the departed Holy Father wondered – whether God has destined me, through my children, to bring glory to Italy. My children!' Her voice broke suddenly. 'I have no children. I had hoped . . .' She felt her control snapping. She burst out: 'My husband is enamoured of a sorceress. They say she is a wrinkled old woman in reality, who appears as a young and beautiful lady. Life is strange and the ways of Fate are incomprehensible. You comfort me, Count, for there is nothing you would not do to serve me and Italy. If ever I were Queen of France, I would not forget – though I know you seek no honours.'

'I seek only the honour of serving our country, Duchessina.'

'You are good, Count; you are noble. We will both remember our country . . . always. We are strangers in a strange land, but we must never forget Italy. Stay and talk with me awhile. How good it is to speak our native tongue! You may sit, my lord Count. Talk to me of Italy . . . in Italian. Talk of our beloved Arno and the groves of olives . . . and the blessed sunshine . . .'

But it was she who went on speaking; and as she talked, it was not Ippolito – once so well-loved – whom she saw in her mind's eye; it was Henry, his eyes shining for Diane, shamefaced and apologetic for his wife.

She told the young Count of her life at the Murate and how she had heard the story of the Virgin's mantle.

'Miracles are made on Earth by those who are great enough to make them,' she said. 'There are some who are selected by the Holy Virgin to work miracles. I often think of my position, and the power that would be in my hands to work good for my country, if my brother the Dauphin passed from this life. He is delicate in health; it might be that God has not meant him to rule this land. And then, were I Queen, I must have children . . . sons . . . to work for the good of France . . . and Italy.'

'Yes, Duchessina,' said the Count quietly.

'But I keep you from your duty, Count. When you wish for conversation, go along to the house of the brothers Ruggieri.

They will have much to show you that is truly marvellous. When I tell them you are my friend — that you and I understand each other — there is nothing they will not give you.'

After he had left her, she found the pain of unrequited love was easier to bear. Perhaps, she thought, it will not always be thus.

✦ ✦ ✦

Heavily cloaked and closely hooded, accompanied by the youngest of her women, Catherine left Les Tournelles and hurried through the streets of Paris. She was going to see the astrologer brothers who lived on the left bank of the Seine close to the Pont Notre Dame. The house could be approached from the street or the river, for at the back its stone steps led down to the water, where two boats were kept moored to carry away any who might wish to leave by a different route from the one by which they had come. Catherine was delighted with the prudence which the brothers had shown by selecting such a house.

Most of the court ladies visited astrologers whose business included the sale of charms and perfumes; but these French ladies visited French magicians. The Italians were not only unpopular in France; they were suspected of all sorts of evil practices. Stories of the reign of terror under Alessandro in Florence were circulated; it was known that Ippolito had been murdered; it was suspected that Clement had died through poison.

The Italians, thought the French, were skilled in all the arts of poisoning.

Therefore, reasoned Catherine, at such a time she would not

wish to be seen making a hurried visit to the house of the Italian sorcerers.

She had impressed on Madalenna, her young Italian attendant, that she wished none to know of their journey this evening to the house of the brothers.

She smiled faintly at the small figure beside her. Madalenna was to be trusted.

They reached the shop, descended the three stone steps, pushed open the door and went into a room in which were benches and shelves where stood great jars and bottles. From the ceiling hung herbs of many kinds; and on the bench lay the skeleton of a small animal among the charms and charts.

The two brothers came into the shop, which was lighted only by a candle that guttered and showed some sign of flickering out altogether. When they saw who their visitor was they bowed obsequiously, thrusting their hands into the wide sleeves of their magicians' robes, and waiting, with bent heads to hear the commands of their Duchess.

'You have my new perfume for me, Cosmo?' she asked, turning to one of the brothers.

'It is ready, Duchessina. I will have it sent to you tomorrow.'

'That is good.'

Lorenzo waited with his brother for her commands; they knew she had not come thus – when she might have sent for them – merely to ask about a new perfume.

Madalenna hovered uncertainly in the background. Catherine, turning to her, said loudly: 'Madalenna, there is no need to stand back. Lorenzo, Cosmo, bring forth the new perfume. I would hear Madalenna's opinion of it.'

The brothers looked at each other. They knew their

Duchess as well as any; they remembered a meek little girl who had asked for an image of Alessandro that she might, through it, bring about the death of that monster. She had something on her mind now.

They brought the perfume. Lorenzo took Madalenna's hand while Cosmo thrust into a bottle a thin glass rod. He wiped the now perfume-smeared rod on Madalenna's hand, bid her wait for a few moments, and both brothers stood back as though spellbound, waiting for the moment when the perfume would be ready for Madalenna to smell it.

And all the time their eyes were furtive. What had brought the Duchess here at such an hour?

'It is wonderful!' declared Madalenna.

'See that it is sent to me tomorrow,' said Catherine. And then: 'You know I did not come here merely to smell a perfume. Lorenzo, Cosmo, what have you discovered for me? Is there any news of a child? You may speak before Madalenna; this dear child knows my secrets.'

'Duchess, there is yet no news of a child.'

She clenched and unclenched her hands. 'But when? . . . When? . . . It must be some time.'

They did not answer.

Catherine shrugged her shoulders. 'I will look into the crystal myself. Madalenna, sit down and wait. I shall not be long.'

She drew aside the heavy curtains which divided the shop from a room at the back. In this room was a large cabinet which the brothers always kept locked and which Catherine knew to contain many secret hiding places. She sat down while the brothers drew the curtains, shutting off the shop and Madalenna. Catherine stared into the crystal; she could see nothing. The brothers waited respectfully.

Suddenly she turned to them and spoke, and they now knew the real reason for her visit. 'There is a young Count,' she said, 'who wishes to serve his country. Should he come to you and wish to talk of his native land – *our* native land – in our native tongue, be kind to him. If he should ask for a love potion to enhance his charms in his mistress' eyes . . . or if he should ask for a draught of any sort, give it him. You may trust him.'

The brothers looked at each other apprehensively. Catherine's eyes revealed nothing; her face held the innocence of a child's.

The court was on the move once more, and this time there was a reason, other than the King's restlessness, behind the move.

Catherine rode with the *Petite Bande*, keeping close to the King and Madame d'Etampes. A place of honour – yet how she longed to be of her husband's suite; but there was no place there for her, since it was ruled by her hated enemy, whom Henry continued to adore. Catherine was hiding her passion and her jealousy with success; she could laugh as loudly as any surrounding the King.

As they halted at various towns and châteaux on their way from Paris to Lyons, there were lavish entertainments for the amusement of the King. Madame d'Etampes and the Queen of Navarre put their heads together to devise plays and masques. Countless beautiful girls had been brought with them, and there were some to be found on the way. They danced before the King: they tried to secure his interest by boldness and modesty in turn; but Francis was half-hearted, for war was spreading over France, and it was the invasion by the Emperor's troops, of the fair land of Provence, that was sending the court hurrying from Paris down to Lyons.

It was in Lyons that Catherine betrayed herself.

She was with her women in her apartments when Henry came in. Her heart beat in the mad fashion it was accustomed to when he was with her. She hastily dismissed her women, trying to suppress the emotion which possessed her.

He said: 'I am afraid I disturb you. I am sorry.'

'There are occasions when it is good to be disturbed.' They were alone now and she could not prevent her eyes shining with an eager passion. She added breathlessly: 'I pray to the saints that there may be many such disturbances.'

He looked at her in a puzzled way, not comprehending. She felt slightly impatient with him; but oddly enough she loved him the more for that slowness of wit which exasperated his father.

'Pray be seated, Henry,' she said, tapping the window seat and sitting there, making room for him as she drew in her pearl-embroidered skirts.

It was unbearable to have him so close and to feel that he was so far away. Was he thinking now of Diane? She doubted it, for he looked unhappy, and he was never unhappy thinking of Diane.

He said: 'This is a sorry state of affairs.'

She touched his arm, and although she knew he hated to be touched by her, she could not withdraw her hand. But now he did not seem to notice. He went on: 'Have you not heard the news? Montmorency is retreating before the Imperial troops. Tomorrow my father leaves for Valence.'

'Oh, another move? I was thinking I have scarce seen you since we left Paris.'

She could not keep the reproach out of her voice; her eyes

were hot; she was seeing herself, tossing and turning in her bed, awaiting a husband who did not come, picturing him with Diane, asking herself, Why? Why should it be Diane and not Catherine? How could she listen to his talk of war? When he was near her she could think of nothing but love.

Her voice sounded high-pitched. 'Has the King spoken to you again?' she asked. 'We see so little of each other, it is small wonder that we have no children . . .'

He did not move, and she realised he had not even heard what she said. He could not follow two lines of thought at the same time; if something was on his mind he could hear and see nothing else.

'Montmorency is burning and destroying everything as he retreats, and there will be no stores of food left for the advancing enemy. Men, women, children — French, all of them — are left starving after the armies have passed through . . .'

She interrupted him. 'But that is terrible. I have heard that Montmorency is cruel and that his men obey him through fear!'

'It is the only way,' said Henry. 'Montmorency is a great man. His policy is the only safe policy. But for Montmorency the Spanish devils would be in Lyons now. I would I could go and fight with him.'

She was pleased. If he went to fight, he must leave Diane.

She slipped her arm farther through his. 'There are soldiers enough, Henry,' she said softly.

'My father has said that if he needs the Dauphin he will send for him. I wish he would send for me! But he hates me. He knows I long to fight; therefore he says, "You shall not fight!" And the enemy is at our gates. But for my father's folly there would be no war. Long ago Milan would have been ours!'

Catherine's eyes went to the door. She longed for Henry's

confidences, but she dared not let it be known that she had said, or even listened to, a word against the King. Francis' favour was easily won by some; it was equally easily lost; and she must not forget that it was only through a lucky chance that Henry was speaking to her thus. He had come to the apartment not thinking of her; and he had found her there, and being unusually excited by the closeness of the war, had wished to talk to someone – even Catherine.

She said: 'Lower your voice, Henry. There are spies everywhere, and what you say might quickly be carried to your father.'

He shrugged his shoulders. 'This desire of his for Italy – it is like all his desires. No matter what stands in his way, he will do anything – cruel, foolish, it matters not – anything to get his desires. As it is for women, so it is for Italy. There is no right or wrong for my father where his desires are concerned. When Monsieur de Chateaubriand objected to my father's immorality with Madame de Chateaubriand, he took the man by the throat and threatened to cut off his head unless he gave up the woman. He must lose either his head or his wife.'

Catherine laughed, loving this intimacy. 'So he kept his head. Sensible man!'

'I hate the life my father leads!' said Henry. His mouth was prim and Catherine wondered about his love-making with Diane. 'He chooses the most degraded people to surround him. Madame d'Etampes should be banished from court.'

Catherine's smile was noncommittal. The King's mistress was supposed to be her friend.

Then Henry spoke again of his father who was for ever reaching out his hands to Catherine's native land of grapes and olives and the finest artists in the world. He was reckless when he should be cautious – so said his son – bold when there was the greatest need for hesitation.

Catherine understood that glittering personality far better than did his son. She knew that over the brightness which surrounded him lay the shadow of Pavia. There was hardly an hour in the King's life when he did not remember that defeat, and he would feel that nothing but the conquest of Italy would wipe out the humiliation. It was Pavia that made him reckless, eager as he was for that military success which would put him right with the world; it was Pavia that made him hesitate, reminding him that disastrous defeat must never be repeated. Pavia had made of the century's greatest lover its most incompetent general.

'The Emperor,' Henry was saying, 'has made a triumphant return from the East. He has twice defeated Barbarossa; he has taken Tunis, and the whole of the Christian world rejoices because he has brought with him many who were made slaves to toil for the barbarians. And what has my father done? He looks about him for an enemy of the Emperor – and makes a treaty with the Turks! With infidels! This Most Christian King! He'd make a treaty with the Devil to get a woman or a country.'

'I beg of you, Henry, my dear Henry, speak quietly. If it should get to the King's ears . . .'

'Then should he hear the truth for once. I do not think that would harm him.'

'He is angry,' said Catherine gently, 'because Milan was promised to us through our marriage. But then, my kinsman died.'

She looked at Henry anxiously. Did he hate his marriage because of Clement's untimely death, as did the rest of France? How she longed for him to tell her that he was pleased with their marriage, that he was happy to be united to her, even though she had not brought him the promised riches.

He did no such thing. He could only think of his father's disastrous military campaign.

'Milan was scarcely defended at all!' he said. 'We could have taken it. But my father hesitated, and now . . . it is too late. Would I were there. I would have taken Milan . . . and held it.'

'You would!' she cried. 'Oh, Henry, you would do brave things, I know. I should be so proud of you . . . so honoured that my husband was known throughout the world for his resource and his courage.' He did not move away from her. She said eagerly, thinking of the love potion she had in her drawer, awaiting a moment when she could give it to him: 'You will take some refreshment, Henry?'

He shook his head. 'Thank you, no. I cannot stay now.'

She should have let him go then, but she was intoxicated by the pleasure of having him with her. 'Henry, please, *please*. Share a cup of wine with me. I scarcely ever see you.'

'I . . . I have not the time,' he said firmly.

Her control snapped. She cried: 'You would have, did you spend less time with Madame La Grande Sénéchale.'

He coloured hotly and he looked at her with distaste. 'She is an old friend,' he said with hauteur.

'Indeed she is. Old enough to be your mother. Madame d'Etampes says she was born on the day the Sénéchale was married.'

Henry's eyes flashed dangerously. 'I do not care to hear what that harlot says, and I should advise you, in view of your position, to choose your friends more wisely.'

She faced him; she was so miserable that she could not hide her anger.

'You have forgotten, Monsieur, that the lady is the most influential at court.'

'I have not forgotten that she is the most immoral.'

'Why should it be more immoral for the King to have a mistress than for the King's son to leave his lawful wife . . . night after night . . . for the sake of . . . an old friend!'

He was white with anger. He did not know how to deal with this situation. He had done his duty and it had not been easy; but if she were going to make such scenes as this it was going to be harder still.

And then she began to cry; she flung her arms about his neck, for when her control broke suddenly the floods seemed to flow the faster for having so long been pent up.

'Henry,' she sobbed, 'I love you. I am your wife. Could we not . . . could we not? . . .'

He stood rigid. 'I think there has been some . . . misunderstanding,' he said, and his voice was cold as icicles in January. Pray release me, and I will explain.'

She let her hands fall to her side, and stood staring at him, while the tears started to roll down her cheeks.

He moved towards the door. 'You have misunderstood,' he said. 'Madame la Grande Sénéchale is a great friend of mine and has been for years. Our relationship is one of friendship only. She is a lady of great culture and virtue. Pray do not let me hear you slander her again. It is true that you are my wife, but that is no reason for vulgar displays.'

'Vulgar!' she cried through her tears. 'Is love then . . . vulgar?'

He was all eagerness to get away. She deeply embarrassed him. She tried to fight off the heartbreaking emotion that was racking her, but she could not do it. She had made a grave mistake, but having made it, she was reckless, not caring what she did. She knelt and caught him by the knees.

'Henry, please don't go. Stay with me. I would do anything to please you. I love you . . . far more than anyone else could possibly love you. It is only because our marriage was made for you by your father that you do not like it.'

'Please release me,' he said. 'I do not understand you. At least I thought you reasonable.'

'How can one be reasonable and in love? There is no reason in love, Henry. It cannot last, can it, this infatuation for a woman old enough to be your grandmother?'

He threw her off, and she allowed herself to fall back heavily on the floor. She lay there crying while he strode out of the room. But as soon as the door closed she realised how stupidly she had been behaving and still was behaving. This was not the way.

She got up slowly and dragged herself to the bed. She threw herself on to it and sobs shook her body – but they were silent sobs.

After a while they stopped. One does not weep, she said to herself, if one wishes to succeed. One makes plans.

✤ ✤ ✤

Henry did not come near her for several days after that, and she felt that if she left her apartments and mingled with the men and women of the court she might betray something of this heartbreaking jealousy. She prayed, on her knees and as she went about her rooms, for the death of Diane. 'Perhaps, Holy Mother, some terrible sickness that need not kill her, only disfigure her . . . Guide the hand of Sebastiano di Montecuculi. Put the right thoughts into his head. It would be for Italy, Holy Mother, so there could be no sin in it.'

Madalenna brought news to her.

'The King has sent for the Dauphin, Madame la Duchesse. He is to go to his father in Valence. This is bad, people are saying. They say things are very bad for France.'

But on the day the Dauphin was due to leave for Valence Henry came to the apartment. She was lying on her bed feeling tired and heavy-eyed. How she wished that she had been up, her hair neatly braided, herself perfumed and elaborately gowned.

He came and stood by the bed, and he was almost smiling, so that it seemed as if he had completely forgotten their last encounter.

'Good day to you, Catherine.'

She held out her hand and he kissed it, perfunctorily it was true, but still he kissed it.

'You look happy, Henry. Is the news good?' Her voice was flat; she was setting a firm guard over her feelings.

'For the armies, it is bad,' he said. 'But for myself, good; for I think I may shortly be joining my father in Valence.'

'You . . . Henry . . . to go with the Dauphin?'

'Francis has taken to his bed. He is sick. He cannot leave yet to join my father.'

'Poor Francis! What is wrong?'

'Very little. I have hopes that my father may command me to take his place.'

'He will doubtless wait a day or so. What ails your brother?'

'He has been playing tennis in the sun. He played hard and was thirsty, and, as you know, he drinks only water. That Italian fellow took his goblet to the well and brought it back to him full. He drank it all and sent the man back for more.'

Catherine lay very still, staring at the carved goddesses and angels on the ceiling. 'Italian fellow?' she said slowly.

'Montecuculi. You know, Francis's Italian cupbearer. What does that matter? The heat and the water made Francis feel ill, so he retired to his rooms. My father will not be pleased when he hears the news. He will upbraid him for drinking water.'

Catherine did not answer. For once, when Henry was with her, she was scarcely aware of him, for she could see nothing but the fanatical eyes of Montecuculi.

✤ ✤ ✤

The whole court was mourning the death of the Dauphin. None dared carry the news to Francis, who, in Valence, knew only that his son was sick.

The shock was overwhelming. The young man had been alive and well only a few days before. True, he was not exactly virile, but he was strong enough to play a good game of tennis. His death was as mysterious as it had been sudden.

The court physicians agreed that his death must have been due to the water he drank. All those about the young man had been shocked by his preference for water, which he drank immoderately, while he rarely took a drink of good French wine. He had been overheated and told his Italian cupbearer to bring him water.

His *Italian* cupbearer!

Now the court had begun to whisper. 'It was his *Italian* cupbearer, you see.'

The King had to be told, and it fell to the lot of his great friend the Cardinal of Lorraine to break the news; but eloquent as the Cardinal was – and never yet had he been found at a loss for a word – he could not bring himself to tell the King of this terrible tragedy. He stood before his old friend, stammering that the news he had was not very good.

Francis, crossing himself hastily, and thinking immediately of his eldest son whom he knew to be ill, said: 'The boy is worse. Tell me. Hold nothing back.'

He saw tears in the Cardinal's eyes and commanded him to speak.

'The boy is worse, Sire. We must trust in God . . .' His voice broke and the King cried out: 'I understand. You dare not tell me that he is dead.'

He stared at those about him in horror, for he knew that he had guessed correctly.

There was silence in the room. The King walked to the window, took off his cap, and, lifting his hands, cried: 'My God, I know that I must accept with patience whatever it be Thy will to send me; but from whom, if not from Thee ought I to hope for strength and resignation? Already hast Thou afflicted me with the diminution of my dominions and the defeat of my army; Thou hast now added this loss of my son. What more remains, save to destroy me utterly? And if it be Thy pleasure to do so, give me warning at least, and let me know Thy will in order that I may not rebel against it.'

Then he began to weep long and bitterly, and those about him wept in sympathy and dared not approach him.

In Lyons the whispering campaign had started. Catherine was aware of it first in the looks of those she passed on the staircases and in the corridors. People did not look at her, but she knew they looked after her when she had passed.

Madalenna brought her the news.

'Madame la Duchesse, they are repeating that his cupbearer

was an Italian. They say that had they not let the Italians into their country their Dauphin would be alive today.'

'What else do they say, Madalenna? Tell me everything . . . whatever it is they say you must tell me.'

'They say that there is another Dauphin now . . . a Dauphin with an Italian wife. They say the future Queen of France will be an Italian. They ask if it was the Italian count who killed the Dauphin.'

It was not long after that when Count Sebastiano di Montecuculi was arrested.

* * *

Against his father's order, Henry rode to Valence. Francis was inclined to be indulgent in his sorrow. Now he must look at this son, whom he could never love, in a new light. Henry was the Dauphin now. He was precious. Francis could not help feeling that some ill luck was dogging him and he trembled for his remaining sons.

'Foy de gentilhomme!' he said to Henry. 'Methinks I am the unluckiest man in France – my army defeated and my Dauphin dead!'

Then the soldier in Henry spoke. 'Your army is not defeated yet, Father, and I am here to try to prevent that. You have lost one son, but you have another who stands before you now.'

Then Francis embraced the boy, dislike temporarily forgotten.

'Pray, Father, allow me to join Montmorency at Avignon.'

'Nay!' cried Francis. 'I have lost one son. I must guard well what remains.'

Henry would not let the matter rest there and after a while

he succeeded in persuading his father to let him join Montmorency.

And then it was that Henry formed his second friendship, and one almost as strong as that he felt for Diane.

Anne de Montmorency was as stern a martinet as ever commanded an army, and a devout Catholic, most punctilious where his religious duties were concerned. Henry thought him like an avenging angel; and the soldiers – abandoned, vicious as they were – were terrified of him. Food might be short and pay not forthcoming, but Montmorency never relaxed that wonderful discipline which was the admiration of all who experienced it. God was on his side, he was sure; violent he was; cruel in the extreme; and the boldest trembled before him. He had no mercy on delinquents. There was not a morning when he omitted to say his Paternosters, and hardly a day when he would not have a man tortured, hanged, or run through with a pike for a breach of discipline. Indeed, it was when he said his prayers that he seemed to grow more vicious. He would stop muttering them and shout, 'Hang me that man!' or 'Run your pike through that one!' There was a saying in the army, 'Beware of Montmorency's Paternosters.'

To young Henry this man seemed wonderful. As for Montmorency, he was so delighted to see the young Prince instead of the King, that he could not hide his relief, and made much of the boy. Ever since Pavia the Army had been afraid as soon as the King entered its midst. Francis was unlucky, they said; the saints had decreed that he should be defeated in war. Moreover, Henry was without that bombastic nature which characterised so many of his rank; he wanted to be a good soldier and was ready to place himself entirely under Montmorency's command.

But Francis did not delay his coming. Very soon after Henry's arrival in Avignon, the King followed his son there. This time Francis was not unlucky, and France was saved – though not through force of arms. The imperial troops, owing to the tactics of Montmorency in destroying towns and villages as he retreated, were starving and dying in thousands. There was only one course open to them – retreat.

Should he pursue the fleeing Spaniards and their mercenaries? wondered Francis; and he hesitated as he had done so many times before. He wanted to get back to Lyons, to look into this matter of the death of his eldest son, to discover if the rumours that he had been poisoned contained any truth.

So there was a temporary lull in the fighting.

Henry said when he took leave of Montmorency: 'You can be sure that whatever happens I am, and shall be all my life, as much your friend as any man.'

Montmorency kissed the boy on both cheeks. Henry was learning what a vast difference separated a Duke from a Dauphin, a second son from the heir to the throne.

In his prison cell, Montecuculi awaited the coming of his torturers. He had spent the hours in his dark cell praying that he might have the courage for the ordeal through which he knew he must pass.

How easy it was to imagine oneself a martyr! How tedious, how shocking the reality! To see oneself going boldly and defiantly to execution for the love of one's country – that was glorious. And the reality? Humiliating torture that carried a man to the gates of death, and cruelly brought him back to life that he might make the journey again and again, that he might learn how his poor body lacked the strength of his spirit. In place of that loud, ringing tone, 'I will not speak!' there must be groans and screams of agony.

Sweat ran down the handsome face of Montecuculi, for men had come into the cell now and the doctor was there to examine him, and discover to what lengths they might torture him without killing him and destroying the only means of discovering the truth of the Dauphin's death.

Chairs and tables were brought into the cell while the doctor conducted his examination; with a horror that made him want to retch, Montecuculi watched two shabbily dressed men bring in the wedges and the planks.

'How is his health?' asked a businesslike little man who seated himself at the table and set out writing materials.

The doctor did not speak, but Montecuculi knew the meaning of the grim nodding of the head.

After a few minutes the doctor went out to an adjoining cell to wait in case he should be needed during the torture.

A tall man in black now approached the Count. He said: 'Count Sebastiano di Montecuculi, if you refuse to give satisfactory answers to the questions I shall ask, it has been decided that it will be necessary to put you to the torture – ordinary and extraordinary.'

Montecuculi trembled. He knew the meaning of this. He understood what the planks and wedges meant; they were to make what was known through the country as The Boot; and into The Boot his legs would be packed; then the torture would begin.

While they were preparing him there was a commotion outside the cell, and as a tall figure, in clothes that glittered with jewels, came in, all those in the cell stopped what they were doing to bow low. The King looked incongruous in that dark chamber of horror. Francis looked grave; for his times, he was not unkind, but he had suffered deeply at the loss of his son and he had vowed that he would do everything in his power to avenge the murder; he had, therefore, come in person to hear a confession wrung from the lips of the man he believed to have murdered the boy.

'Is everything in readiness?' he asked, taking the chair which was immediately brought for him.

'Sire, we but await your commands to proceed.'

The executioner, whose face was the most brutalised it had ever been the young Count's misfortune to behold, bound him with ropes; and when this was done the man's two assistants each fitted a leg into a boot, and the cords about them were tightened by means of a wrench.

'Tighter!' growled the executioner; and the Count was in sudden, excruciating agony, for so tightly were his legs compressed that all the blood was thrown back to the rest of his body. He screamed and fainted. When he opened his eyes, the doctor was standing over him, applying vinegar to his nose.

'Here's a good beginning!' chuckled the executioner. 'Lily-livered Florentines! They paint pretty pictures, but they faint before the torture begins! Better speak up, boy, and save our lord the King another moment in this cell.'

There must be a wait, the doctor said, before the wedges were driven in, for it would take several minutes before the circulation was normal. Francis brought his chair closer to the young man and talked to him not unkindly.

'We know, Count, that you acted under instructions. You are a foolish young man to suffer for those who should be where you are now.'

'I have nothing to say, Sire,' said Montecuculi.

But Francis continued with the attempt to persuade him to speak until it was declared time to drive in the first of the two wedges.

'On whose instructions,' said the tall man in black, 'did you give the Dauphin poison?'

Montecuculi shook his head; he would not speak.

One of the men was ready at the Count's knees, the other opposite him at his ankles; the cases in which the legs had been placed were so tightly bound that they would not give. There was a sickening crunch as the bones were crushed to make room for the wedges.

Montecuculi swooned.

They brought him round with vinegar and asked the question again. The third and fourth wedges were driven in, and Montecuculi knew, as his pain-crazed brain sought to cling to reason that he would never walk again.

'Speak, you fool!' cried the man in black. 'You've had the Question Ordinary. It'll be the Extraordinary next. Speak. Why shield your masters?'

The physician was bending over him, nodding in his grim and silent way. The Count was young and healthy; the continuation of the torture would, he thought, very likely not kill him. He could be questioned to the limit today; if that failed to wring an answer from him, the water torture would be tried later.

Montecuculi's mind had one thought now; it was to save his tortured body more pain. He was reminding himself as he seemed to sway between life and death that he had achieved that which he had set out to do. Thanks to him, France would have a Medici Queen. If he implicated her, he would have killed and suffered in vain. Yet these people would not believe him innocent! They had found poison in his lodging; that, and the fact that he was an Italian, was sufficient to mark him as guilty in their eyes. He dared not implicate Catherine and Catherine's astrologers, but if they persisted in the greater torture he did not know how he could endure it, for what he had suffered so far was the Ordinary Question – the driving in of four wedges only. The Extraordinary would be the driving in of four more. He yearned to be a martyr; he yearned to die for Italy; but how could he endure this continued agony? His body was weak with suffering; he could feel his resistance weakening also.

The King had folded his arms and was sitting back; he did not take his black eyes from the Italian's face.

The men were ready with the fifth wedge.

The King held up his hand. 'Speak!' he said gently. 'Why suffer this? You will speak in the end.'

Montecuculi opened his mouth. He sought for words, but he could say nothing, for his brain was numbed.

The King shrugged his shoulders. The man was ready with the first wedges of the greater torture.

Agony . . . horror . . . pain engulfed the Count. If only it were death, he thought.

Then he raised his hollow eyes to the bright ones of the King and began to talk.

Catherine, alone in her apartment, felt ill with anxiety. They were torturing Montecuculi. What would he say? How could he, suffering exquisite torture, stop himself from implicating her? What when they took Cosmo and Lorenzo Ruggieri?

Those two – clever as they were – could never endure torture. Confessions would be wrung from them as well as from the Count.

They would blame her. The whole country was ready to blame her. What would they do to the Dauphiness who had inspired murder?

What a fool this man was! What a stupid, blundering fool! Did he think to kill the Dauphin and have no questions asked? She had not meant him to kill the Dauphin. It was not ambition that had prompted her to speak to him. She saw now how easily he had misunderstood. The fool, to think he could so lightly remove the heir to the throne of France.

And now . . . she was Dauphiness; if she passed through this trouble she would be Queen of France. A miracle indeed! But it had gone wrong somewhere. She had asked for love and she had been offered a crown.

Already they were suspicious of her. From Duchess to Dauphiness through the mysterious death of the King's eldest son! They were whispering of her, watching her, suspecting her, only waiting for the condemnation which they felt must come, once the Italian Count had been put to the torture.

What would they do to her? Of a surety she would be banished from France. They would not keep an Italian murderess in their country.

Oh, Montecuculi, you fool! You and your silly martyrdom! Where will that take you now? Where will it take me?

She looked at her pale face in her mirror. If I lost Henry now, she thought, I should pray for death; for in truth, I do not care to live without him.

The court gathered together for a great spectacle. All the highest in the land would be present. Stands were erected and the royal pavilion was hung with cloth of gold.

Catherine, in her apartments, heard the shouts outside her window. She dressed herself with great care. Her dress was studded with pearls; her corsage rich with rubies. How pale she was! Her thick skin, beautiful in candlelight, looked sallow in the glare of the sun. She had changed in the last few weeks, and the change was there in her face. It was subtle, though; none would see it but herself. There was craft about the lips, a hard brilliance in the eyes. She realised what agonies she had suffered when she had heard Montecuculi had been arrested, what terrible fears had beset her when she had heard they were torturing him. But the saints had been merciful to Catherine de' Medici. They had put wisdom into the mind of the suffering man. He had invented a good story that was not too wild to be convincing; and so he had saved Catherine. He had told the King and his torturers that he had taken instructions from two Imperial generals, and that they had had their instructions from a higher authority. He had even given the names of the Imperial generals. That was clever, for how could the French touch Spanish generals! He had also said that his instructions were to poison all the sons of the King and the King himself. Very clever. Montecuculi was not such a fool.

But the people of France still believed her to have been involved in the Dauphin's death. She was an Italian with much to gain, and that was good enough grounds, in their eyes, for murder. Yet I am innocent of this, she assured herself. I never thought to remove poor Francis.

She could hear the trumpeters now, and Henry came in to

escort her, for on a ceremonial occasion such as this he could not sit with his mistress. He looked noble in his splendid garments; but he frowned at his wife and she sensed his uneasiness.

'The air is thick with rumour,' he said, and his glance seemed distasteful as it rested upon her. 'Would my brother were alive!' he continued with great feeling. 'Why should those guards have wished to destroy my family?'

Catherine went towards him eagerly and slipped her arm through his. 'Who knows what plans are afoot?' she said.

'They are saying the Italian lied.' Now he would not look at her.

'They will always say something, Henry.'

'I would my father had not arranged this spectacle. Or I would that you and I need not be present.'

'Why?'

He turned to her. He looked into her dark eyes that seemed to have grown sly, secretive. She repelled him today more than she usually did. He had thought he would get used to her; he had even begun to think that he *was* getting used to her, but since the mysterious death of his brother he did not want even to look at her. He did not understand her; and how could he help knowing that her name figured largely in the whispering scandal now circulating through Paris, through Lyons, through the whole of France? She was queer, this wife of his. She, who was calm and self-contained in company, was an entirely different person when they were alone. Now, when shortly they must see a man suffering a horrible death, her eyes gleamed and her fingers twitched with eagerness as she plucked his sleeve. He did not understand her; he only knew that when he was with her, he was filled with a nauseating desire to escape – escape from the clinging hands, the pleading eyes and the lips, too warm and moist, which clung over-long to his flesh.

'Why?' he repeated impatiently after her. 'You know why. You and I stand to gain so much by my brother's death. Had he lived, I should have remained a Duke, you a Duchess; now, unless the poisoned cup is being prepared for us, we shall be King and Queen of France one day.'

She said in that low, husky voice which she reserved for him: 'I have a feeling that my husband will one day be the greatest King France has ever known.'

'He would have been happier if he had been born to kingship, and had not to step into his murdered brother's shoes.' He turned abruptly; he was afraid that what was being whispered about her was true! He found, to his horror, that he could believe it. 'Come!' he said coldly. 'Let us not be late, or there will be my father's anger to face.'

They took their places in the glittering pavilion. Catherine knew that all eyes were on her; and in the hush that followed she heard the faint rustling of silk and brocade, and the whispering of voices.

Diane sat with the Queen's ladies, upright, haughty, and magically beautiful, so that Catherine's control threatened to desert her, and she felt like crumpling into tears. It was not fair that she should be so old and yet so beautiful. What chance had a young girl, inexperienced in the ways of love, against such a one? Oh, Montecuculi, she thought, you have given me the promise of queenship when what I wanted was to be a beloved wife and mother!

She moved closer to the jewelled figure of her husband. Was it her fancy, or did he move slightly away from her? His eyes went to Diane, and now he was the devoted lover whom Catherine wanted for herself.

I hate her! she thought. Holy Mother of God, how I hate her! Help me . . . help me destroy her. Send a blight to destroy that bright beauty; send humiliation to lower that proud head . . . Kill her, that the one I love may be mine. I wish to be a Queen and a well-loved wife. If this could happen to me I would give my life to piety. I would never sin again. I would lead a blameless life free from even venial sins. Holy Mother, help me.

Oh, Henry! Why do I, so carefully nurtured, so balanced, so controlled, why do I have to love you so madly when you are enchained by that sorceress!

The heralds were trumpeting, and everyone was rising in his or her seat for the ceremonial entry of the King and Queen.

Francis looked weary. He was mourning both the death of his son and the devastation of Provence. Catherine, watching him, prayed that he would not be influenced by the whisperings concerning herself.

She sat back now, for the wretched prisoner was being carried out. Could that be handsome Montecuculi! He was unrecognisable. He could not walk, for both feet had been crushed to pulp in the cruel Boot. His once clear brown skin was yellow now; in a few weeks they had changed him from a young to an old man.

But Catherine was quick – and greatly relieved – to see that he had retained that noble and fanatical air. Bruised, bleeding, and broken he might be, but he wore his martyr's crown. She had not been mistaken in her man. He knew what terrible death awaited him, but he was resigned; perhaps he felt that his greatest torture was past. Four strong men were leading out four fiery horses; they needed all their strength and skill to hold the animals. Catherine's mind switched back to a scene in the Medici Palace when she had sat with her aunt and the Cardinal and watched the death of a faithful friend.

She had shown no emotion then. It had been important that she showed none. Now, it was far more important.

Each of the Count's four limbs was attached to a different horse. Now . . . the moment had come. Young girls leaned forward in their seats, their eyes wide with expectation and excitement; young men caught their breath.

Now!

There was a loud fanfare of trumpets. The horses, terrified, galloped in four different directions. There was a loud cry like that of an animal in the utmost agony; then a deathlike silence broken only by the thudding of horses' hoofs. Catherine stared at the horses galloping wildly about the field, attached to each a gory portion of what had been Count Sebastiano di Montecuculi.

She was safe. Montecuculi could not betray her now. And the Dauphin Francis was dead and in his place was Henry, before whose Italian wife shone the throne of France.

Chapter VI

THE LOVE CHILD

Three women who watched the horrific spectacle knew that from now on their lives would be different.

Anne d'Etampes left the pavilion feeling apprehensive. For ten years she had ruled the King of France and, through him, France. There was no one in the land more important than herself; even men such as Montmorency and the Cardinal of Lorraine, if they wished to enjoy the King's favour, must first seek that of his beloved Duchess. The most beautiful woman of the court, she was also one of the cleverest. Francis had said of her that among the wise she was the most beautiful, and among the beautiful the most wise. She saw her power now, hanging by a thread; and that thread was the life of the King.

The King and the new Dauphin, it would be said, were as different as two Frenchmen could be; but in one important point there was a similarity. Francis, all his life, had been guided by women; in truth, he had been ruled by them, but so subtly that he had never realised it. In his youth there had been his mother and later his sister; their rule had been overlapped by that of Madame de Chateaubriand, who, in her turn had been ousted by Anne herself. These four women had one quality in common; they were all clever; Francis would not have tolerated them if they had not been. So much for Francis. And Henry? He was of a different calibre; there had been no loving parent and sister in his childhood; instead, there had been Spanish guards to jeer at him. But the woman had appeared at the right moment, a woman who had those very qualities which delighted the father – beauty and wisdom; and more completely under the sway of a woman than Francis had ever been, was young Henry in the hands of Diane de Poitiers.

There was more in this hatred of Diane and Anne for each other than mere jealousy. They were each too clever to care that the other might be considered more beautiful, except where beauty could be counted as a weapon to gain the power they both desired.

The more intellectual of the two women was Anne. Writers and artists of the court were her close friends, and they, like herself, were interested in the new faith which was beginning to spread over the continent of Europe. Anne passionately wished to see the Reformed Faith brought into France. She had many with her; all the ladies of the *Petite Bande*, for instance, and they were the most influential in the land; then there was her uncle, the Cardinal of Melun, and Admiral Chabot de Brion. The Admiral was more than a supporter, for, believing in the equality of the sexes, Anne saw no reason why, since Francis was unfaithful to her, she should remain faithful to him.

Diane, the enemy of the Reformed Faith, had sworn to fight against it. Montmorency, now the closest male friend of the Dauphin, ranged himself with his young friend's mistress. The Cardinal of Lorraine supported Diane, with three of his nephews, young men of great energy and ambition: these were Francis, Charles, and Claude, the sons of the Duke of Guise. With such adherents, Diane could feel strong even against the most influential woman of the court.

So Anne, thinking of these matters, wondered afresh what mischievous enemy of hers had, by proxy, slipped the poison into the Dauphin's cup.

But there was nothing to be done but wait and watch, and lose no opportunity of ousting her rival. The Dauphin was young; the woman was old; and the little Italian was not without charm.

Yet, comfort herself as she might, Anne could not help but see herself as the moon that is beginning to wane.

As Henry led Catherine back to their apartments, she also was thinking of the change that had come over her life. Her face was impassive; she gave no sign that the scene she had just witnessed had aroused any emotion in her. Henry looked yellowish-green. He had seen death before; he had seen even such cruel death; but this touched him more deeply than anything he had ever seen before. He wished he had not so much to gain from his brother's death.

Catherine turned to him as soon as they were alone. 'How glad I am that it is over!'

He did not speak, but went to the window and looked out. Surely, thought Catherine, he must be glad. A short while ago a Duke, now a Dauphin – with the crown almost within his reach. He must be secretly rejoicing.

She went to him and laid a hand on his arm. She was sure he did not notice her touch, since he did not draw away from her.

She said: 'Now it is avenged, we must try to forget.'

Then he turned and looked into her eyes. '*I* cannot forget,' he said. 'He was my brother. We were together . . . in prison. We loved each other. I could never forget him.'

His lips trembled, and, seeing him softened by his memories, she sought to turn the situation to her advantage. 'Oh, Henry, I know. He was your dear brother. But you must not grieve, Henry, my love. You have your life before you. Your wife who loves you . . . and longs to be a wife in very truth.'

She saw at once her mistake. She who was sly in intrigue was clumsy in love; intrigue was natural to her, but love, coming suddenly, she did not understand its ways.

He disengaged himself. 'I would I knew who had killed him,' he said; and his eyes glowed as they looked straight into hers. She flinched and he saw her flinch.

He turned from her quickly as though he wished to put as great a distance between them as possible, as though when he was near her he could not rid his mind of a terrible suspicion.

'Henry . . . Henry . . . where are you going?' She knew where he was going, and the knowledge enflamed her, robbing her again of that control which she had learned was her strongest weapon.

He said coldly: 'I do not think it necessary that I should keep you informed of my movements.'

'You are going to her again . . . again. You desert your wife on such a day . . . to go and make sport with your mistress.'

She saw the hot colour creep up under his skin; she saw his mouth set in the prim line she knew so well.

'You forget yourself,' he said. 'I have told you that Madame la Grande Sénéchale is not my mistress. She is my greatest friend whose calm good sense gives me great relief from the tantrums of others which I must endure from time to time.'

He was gone; she stared after him. He lied! She was his mistress. How like him to lie on such a matter, because he would think it was the noble and chivalrous thing to do! But he was noble and chivalrous in very truth.

So on this day when she found herself the Dauphiness of France, Catherine, being in love, could forget her new exalted rank and must concern herself solely with the relationship of Henry and Diane.

I will find out if he speaks truth! she vowed. If I have to hide in her apartments, I will find out.

✤ ✤ ✤

Diane, leaving the pavilion, accompanied by her women, was considering her new importance.

When they reached her apartments, she made her women kneel and offer prayers for the soul of the Count. She knelt with them, and when the prayers were over, she bade them disrobe her; she said the spectacle had made her feel a little ill, and she wished to be left to rest awhile.

She watched these women of hers closely. Annette, Marie, and Thérèse had always shown her the utmost respect, but did she now notice in their eyes something more? Perhaps they were realising the change that had come into her life, for indeed they would be stupid if they were not.

'Bring me a cushion here, Thérèse. Thank you.' She was always courteous to them and she knew that they would have loved her if they had not been a little afraid of her. They believed her to be a sorceress. 'Just put that rug lightly over me, Annette. I do not wish to be disturbed.'

They hesitated.

'Yes?' Diane studied her long white fingers, sparkling with jewels. On the first finger of the right hand, she wore a ruby, a present of Henry's.

'If it should be Monsieur d'Orléans, Madame?'

Diane raised her eyebrows and Annette blushed hotly. 'Forgive me,' muttered Annette, 'I meant Monsieur le Dauphin.'

'If it should be the Dauphin,' said Diane, 'you may come and let me know. Then I will tell you whether or not I will see him. For anyone else, remember, I am not to be disturbed.'

They left her, and she smiled to think how they would now be whispering about her, awed because she made no difference in her treatment of her lover now that he was the heir to the throne.

Little had she thought when, at the King's command, she had held out the hand of friendship to his son that she would, one day, become the most powerful woman in France. The King was far from well; and when he was gone, Henry, her Henry, would triumphantly mount the throne; and it would be for her to see who was at his elbow then, for her to say who should have a strong hand in the management of affairs.

Madame d'Etampes, that insolent harlot, should be banished from the court; she should pay for all the insults she had dared to throw at Diane de Poitiers. All that pleasure was to come. Diane, closing her eyes, saw herself beside the young King, receiving the homage of his subjects in place of the pale-faced, insignificant Italian girl. What a mercy the child was meek. Some wives might have made themselves very unpleasant.

At whose command had Montecuculi poisoned young Francis? Was it true that he had received instructions from the

Imperial generals? It was possible. People thought that Henry's Italian wife had a hand in the matter; but they were ready to blame any Italian and they did not know the self-effacing child. They had heard stories of poisoning and violence in Italy and they were ready to look upon all Italians as murderers.

The expected knock intruded on her thoughts.

'Madame, Monsieur le Dauphin is here.'

'Bring him to me in five minutes,' she instructed.

Her women marvelled together. She did not hesitate to keep the Dauphin waiting – the Dauphin who was almost the King!

Diane took a mirror and looked at herself. She was wonderful. She was not surprised that they thought her a sorceress. No sign of fatigue; her skin as fresh as ever; her dark eyes clear. She threw back her long hair and put down the mirror, as, the five minutes up, the door opened and Henry came in.

He came to the bed and knelt.

'My dear!' she said.

He kissed her hands in the eager way he had never lost. He was, though, no longer the quiet boy; he was an impatient lover. But he did not forget that, though he had been raised to a dizzy eminence, she was still his goddess.

He rose and sat beside her on the bed. She took his face in her hands and kissed it.

'You may be the Dauphin of France,' she said, 'but never forget you are my Henry.'

'The Dauphin of France,' he said, 'what is that? But when you say I am yours I am the happiest man in France.'

She laughed softly. 'Ah! So I have taught you to make gallant speeches then?'

He turned his face to hers, and with a gesture which reminded her of the boy he had been such a short while ago, he buried his face against the soft white satin of her gown.

There was a short silence before he said: 'Diane, who instructed that young man to kill my brother? I would I knew.'

Looking down at his dark head, she thought, Does he know? Does he suspect someone?

'Henry,' she said in a whisper, 'you cannot think of any who might have done this thing?'

And when he lifted his face to hers he said simply: 'There are some to whose advantage it has been. Myself, for instance.'

No! she thought. It was nothing. He knows no more than I do. If he did, he would tell me; there are no secrets between us.

'Promise me, my love,' she said, 'that *you* will never drink rashly. Let everything . . . *everything* . . . be tasted before it touches *your* lips.'

He said quietly: 'I have a feeling that I am safe, Diane.' Then he turned to her eagerly as though he wished to banish unpleasantness in the happiness she could give him. 'Let us forget this. Francis is dead. Nothing can bring him back. I pray God that if it is ordained that I should wear the crown, I shall do it with honour; and if I am unworthy, I can only hope that it will be taken from me.'

She caught him to her suddenly. She knew that he had had no part in the murder of his brother. She knew that in her lover she was lucky, for being a practical woman she could not help thinking, as she lay in his arms, of the glorious future which awaited the uncrowned Queen of France.

By the spring of the following year, the speculation over the Dauphin's death had, in a large measure, ceased. One of the accused Imperial generals had been killed in battle before he could hear the charge against him; as for the other, he had declared it was ridiculous. There was for a time much discussion as to what should be done about bringing the accused to justice, but eventually the matter was dropped. The Imperialists of Spain laughed the accusation to scorn; and the French could not but feel half-hearted about it. And as no discussion would bring young Francis back to life, the King preferred to forget.

Catherine knew that there were still many to whisper about 'the Italian woman', as they called her throughout France; there were still plenty to believe that she was involved in the plot that had destroyed Francis and put her husband within easy reach of the throne.

She used her young woman Madalenna to spy for her. Poor, silly little Madalenna! She was afraid of her mistress, seeing in her something which others, who did not live so close to her, failed to observe. It fascinated the child, but it was the fascination of a snake for its prey. Many tasks had been allotted to her and these often led her into strange places. Once she had been obliged to hide in the apartments of the Grande Sénéchale herself when the Dauphin visited her, and had had to report to her mistress everything she had seen and heard. The girl had been terrified of being discovered; she could not have imagined what would have happened to her if the Dauphin or the Sénéchale had become aware of her presence in the cupboard in which she had shut herself. But, terrified as she was of these tasks which were set her, she was more terrified of her mistress, and for that reason they were performed with careful craft. Madalenna was not sure what it was about her mistress that so frightened her. It might have been because of what lay beneath her smiles and her fine manners, her humility with those about her; yes, beneath that correct and smiling façade there was, for one thing, a passionate love for the Dauphin, and for another, a delight in discovering what was not meant for her eyes and ears; there was craft instead of guile; there was fierce pride instead of humility. And because Madalenna knew that there was much else besides, she was afraid. She remembered how her mistress's eyes had glistened after that sojourn of Madalenna's in the Sénéchale's cupboard; her eyes glittering, her lips tightly pressed together, the Dauphiness had insisted on hearing each indelicate detail, as though begging for what must have been torture, to go on and on. It was uncanny, thought Madalenna; and often when her thoughts turned to her mistress, she would cross herself.

She was glad now that the Dauphin was away from court.

Henry was at Piedmont. The French had invaded Artois and had enjoyed a successful campaign; but restlessness quickly overtook the King, and no sooner did he find himself among his soldiers than he longed for the comfort and luxury of the court, the intellectual conversation and the voluptuous charm of his mistress. So he had called off the war, disbanded his army with the exception of a garrison which he left in the town of Piedmont under Montmorency and Dauphin Henry, and returned to Paris, where the court was *en fête* to welcome him.

Summer came, and Fontainebleau was beautiful in summer. Francis, as restless as ever, found some peace in this palace among his statues and paintings. He would spend much time, between bouts of feasting and love-making, marvelling at his

Italian pictures – Leonardo's Gioconda, Michelangelo's Leda, and Titian's Magdalen among them. Then he would tire of his masterpieces temporarily, and there would be a spate of comedies and masques, balls and feastings; or he would ride out in the forest and spend days with his *Petite Bande*.

Catherine was no more at peace than was the King, though none would have guessed it. When he rode out to the chase, she was often beside him. He liked to show her his master-pieces and discuss them with her, since many of them were works of her countrymen. It was one of his pleasures to hear her speak of Florence; and they would often chat in Italian.

But the love of her husband meant so much to Catherine that she would have gladly bartered the friendship of the King for it. She dreamed of Henry, longed for him, and although she was delighted that, being in Piedmont, he was not seeing Diane, she longed for his return.

Madalenna brought the news to Catherine. It was the sort of news, Catherine thought grimly, that she would be the last to hear.

'The Dauphin, Madame la Dauphine, is enamoured, they are saying, of a young Italian girl . . . a merchant's daughter of Piedmont. She is very young and they say very beautiful, and he visits her so often that . . . that . . .'

Catherine gripped the girl's wrist; there was in her eyes that fierceness which mention of Henry always put there. 'Come, come, Madalenna, that *what*?'

'They say, that there is to be a child . . . and that the Dauphin and the lady are very happy about it.'

Catherine let the girl's arm drop. She walked to the window and looked out. She did not want Madalenna to see the tears which had come to her eyes. Madalenna must think of her as strong . . . cruel if necessary, but always strong. So he had fallen in love! And the court was whispering of it, delighting in this fresh scandal which was wounding further Catherine de' Medici's already tortured heart. He had escaped at last from his aged charmer . . . but not to his wife, who loved him so fiercely that when she thought of him she lost all her control. Oh, the humiliation! Was she to be humiliated for ever? That it should be a girl of her own race – a young girl, younger than herself! A merchant's daughter of Piedmont, and Catherine, his wife, was a Medici of Florence – a Medici and a Queen-to-be; yet he could not love *her*, and *she* could not have his child!

She closed her eyes, forcing back the tears.

Madalenna stammered: 'I . . . I thought you would . . . wish to know. I hope I did no wrong.'

'Have I not told you that all the news you gather must be brought to me? Now, Madalenna, tell me everything. What is the court saying concerning my husband and his newest mistress?'

'I . . . I do not know.'

'You need not be afraid, Madalenna. The only time when you need be afraid of me is when you hold anything back.'

'They are laughing at . . . the Sénéchale.'

Catherine burst into loud laughter which she suppressed almost immediately. 'Yes? Yes?'

'Though some say she never was his mistress, and that she but mothered him, tutored him . . . and since she is but his great friend and adviser, this matter will not change their relationship.'

Catherine put her face close to that of the girl. 'But *we* do not say that, eh, Madalenna? Those who say it have no sly little maid to hide in cupboards and spy on those two in their tender moments.'

Madalenna flushed and drew back. This was another of her mistress's traits which frightened her – the loud laughter, the sudden coarseness of one who to the world outside her apartment was so demure, one might almost say, prudish.

'I should not have done it, Madame, but for your orders,' said Madalenna.

'But you remember, Madalenna, that when you obey orders you work for yourself. If you were found – shall we say in a cupboard? – you would doubtless have some story to tell. There will be need, I doubt not, when the Dauphin returns from Piedmont, for you to hide in yet another cupboard.' Catherine laughed again. She pinched the girl's cheek. 'Have no fear, my child. You will work well. And I shall reward you by keeping you beside me. You would not wish to return to Florence, Madalenna. Life is very cruel in Florence. You never saw my kinsman, Alessandro. Any, Madalenna, who would leave Paris for Florence would not be in their right senses. And who would go back to Italy when they might stay in France? Do not fret. You shall stay. Now tell me what was said about me.'

Madalenna swallowed and looked at the floor. 'They say it is odd that he can get this humble girl with child . . . and not his wife.'

'What else?'

'They say he has a fondness for Italian . . .'

'For tradesmen, eh? Do they not say their merchant Dauphiness has given him a taste for trade?'

Madalenna nodded.

'But it is not at their Dauphiness they mock, is it, Madalenna? It is at Madame Diane, is it not?'

'Madame d'Etampes is delighted. There is to be a great ball

in honour of the King,' she added quickly, hoping to divert Catherine's attention.

'In honour of the Piedmontese!' said Catherine, laughing again.

But when she dismissed Madalenna, she wept a little, sitting upright that she might more easily hold back her tears. The girl's name was Filippa; she had heard it mentioned without knowing why people discussed her. Filippa, the Piedmontese. She tried to see those prim lips kissing the imagined face, which must be very beautiful – dark, soft, Italian beauty; Italian love that was quick and passionate, as fiercely demanding as her own.

How cruel was life! It seemed more cruel that it should have been an Italian girl, and so young. Where do I fail? she asked herself again and again. Why should he love an unlettered girl of my own race, and despise his noble wife?

But when she joined the masque and overheard the whisperings, the sly jests, the allusions, she was happier, because she believed this to be Diane's tragedy rather more than her own.

Henry was coming back to Paris, and Catherine was filled with eager anticipation that alternately soared to hope and dived down to despair.

She spent much time at the secluded house that backed on to the river. Special perfumes were made for her; she had become practised in the art of using cosmetics. Henry, she was determined, should find a different Catherine on his return.

He was seducible; the little Piedmontese had proved that. She would win him from the girl as the girl had won him from Diane.

She was pretty now; she smelt deliciously of the strange perfume which the Ruggieri brothers had made especially for her; she felt her spirits rise when she heard the trumpets and horns of Henry and his company as they rode through the streets of the capital.

With madly beating heart she went down to the court of the Bastille where the King would ceremoniously receive his son. The walls were hung with the loveliest of French tapestry for this occasion, and the hall was illumined by a thousand torches. There was to be a banquet, followed by a ball.

Francis, who loved such occasions, looked younger than he had for some weeks, and his magnificence outshone that of all others.

Henry came into the court on a flourish of trumpets; he went at once to the King, who embraced him warmly and kissed him on both cheeks. Then Henry received the Queen's embrace.

'And here,' said Francis, putting an arm about Catherine and bringing her forward, 'is our dear daughter and your beloved wife, who, I need not tell you, has been living for this day since you left her side.'

Catherine, her heart hammering under her elaborate corsage, lifted her eyes shyly to her husband's face. He embraced her formally. She saw in him no delight at seeing her again. She told herself that he was hiding his pleasure, that he was ashamed, perhaps, because of the scandal which he would know had preceded him to court. Yet she knew that she was deceiving herself.

'Henry . . .' she whispered, so softly that none but he could have heard.

He gave no response. He stepped back, prepared to greet

others who came forward to kneel and kiss the hand of their future ruler.

Soon it would be the turn of the Grande Sénéchale to kneel and do homage to the Dauphin; and not only was Catherine watching, but she knew that, all about her, sly eyes would be turned towards those two, that jewelled fingers would be preparing to nudge silk-clad ribs; the whole court, not excepting the King and Madame d'Etampes, would be waiting to see the greeting between these two.

And now . . . Diane. To Catherine, she had never seemed so beautiful as she did at this moment. Her black-and-white gown was decorated with pearls; there were pearls in her raven black hair. Serene, and completely sure of herself, she did not betray for a moment that she was aware of the interest she was creating, although, of course, she knew that everyone in the hall was watching her.

If Diane was capable of hiding her feelings, the young Dauphin was not. He flushed and his eyes shone, so that it seemed to those close observers that he was no less in love with her than before. But into his eyes had crept a certain misery, a wretchedness and shame. There was a faint titter, which the King's sharp glance immediately suppressed, though he himself was laughing inwardly. Henry looked like a remorseful husband, he thought.

Diane rose, smiling; she said her words of welcome as everyone else had, and then she turned and gave her attention to the eldest son of the Duke of Guise. The Dauphin's miserable eyes followed her.

The King commanded his son to sit beside him as he had much to say to him concerning military affairs.

The comedy was ended.

At the banquet which followed, Henry must, for courtesy's sake, sit next to his wife, while Diane took her place with the Queen's ladies. But everyone – and Catherine more than any – noticed that his eyes kept straying towards that regal figure in black and white, and that Diane seemed very happy talking to the Queen and her ladies of the charitable schemes they intended to carry out.

After the banquet Diane seemed to avoid the Dauphin, and kept at her side those redoubtable allies of hers, the young de Guises.

Catherine took an opportunity to slip away from the festivities. She called Madalenna to her. The girl's eyes were round with fear; she had been dreading the return of the Dauphin; she knew, before she was told, what would be expected of her.

'Go,' said Catherine, her eyes glittering in her pale face, 'go to the apartments of the Sénéchale. Make sure that you are hidden. I wish to know everything that takes place between them.'

✤ ✤ ✤

When Diane retired to her apartments, Henry followed her after a short interval.

Diane was smiling serenely while her women asked her if they should help her disrobe.

'Not yet, Marie. I think I may have a visitor.'

She had hardly spoken when there was a tap on the door.

'Marie,' she said, 'should it be the Dauphin, tell him I will see him. Bring him in and leave us.'

Henry came shyly into the room, and she was reminded vividly of the boy whom she had met in the gardens on the first occasion when they talked of horses.

Diane, smiling graciously, held out both her hands. Her women went out discreetly and shut the door.

'I am so happy that you are returned,' said Diane.

'And I . . . am wretched,' he answered.

'Henry, that must not be. Please do not kneel to me. Why, it is I who should kneel to you. Come, sit beside me, as you used to do, and tell me what it is that makes you so wretched.'

'You know, Diane.'

'You mean the young Italian girl at Piedmont?'

He burst out: 'It is true, Diane. All they say is true. I cannot understand myself. It was as though some devil possessed me.'

'Please do not distress yourself, Henry. You love this girl?'

'Love? There is only one I love, only one I shall ever love in the whole of my life. I knew that all the time. But I was lonely, longing for you so much. Her hair was raven black, and it grew like yours, in ripples. You were not there, Diane, and I tried to grasp at what seemed like your shadow.'

She smiled at him, and, looking at her, he wondered how he could ever have thought the little Piedmontese could have resembled her. There was no one on Earth who could compare with Diane.

'My dear,' she said, gently and caressingly, 'there is no need to be sad. You went away, but now you are back. That, it would seem to me, is a matter for rejoicing.'

'You will forgive me?' he pleaded. 'You will understand? It was a passing fancy – quick to demand satisfaction, and when satisfied, I found that it had gone. It grew out of my longing for you.'

'I always knew that,' she told him. 'For me and for you, there is one love and one love only.' She turned towards him, and took him into her arms. 'There is no talk of forgiveness, my love,' she went on. 'They whispered; they jeered. Madame d'Etampes, you know. It might have been humiliating . . . for some.'

'How I hate that woman! That they should dare to humiliate you, and that I should be the cause of it, grieves me deeply. It makes me hate myself. I wish I had been killed in battle before that happened.'

She kissed him tenderly, as she had done in the beginning of their relationship. Henry's love for her was fierce and passionate; hers for him held in it a good deal that was maternal.

'Then would it have been my turn to be desolate,' she said. 'There is one thing I could not have borne . . . and that is that you did not come back to me.'

They sat down with their arms about each other.

'Diane . . . it is forgiveness, then? It is as though . . . that never happened?'

'There is nothing to forgive. It is, as I always knew, and you have just explained, a nothing . . . a bagatelle. You were lonely and she was there, this pretty little girl, to amuse you. I am grateful to her because she made you happy for a time. Tell me this, you would not like her brought here . . . to Paris?'

'No!'

'You no longer love her?'

'I love only one; I shall always love only one.'

'Then you no longer desire her?'

'When I realised what I had done, I never wanted to see her again. Oh, Diane, my only love, can we not forget it happened?'

'We cannot do that, for I have heard that there is to be a child.'

He flushed a deeper red.

She laughed. 'You were ever one to forget your status, Henry. That child will be the son – or daughter – of the King of France. Had you forgotten that?'

'I am filled with shame. You are so good, so beautiful. You understand this wickedness of mine just as you understood my weakness, my folly, my shyness, and my shame. When I am with you, I cannot help but be happy, even though I have soiled this beautiful union of ours by my infidelity.'

Diane snapped her fingers. Her eyes were brilliant; her mouth smiled, for she was thinking that the court would soon be realising that it had laughed too soon. She was going to take charge of this matter. It pleased her that the court should see her as Henry's beloved friend rather than his mistress; the first and most important person in his life, his spiritual love.

'My darling,' she said, 'the child must be looked after; it must be educated in accordance with its rank.'

'Its rank!'

'My dear, it is *your* child. That alone makes it of the utmost importance in my eyes. Henry, have I your permission to take charge of this matter? When the child is born, I wish to have it brought into France. I wish, personally, to superintend its education.'

'Diane, you are wonderful!'

'No,' she said lightly. 'I love you and would see you respecting yourself, taking to yourself that honour which is your due.'

He put his arms about her. 'I dreamed about you,' he said. 'I thought of you continually, even when I was with her.'

Diane had slid into his arms. She had put aside the practical Frenchwoman now; she was ready to receive his adoration, which, from experience, she knew would quickly change to passion.

❧ ❧ ❧

Catherine did not see her husband until the next day. Madalenna had managed to slip out of Diane's apartment when the lovers were sleeping, so Catherine knew what had taken place.

She spent the night weeping silently. She knew that she had been wrong to hope. The clever witch had only to smile on him to cast her spell over him.

He appeared next day, flushed and triumphant, the forgiven lover who understands that his peccadillo is to be forgotten; he was wearing the black-and-white colours of Diane.

The court admired the Sénéchale more than ever; Catherine's hatred for her was greater. Madame d'Etampes was disappointed; more, she was worried.

When the little Piedmontese gave birth to Henry's baby, the Sénéchale kept her word; she had the child brought to her and made arrangements for its upbringing.

It was a girl, and, to the amazement and admiration of many, the Sénéchale had the child christened Diane.

❧ Chapter VII ❧

THE FRIGHTENED DAUPHINESS

There was tension at Loches. Everyone felt it, from Anne d'Etampes to the humblest worker in the kitchens. Diane, in continual conference with her young friends, the de Guises, seemed to have grown an inch taller and a good deal more haughty. She saw herself clearly now as the power behind the throne. Catherine, outwardly meek, felt a new strength within her. But for her, these two women who believed themselves to be so far above her in wit and intelligence would not be in their present position! It was stimulating to shape the destinies of others, even while, because one worked in shadow, one must be treated as though of no account.

Icy December winds were whistling through the bare branches of the trees in the palace gardens, and the snow was falling.

The King lay ill; and many believed he would never leave his bed.

It was not only the court that was uneasy; it was the whole of France. And it was not only this illness of the King's that gave rise to tension. The Dauphin, with Charles of Orléans,

175

Montmorency and a retinue of noblemen, was travelling south to welcome Charles V of Spain into France. And the illness of Francis, together with the friendly invasion of Francis's perennial enemy, was sufficient to set tongues clacking, while speculation as to the wisdom of this unprecedented visit was offered in all the wine-shops from Paris to Le Havre and from Le Havre to Marseilles.

It was that stern Catholic, Anne de Montmorency, who was responsible for this friendly overture to Charles V. He had, on the illness of the King, taken over the reins of government, and when he had done this, he acted promptly. He had broken off friendly relations with the English and the German Princes, the Turks and the Duke of Cleves. He had persuaded Francis that alliance with Spain might mean the acquisition of Milan – which the death of Clement had snatched from the King just when he had thought the marriage of the Medici girl and his son Henry had brought it to him – and Francis could always be dazzled by the very name of Milan. And when Charles V had to journey from Spain to Flanders to subdue his rebellious subjects in the latter country, what better gesture of friendship than to offer him safe passage through France, which would mean such saving of Charles's time and pocket!

The invitation given was accepted – with a lack of ease on both sides; and so, Henry had ridden off rather sullenly for, much as he admired and respected his friend Montmorency, he could not relish the idea of welcoming as a guest of France, the man who had once held him a prisoner.

Courtiers huddled round the great fireplaces at Loches discussing the coming of the King of Spain and the possible departure of the King of France. There was a gloom about the palace. Loches, set on the top of a lofty rock, with a dark history of misery and pain that seemed to cling to it, with its underground dungeons, its torture-rooms, its noisome pits and its *oubliettes*, was hardly the pleasantest of French châteaux. There was scarcely a member of the court who did not long to return to Fontainebleau. The fact of the King's being sick meant that lavish entertainments ceased, and that young ladies who had taken on airs with royal favour, now seemed to shrink as they moped in corners. The court of France lost half its vitality when its King lay sick.

Catherine sat on a stool stretching her hands to the blaze while she listened to the conversation of those about her.

Young Guy de Chabot, the son of the Seigneur de Jarnac, was a gay and dashing fellow, reckless in the extreme, a young man who gave himself up to the pleasures of love-making as fervently as men like Montmorency gave themselves to soldiering. He was talking now to a handsome captain of the Guards, Christian de Nançay, another such as himself. Idly Catherine listened to their conversation.

'The King,' said de Chabot, 'should choose his women with greater care. Depend upon it, La Feronnière has brought this sickness on him.'

'My friend,' whispered de Nançay, 'there you speak truth. The woman is herself suffering at this very time.'

'Our King has his enemies,' went on de Chabot. 'One understands that the husbands and fathers of those whom he seduces cannot find it in their hearts to love him as easily as do the wives and daughters. Odd, is it not, and can at times be inconvenient. I have heard that the husband of La Feronnière arranged that the woman should pass this little trouble on to our lord King.'

De Nançay snapped his fingers. 'My God! The King has suffered from the disease for many years. This is merely a recurrence of an old malady, depend upon it.'

They knew Catherine heard them, but what did they care? The quiet little mouse was of no consequence.

Anne d'Etampes strolled up to the two young men. They were at once alert; rumour had named them both as her lovers. They bowed; they kissed her hands; they were, thought Catherine, rather ridiculous in their efforts to outdo each other. Anne had that quick smile, which held so much promise, for both of them. They were two of the most handsome men at court, and Anne was very fond of handsome men.

Catherine watched them, joking, laughing, gaily flirting. Anne was beautiful, and only the closest observer, such as Catherine, saw how very worried she was.

Diane came to the fireplace and with her was Francis de Guise and Marot the poet. Princess Marguerite, the King's daughter, joined them; and as they settled themselves about the fire, Catherine found herself drawn into the group.

The tension had heightened. It always did when these two women on whom the court looked as rival queens found themselves together.

Diane, very lovely in black and white, wearing on her finger the great ruby which Henry had given her, showed that she saw herself as the rising queen. Anne, in blue that matched her eyes and showed her lovely fair hair to perfection, was more beautiful, more gay than Diane. The setting sun, thought Catherine, watching avidly that she might not miss a gesture, is often more magnificent than when it rides the sky.

'What gallant courtiers you must find Monsieur de Nançay

and Monsieur de Chabot,' said Diane slyly. 'They are always at your side.'

'Indeed they are,' retorted Anne. 'I fear there are some who envy me the smiles that come my way.'

'Then that is wrong of them!' cried Diane. 'I always say that Madame la Duchesse d'Etampes has earned well her favours.'

'Madame la Grande Sénéchale is kind indeed. I myself have said the same of her.'

The little circle was uneasy. In a moment they would be called upon to take sides, always a dangerous matter. De Chabot nervously turned the subject to the coming of Charles V. He declared himself eager for a sight of the ogre.

'A strange thing,' said Princess Marguerite, 'that he should be coming as my father's guest – the man who imprisoned my father and my brothers. It is beyond my understanding.'

'But it all happened long ago!' said de Guise. 'It is one of those things best forgotten.'

'Yes,' said Anne; 'it happened long ago. Sénéchale, you will remember more clearly than any of us. You were a wife and a mother at the time; I was but a child.'

Diane said: 'You must have been very talented, Madame d'Etampes. I believe, at the time of the King's imprisonment, Madame de Chateaubriand was jealous of you on the King's account.'

'An uneasy matter for Frenchmen,' said de Guise quickly, 'to have the Spaniards on their soil, even though they come as friends.'

'A far more uneasy matter for Spaniards!' put in the poet Marot.

'I wish they would hurry and reach us. How dull are the days of waiting!' Anne laughed as she spoke, but she did not feel like laughter. The Sénéchale, with her boldness, always disturbed her, always made her feel that her days of power were fast approaching an end.

'I had thought Madame d'Etampes could not find the days – nor the nights – dull,' said Diane quietly.

'It is true that I was born with gaiety in my heart,' said Anne. 'But I should like to see the party here. I long to clap eyes on the mighty Charles.' She noticed Catherine sitting there. 'Our little Dauphiness would wish to see her young husband, is that not so, Madame la Dauphine?'

Catherine shrugged her shoulders.

'Shame!' cried Anne. 'Did there speak the dutiful wife?'

Catherine did not know what had come to her. She had been thinking of Henry while they had been talking and, seeing Diane there, hating her so fiercely, realising that even in a battle of words with Anne she could shine, she had felt her hatred submerging her control.

She forced herself to laugh now.

'Dutiful?' she said bitterly. 'Should I be dutiful? Ask Madame la Sénéchale with whom he spends his days and nights.'

Anne was delighted. There was a smile on almost every face. The little Medici had been able to discomfit Diane as Anne d'Etampes had failed to do.

Diane, to her annoyance, felt a faint colour rise to her cheeks. She hated any reference to her love affair with the Dauphin; she would have everyone believe that she was his spiritual adviser.

Anne tittered. 'Well, we may take the word of the poor, deserted little wife.' She went to Catherine and put an arm round her. 'Why, my little one, I weep for you. But never mind, for he will come back to you. You are so docile, so charming, and so *young*!'

Diane said: 'I am sorry, Madame la Dauphine, that you have felt deserted. When the Dauphin returns perhaps I may persuade him to leave you less alone.'

Diane rose and walked away. There was a silence that lasted for a few seconds before everyone began speaking of the preparations for the reception of the Spaniards.

❖ ❖ ❖

Catherine knew that she had been wrong. Diane was planning to remove her, for she had discovered that Catherine was not the submissive wife she had been believed to be. Catherine harboured grudges; she was inclined to be possessive. Diane had tolerated the Italian girl because she had believed her to be of no importance. But no one insulted Diane with impunity.

Catherine was afraid. Life was too difficult. One was careful, watching every word, every look – and then came an unguarded moment and the work of years was forgotten.

Henry returned to Loches, and Catherine's fear increased. She could find no pleasure in the rich displays which were arranged for the guests. The banquets, balls, the plays, and tournaments meant nothing to her. Henry was looking at her with hope in his eyes, and the hope was that he might rid himself of her for ever. She, for a moment of folly, was to blame. Her hatred had triumphed over her common sense, just as love so often had in her scenes with Henry.

The court left Loches and travelled by stages to Paris. What a magnificent reception was afforded the Spaniard! Catherine watched it all listlessly. What were the schemes and plots of others when her own life was threatened? She watched the entry of Charles into Paris; she was with the King and Queen at one of the windows of the Hotel de Montmorency in the Rue Saint-Antoine; yet it was not at the Spaniard she looked, but at the young man who rode beside him – her husband, who was beginning to hate her and long to be rid of her; and indeed, since she had shown unfriendliness to his mistress, Catherine believed he was turning over in his mind how he could do this. She watched the uneasy Charles presented on behalf of the city with a huge silver figure of Hercules draped with a lion's skin of gold; at Notre Dame she heard a *Te Deum* sung for him; but she was unimpressed by these ceremonies, for all she could think of was, what will become of me now?

The whole court was laughing because, during a hunting party, the young and mischievous Duc d'Orléans had leaped on to the horse which was being ridden by Charles V and shouted: 'Your Imperial Majesty is my prisoner!' And Charles, feeling that that moment which he had dreaded had come at last, cursing himself for a fool to have entered his enemy's country, galloped off through the forest with the young Duke clinging to him. How chagrined was Charles to learn that this was the boy's idea of a joke! And how his French hosts laughed at his expense! But in Catherine's heart there was no room for laughter, since this new fear for her fate had possession of it.

In spite of the gaiety and festivities, the men and women of the court had time to whisper, and their whispers concerned the little Italian Dauphiness.

Catherine, knowing they whispered, would lie awake at night and wonder. Was it true that a divorce was being planned?

It was some time ago that she had heard of Alessandro's death. He had been stabbed by an obscure relative of hers, who had immediately become the hero of Florence. The young assassin's sister had been used as a decoy, and Alessandro had died as violently as he had lived.

What perilous lives we lead, we Medici, she thought. Clement, Ippolito, Alessandro – they had all died suddenly, and the last two had certainly been murdered.

Was she any more secure than her relatives?

They would not kill her; yet she believed she would prefer death to what they were proposing to do.

She thought of the aunt of this Charles whom France was now honouring with feats and ceremonies. That aunt had been another Catherine – Catherine of Aragon, and wife of the King of England. *She* had been divorced because she could not bear a son. And again, ostensibly for the same reason, that King's second wife, having no powerful relatives to protect her, had lost her head. Catherine de' Medici had now no powerful relative to protect her.

They would not kill her. She would not care if they did. They would divorce her, and banish her; and she would never see Henry again.

'All these years married,' they were saying, 'and no child! What good is such a wife to the heir to the throne? He can get children; witness the Piedmontese. For such a one as this Medici, there is only one thing: divorce!'

She wept; when she was alone she stormed. How could she get children when she scarcely ever saw her husband!

She had not thought it possible for her hatred of Diane de Poitiers to grow; but, during the visit of Charles of Spain, she learned that it could.

183

Francis, having shaken off sickness once again, and feeling stimulated by the passing through France of his enemy, spoke to Catherine of the relationship between herself and Henry, as she rode beside him when they were out with the *Petite Bande*.

Anne had stayed in the palace that afternoon; she was feeling tired, she said. Francis missed her; he had asked his little daughter-in-law to ride with him, since he felt it his duty to speak to her. It was an unpleasant duty, and he wished to have done with it as soon as possible. Seven years married and no child! A grave matter for a Duke of Orléans; a disastrous one for a Dauphin of France!

'Catherine,' he said, 'this is a sorry state of affairs. All these years married . . . and no sign of a child. Can you explain it?'

'I can only say, Sire,' she answered sadly, 'that if the Dauphin were with me as much as he is with the Sénéchale . . .'

The King sighed. 'That boy angers me,' he interrupted. 'How like him this is! He is heir to the throne, and he sets his responsibilities light beside his infatuation for a woman. It is incredible.'

'Sire, I had hoped his infatuation would not last so long.'

'With that boy anything is possible. Well, Catherine, something must be done, you know. Seven years is a long time. I should have thought it was impossible for him to get children, but for the affair at Piedmont. You must not be outdone by your young fellow country-woman, daughter.'

He whipped up and rode away. Catherine was in no mood to amuse him. He left her desolate. So he was turning against her, she felt. His voice had sounded less cordial than usual. 'You must not be outdone . . .' Undoubtedly he had emphasised the '*must*'. He meant that if she did not soon become *enceinte* she could not remain married to his son.

And if I were not married to Henry, thought Catherine, I should no longer wish to live.

The King was moody today; had he already decided on the divorce?

She need not have worried. Francis had not given her another thought. He was feeling too unwell to enjoy the chase; and again he was thinking wistfully of the days of his youth. He was thinking also of Anne, and wondering why she had not accompanied him this afternoon. How did she, who was still young and so beautiful, feel towards this aged man that he was fast becoming? The love of a mistress could not be counted on as could the love of a mother and a sister. Marguerite, Queen of Navarre, had been ambitious for him; Anne was ambitious for herself. He remembered now, how, in the first years of his love for Anne, she had demanded the jewels which he had given to his former mistress, Madame de Chateaubriand; not, she said, because of their value, but because of the beautiful devices engraved on them, which the King's sister had composed. He had been completely under the spell of Anne, and had asked Madame de Chateaubriand to return the jewels. But Anne had been cheated then, for the Chateaubriand had outwitted her by having the jewellery melted down so that the inscriptions written for her should not be passed on to another. He had admired his former mistress for that gesture; but Anne had been furious with him and with her. Anne was always imperious, always sure of herself. She was beautiful still and many admired her; that should be so, for Francis must have of the best; but he often wondered if the admiration of those about her was expressed more actively when he was not present. His thoughts went to Admiral Chabot de Brion, Christian de Nançay, Guy de Chabot, and others – even including the poet Marot.

And yet, although he could not trust her, he was unhappy without her. If he accused her of infidelity, she would immediately refer to his own failing in that respect. The sexes were equal at the court of France. It was not for the most promiscuous man in France to complain of his mistress's lovers.

He could find no pleasure in the hunt without her, so he decided to cut short the afternoon's sport and return to her.

The first thing he did when he reached the palace was to go straight to Anne's apartments. There he found one of her women, Mademoiselle de Colliers, in a state of great agitation; she stammered and blushed, and even dared to attempt to detain him. He brushed her aside and went into Anne's chamber, where Christian de Nançay was hastily struggling into his clothes. Anne, in a wrap of cloth of silver, her fair curly hair in disorder, was, he saw at once, completely at a loss. Mademoiselle de Colliers came running into the room. The girl was more frightened than the guilty pair.

Francis, the purple blood in his face, his heart pounding, summed up the situation at once; the afternoon was hot and oppressive, and the girl was terrified because, having been set to watch at one of the windows for the King's return, she had fallen into a doze and had awakened only when it was too late to warn her mistress.

Now this sort of thing was very amusing – when it happened to anyone else.

Anne was guilty; he only had to look at her to see that. De Nançay looked like a man who knows his career is ruined; as for the girl, she was so beside herself that she knelt at the King's feet, embracing his knees, lifting her young imploring eyes to his.

He strode to the window and called for his guards. He kept his back on the three people in the room, and stood there looking down on the courtyard. He felt too ill for anger. He had suspected something of this. He was seeing himself, old, tired, and ill, compared with this vigorous young captain of the Guards. This would not have happened ten years ago . . . five years ago. He understood perfectly. It was no use blaming Anne because she contrived to amuse herself with the handsome young man while the tiresome old one was out of the way. He would have done the same himself. He saw the situation too clearly for his anger to remain.

He was all-powerful; he could imprison the young man; he could cast off Anne. And what then? How would he replace her who was irreplaceable? Anne would lose her position as first lady in the land and he would be wretched without her.

The guards were coming into the room.

He turned, assuming great anger, and pointed to the captain. 'Arrest that man!' he said. 'Let him reflect in prison on the impropriety of conducting here, in her mistress's own room, an intrigue with an attendant of Madame d'Etampes.'

The guards seized young de Nançay, who was now feeling considerably relieved in his mind.

'Get up,' said Francis to the girl, 'and leave us.'

Thankfully she scrambled to her feet and hurried off.

Francis turned to Anne. 'I think you will agree,' he said, as the door closed leaving them alone, 'that my conduct was as restrained as yours has been abandoned.'

Anne was nonplussed, and he was delighted to see her at a loss. He would punish her now by keeping her in doubt as to her fate.

The story of the King's discovery of de Nançay with his mistress leaked out. Poor little Mademoiselle de Colliers had not, as she feared, lost her reputation. Everyone knew who was the heroine of that little farce. De Nançay had been the favourite's lover for weeks. Malicious stories were bruited about, not only concerning Christian de Nançay – who was very soon released – but all the young noblemen who circled about Madame d'Etampes; and these stories originated from Diane's supporters.

Catherine was too deeply concerned with her own troubles to pay much attention to the skirmishes between the mistresses of the King and the Dauphin until she suddenly realised that she might turn this state of affairs to her advantage.

Anne was her friend; they were often together; it was not difficult to plant ideas in Anne's fertile mind.

Catherine said, as they rode together in the *Petite Bande*: 'How the King loves the Duc d'Orléans! I think it would need very little to make him pass over the Dauphin in favour of Monsieur d'Orléans. I am sure he wishes young Charles were his elder son and Henry the younger.'

Anne gave her a swift glance. What a stupid little thing the Italian girl was! she was thinking, as Catherine meant her to. The silly creature . . . to sow such seeds! Of course it was not possible . . . But was it? Could Anne, she asked herself, persuade Francis to disinherit his elder son in favour of the younger? Would the law of France allow even its King to meddle with the line of succession? If it could be done, it must be done. It would make all the difference in the world to Anne d'Etampes if Charles of Orléans became the King of France instead of Dauphin Henry. With Charles on the throne, Madame de Poitiers would be of no consequence whatever.

And this Italian child would be of no importance either! She really was stupid to put such an idea into the mind of one who, if it were possible to bring it about, alone could do it.

She did not know how violently Catherine's heart was beating; nor did she realise that the Italian had noticed the disturbing effect her words had had.

Catherine's plan was desperate; but the plan suited her need. Now it was for Madame d'Etampes to start courting young Charles of Orléans, and then Diane must realise that it was imperative for Catherine to have a child at once.

Alert herself, she set Madalenna to watch. Catherine missed little. She watched Diane and Anne; and she knew that she herself was more clever than either of them. Diane had not yet realised why Anne was making herself so pleasant to Charles. She would soon, though; and then, thought Catherine, Henry will come to me, ready to give me a child.

How stimulating it was, this working in the dark! And how foolish were those two women to show so openly their antagonism to one another. Catherine watched their manoeuvres, and smiled secretly.

Diane successfully brought ruin on the Admiral Chabot de Brion. He had been filling his coffers with State money, but in Diane's eyes his sin was that he was a secret lover and ardent supporter of Anne. With admirable adroitness, Diane secured his banishment from court before Anne could successfully intervene. Anne naturally sought immediate retaliation, and she set herself the task of bringing about the disgrace of none other than the great Montmorency.

She could not have done that, Catherine knew, had not events played right into her hands. Francis had tried to keep out of these women's quarrels which were dividing his court.

When his health improved, he promised himself, they should be stopped. The Catholic party who supported Diane! The Reformed party that clustered round Anne! He would show them that there should be one party and one party only – the King's party.

But Francis could now see that Charles V of Spain had no intention of keeping the promises he had made when he was the guest of France. One of the reasons he had been invited to use French soil as though it were his own was because of a hint he had previously given as to the future of Milan. He had suggested that young Charles of Orléans might marry the daughter of Ferdinand of Austria, and, to show his approval of the proposed match, had said that he would dispose of the duchy and state of Milan in such a manner that the French King would have every reason to be content. How could he have said more clearly that the Milanese should be given to Francis by way of his young son! But after journeying through France and subduing Flanders, Charles V had changed his mind. He did not now feel quite so dependent on the friendship of France, and he calmly suggested that Francis should renounce all claims to the Milanese, in return for which he would give his eldest daughter to the Duke of Orléans, and the Netherlands would be her dowry, to come to her after his own death.

The very mention of Milan always moved Francis deeply. To think that the long-desired possession had been dangled before his nose, only to be snatched away, infuriated him. And when he learned that Charles V had bestowed Milan upon his own son Philip, Anne was beside him, whispering in his ear.

'You may depend upon it, Montmorency knew of Charles' perfidy from the beginning. He deliberately disguised it. He does not wish the Duke of Orléans to have Milan, since then he would become too powerful to please his brother the Dauphin. It is not you, Francis, for whom Montmorency works; it is for Dauphin Henry. Have you not seen the friendship between them? Sire, are you to stand by and see them work together against you?'

The result of this was that Francis, to the rage of Diane and Henry, and to the delight of Anne, banished the once-favoured Montmorency, the great general, the Constable of France, to his château in the country.

Anne had won the bigger battle.

The fight continued. The mighty war of religion had started in France.

Catherine, watching closely, saw that Anne d'Etampes was becoming more and more friendly with Charles of Orléans.

The entire court was discussing the unsatisfactory state of the Dauphin's marriage. What use was it – this fruitless union? Why had there not long ago been a divorce?

It was obviously the fault of the Italian. Henry had proved his manhood in Piedmont.

It was Diane who fostered such talk. The Italian had shown some spirit; she was the friend of Madame d'Etampes. If Catherine was not the meek wife Diane had hitherto believed her, then Diane wished her removed.

Anne was sympathetic. She hinted to Catherine that she would plead her case with the King. She would do this, Catherine knew, because it suited her for the Dauphin to continue with this childless marriage. If there was a divorce and a new marriage for Henry – a marriage which produced children – how then could she persuade the King to displace

Henry for Charles of Orléans? Catherine knew that that plan had taken deep root in Anne's mind; if only Diane would realise it, Catherine was sure she would cease to agitate for a divorce.

Outwardly calm, Catherine was becoming inwardly frantic. She saw herself the divorced woman – she, who had already come very near to being Queen of France – banished to Italy to live her life there. She was twenty-three; for nine years she had fought a battle for her husband's love; was she going to fail now?

She did not now weep. Instead, she looked back over the years and saw her mistakes. She should never have shown Henry her wild, passionate longing for him. She ought to have known that, as he was in love with another woman, it would repel him. But how could she – child that she had been – have known that? She had known nothing of human relationships, nothing of love.

'Holy Virgin!' she cried. 'Could I but go back to be a child bride again, how differently I should behave!'

But what was the use of hoping for a chance to start again. That sort of miracle never happened. The only miracles that happened were those you made yourself. She must do something. But what?

Kill Diane? Willingly would she do that. Happily would she mix the draught that would kill her rival. But what good would that do? She dared not, even after all these years, be involved in another murder. There were many at court who would never forget how Dauphin Francis had died. Caution . . . caution all the time. But she must do something. She must make a miracle.

How? She was beside herself with grief and terror.

Passionately she loved this country, with a steadier, but none the less deep love than that with which she loved her husband. To love a person, she knew, must always be weakness, for even if love was returned, the person could die or change; but to love a country was not a foolish thing, because a country had no fluctuating feelings towards one.

Amboise, Blois, Chenonceaux. She saw that stately panorama of castles come and go before her eyes. She saw Paris and the Seine and Notre Dame; she saw the palace of Les Tournelles and the torch-lighted hall of the Bastille; she saw the Louvre and glorious Fontainebleau. Leave these for the gloomy Medici Palace or the sombre, walled-in convent? Never!

Who would help her? Who save her? There was one with whom the final decision lay. He had been kind to her; he was always chivalrous. A forlorn hope, but the only one left to her.

She looked at her face in the mirror and saw there the marks of grief. Never mind. Her grief this time should be her weapon.

She had made up her mind and did not hesitate. In a very short while she would know success or failure. She was gambling on what she knew of the King's nature. The result would depend entirely on how deeply he desired the divorce; if his mind was made up, nothing she could do would influence him.

She went to his apartment and sent a message in to him by one of his pages, begging to be allowed to see him alone. She was set to wait in an antechamber sumptuously furnished, as were all the rooms of his apartments. She let her fingers stroke the velvet hangings; there was no luxury in the world like that to be enjoyed at the court of France. It was the gayest, most amusing, most intellectual court in the world. Here women were not merely pretty ornaments to make pleasant a masculine world; they took their place side by side with men. This was the home she had grown to love.

'The Virgin help me!' she murmured. 'I shall die if I am banished from the man and the land I love.'

The King was busy with some of his ministers and an hour of suspense elapsed before she was taken in to him. She bowed before him and, lifting anguished eyes to his, she begged that she might speak to him alone.

Those kind, tired eyes with the bags beneath them understood her glance of appeal. He waved his hands towards the Cardinal of Lorraine and his Grand Chamberlain, the Comte de Saint-Pol, and the other noblemen who had made no attempt to leave him.

'I would be alone with my daughter,' he said.

Catherine gave him a grateful, tremulous smile, which he returned; and then seeing his jester, Briandas, who looked upon himself as a privileged person, still sprawling in the window seat, he shouted: 'You also, Briandas. Get you gone.'

'Sire?' said the impudent fellow, raising his eyebrows, 'I had thought you would wish me to remain to chaperon the lady.'

Francis signed him to leave, and, bowing low and ironically, the jester went out.

'Now, Catherine, my little one!' The charming voice, tenderly soft, sent Catherine into floods of genuine tears.

It was rarely that Francis could witness, unmoved, a woman's distress. 'Catherine, my dear one, what is it?'

She knelt and kissed his feet. He lifted her and looked with concern at her tear-blotched cheeks. He took a perfumed handkerchief and wiped her eyes.

She sobbed: 'You are so good. I could not live without the joy of serving you.'

Now this was charming, thought the King. This was delightful. She had always been able to choose her words well. This was a tender little love scene – platonic love – the most comfortable of loves. The admiration of a daughter for her father, made more exciting because the daughter was not of his blood.

'Tell me all, little one,' he said. 'Have no doubt that I will do all in my power to help you.'

'Sire, my honoured and beloved lord, I beg of you to forgive me this familiarity. It is the thought of being banished from your shining presence that gives me the courage to speak to you. I love this land; I love it through its great and glorious King. I have been happy here. It is true I have no children and my husband is bewitched by one old enough to be his mother. These are tragedies; but because on occasions I have won a smile of approval from your royal lips, I have been happy; because, in my small way, I have given my gracious King some pleasure, my life has seemed to be worth while. I do not come to plead for what you would not willingly give, because if it were not your gracious pleasure, it could not be mine.'

'Speak, my dear,' he said. 'Tell me everything that is in your mind.'

'If it be your will that I should retire to a convent, then, though my heart be broken, this would I do. If it should be your will that I should remain here to serve you, then I shall be the happiest woman in France. But, Sire, whatever your command, I shall, to my utmost power, carry out your wishes, for though to be banished from your presence will be to me a living death, I am wise enough to know that there is no joy in my life but that which comes to me through serving you.'

Whereupon she again fell to weeping bitterly, for she was very frightened indeed. But she felt herself lifted on to the royal knee and rocked in the royal arms as though she were a child. Hope came back, so bright, that it was more dazzling than the rubies and sapphires on the royal doublet.

Francis was thinking quickly. He had almost made up his mind to the divorce. As he wiped her tears he was thinking: if Henry spends too much time with one who is too old for child-getting and in any case could only give him bastards, let Henry stay childless. Then, on the death of Henry, would young Charles, if he still lived, mount the throne.

How pleasant it was to play the chivalrous role when one could feel that it did not after all involve any great folly. He could please the little daughter who showed her affection so charmingly, and at the same time he could please Anne. It was rarely one had the experience of pleasing two women at the same time.

'My child,' said the King, 'God has willed that you are my daughter-in-law and the Dauphin's wife; therefore, who am I to have it otherwise? Rest happy, my child. Perchance it might, ere long, please God to accord you and the Dauphin the grace which you desire more than anything in the world.'

Catherine lifted eyes to his face that, while full of tears, seemed radiant with joy. Her mind was working quickly. It was only postponement, she knew; but it would mean at least another year of grace. And who knew what might happen in a year?

She seized his hand and covered it with kisses. She was incoherent – purposely so – because she wished to drop the ceremonious approach and tell the King of her adoration of his gracious self.

She begged he would pardon her for her indiscretion. She thanked him again and again; she asked nothing but to stay near him, to see him each day, to listen to his poetry and his songs.

Catherine marvelled at herself. How calm she was now! How cleverly she had enacted this scene! Each word she had uttered had been the right word. How sad, how tragic, that she who could so bemuse the clever father, must expose herself so pitifully to the simple son!

At last he dismissed her; they parted with vehement protestations of devotion on her part, gracious admission of affection on his.

Here was defeat for the Catholic party. The King had given the Dauphiness a reprieve.

✦ ✦ ✦

Diane was alarmed. She had noticed Anne's growing friendship with young Charles of Orléans. The King seemed to dote on that young man more than ever, whilst his distaste for his elder son seemed more marked. Francis had postponed – indefinitely it would seem – this matter of the divorce. Could this mean that Anne was trying to persuade her royal lover to juggle with the succession, to set his younger son above his elder? Surely that had never happened during the whole history of France; but who knew what a King, weakened by disease, priding himself on his chivalry, might not do for a woman with whom he was infatuated?

Diane saw immediately what she must do. She must make every effort to turn the barren marriage into a fruitful one.

She begged an audience with the Dauphiness.

Catherine received her in her apartments, and they talked idly of Italy and the artists of that country; but Catherine guessed why she was honoured by this visit from her husband's mistress, and, in spite of her excitement, she felt the humiliation keenly.

Looking at the serene, lovely face before her, mad thoughts whirled in Catherine's brain. She wondered if she might arrange for men to enter the woman's chamber whilst she slept, and then mutilate or even murder her.

I hate her, thought Catherine, as she smiled sweetly. She little knows that I have set Madalenna to watch them together. She would have me think that they are platonic friends. Little does she know that I have seen through Madalenna's eyes. Would I could find some way of seeing them together myself.

'Madame,' Diane was saying, 'you are fully aware of my friendship with the Dauphin. It is of such long standing. I have been a mother to him.'

A lewd, incestuous mother, thought Catherine bitterly.

'Our friendship began when he was very young, and it will endure to my death, for I am older than he is, and it is almost certain that I shall die before him.'

Would it were tomorrow! How I should rejoice to see you, a dagger through your heart, and your black-and-white gown stained with your blood! And those serene features, serene no longer, but twisted in the agony of death! I will insist that Cosmo or Lorenzo find me a poison that will make a victim die a long and lingering death which will seem to be the result of a natural malady.

'I know him so well,' went on Diane. 'I know his thoughts

even when he does not confide in me — although he does confide in me frequently. Now, my dear friend, it is imperative that you and the Dauphin have children. I am your friend — your very good friend — and I tell you so.'

'Madame, you tell me nothing new. The whole court knows that I pray each night for a child.'

'The Dauphin is rarely with you,' smiled Diane. 'His presence would be more effective than your prayers.'

She paused, but Catherine forced herself to silence, while her thoughts raced on. And why is he not at my side? Because you are luring him from me. I hate you. If I had a poisoned draught, how gladly would I force it down your throat!

How meek she is, thought Diane. Really I wonder that I thought her worth removing. That little outburst was nothing. It was to be expected. It was because she made it before my enemies that it seemed important in my eyes. She is the very wife for Henry. They must have children.

Diane was smiling, picturing the birth of Catherine's children. Diane herself would supervise their education, choose their nurses and their teachers. They should be hers as surely as was their father.

'Madame la Dauphine,' continued Diane, 'I think I know why the Dauphin is chary of visiting your chamber. Will you forgive the frankness of one who longs to be your friend, who yearns to help you, who wishes to see your nurseries full of healthy babies?'

Catherine bowed her head to hide the violent hatred in her eyes.

'Then I will tell you. When the Dauphin visits you, be not too loving. You are fond of him, I know, and his visits are so rare; but do not make too much of them. Let him think that it is with you as it is with him . . . a duty, not a pleasure. I think he would come more often if you did that.'

Catherine's cheeks were flushed, not with modesty at the discussion of a delicate matter – as Diane believed – but with fury. So he had told this woman of her passionate entreaties, of her declarations of love, of her tears, of her desire! He had told all that to her enemy!

She had need of all her control to stop herself slapping that calm and arrogant face. But she must remember that the King had only postponed her banishment. She could not continue to hold her place if she did not bear a child. This hated enemy alone could help her to that goal. Therefore must she smile and simper; therefore must she pretend to respect one whom she hated. This bitter humiliation was the price asked for ultimate power. Once it was hers, it would be her happy lot to turn the tables on this woman, and every insult should be paid for with interest.

So the girl with the meek smile and flushed cheeks listened to the advice of her husband's mistress; and that very night the Dauphin visited her. So urgent was her love that she was happier to have him on these terms than not at all.

And so, every night, from then on, at his mistress's command, Henry visited his wife.

Catherine followed Diane's advice, and she found that after a while Henry became almost friendly. He consoled himself and her. 'A duty, a necessary act. Once you are pregnant we shall have a long respite until it is necessary to think of the next one.'

What romance for a passionate girl! When he left her she would weep until morning.

But in less than a year after her tearful and touching scene with the King the court was ringing with the joyous news.

'Madame la Dauphine is *enceinte*! Let us pray the saints that it is with a male child!'

✤ ✤ ✤

Three hundred torch-bearers lined the route from the King's apartments to the church of the Mathurins. It might have been midday, such light did they give. In the procession which was led by hundreds of the gentlemen of the households of the King and the Dauphin, came the King of Navarre, and the Dukes led by Monsieur d'Orléans, with the Venetian Ambassador and the Papal Legate with other cardinals and priests. These were followed by the Queen, the Princesses led by Marguerite, the King's daughter; Madame d'Etampes – showing no sign of the chagrin she was feeling – was more extravagantly dressed and more beautiful than any; and in the midst of these ladies, the royal baby was carried.

The church was decorated with finest Crown tapestries, and in its centre was a circular platform covered in cloth of silver; and on this platform stood the Cardinal of Bourbon waiting to perform the baptismal ceremony.

As soon as the procession had reached the church, the King set out; the sounds of tumultuous cheering seemed to shake the foundations of the church, as, smiling graciously, acknowledging the acclaim of his people, the King reached the Mathurins to act as godfather to the little boy who was named after him.

On the circular dais stood the Duc d'Orléans, the second godfather, and Princess Marguerite, the godmother. The baby seemed lost in his magnificent christening robes – a tiny, red, wrinkled-faced creature, a future King of France.

When the ceremony was over, the baby, surrounded by the ladies of the court, was taken back to the palace. The feasting and rejoicing that must crown such an important event had begun. There must be balls and masques, dancing, plays, jousts to celebrate this addition to the House of Valois. Little Francis was the toast of the hour.

But there was none more delighted with him than was his mother. She watched him in wonderment – this shrivelled little creature who had given her security.

She held him fiercely to her breast. Her little Francis! Henry's son!

But even as she did so, fear came to her. He seemed so small and fragile. There must be more sons to make his mother feel safe.

✦ Chapter VIII ✦

THE HOLE IN THE FLOOR

*I*t was April at Fontainebleau. In her beautiful bed with its
rich hangings of brocade and wonderfully woven
tapestry, lay the Dauphiness. Her eyes were lustreless,
her fair hair spread out on the pillows; her thick pale skin
seemed almost yellow in the sunlight; otherwise she showed
little sign of the ordeal through which she had recently passed.
She was strong and young; and childbearing was easy for her.

She was not discontented as she lay there, although she
wished that her Elisabeth had been another boy. Still, there
would be boys yet. There would be many children. She
allowed her lips to curl cynically, for Madalenna, sitting at her
tapestry in the window seat, was intent on her work, and could
not note her mistress's expression. Diane had decreed that the
Dauphin should be the father of many children; therefore it
would be so. As for Catherine, she had proved, by producing
these two children, born within two years of each other, that
she was no barren wife.

How lucky she was that her husband's mistress had decided
to allow his wife to bear his children! He visited her apartments
regularly – on his mistress's instructions – albeit he came like

a schoolboy going unwillingly to school; but nevertheless he came.

It was senseless to nourish this bitterness. She should congratulate herself. She had a son and a daughter and there could no longer be any suggestion of divorce.

Everywhere in France – unpopular as she was – she was regarded as the future Queen. She was – though still called 'the Italian woman' – the Dauphin's wife; and France was beginning to take its Dauphin to its heart.

Henry had proved himself an excellent soldier in the last few years, for the King could not leave his war with Charles V for very long; and Henry took a big part in it. He was without much imagination, but he was as brave as a lion; he was kindly too, a just disciplinarian; he was the sort of leader men liked to follow; and eager as he was to prove a worthy general in his father's eyes, he rarely erred on the side of recklessness. His men were fond of him, and the sober backbone of the country liked him. France adored its licentious, charming, and artistic King; it was hoped that he would live long to enjoy his pleasures; it was gratifying to hear of the works of art he had collected and to know that he employed the best artists in the world to beautify his palaces; it was amusing to hear of the erotic joys, of the beautiful women who delighted him in mirror-panelled chambers. But the splendours of Francis were costly, and it was comforting to look forward to a more sober court under the King-to-be.

There would be, to some degree, a return to morality. The Dauphin, it was true, had a mistress; but the relationship between them was like that of husband and wife. Nor did the people blame the young man for taking a mistress, for was he not married to 'the Italian', and that, in the eyes of good French men and women, was ample reason for choosing a French mistress. Yes, France was well pleased with its Dauphin.

Catherine was also pleased with her Dauphin – desperately, maddeningly pleased. Her passionate love had increased rather than diminished with this greater intimacy between them. Oh, how hateful it was to think that he came to her because Diane sent him!

But she had her babies now.

'Madalenna!' she said. 'Bring me my baby.'

Madalenna rose and went to the cradle – a magnificent affair of cloth of silver, decorated with ribands and laces.

Catherine's face softened as the child was brought to her. She held out her arms and took the little Elisabeth into them.

'Is she not a beautiful child, Madalenna?'

'She is indeed,' said Madalenna.

'I fancy she has a look of her father about her.'

'It is too early to say yet,' said Madalenna.

'Oh come, Madalenna, look at her nose.'

'You think it is the Valois nose?'

'Do you? Perhaps. But I am sure those are the Medici eyes.'

'Ah, Madame la Dauphine, it will be well for her beauty if she has the Medici eyes.'

Catherine kissed the small face. 'It is to be hoped also that she has the Medici nose,' she said, 'for I declare, Madalenna, the Valois nose is impressive and noble for a man, but somewhat overpowering, do you not think, for a little girl?'

Madalenna laughed gaily. How happy she was talking thus to her mistress. It seemed to her now that the Dauphiness was just a happy mother, not that cold, frightening mistress who sent her on secret hateful missions.

'Go to the nursery, Madalenna, and bring young Francis to

me. I would have both my children with me. Go and tell him his mother wishes to show him his little sister.'

Madalenna went, and in a few moments returned with the little Prince. He was just over two years old, small for his age, with a delicate air. He was rather a pampered little boy, for his great, glittering grandfather, whose name he bore, had taken a fancy to him; and that meant that everyone else at court must do the same.

'Come here, Francis dear,' said his mother; and he came and stood by the bed, his great eyes fixed on her face. He seemed to regard her with awe; she would rather it had been with affection. It was strange, but the awkwardness which she felt with the father seemed to come between her and the child.

'Look, my little one,' she said, 'here is your baby sister.'

But he could not keep his eyes on his sister; they kept coming back to his mother's face.

'Is she not a beautiful little baby, my Prince?' demanded Madalenna; and Catherine noticed how naturally the boy could smile and nod at Madalenna. Why was it that he was at ease with others and not so with herself? Perhaps she was spoken of with awe in the nursery. Was she not the Dauphiness? But that was not the reason. Young Francis had no fear at all of his father; he would climb all over Henry and chuckle with glee as he pulled his beard. The child was equally at home with the King himself. Catherine had seen him try to pull the jewels off his grandfather's coat, for which he had received a friendly tap on the cheek, and had been thrown to the ceiling with a 'Ha! My young robber! So you would steal the Crown jewels!' No! There was something strange in the child's feelings for his mother, something she could not understand.

'Madalenna, lift him on to the bed.'

He sat there uncomfortably, she thought; as though, while she fascinated him, he was afraid to get too close.

'Why, Francis,' she said, 'it is pleasant to have you here like this. You . . . and your sister . . . and your *maman*. Is it not, my little one?'

He nodded. He was staring at the ruby on her finger.

'Ah! Is it not beautiful, Francis? It was a gift from your papa.' She took off the ring and gave it to him.

Now he smiled. 'Pretty!' he said; and tried to put it on his little finger.

'You must wait, must you not, until you are a grown man. Then, my son, you will wear many beautiful jewels.' She saw him, a grown man, loving his mother. She could not bear to see him as the King of France, for that would mean that Henry was no longer King. She could not imagine a world that did not contain the joy and agony of loving Henry.

She took off more rings and he played with them on the bed.

She thought: he is not really afraid of me. I could soon make him love me.

He was laughing as the rings slipped from his fingers into the bed.

'Too big,' he said. 'Too big for Francis.'

And she seized him and kissed him suddenly and passionately, until she noticed that he had stiffened. She released him at once, while she wondered bitterly why it was she found it so hard to make people love her – even her own children.

She must remember not to be too demonstrative with young Francis.

'Try on this one,' she said; and she pulled a sapphire ring from her finger.

He was chuckling over the jewels when Diane came in.

'You will forgive this intrusion, Madame, I know,' she said.

Catherine's face was set into the fixed smile she had always to show Diane. Fierce hatred was in her heart. How dare the woman come bursting into her private apartments! How dare she? That was easy to answer. Every bit of happiness that Catherine knew was doled out to her by this woman. 'Your husband shall make love to you tonight.' Make love! There was no love-making, only child-making. '*I* will insist that he comes!'

I am nothing to him, thought Catherine; and she is all. What would I not give to see her lying dead?

'It is a pleasure to see you, Madame,' said Catherine. 'How well you look.'

Diane rustled regally to the bed and kissed Catherine's hand.

'And you, I am sad to see, do not look so well. You have overtired yourself.' Diane glanced at Madalenna. 'I had given instructions that Madame la Dauphine was to sleep this afternoon.'

'You must not blame Madalenna,' said Catherine. 'She obeyed her mistress and brought my son to me.'

Diane was playful and firm all at once. She clicked her tongue. 'It was very wrong of you to so tire yourself. And young Francis was to stay in his nursery. He has not been well these last days, and I did not wish him to be carried through the corridors. Hello, my little one.'

The boy smiled. 'Look!' he said; and he held out a ring.

'That is beautiful. And what are you doing with *Maman*'s rings, eh?'

Catherine felt as though she wanted to burst into tears, for Francis looked at Diane as though she were his mother.

'Come along,' said Diane. 'We are going back to the warm nursery; and if you are very good I will tell you a story. Madalenna, cover up your mistress, and put the baby in her cradle. Madame la Dauphine must not tire herself so. Oh yes, I know she is feeling better.' This was to Catherine. 'But we want no ill effects to spoil our pleasure in Madame Elisabeth's arrival.'

She picked up young Francis, and Catherine noticed how willingly he left the rings to go to her. She longed to snatch him from her arms, to shout: 'You have my husband! Leave me my child!'

But instead she smiled and murmured: 'You do too much for me . . . and my family.'

Diane, if she saw subtle allusions, knew when to ignore them. 'Indeed no. I count myself favoured to serve you and the Dauphin. Now say "*Au revoir*" to *Maman* — there is a good little fellow.'

Was it Catherine's imagination or did young Francis say '*Au revoir*' with something like relief?

As Diane and Francis left, Madalenna obediently took up little Elisabeth and laid her in her cradle.

Catherine lay back on her pillows. She set her mouth into a smile while she thought of her hatred of Diane.

Madalenna stitched quietly in the window seat; the baby slept, and as the afternoon wore on, Catherine lay still thinking of how much she hated her enemy.

As soon as she was well enough to travel, Catherine left Fontainebleau to join the court at Saint-Germain-en-Laye.

When she was there she sent for Cosmo and Lorenzo Ruggieri. She wished, she said to discuss with them her daughter's horoscope.

When they came to her she dismissed all her attendants.

'Speak in Italian,' she said, 'and quietly; for what I have to say to you two must be heard by none other.'

They begged her to proceed.

'How,' she asked, 'can I rid myself of an enemy and seem to have no hand in her going?'

The two brothers looked first at each other and then at Catherine; they were worried.

Cosmo was the first to speak. He said: 'Duchessina, there is one enemy of whom you could not rid yourself without the gravest suspicion. Is it of her we must speak?'

She did not answer. She knew that he was right; but she wished to ease her jealous soul by talking of the impossible.

'It matters not who it is,' she said imperiously as the two brothers were waiting for her to speak.

'I crave pardon, Madame la Dauphine,' said Lorenzo firmly, 'but we cannot agree that it matters not.'

'There are poisoned perfumes,' she said.

'Dangerous!' answered Cosmo. 'They may fall into the wrong hands.'

'Lip salve,' she suggested.

'As dangerous as perfume,' Lorenzo put in. 'Very easily traced to those who supply it.'

'There are gloves so cleverly poisoned that a victim has only to draw them on and death follows,' she said.

The brothers nodded and were silent; but their lips, she noticed, were tightly compressed.

'And then,' she went on, 'there are books. It is but necessary to turn the leaves and the poison enters through the skin and the victim dies. In Italy we know how such things are done.'

'It is necessary for Italians to be cautious,' said Cosmo. 'We are not loved in this land.'

'I thought you two would work for me,' she said.

'We have sworn to serve you,' said Cosmo.

'With all our hearts and minds,' echoed Lorenzo.

'But always with caution, dear Duchessina,' finished Cosmo. 'Oh, dear lady, if aught happened to the one you wish removed, every finger would point to you. All know the position she holds. All understand how deeply she has humiliated you. Why, if she were to die a natural death tomorrow, there would be those to look askance at you. Rather you should employ us to keep her alive than to remove her.'

She stared before her. 'I see . . . that you are right, my dear wise friends. Let us talk of my daughter's future.'

The brothers were greatly relieved. They knew of the raging emotion beneath the calm of their mistress. They were often afraid that she would wish them to act rashly. At the time of Dauphin Francis' death they had suffered agonies of suspense; they had expected to be arrested and put to the torture. The Dauphiness would be a fool if she tried to remove the Sénéchale.

'Come,' said Catherine. 'Will my daughter make a good marriage?'

But how could she be interested in her daughter's future! It was that of herself and her husband that mattered most to her. Henry's hatred would be unrelenting if anything happened to Diane, for he would be the first to blame her.

What folly was love that brought nothing but misery and jealousy! If only she could curb her emotions for that silent prince, her husband. How cruel that she, Catherine de' Medici, so clever, so accomplished in many ways, should be such a fool in this one!

She did not listen to the brothers. She wanted to shout at them: 'I do not care. I love my husband so much that there is little left for others . . . even my children.'

She dismissed them since they would not talk to her of how she could remove Diane. She shut herself into her chamber and tried to rest.

She made resolutions. In future she would try to see the faults of Henry. She would try to return indifference for indifference. What if she took a lover? She laughed. Respect she could inspire . . . and awe. But love? Had any other loved her? Ippolito? Doubtless he had thought that as they were Medici cousins they would run well in harness. Nobody loved her. She was alone. Even the lowest serving girl had a lover. Even those who lived in hovels down by the river were loved by someone. Yet, the future Queen of France must remain unloved; and even her child turned to another woman in preference to herself.

'Where do I fail?' she asked herself as she watched the evening shadows fall across the windows.

How lonely she was! Her women had left her for the night, and Henry would not come. She laughed bitterly. With one child but a few weeks old, the time was not ripe for the begetting of another.

She lay sleepless, listening to the palace settling down for the night. She heard the sound of voices in the garden. Some lovers lingering there? A soft footfall in a corridor. Lovers' meetings? The shutting of a door; the creaking of a board. All over the palace there would be lovers. The King and Madame d'Etampes. The ladies-in-waiting. The Gentlemen of the Bedchamber . . . all the noble men and women of the royal household. Madalenna perhaps. Some secret assignations; some legitimate love. The Dauphin and Diane. Why, their relationship was of such long standing and so discreetly conducted that it was almost a marriage.

She laughed bitterly and got out of bed. She wrapped a rich velvet gown about her and threw back her long fair hair.

I am not ill-favoured, she thought. I am more than twenty years younger than she even says she is! Why, oh why, should I be left alone?

Diane's apartments in this palace were directly below her own. She had felt exultant when she had heard that, and had promised herself the fulfilment of a wish which had long been hers.

Shortly before the birth of Elisabeth, she had brought in an Italian workman, a servant of the brothers Ruggieri, and had had him bore a hole through the floor of her room and the ceiling of Diane's. The work had been done when the court was in residence at Les Tournelles; and so neatly had it been executed that, if the spy-hole between the two floors was not very carefully looked for, it would not be noticed. The workman was an artist in his way, and the hole in the ceiling was set within a beautiful carving of flowers so that it seemed to the casual eye to be part of the decoration. On Catherine's floor it was carefully covered by a rug over which she kept her writing desk. She was just able to move this desk herself; then it was a simple task to lift the rug, put her eye to the hole, and see a good deal of what went on in the room below.

When the court was at Saint-Germain and Diane was with it, ostensibly in attendance on the Queen, Catherine would lock her doors, lift the desk, remove the rug, and watch through the spy-hole.

The sight of her husband and his mistress together, while it tortured her, yet fascinated her; and while she knew they were together, she could not resist watching them.

Through the spyhole, she saw a new Henry, a new Diane. Sometimes she laughed to think that she shared their intimate secrets; more often she wept. She knew that she would be a happier woman if she brought back her Italian workman and bid him fill up the hole.

But again and again she returned to the torture.

And on this night they were together – her husband, dark and lithe, Diane with her milk-white skin and raven hair.

Catherine wept bitterly as, cramped and stiff, she kept vigil at the spy-hole until they slept.

Catherine could see no escape from her enemy. She believed now that Henry would be faithful to Diane till death. If only Anne d'Etampes could prevail upon the King to banish Diane from court!

Tension between the King and the Dauphin was growing. The war between France and Spain had come to another halt with the Treaty of Crépy; and the two court parties – the Reformed party and the Catholic party – were at odds concerning the treaty. The King had agreed to it, and the Dauphin was against it. Henry believed that had he been allowed to fight on, he and his troops would have been more than a match for those of Spain. But Francis, with Anne and young Charles of Orléans, was delighted with a treaty which offered the young Prince a choice of two brides – Charles V's daughter, the Infanta Maria, or his niece, the daughter of Ferdinand of Austria. And he was to be allowed four months in which to decide. With the Infanta went the Netherlands, but only on the death of Charles V; with Charles's niece went Milan, but only when an heir was born to the couple.

Henry pointed out that these terms were much the same as had been offered previously. What, he demanded, had they gained by the sacrifices of the war which they had been pursuing for so long? The boy was right, thought Francis; but he was weary of war. He wanted to see young Charles settled; and Anne was continually pointing out that the Dauphin's objections to the treaty meant that he did not wish to see his brother too powerful.

Henry's apartments, with those of Diane, had become the headquarters of the Catholic party; and one evening, not long after the signing of the Crépy Treaty, Diane and Henry were supping rather more merrily than usual with a group of their closest friends.

Catherine was not of the party; she remained in her chamber. She had, earlier in the day, spoken of a sick headache. She had set Madalenna to watch and report all that was said at Henry's supper table. The girl must wait in an antechamber, hide herself in the hangings and make sure that she was in a spot where she could overhear what was being said.

Catherine waited wretchedly. Madalenna did her work well, for all that she hated it. She dared do nothing else. Catherine smiled coldly, recalling the frightened face of Madalenna. She, Catherine de' Medici, might not know how to win people's love, but she knew how to make them tremble.

She hoped Madalenna would have something worthwhile to report; if Diane would only say something which would, if repeated, be construed as treason against the King! What joy if she were banished. But then, if she were, Henry would follow her into exile. Still, as Dauphin, there were duties at court which he could not neglect. She was tempted to tell Anne something of her love for her husband and her hatred of his mistress. The venomous feelings they both had for Diane should make them the closest allies. But she hesitated, reminding herself that no one must know her mind, for it had always been advantageous to work in the dark.

Madalenna came breathlessly to her and Catherine rose from her chair.

'Madalenna! Why have you left your post?'

'Madame la Dauphine, Monsieur de Vieilleville has just left the Dauphin's table. He said that he was unwilling to be a party to the Dauphin's indiscretion. There is a fine scene in there . . . and . . .'

'What scene?' demanded Catherine. 'What have you heard?'

'It began when they talked of the King and said what a fine man he once was, and how sadly he is changing, and how in the last months his health is seen to be failing . . .'

'Yes, yes. We know all that.'

'Well, then the Dauphin said that when he was King he would bring back Anne de Montmorency, and there was applause round the table. Then he told Monsieur Brissac that he should be Grand Master of the Artillery and Monsieur de Saint-André that he should be Grand Chamberlain.'

'What folly!' cried Catherine. 'What if this comes to the King's ears?'

'That is what Monsieur de Vieilleville said. He said that the Dauphin was selling the skin of the bear before the bear is killed. And he begged leave to go.'

'You have done well, Madalenna. Why, the Dauphin and the Sénéchale have done enough, I'll swear, to get themselves banished from the court . . . You need not go back. Stay here. Tell none what you have heard, or they would ask you how you heard it, and that, little Madalenna, would not be easy for you to explain.'

Madalenna flushed hotly and Catherine smiled at her. She slipped out into the corridor which separated her apartments from those of her husband and, seating herself in a window seat, she waited.

She did not wait long before she saw the King's jester, Briandas, creep silently out of the Dauphin's apartment.

'Good day to you, Briandas,' she cried. 'You have a guilty air! What secrets have you been listening to in there?'

The man seemed astonished; he had lost his native wit.

He stammered: 'Secrets? Why, Madame la Dauphine . . .'

Catherine said slyly: 'And what post, Briandas, is to be yours when mine is Queen of France?'

'You have sharp ears, Madame la Dauphine.'

'News travels fast in palaces, Jester.' She stared at her beautiful white fingers. 'Do you think Saint-André will be a better Grand Chamberlain than Saint-Pol?' She continued to study her fingers. 'I know not what the King will say to these changes. I fear he will not be overpleased with those who applauded them. They might find that they lose their heads before they attain their posts. What think you, Jester?'

'It is true,' said Briandas, 'a post would be of little use to a man without a head.'

'All those present would be under suspicion.'

'Is that so, Madame la Dauphine? Methinks you are right. Only a humble man such as myself would be safe.'

'It is not wise to be too humble, Briandas. I myself am humble, yet had I been at that table, I know what I should be doing now instead of exchanging this chatter.'

'What would you be doing, Dauphine?'

'I would go to the King and make sure that he knew I was a loyal subject. A King-that-is is more to be feared than a King-to-be. For if you lost your head today, it would not matter to you who was King tomorrow.'

'I see you are my friend, Madame.'

'I am the friend of the humble and meek.'

The jester's eyes kindled as he bowed low.

Catherine watched him make his way to the King's apartments.

Francis was at supper with Anne, the Cardinal of Lorraine and several of the officers of the Crown, including Monsieur de Tais, the Grand Master of the Artillery and the Comte de Saint-Pol.

The jester addressed the King without ceremony.

'God save you, Francis of Valois!' he cried.

Francis, startled by such an insolent address, even from his jester, demanded to know the meaning of it.

'Why,' said Briandas slyly, 'you are King no longer. I have just had this proved to me. And you, Monsieur de Tais, are no longer Grand Master of the Artillery; Brissac is appointed. And you, Monsieur le Comte de Saint-Pol, are no longer Grand Chamberlain, because Saint-André is. Montmorency is soon to be with us again. Begone, Francis of Valois. I call God to witness, thou art a dead man!'

The King rose; he took the jester by the collar and shook the little man.

'*Foy de gentilhomme!*' he cried. 'You will explain more fully what you mean, or feel my steel in your heart. Speak, man, if you wish to live another minute.'

'The King is dead!' cried Briandas. 'Long live King Henry of Valois!'

The King's face was purple.

Briandas hurried on: 'With these ears I have heard. King Henry and Queen Diane are already mounting the throne.'

But the King had had enough of this folly and told the man to speak seriously of what he had heard. When Briandas had finished, Francis stood glowering before him.

Anne laughed. 'So he has dared to speak his evil thoughts aloud. Depend upon it, this is Madame Diane's will. She can no longer wait for her queenship.'

But there was no need to goad Francis. Catherine, who had quietly entered the room during the uproar, saw that his blood was up. She laughed silently, for she had heard Anne speak of Diane. Surely now there would be no place at court for Henry's mistress; and surely the Dauphin would not be allowed to stay away too long.

Francis was preparing to show Henry whether or not he was dead. He shouted for the captain of his guard and ordered him to bring with him forty of his archers.

At their head, with vengeance in his heart, the King set out for his son's apartments.

But Diane's spies were as alert as Catherine's; and Henry had been warned of his father's anger ten minutes before Francis reached his apartments. He and Diane had left immediately for Anet.

So when Francis, with his archers at his heels, kicked open the door of his son's apartments, there was no one there but the lackeys clearing away the remains of the feast. Francis took hold of the first one he could lay his hands on and shook him until the man's face was as purple as his own.

'Where is your master?' he cried. 'Speak, you fool, or by the Virgin I'll slit your throat.'

'Sire . . . my gracious King . . . he . . . left . . . ten minutes gone.'

Francis threw the man from him. 'So he has flown. That is well for him, and for his friends who yearn to take the shoes of their betters. Get you gone . . . all of you!' He turned on the trembling lackeys, flourishing his sword. He signed to his archers, and they began chasing the unfortunate lackeys, who now had one thought, and that to hide themselves from the King's anger. The only way in which they could escape was by leaping out into the courtyards through the windows, and this they did; whereupon the King and his archers threw the remains of the feast after them; and, the royal anger being not at all appeased, the glass, plate, and cutlery followed. After that the chairs, tables, and mirrors were hurled out on to the cobbled courtyard. Then the King snatched up a halberd and slit all the beautiful tapestries that adorned the walls, his rage for once being greater than his love of the beautiful.

As he slashed, he seemed to hear the insolent voice of his jester. 'God save you, Francis of Valois!' and then: 'I call God to witness, thou art a dead man!'

And he knew that, had he been younger, he would not have been so angry. It was because he felt himself to be near the grave that he was infuriated by being reminded of it.

He was unhappy.

Catherine was also unhappy. She had succeeded in driving Diane from court, but she should have known that the mistress would take Catherine's husband with her.

❧ ❦ ❧

The King of France was a sad man. He could not find it in his heart to forgive a son who was so obviously awaiting his death with eagerness. Henry stayed at Anet for four weeks before he dared show himself at court, and then there was much coming and going between Fontainebleau and Anet, until at last the ailing King had seen that he must be reconciled with his heir. All the same, he had little affection for him; and he kept young Charles closer to him and doted on him more than ever.

But Henry could be useful to his father, for he was a good soldier; and peace with Spain did not necessarily mean peace with the English. So Henry came out of his brief exile to help his father in the struggle with the enemy across the Channel.

There was a wild attempt to invade the coast of Sussex and another to invade the Isle of Wight – both of which were failures. There was another and unsuccessful onslaught on Boulogne – a fruitless endeavour to recapture the town from the English.

It was when he was encamped near Abbeville that one of the greatest tragedies of his life overtook Francis.

The weather was hot, for it was August, and from the steaming streets of the town rose the smell of putrefaction. It was not long before the dreaded news was running through the camp. The plague had come to Abbeville!

Francis hastily gave orders that none was to go into the town. He knew that this was the end of his campaign. He could fight an army of men; he could not fight the plague. He must, as soon as possible, treat with the English, seek allies, and strengthen every fortress in France.

He lay in his luxurious bed – for even in camp, his bed must be luxurious – and thought sadly of his reign which had begun so brilliantly and now seemed to be ending in gloom. He wondered if sober-sided Henry would recover everything that his father had lost.

And while he lay there, news was brought that the young and handsome Count d'Enghien craved an audience; and when the young man came, the King saw at once that his face was blotched with weeping.

He knelt, but would not approach the King; and something in the strangeness of his demeanour put terrible fear into the heart of Francis.

'What is it, man?' he demanded.

The young Count sought for words, but he could only sob; and the King, raising himself on his elbow, spoke first harshly and then gently, bidding him state immediately what news he had brought.

'Sire, last night, I went to the town.'

'What?' roared the King. 'You knew the order?'

'Sire, it was by order of the Duke of Orléans that I went.'

The King smiled wryly. Young Charles, the reckless, the brave, had no doubt declared he was afraid of nothing, not even the plague. What a boy he was with his pranks and his mischief! But this was serious. He must be punished for this. And what was wrong with this bright young man – a favourite of Francis'? Why did young d'Enghien kneel there snivelling like a girl?

Francis was uneasy. He ordered the young man to continue.

'We went to the house of a merchant, Sire.'

'Get on. Get on!' cried Francis.

'There was a girl there – the merchant's daughter. The Duke had seen her and fancied her.'

'Well?'

'She had died, Sire . . . of the plague.'

'You fool!' shouted Francis. 'You come here to me and boast of this silly escapade. *Foy de gentilhomme*, you shall pay for this. I'll clap you into prison. You idiot! You fool!'

'That is not all, Sire. The dead-cart took her as we reached the house, and . . . the Duke insisted we go inside. He thought it was a trick of her father's to hide the girl, Sire.'

Francis felt suddenly ill. He knew that the count was trying to break some tragic news. He was trying to tell him gently, gradually. Francis opened his mouth to shout, but no words came.

'We saw the bed, Sire, the bed on which she died. The Duke, continuing his belief that the girl was being hidden from him, slit the bed with his sword. Sire, the feathers flew about the room . . . they covered us . . . The feathers from a bed in which a girl had recently died of the plague!'

'My God!' groaned Francis; and now he dared not look at the young man.

'Her father seemed to watch us, Sire, but he did not see us, I think. He, too, was smitten by the plague.'

Francis leaped off the bed. 'Stop babbling, you fool. Where is my son?'

D'Enghien was on his feet, barring the King's way. 'Sire, you cannot go to him. You *dare* not go to him.'

Francis pushed the young man aside. He could feel the sweat in the palms of his hands, as he ran towards the tent of his younger son.

Those who stood outside it tried to stop him. He shouted at them. Was he, the King, to obey *their* orders! They would stand aside or take the consequences.

Oh misery! There on the bed lay his sweet son Charles. Was this the boy he had smiled on only yesterday morning?

'Charles!' he cried brokenly. 'My dearest son. What folly is this? . . .' But his voice broke, for the eyes that were lifted to his did not recognise him.

D'Enghien had entered the tent and was standing beside the King. He was weeping silently.

'The priest bid us leave the town,' said the young man as though he talked to himself. 'He was right . . . when he said we danced with death . . .'

Francis turned on him. 'Something must be done!' cried the King. 'Where are our doctors . . . our physicians?'

But as d'Enghien lifted his wretched eyes to those of the King, they both knew that nothing could be done.

✤ ✤ ✤

To be old when you had been so gloriously young, to have no love of life when you have worshipped it with every breath in your body – that, thought Francis, was a sad plight for a man to come to.

God had deserted him. He was unlucky in battle; the sons he had loved had been taken from him, and the one who irritated him at every turn was left. His mistress was unfaithful to him, and he no longer had the energy, nor desire, to seek others. A day at the chase tired him. What was left to a sick old man who had once been a vigorous youth?

Sorrowing he had returned to Paris after the death of Charles; but though a bereaved father, he was still a King, and he must remember that Charles could no longer bring glory to France through a rich marriage, and that once more Milan had been dangled under his nose only to be snatched away when he was preparing to grasp it. So France and Spain must go to war again.

Peace was made with the English, fortresses strengthened, new allies sought, as Francis prepared to renew his claims on Milan.

But, missing his son bitterly, he could only be half-hearted about war.

He had the young Count of Enghien with him constantly, that they might talk of Charles. The Count had known the boy better than any other had, for they had been the closest friends. Francis made the young man go over and over those last hours of Charles's life. Francis saw the taverns where they had caroused with men and women eager to snatch a few hours of riotous life before death took them; he saw the death-cart rattling over the cobbles, and the priest walking before it, muttering prayers for the dead and the dying; he heard the tolling of the bell; but most vivid in his mind was the imagined picture of that macabre scene in the dead girl's bedroom, with young Charles – so vital, so beautiful then – shouting as he plunged his sword into her bed, until the polluted feathers flew about him like a snowstorm.

'You and I loved him better than did any others,' said Francis to the young Count. 'There is none to whom I would rather speak of him than to you.'

So d'Enghien came into the King's personal service, and stayed with him; and after a few months, Francis felt that the young man filled, in some measure, the terrible gap which the death of Charles had made in his life. He reflected bitterly that it was strange he should find comfort in this young man while his own son Henry had nothing to offer him.

Elisabeth was nearly a year old, and it was time she had a successor. Henry, at Diane's command, was coming to Catherine regularly now; and each night, she perfumed herself, put flowers in her hair, wore her most seductive garments, and prepared herself to greet her husband.

As for Henry, familiarity bred tolerance. He no longer saw her as the repulsive young girl who had come to him at the time of his brother's death. He did not like Catherine, but he had learned not to dislike her; and Catherine felt that from dislike to indifference was quite a big step forward. Give her time – for time was on her side, not Diane's – and she would one day win him. She need have no fear that she would be banished now, and her life could be spent at his side. She must go on pretending for a while that she did not care that her husband in name was Diane's in truth; and that the children whom she had borne were Diane's to love and cherish and plan for. She must try not to brood because it was Diane who was always at their cradles when they were sick and that it was Diane who gave instructions; Diane to whom young Francis turned when he was in trouble or wished to ask a question. She must not feel bitter when little Elisabeth clucked with pleasure to be taken on to that sweetly smelling black-and-white satin lap.

Instead, she must wait, seeking every advantage that might result in Diane's downfall and her own closer intimacy with Henry. She would rise – or stoop – to anything that would bring about such changes; she would neglect nothing, however seemingly insignificant.

Henry would soon be with her. He spent an hour each night with Diane before he came to her. That was the jam to sweeten his pill, thought Catherine bitterly. He was longing for her to tell him that she was expecting another child, for then these duty visits of his could cease, and he could go to Anet – his real home – and there stay with his beloved mistress and not have to give a thought to his wife.

Even if it were so, thought Catherine, I would hold back the news until I could no longer conceal it.

What could she say tonight to keep him with her a little longer than he usually stayed, to show him that she was cleverer than Diane, more capable of ruling a man or a country?

She thought of the court. The biggest scandal at the moment was Madame d'Etampes' love affair with Guy de Chabot, one of the most fascinating of young men. He was married to one of the sisters of Anne d'Etampes, but the King's favourite was not inclined to let this small matter stand in the way of her pleasure. How, wondered Catherine, did Anne draw men to her? In spite of flagrant infidelity, the King continued to cherish her; and yet, Catherine, who was true and loyal, who would give everything she possessed to win her husband's regard, was ignored and slighted!

Henry came in. She lay back on her cushions and looked at him yearningly. How he had changed since she had first seen him in Marseilles, a shy, sullen boy! Now he was a man – the heir to the throne, a man of dignity, slow still, but one to inspire respect. His black hair had a few silver threads in it, although he was only twenty-seven.

Tonight, she decided, she would speak to him of Anne d'Etampes and her lover; passionately, she wished him to know that although, outwardly, she was Anne's friend, she wished to serve none but him. In his presence humility always possessed her. She wanted to tell him that, if he commanded it, she would serve Diane. She felt the old indiscretion coming to the fore. If she did not curb her tongue she would be telling him soon how she set Madalenna to spy on the people of the court. She would tell him that she would put all her spies at his disposal – for Madalenna was not the only one.

She checked herself in time.

'Is it not scandalous how Madame d'Etampes conducts herself!' she said. 'The whole court is talking of this latest love affair.'

Henry lifted his shoulders as though to say he was past being disgusted with the most disgusting woman in France.

'This de Chabot!' went on Catherine. 'Is it not marvellous how he can live in a style rich enough for Anne d'Etampes? The King has given that lady very expensive tastes, I fear.'

Henry was never one for scandalous gossip, even about his enemies. He did not answer. He took off his coat and flung it across the chair, for he dispensed with the help of attendants when visiting his wife. Everything connected with this painful duty, he did in a shamefaced way. He visited Catherine's apartments as though they were a bawdy house; in Diane's he was natural and at home.

Catherine noted this, and violent anger surged up within her, but she was learning to suppress it as soon as it came, reminding herself that one day all insults should be paid for.

Henry might not like gossip, but she could see that he, too, was wondering how de Chabot found the money to live in grand style. He would repeat, to Diane, what Catherine had said, and Diane would see that this was circulated to the discomfiture of Anne. And might it not be that Anne, in that tricky way of hers, would turn the tables on Diane? That was what Catherine hoped, and every small pin-prick inflicted on Diane was worth a little trouble.

'His father, the Seigneur de Jarnac, has made a very profitable marriage, I hear,' went on Catherine. 'This rich stepmother of de Chabot's is young and charming, too. It may be that it is she who makes it possible for the young man to live as he does at court.'

Catherine looked at Henry appealingly. She was telling him: You see, I have means of finding out everything that goes on. If you would but link yourself with me, my darling, you would discover how I would serve you.

'How like him that would be!' said Henry contemptuously. 'I verily believe he is the kind of man to live on a stepmother!'

He blew out the candles and came to the bed.

She was trembling, as she always trembled; and she tried not to think of what she had seen through the hole which, at Saint-Germain, connected her apartments with those of Diane.

A stir of excitement ran through the court; the King spoke of it to his new favourite, d'Enghien, with irritation. Madame d'Etampes and her lover, de Chabot, were both furious and afraid. Catherine, whilst appearing to be unconcerned, looked on with delight. Now she was in her favourite role. Unseen, she had stirred up trouble, and now she could watch the effect, while none realised that she had had a hand in it.

The matter concerned de Chabot and the Dauphin himself.

It had happened in this way: surrounded by courtiers and ladies of both the Reformed and the Catholic parties, Henry had found de Chabot at his side. De Chabot's dress was as magnificent as that of the Dauphin, and Henry had been filled with a violence of feeling such as he rarely experienced. Here was this popinjay, deceiving the King with the woman Henry hated more than any other, since she was the declared enemy of Diane.

Henry, remembering a conversation he had had with Catherine, said impulsively: 'How comes it, de Chabot, that you are able to make such a show of extravagance? I know the revenues which you enjoy are not great.'

De Chabot, embarrassed by this question, which was totally unexpected, said: 'Sir, my stepmother keeps me in everything I require. She is a most generous lady.'

Henry shrugged his shoulders and turned away.

As soon as Diane heard of this matter, she realised how ill-chosen had been de Chabot's words; she saw at once a chance to spread a scandal concerning the latest and favourite lover of Anne d'Etampes.

Diane started the whispering through the Catholic party.

'My dear, de Chabot has admitted to the Dauphin that he is the dear friend of his stepmother.'

'She keeps him! Well, he is a handsome one, that! And that old man, his father, must be very feeble.'

When de Chabot heard how his words had been mis-construed, he hurried home to his father's château, where he managed to convince the old man that there was no truth in this mischievous scandal. And, returning to court, he was deter-mined, cost what it might, to avenge the insult.

Now was the turn of the Catholic party to feel discomfited. Diane had not expected de Chabot to be so insistent. The young fool had declared he would not be satisfied until he had faced his slanderer in the lists. He cared not that what he was saying was tantamount to challenging the heir to the throne.

Catherine laughed to herself when she was alone. Henry was in an embarrassing position. And who had led him there?

Diane! Was it not true that she had spread the scandal so that de Chabot must demand satisfaction? People were saying that this time Madame Diane's hatred for Anne d'Etampes had put the Dauphin in a very unpleasant situation. They did not know that it was meek Catherine who had sowed the seed.

It was intolerable. This foolish de Chabot, reasoned Diane, was thirsting for a fight. It was illegal to challenge the heir to the throne. The fool should have known that. He could not be allowed to go about demanding satisfaction, for although he did not mention Henry's name, all knew to whom he referred.

Competently Diane looked about her for a scapegoat, and her thoughts rested on a certain Francis de Vivonne, a good-looking young man with a great reputation for military valour. He was reckoned to be the best swordsman in France and its finest wrestler. At one time he had been a favourite of the King's; but he was essentially an ambitious man, and he preferred to bask in the warmth of the rising sun while seeking to avoid the scorching rays of that which was about to set. He was just the man who would eagerly seize a chance of gaining the favour of a man who must shortly be King.

Diane sent for the man and told him her wishes; and that very night, when the company had eaten and the banqueting hall of Les Tournelles was filled with men and women of the court, de Vivonne swaggered up to de Chabot and caught him by the arm.

'Monsieur de Chabot,' he said in a loud voice, 'it has come to my ears that you are eager to defend your honour against one who has spoken against it.'

There was a hushed silence in the hall. De Chabot first flushed, then grew pale. The King leaned forward in his chair, his brows drawn together in a frown. Anne d'Etampes had turned pale. Henry had flushed scarlet; and Catherine, feigning surprise, wished that she could burst into her gusty laughter.

De Chabot spoke at length. 'It is true that lies have been bruited about concerning me. I shall not rest until I have had satisfaction of the man who has spoken against me.'

Henry's face went an even deeper shade of scarlet, but Catherine noticed miserably that his eyes went to Diane as they used to do when he was young and uncertain how to act. Oh, what would she not have given for him to have turned to her like that!

De Vivonne, now assured that he had the attention of all, broke the silence. 'I am that man, de Chabot. It was to me that you cynically boasted of the impropriety which you thought it proper later to deny.'

De Chabot's sword was out of its sheath. 'You lie!'

Immediately de Vivonne's sword crossed his.

'I speak truth. Come, you have declared yourself eager to avenge your honour. Here is your chance . . .'

The King rose in his chair.

'Stop! Come here, both of you. How dare you cross swords thus unceremoniously in our presence!'

They put away their swords and came to stand before the King.

'I will hear no more of this matter!' said Francis. 'I am weary of it. If you value your freedom, go your ways in peace.'

The two men bowed. They mingled with the crowd.

Francis saw that Anne had momentarily lost her poise. She was terrified. She was in love and her lover had been challenged by the most skilful dueller in the country. It was said that certain death was the fate of any who fought with de Vivonne.

Catherine, watching her, understood her feelings, for was she not also in love? She saw Anne's glance at Diane, saw the hatred flash between them. Diane was smiling serenely. She thought she had scored a victory. But one day, Diane, thought Catherine, there will be no victory for you, no triumph; only bitter humiliation and defeat.

'Enough of this foolery!' cried Francis. 'Have the musicians in and we will dance.'

❖ ❖ ❖

Anne paced up and down the King's private chamber while Francis lay back watching her. Her fair curly hair was in disorder and one of the flowers which adorned it had slipped down to her ear. Her agitation made her all the more delightful in his eyes. She was no longer young; but Anne would never lose her beauty, never lose her charm. He liked to see her thus, worried, frightened; it made her seem vulnerable and very human. De Chabot's youth might please her; but she was realising that Francis' power was the more important, since only through it could she continue to enjoy the former's youth.

He thought of her in various moods, in various situations. How delightful she had been in the first months of their love – enchanting him with her perfect body and her agile mind; she had brought new delights to a man who thought he had tasted all. And now old age had attacked him, and the coming of that old monster had been hastened by this pernicious malady from which he could not escape. He thought of her – retaining *her* youthful energy with de Chabot, with de Nançay. And he doubted not that if he made inquiries other names would be mentioned. But he did not wish to know. She was a part of his life and it was a part he could not do without. It was more kingly to shut his eyes to what in all honour he could not face, to feign ignorance of matters which he did not wish to know.

That he knew of her infidelities now merely made her shrug her shoulders. Her position was in any case precarious. She feared his death, not his displeasure.

This, thought Francis, is the tragedy of old age. It is a king's tragedy as well as a beggar's. Who would have believed, twenty years ago, that I, Francis, the King of France, with the power of France behind me, would allow a woman to deceive me while I pretend to deceive myself!

Henry, the King across the water — what would he have done in like case? Would he have been so deceived? Never! Francis remembered another Anne with whom, in the days of his youth, he had flirted and whom he had sought to seduce; he remembered her later at Calais — black-eyed and beautiful, proud with the promise of queenship. That Anne had lost her head because the King of England believed — or pretended to believe — that she had deceived him. Then there had been little Catherine Howard on whom that King had doted, and yet she too had been unable to keep her head. Now, had the King of France been such another as the King of England, *his* Anne might have feared to take lovers as she did. But alas! — or should he rejoice because of it? — Francis the First of France was not Henry the Eighth of England. There were two things they had in common nowadays — old age and sickness. It was said that old Henry's present wife was more of a nurse than a wife. Well, he, Francis, was full of faults, but hypocrisy was not among them. With him the power of seeing himself too clearly had amounted almost to a fault; it had certainly brought its discomforts.

He bid Anne come to him and arrange his perfumed cushions.

She said: 'Is that better? Are you comfortable now, my beloved?'

He took her hand and kissed it.

'How many years have I loved you?' he said. 'It started before I was a prisoner in Spain.'

Her face softened and he wondered if she also was remembering the glowing passion of their days together.

'You wrote me verses in your Spanish prison,' she said. 'I shall never forget them.'

'Methinks the professional verse-maker could do better. Marot, for instance.'

'Marot writes verses for all and sundry. It is the verses that are written by the lover to his mistress that have the greatest value.'

She smoothed the hair back from his forehead and went on: 'My dear, this duel must not take place.'

'Why not?' He supposed he would give way, but he was going to frighten her first. 'It will give the people pleasure,' he went on. 'Do I not always say they have to be amused?' He smiled at her. 'I am hard put to it to think up new amusements for my people. And here is a ready-made entertainment. A public combat. What could be better?'

'It would be murder.'

'And how my people enjoy to see blood spilt! Think of it, my darling! There will be those who gamble on de Chabot and those who wager on de Vivonne. A gamble! A duel! I'll wager Monsieur de Vivonne will be the victor. It is true, my love, that he is the finest swordsman in France. I was better . . . once. But alas! I have grown old and others take my place . . . yes, take my place.'

She narrowed her eyes, whilst his smouldered. She knew he was thinking of de Chabot's making love to her, as de Nançay had been when he discovered them. He would be amused to have her lover murdered by the best swordsman in France, for de Vivonne would avenge the King's honour as well as that of the Dauphin.

She repeated: 'It would be murder.'

'Oh come, my love, your opinion of de Chabot is unworthy of him. He is not such a poor, craven fellow that he is going to fling aside his sword and beg for mercy as soon as de Vivonne holds his at his throat.'

'He is no craven, certainly!' She spoke with vehemence.

'Then doubtless he will give a good account of himself,' said the King.

'He will, but still it will be murder.'

'Do not distress yourself, my love. The young fool will have brought this on himself. What matters it if he *is* his mother's lover? Who should care?'

'His stepmother!' she said.

'Mother . . . stepmother . . . I do not care. But the fellow should not have made such a fool of himself. He should not have gone about lusting for revenge.'

'It was natural.'

'How gracious of you to champion the young fool, my dear. So charming of you to take so much trouble to save his life.'

She said: 'It is of the house of Valois that I think.'

He raised his eyebrows. 'How so?'

'Sire, you know this is not de Vivonne's quarrel. It is the Dauphin's.'

'What of that?'

'It demeans your royal house that another should take up the Dauphin's quarrel.'

'Yet this young man declares his honour must be avenged.'

'He is young and hot-blooded.'

The King looked at her slyly. 'I'll warrant he is; and for that very reason it would seem he finds favour with some.'

'Francis, you must stop this duel. This kind of combat cannot take place without your consent. I implore you not to give it.'

There were tears in her blue eyes; he could see the beating of her heart disturbing her elaborate bodice. Poor Anne! Indeed she loved the handsome fellow. She was asking for his life as she had once asked for Madame de Chateaubriand's jewels.

She threw herself down beside him, and, taking his jewelled hand, kissed it; she laid her face against his coat.

Odd, thought the King. The King's mistress pleading with the King that he might spare the life of her lover. Amusing! The sort of situation Marguerite might have put into one of her tales.

He drew his hand across the softness of her throat as though it were a sword to sever the lovely head from the proud shoulders.

'Why do you do that?' she asked; and he replied: 'I was thinking of my old friend, the King of England.'

She laughed suddenly with that quick understanding which had always delighted him. He knew all. De Chabot was her lover, and she was pleading for his life because she could not bear to be without him.

He joined in her laughter.

'Dear Francis!' she said. 'I would that we could start our life together all over again. I would that this was the first evening we met. Do you remember?'

237

He remembered. There was no woman he had loved as he had loved Anne d'Heilly. He was getting old and he had not long to live; and Anne saw, staring her in the face, a future at which she dared not look too closely.

She clung to him.

'Francis . . . let us be happy.'

So much had she given him; so much would she continue to give to him; and all she asked in return was complaisance and the life of her lover. So how could he, the most chivalrous of men, refuse to give her what she asked?

All during the last months of that year there was uneasiness throughout the court. The old order was dying. People were wondering what changes would be made when the new king came to the throne.

Anne, having saved the life of her lover when Francis refused his permission for the duel between him and de Vivonne to take place, enjoyed a temporary respite. She knew it could not last. The King's bouts of illness were growing more and more frequent; he did not care to stay in any place for more than a few days now. He hunted often, although he was too ill to enjoy the chase; but he always said that he would go, and if he was too old and sick to ride he would be carried there. Anne prayed daily for his health. The Reformed party watched uneasily while the Catholic party waited hopefully.

Catherine had felt stimulated by the de Chabot affair, which she herself had cunningly brought about. She felt that if she wished it, eventually she could make puppets of all these people about her while she herself was the puppet-master.

She longed for power. She would use all her cunning to

achieve it. If the love of her husband and the affection of her children were denied to her, why should she not work for power?

She had learned to work in the shadows.

She watched the King growing weaker with each passing day. She was tender to him, solicitous, showing great eagerness to serve. And she smiled, remembering that in her wisdom she had made friends with Diane and, because of that great and deeply humiliating effort, she now had children, so that she need not, as poor Anne d'Etampes, fear the death of Francis. Those children, who had come to her out of her wisdom and her cunning, had given her the security for which she had once had to plead with the King.

Up and down the country went the court at the bidding of its restless King. A week at Blois; another at Amboise; to Loches, to Saint-Germain, and back to Les Tournelles and Fontainebleau. And then . . . on again.

✦ ✦ ✦

It was February and the court had travelled down to Mantes and come to rest at the Château of La Roche-Guyon. Here they would be forced to stay awhile, for the snow was falling incessantly and the sky was still heavy with it. Great fires were built up in the huge fireplaces; Anne, with Catherine and other members of the *Petite Bande*, put their heads together in order to devise some means of diverting the King from his gloom.

They planned masques and plays; there was dicing and cards; balls, when the company planned extravagant and fantastic fancy dresses. But the King would not be amused; he hated to be forced to stay in one place when he wished to move on, and the King's mood, as always, was reflected in his courtiers. They stood about in melancholy groups asking themselves and each other what they could possibly do to relieve the tedium. They were like fretful children, Catherine thought, with too many toys. As for herself, what did she care if the snow kept them prisoners here. Henry was here and Diane was here. It made no difference to her whether they were at Les Tournelles or Loches, Fontainebleau or La Roche-Guyon. She still had her hours of agony to endure when the Dauphin was, as she knew full well, making love to Diane; she still had her moments of hope when ceremony demanded that he sit beside her or dance with her; there was still the bitter-sweet hour when he dutifully came to her apartments. And to set beside jealousy there was always hope; and neither of these emotions could be altered by place or time.

The snow was piling up high in the courtyards; it lay along the castle walls. Never had the old château seemed so gloomy, and the King was growing more and more irritable, bursting into sudden temper over matters which would once have called forth nothing but a grunt of amusement.

It was midday and they had just eaten heavily; the old were drowsy; the young were fidgety. Why, asked one young nobleman of the Count d'Enghien, could not the King go to his chamber and sleep, or perhaps take a beautiful girl to keep him company — two beautiful girls? He had but to tender the invitation.

The Count replied sadly that the King was not the man he had been.

'Come here, Catherine my dear,' said Francis, 'and sit beside me. Can you not think of some game we might play to relieve this tedium? Of all my châteaux, I think that after this I shall hate La Roche-Guyon most.'

Catherine looked at Anne, who was sitting on the other side of the King's chair. Anne lifted her shoulders; she was listless. The King looked very ill today.

'There is nothing, Sire, but to watch the snow and be glad that we are in this warm château and not out there in the cold,' said Catherine.

'The child would bid me count my blessings!' said the King. 'Why, in the days of my youth we had some good fights in the snow.'

'Sire, let there be a fight now!' cried Catherine.

'Alas! I am too old to join in it.'

'It is pleasanter to look on at a fight than to take part in it,' said Anne. 'Come, you slothful people. The King commands you to fight . . . to take up arms against each other . . . '

'Armfuls of snow!' cried Catherine. 'A mock battle. It will be amusing.'

Francis with Catherine, Anne, Diane, and other ladies and some of the older men, ranged themselves about the windows while the young men rushed out to the courtyards.

Catherine, watching the fight, smiled to herself. Even in a game, it seemed, there must be two parties. D'Enghien was the leader of the Reformed party; d'Enghien for the King and Anne. For the Catholic party and Diane . . . Henry of course, and with him the dashing and imperious Francis de Guise. It was the latter who concentrated his shower of snowballs on the Count. Henry, as Dauphin, must necessarily keep aloof. The two young men, de Guise and d'Enghien, were the heroes of the fight. Diane was watching them closely; and Catherine watched Diane.

'Bravo, Count!' cried the King when his favourite scored a neat hit.

'And bravo, de Guise!' Diane was bold enough to shout when that handsome fellow threw his snowballs with accuracy.

Even there, in the group surrounding the King, there was evidence of the two parties. Only one person kept silent – the wise one; she who was content to be thought meek and humble, and in reality was more cunning than any.

Catholic against Protestant, thought Catherine. The d'Etampes party against Diane's party. De Vivonne against de Chabot. The fools, thought Catherine, to take sides in somebody else's quarrel. The wise worked for themselves.

The King noticed the silence of his daughter-in-law and, drawing her to him, whispered: 'Why, Catherine, whom do you favour – my charming Count or that handsome rogue de Guise?'

'I favour the winner, Sire,' said Catherine, 'for he will be the better man.'

Francis held her wrist and looked into her eyes. 'Methinks there is great wisdom behind those charming dark eyes. I say let them fight this out with snowballs – fit weapons for such a quarrel.'

The fight went on. It was too amusing to be stopped. Even the King forgot his melancholy. Catherine laughed aloud to see dashing de Guise sprawling in the snow; and when Diane turned cold eyes upon her, she laughed equally loudly to see young d'Enghien go head first into a snowdrift. Catherine's eyes met those of Henry's mistress, and Diane smiled. You suppose, Diane, thought Catherine, that I am of no account. *I* am too humble to take part in your petty quarrels. To a simpleton such as I am, this is but a snow-fight – nothing more.

Diane said: 'Good fun, this snow-fight, is it not, Madame?'

'Most excellent fun,' replied Catherine.

And she thought: nothing is forgiven. Every pin-prick, every small humiliation, is noted; and one day you will be asked to pay for them all, Sénéchale.

The battle had taken on a new turn. One man found a stone and threw it; another discovered a goblet which had been left in the courtyard, and aimed it at the head of a man in the opposing party. The first blood was then shed. It brought laughter and applause from the onlookers.

Now some of the fighters had come inside the castle and were throwing cushions at one another. The King and the watchers were so overcome with laughter that they encouraged the fight to grow wilder and wilder.

A stool went crashing through a window; it was followed by others.

'Come!' cried Francis. 'Attack, men!'

No one but Catherine noticed Francis de Guise disappear from the fight. She, only, knew that something significant was about to happen. If she could but slip away, send a command to one of her women to follow Monsieur de Guise!

All manner of articles were flying out of the windows now. A china bowl splintered on the head of one young man, who staggered, looked startled and then fell unconscious on the snow.

'Carry in the wounded!' cried Francis.

Even as he spoke, pots and pans were flying out of the windows, followed by chairs and small tables.

The King roared with laughter.

'What a merry turn to a snow battle!' cried Anne.

And the comedy was suddenly turned to tragedy. Catherine need no longer wonder as to the disappearance of Monsieur de Guise.

Suddenly, crashing down from an upper window came a heavy chest.

The Count was standing immediately beneath the window from which it fell. There was a warning shout of horror in which the King joined, but it was too late. D'Enghien, startled, looked up, but he could not escape in time. The chest fell on top of him; and his blood gushed startlingly red over the whiteness of the snow.

❖ ❖ ❖

That sad year sped by quickly for the King of France. There seemed little left to live for. 'I have but to love, and misfortune overtakes my loved ones!' he said. 'When I grew to love my son Francis, he died suddenly and mysteriously. My beloved Charles was a victim of the plague. And now this handsome boy, who in some small measure took their place in my heart, has been cruelly done to death in a sham battle.'

He sought to forget his grief in gaiety. There was a long meandering from castle to castle. The tempo must be speeded up; there must be richer food at his tables; stronger wine must flow; the women surrounding him must be more beautiful; the morals of his court the more depraved. His dress was more extravagantly jewelled. The sparkle of diamonds must make up for the lack-lustre of his eyes, the red of rubies for the pallor which had touched his face. Wit and wine, women and love, music and poetry – they must be his to enjoy. His must still be the most luxurious and the most intellectual court in Europe.

It was February, exactly a year after the death of the Count, a cold and snowy February to remind him of the tragedy.

The Court was at Saint-Germain-en-Laye; and at the head

of his banqueting table, Francis sat – his Queen on his right, Anne on his left.

Catherine, in her place at the table, was thinking that not now would she change places with the King of France. His day was fast ending and it was the turn of others to enjoy great power. Henry. Diane. And Catherine de' Medici?

When the banquet was over and the company danced, Catherine assured herself that hers would be the brightest destiny. She had learned to hide her light under a bushel until the time came for her to show it; then should its brightness dazzle, not only the men and women of France, but of all Europe.

Outside the snow was falling fast; inside the castle, the heat was unbearable. Bodices slipped from shoulders; eyes gleamed in torchlight. Anne sat beside the King and with her was Catherine. Neither cared to dance. Catherine, her hands meekly folded in her lap, knew that Henry was whispering to Diane as they sat among their friends and supporters; Catherine gave no sign that she as much as saw them. Anne was watching de Chabot with a red-headed beauty, and there was smouldering jealousy in her eyes; the King was aware of Anne's jealousy. It gave Catherine a feeling of comfort to know that for once the King and his mistress were experiencing the same bitter emotion as she did herself. It gave her a feeling of satisfaction to realise that long endurance had taught her to hide her feelings far better than they could.

A messenger came while the dance was in progress. He craved the King's permission to speak, and on receiving it, he announced the death of the King of England.

Francis stared before him. 'Dead!' he said. 'So he is dead then.'

He beckoned to an attendant and bid him look after the messenger and feed him well.

'I had been expecting this,' said Francis. 'He has been long sick.'

'The end of an old enemy,' said Anne. 'I wonder how he will face his Judge. We must do a masque: "The King of England at the Judgement Seat". What think you?'

But Francis was silent.

Anne pressed his hand and said: 'This saddens you, my love.'

The King smiled. 'We were of an age,' he said. 'My old friend; my old enemy. He has gone whither I shortly must follow.'

Catherine said: 'I beg of you, Sire, say not so.'

'There, my little one. Do not be distressed. It is something we must all come to, and I but happen to be a step or two nearer than you and Anne here.'

Anne's lips were tight. 'I beg of you not to speak of it,' she said.

'And I beg of you, my darlings, not to be distressed,' he said lightly. 'Catherine, you are safe now, my child. You have a son and a daughter. Get you more of them. I will speak to Henry of you, sweet Anne. He is a good and honest fellow. He will see no harm comes to you.'

Anne's lips twisted wryly. Ah, thought Catherine, it is not Henry she fears. This is ironic justice. For long she has guided the King's hand to the disgrace of many; now she herself must be disgraced because there will be a new woman to guide a new King's hand. And that new King is my husband. Anne's years of plenty would be paid for. And one day, so should Diane's.

A shadow had fallen over the merry-making because the King of England was dead.

'I remember him well,' mused Francis. 'At Guisnes and Ardres. Big and red and blustering . . . a fine figure of a man . . . a handsomer it would have been hard to find, if you liked the type. I threw him in a wrestling match; and never have I seen such anger. We were like the bull and the panther. One morning I went to him before breakfast and I had him at my mercy. I called him "My prisoner" and I gave him his shirt with my own hands. You should have seen his face, my darlings. When my dear boy Charles mounted the Emperor's horse to tease him, the expression on the Imperial countenance took me back in years, and I remembered the King of England.'

'You should not be sorry at this man's death, Francis,' said Anne. 'He was no friend to you.'

'It is a strange feeling. Our lives seemed intwined. And now he is dead. The same disease took him as will take me. There was much we had in common. Each in his country the supreme ruler. Each with his love of women. Though I fancy I am more lenient to the women I love than he ever was. He took them to church and took them to bed, and from bed to block. I dispensed with church and block.'

'He was a monster,' said Anne. 'Let us waste no sorrow on him. His poor wife is rejoicing, I'll warrant. She still carries her head on her shoulders, thanks to the timely death of her lord husband.'

'They say,' put in Catherine quietly, 'that she was happy to be a nurse to him. They say it was safer in England to be the King's nurse than the King's wife.'

'Yet she – good nurse though she was, poor lady – has, I understand, been hard put to it to keep her head upon her shoulders.' Anne smiled at the King. 'Come, Sire, away with your grief. Let us do the play we did last week. How it made you laugh! I'll warrant I can freshen it up a bit and give you one or two surprises.'

'Yes, do it, my darling. And let Catherine help you.'

So they did the play, and the King laughed merrily; but it was noticed that he retired to his apartments earlier than was his wont. And when he was there, his prayers were longer than usual; and it seemed that the death of the King of England had cast a prophetic gloom over his mind.

Catherine was planning her dress for the fancy dress masque. She would be Circe.

'Let us be masked,' she had begged Anne. 'It is so much more amusing. You dance with . . . you know not whom.'

Anne had agreed. She let Catherine make arrangements now. Poor Anne! She was growing more and more sick at heart; the King was visibly weaker.

It was his suggestion that there should be a masque. 'A carnival!' he had cried. 'The gayest we have ever had!'

Thus he thought to snap his fingers at death.

Planning her costume, Catherine thought of him, thought of what his passing would mean to her. Queen of France . . . in name. The real queen would be Diane. She could continue to hope. There was hope in every stitch she put into her costume. She would be Circe – gay and bold. She would discover what Henry's costume would be. There were plenty of spies to bring that news to her. She would go to him, not as Catherine, but as Circe, and she would try to make him desire her. She laughed at herself. As if that were possible! But why not? Once a little

Piedmontese had made him love her. A love potion slipped into his wine? Oh, she had lost her faith in love potions. But as she stitched and thought of the masked ball that would take place when they reached Saint-Germain, she continued to dream and hope.

She was feverishly impatient for Saint-Germain. They had travelled through Chevreuse and Limours to Rochefort. How restless was the King in his determination to throw off pursuing death.

He talked continually of death, if not to Anne, to Catherine.

He talked of his achievements. He told his daughter-in-law how he had changed the face of France. He spoke of the palaces he had created and those he had altered. He had, he reminded Catherine, brought a new and intellectual life to his country.

'Catherine,' he said pathetically, 'I have done much that was wrong, but a few things that were good. It was I who aroused new interest in learning – an interest, my darling, which was stifled to death in the years before me. I am the father of the new life. I fertilised the seed; I cherished the young child. Will the world remember that when I am gone? Catherine, what do you think: will they forget Pavia, my mad pranks, all that France lost; will they forget the mirrored baths of which they love to whisper, the black satin sheets that made such a delightful background for the whitest limbs in France? Oh, little daughter, shall I be remembered as the man who loved learning or lechery?'

Catherine wept with him; she thought of him in all his magnificence when she had first seen him, but even then he was an ageing man. Poor, sad King! But old kings must go to make way for new ones; and as she knelt and let her tears fall on to his hands she was thinking of Henry in a costume as yet unknown to her, his eyes burning through his mask with his sudden passionate love for Circe.

But as the cavalcade travelled on, with one of those sudden fits of restlessness the King decided that before going to Saint-Germain for the carnival, he wished to turn aside and stay for a while at the castle of Rambouillet. He would have a few days' hunting there with his *Petite Bande*; and after that they would continue to Saint-Germain for the gayest carnival the court had ever known.

There were more days to dream, thought Catherine. She did not greatly care. She guessed that Circe could never take the lover from Diane; but while they dallied at Rambouillet she could pretend she believed this might come about.

Anne protested at the delay. 'Francis, there is more comfort at Saint-Germain. Rambouillet is so rough. Little more than one of your hunting seats.'

'Comfort?' he had cried; for it was one of those days when he felt a little better. 'It is not comfort I want. It is the hunt.'

But as they neared Rambouillet the King's weariness was great indeed, and it was necessary to carry him to his bed. Once there, he relapsed into melancholy. Would he ever leave Rambouillet? he asked himself.

As he lay in his bed he was frantic suddenly. He must be surrounded by his friends, the brightest and merriest in the court. Let Anne come to his bedside; let the Cardinal of Lorraine be there; all the young people, his son Henry and Catherine, the de Guises, Saint-Pol, Saint-André. Let the musicians come and play.

He felt happier when they were there. He had turned his bedroom into a music-room.

But he was soon weary. He whispered to Anne: 'I would my

sister Marguerite would come to me. I do not see enough of my sweet sister.'

Anne's voice was harsh with tears. 'The Queen of Navarre herself is confined to a sick bed.'

'Then tell her not that I asked for her, or she would leave it to come to me. Beloved sister, my darling Marguerite, it is to be expected that when I am laid low, so should you also be. The saints preserve you, dear sister.'

'Dearest,' said Anne, 'allow me to dismiss these people that you may try to sleep.'

He smiled and nodded.

In the morning he felt better. He was ready for the hunt, he declared.

Anne begged him not to go. Catherine joined in her entreaties, as did other members of the *Petite Bande*. But he would not listen. He smiled jauntily at the bright and beautiful faces of his band; he caressed one and joked with another. He must hunt today. He could not explain. He felt that Death was waiting for him behind the door, behind the hangings. Death had caught the English King; it should not catch Francis . . . yet.

His will was strong. Sickly pale, his eyes glazed, he kept his seat in the saddle. He commanded Anne to ride beside him, and Catherine to keep close. The huntsman's horn and the baying of hounds, he said, were the sweetest music in his ears; and Catherine guessed that as he rode he felt himself to be not the aged man, but the young Francis.

The *Petite Bande* closed round him. They were afraid. Death was the swiftest hunter in the forest of Rambouillet that March afternoon, and each lovely woman, watching her leader, knew that this was the last ride of Francis's *Petite Bande*.

Francis was delirious that night. He talked continually, and it was as though ghosts from the past stood round his bed. Louise of Savoy, his adoring mother; Marguerite of Navarre, his beloved sister; his meek Queens, Claude and Eleonore; the mistresses he had loved best – Frances of Chateaubriand and Anne d'Etampes; his sons, Francis and Charles. He felt the walls of a prison in Madrid enclose him; he knew again the glory of victory, the humiliation of defeat.

He regained consciousness, and with a wry smile spoke of the scandals of his reign.

'A scandalous life I have led, my friends. I will make amends by dying a good death.'

Prayers were said at his bedside, and he listened eagerly to them.

'I must see my son,' he said. 'Bring the Dauphin to me.'

Henry came and awkwardly approached the death-bed of the father whose love he had longed to inspire, and, only succeeding in winning his dislike, had disliked him in return.

He knelt by his father's bed and Francis smiled, all differences forgotten now.

'My boy . . . my only son . . . my dearest Henry.'

Henry sought for the right words and could not find them. But there were tears in his eyes and they spoke more eloquently than any words. Francis was anxious. What advice should he offer his son? He prayed that he would not make the mistakes his father had made.

'Henry, children should imitate the virtues, not the vices of their parents,' he said.

'Yes, my father.'

'The French, my son, are the best people in the world, and you ought to treat them with consideration and gentleness, for when their sovereign is in need they refuse him nothing. I recommend you therefore to relieve them as far as you can of burdensome taxation . . .'

The sweat was running down the King's cheeks. The room seemed hazy to him. His son's face grew dim. He thought of the dangers which would beset this young man. He saw those two factions which could split the country in two; the religious controversy that now, he realised, was but a young sprig in his reign, would grow to a mighty tree whose fruit was bloodshed and misery.

'Holy Mother, protect my boy!' he prayed incoherently. 'Holy Mother, let those about him advise him for his good and that of France.'

He saw Diane . . . guiding his son. He remembered afresh that game of snowballing which had begun so innocently and had ended in heartbreak. It was symbolic. These women's quarrels had amused him. Madame Diane against Madame Anne. But what would grow out of them? Horror and bloodshed. His beloved friend, the young Count d'Enghien, had been crushed to death in the first skirmishes of civil war which would rend his country. The chest was but a symbol. He saw that now. Why had he not seen it before?

'Henry . . . oh, my son . . . why have we come together now that it is too late? Henry . . . beware . . . beware of those about you. There are some . . .'

Henry must put his ear close to his father's mouth if he would catch his words.

'Beware . . . of the Guises. Ambitious . . . they will try to snatch the crown. The house of Guise . . . is the enemy of the house of Valois. Henry . . . closer. Do not be ruled by women . . . as I have been. Learn from the faults of your father. Oh,

Henry, my boy, keep the ministers I have about me. Good . . . honest men. Do not bring back Montmorency. He will strip you and your children of their doublets and our people of their shirts. Henry, deal kindly with Anne. Remember she is a woman. Always . . . be considerate . . . to women . . . but be not ruled by them as was your foolish father . . .'

The King's eyes were glazed, and now it was impossible to hear what he said.

'Father,' said Henry, bending close, 'give me your blessing.'

The King had only time to embrace his son before he left Rambouillet and France for ever.

✦ ✤ ✦

At Béarn, the King's sister, lying in her sick-bed, was overwhelmed with foreboding. Her brother in danger, needing her, and she not with him! She left her bed and prepared to make the journey to Rambouillet. She was ready to set out when the news was brought to her.

Sorrowing, reproaching herself for not being with him, she fell into melancholy. Her life was ended, for he had been her life. She would retire to a convent; in piety only could she find relief from her grief. She was done with life. The King, her beloved, was dead; therefore was she dead also.

Anne, in her own apartments, waited for Diane's revenge. It could only be a matter of days now. Diane would not long delay.

Henry, saddened by the death, yet felt relieved. Never more would he stammer in that presence. Already men's attitudes had changed towards him. They knelt and swore allegiance; they sought to gratify every wish before he knew he had it.

Diane, serene outwardly, was inwardly aware of a deep

pleasure. At last her kingdom had come. She was no longer merely the Dauphin's mistress; she was the first lady in the land.

At Saint-Germain, whither the new King came, after leaving Rambouillet, to make arrangements for the ceremonies that must precede his father's burial, Catherine sat in her apartments thinking of the change this event would bring into her life.

She was pregnant with her third child, but this fact could for some time be hidden from Henry.

She had a son and a daughter; another child was coming; she was the Queen of France. How pleased with her would Clement have been if he could have lived to see this day!

She was safe on the throne of France. That was a matter for the utmost rejoicing; yet there was so much needed to make her happiness complete.

She perfumed herself; she dressed with care; and she waited.

But he did not come, and when she knew that she could no longer hope for him that night, she locked her door and moved the desk and rug and looked down into the chamber below.

Catherine watched them together, saw their embrace, listened to their whispering tenderness, witnessed their passion.

This day she had been raised to the height of her ambition, and yet she must torture herself by spying on her husband and his mistress. Ambition gratified, power would surely one day be hers. It should be her happy fate to bear kings and queens.

And yet, watching her husband with the woman he loved, the Queen of France wept bitterly.

❧ Chapter IX ❧

THE TWO QUEENS

Queen of France! Yet how was her position changed? It was Diane, not Catherine de' Medici, who had, in effect, mounted the throne of France. Everywhere now could be seen the King's initial intwined, not with that of his wife, as etiquette asked, but with that of his mistress. Two Ds overlapping (one reversed) with a horizontal stroke binding them to form an H, 🔲. They were worked into the masonry; they were embroidered on banners; and even on his clothes Henry wore them as an ornament.

Catherine continued to smile and none would have guessed that within her burned a desire to deface those intwined letters whenever she saw them. She pretended, as did the more kindly people who surrounded her, that the letters were two Cs and an H, not two Ds. It made it less humiliating that this could be assumed.

So she went about the court graciously, giving no sign of the misery in her heart. She had her own circle now, and she saw that it was conducted with the utmost decorum. All the ladies and gentlemen who surrounded her went in awe of her. She was an enigma. It was not easy to understand how one, continually subjected to humiliation, could preserve such dignity. At times she would seem almost prim; any sign of misconduct in her women would be immediately and drastically dealt with; and yet there were occasions when a coarse jest could bring forth that loud and sudden laughter. The Queen of France was a foreigner; no one could forget that, and no one could love her. She knew this, and she told herself she did not care. There was only one person in the world whose affection she cared about, and she had come to believe that patience would bring her that. But patience – great patience – was necessary.

She could wait. Thank God she now knew how to wait.

Whilst waiting, she looked about for other interests. There was much that a Queen could do which was denied to a Dauphiness. Francis had talked to her of the alterations he had made to his châteaux. He had found her appreciative and had taught her much. There was one castle in France which Catherine delighted in more than in any other; as soon as she had seen it, it had attracted her. Whenever the court was there, she would play an amusing game of the imagination, planning the alterations she would make if it were hers. The Château de Chenonceaux certainly was an enchanting place; it was unique inasmuch as it spanned the river and was actually built on the arches of a bridge. The effect was delightful, for the castle seemed to be floating above the water like a fairy palace, its keep shaded by protecting trees; water-lilies floated beneath it and reeds and rushes stretched up to its dazzling white walls.

Francis had had plans for beautifying still further this most beautiful of his possessions; but Francis was dead; Henry the King was occupied elsewhere; so why should not the Queen amuse herself?

She found great pleasure in her plans.

Meanwhile, she tried to share Henry's interests, to work patiently and subtly to lure him from Diane. He loved music, and she spared herself nothing in the pursuit of this art. He was particularly interested in chants and hymns, so it was Catherine's delight to discover old ones and have new ones written. But Diane also concerned herself with music, and anything which Diane showed him was, to Henry, always a hundred times more beautiful than anything anyone else could proffer.

Catherine was an excellent horsewoman, and she contrived, between pregnancies, to be present at every hunting expedition. She won admiration, even from Henry, for her courage and good horsemanship, while Diane often remained in the castle to welcome the King on his return. How bitterly did Catherine note the eagerness with which the King always greeted his mistress on returning from a hunt in which she had not accompanied him.

He still came to Catherine at night because, so far, she had been able to keep from him the knowledge that she was once more pregnant.

Now that he was the King, Henry had a respect for his position which almost amounted to reverence. His visits to his mistress' apartments were conducted with great secrecy – as though the whole court did not know of the relationship between himself and Diane. As King, he was naturally more in the public eye than he had been as Dauphin. He would rise at dawn, and the moment he stirred, his entourage would become alive with activity. The highest noblemen in the land, who had been waiting in the antechamber, would enter to salute him; and the man of highest rank would hand him his chemise. His first duty on rising was to pray before his bedroom altar in the presence of the assembled company; but from the moment he arose from his bed, and even while he prayed, the dulcimer and clavicord, the horn and lute would enchant his ears.

After prayers, business followed; and then he would eat. He was no trencherman; he had forgotten how to eat, it was said, when he had been a prisoner in Spain; and it was an art he had never been able to master, rather to the disgust of his fellow countrymen, for the French *cuisine* was fast becoming the best in the world. This did not seem in any way to impair his health; he was fit and strong, and after discussing further business with his ministers of state, he would devote the rest of the afternoon to sport. Usually it was the chase – the most loved of all sports – but he played a good game in the racquet court, and was every bit a sportsman. He had commanded all to forget, while he played, that he was the King; and it was a pleasant sight to watch him while men about him discussed the faults quite openly; and when he had finished the game he would join in the discussion; none was afraid to win a game from the King, because he bore no malice for this, and was delighted to play with men of greater skill than his own.

In the evenings there would be feasting and dancing. It was not wise, said the King's advisers, that the court should be less brilliant under Henry than it had been under Francis. Everyone must know that the court of France was still the court of France – rich, luxurious, arrogant if need be. Perhaps though, the dancing was a little more stately, the etiquette a little more severe.

And afterwards Henry would be conducted to his apartments for his state *coucher*. Poor Henry! He must undress in the presence of his courtiers while the Chamberlain made sure that the bed was properly made; and when he was settled, the usher must bring him in the official keys of the palace and put them under his pillows.

Only then was the King left in peace to make his way to his mistress' apartments. Life was more difficult for Henry than it had been for Francis. Francis had cared nothing for propriety. He would have ordered his courtiers to put ten women to bed with him if he had so desired. But Henry must be sure that he had been left for the night before he could rise and go to his mistress.

How Catherine loved him – for his primness, for his greatness, for his shyness, for his desire to do good! Life was indeed strange when it forced her to give all the affection she had to give to this man who was so unlike herself in every way.

On this night of early summer he came to her apartment which adjoined his own. How stern he looked! So determined to do his duty! They had two children now; she laughed to herself slyly because he did not know that before the year was out they would have a third. Yesterday, she had all but fainted when sitting with her circle, and only her iron control had kept her sitting, smiling in her seat. She was not one to give way to ailments, and she was able to ignore the sickening faintness. She must ignore them, for if she did not the rumours would start. The Queen is *enceinte* once more! And then goodbye to Henry for many months. Goodbye to love – or what did service as love.

Henry was sad because he had recently attended the obsequies of his father, and death would have a saddening effect on one as sensitive as Henry. He had decided to have the bodies of his brothers, Francis and Charles, interred in state at St Denis at the same time as that of his father. It had been an extravaganza, that State burial; no expense had been spared. The three coffins, each adorned with a recumbent effigy of its occupant, were borne outside the walls of Paris to Notre Dame des Champs. The people of Paris had lined the streets to watch the solemn *cortège*.

Many sons, Catherine was thinking as she watched her husband, would have rejoiced, would have said: 'My father is dead, my elder brother is dead; and because of this I am the King.'

But not Henry.

He spoke of the funeral as he sat by the bed. He always chatted awhile before he snuffed out the candles. He was regular in his habits; and he wanted these visits of his to seem natural; he did not wish to hurt her feelings by letting her guess that all the time he was with her he was longing to depart.

He never gave any sign, by word or look, that he was longing for an announcement from her. He was so courteous; it was small wonder that she loved him. But alas, he was so easy to read and it was impossible for one as astute as she was to be deceived.

So he would chat awhile, playing nervously with jars and bottles on her table, then join her, and afterwards chat again and leave her. The interludes were almost always precisely of the same duration. She laughed to herself – painful, bitter laughter.

How many little Valois would people their nurseries before he decided they need get themselves no more? How long before that happy dream was realised – Diane, old and wrinkled, or better still, dead; and the King visiting his Queen not for duty's sake, but for that of love?

'You are sad, Henry,' she said.

He smiled; his smile was shy, boyish, charmingly incongruous in one who was fast turning grey.

'I cannot forget the burial,' he said.

'It was very impressive.'

'My father . . . dead. And my two brothers carried off in the prime of their lives.'

She was not eager to speak of his brothers. Did he even now, when he thought of Francis, think also of her? Suspicion was hard to disperse; it could persist through the years.

'Your brother Charles was no friend to you, Henry.'

'You are right. As I watched the *cortège* and grieved for my father and my brothers, Saint-André and Vieilleville were beside me. They remarked on my grief and Saint-André begged Vieilleville to tell me something that happened many years before at Angoulême. Then Vieilleville told me. He said, "Do you recollect, Sire, when owing to the folly of La Châtaigneraie, Dandouin and Dampierre, the last Dauphin, Francis and yourself fell into the Charente?" I did remember this and I told him so. He then told me how the news that my brother and I were drowned was carried to my father, who was overwhelmed with grief; but in his own apartments my brother Charles was so seized with joy that he was overcome by it. And when he heard that our lives had been saved he was overtaken by a severe attack of fever which experienced doctors attributed to sudden transition from great joy to deep sorrow. Truly Charles was no friend to me.'

She raised herself on her elbow. 'Henry,' she said, 'if he had lived and had married the niece or the daughter of the Emperor he would have been a dangerous enemy to you.'

'That is so.'

'Therefore you should not be sad. King Francis is dead, but

he did not die young, and he had his full measure from life! France never had a better king than you will make, Henry. I pray young Francis will be exactly like his father when on that day, which I trust is far, far in the future, he will take his place on the throne.'

'You are a good and loyal wife, Catherine,' said the King.

That made her happy. I shall win him, she assured herself. I have but to remember to go cautiously.

But how difficult it was to be careful when she was with Henry. With everyone else she was clever and cunning, but in her state of tremulous excitement which her husband aroused, caution deserted her.

She could not resist speaking of Madame d'Etampes, who had hastily left the court, but whose fate was still undecided.

Desperately Catherine wanted Anne to be left in peace. Not that she cared for Anne; she cared for none but herself and Henry. But if she could plead successfully for Anne, if, through her, Diane was not allowed to wreak her vengeance on her enemy, what triumph! 'You are a good and loyal wife!' Those words were as intoxicating as the most potent French wine.

'I was thinking of your father, Henry, and that poor misguided woman whom he loved. He begged of you to spare her. You will respect your father's wishes?'

Immediately she knew she had been wrong to speak.

'You are ill advised to plead for such a one,' he said. 'I have learned this concerning her: she was as great an enemy to me as ever my brother Charles was. He, with her help, was arranging with young Philip of Spain to attack me when I reached the throne. My brother promised to make her Governess of the Netherlands if he married the Infanta. In return for this, she was helping him with money.'

'I . . . see.'

'You see that, being ignorant of what is passing, you should not plead for my enemies.'

'Henry, had I known that she was guilty of this infamy . . . had I known that she had conspired against *you* . . .' In her agitation, she rose from the bed and would have come to stand before him; but as she did so, and stretched for her robe, the dizziness overcame her, and valiantly as she tried to hide it, it had not passed undetected by the sharp eyes of the King; for after all, he was continually looking for the very symptoms that she was trying to hide.

'Catherine, I fear you are not well.'

'I am very well, Henry.'

'Allow me to help you to bed. I will call your women.'

'Henry . . . I beg of you . . . do not disturb yourself. A faintness . . . nothing more.'

He was smiling down at her solicitously almost.

'Catherine . . . can it be?'

His smile was tender now, and how handsome he looked! He was pleased with her; and she longed now, pathetically, to keep his pleasure.

No finesse. No subterfuge now. She wished only to please him.

'Henry, I think it may be. You are pleased?'

'Pleased! I am delighted. This, my dear, is just what I was hoping for.'

She was so happy that his irritation with her had turned to pleasure, even if this did mean her fertility released him from the tedious business of visiting her instead of his mistress.

The uncrowned Queen of France! Surely this was one of the most enviable positions in the land for a practical and ambitious woman to hold. What a happy day for Diane when Francis the King had commanded her to befriend his son!

She received Henry in her apartments, which were more splendid, more stately than those of the Queen.

'How beautiful you are!' he said as he knelt and kissed her hands.

She smiled, fingering the jewels at her throat. A short while ago they had belonged to Anne d'Etampes, presents from Francis. Diane wished that Anne could see her wearing the gems.

Regally Diane dismissed her attendants that she might be alone with the King. They sat together in one of the window seats, he with his arm about her.

'Excellent news, my loved one,' he said. 'Catherine is *enceinte*.'

'That is wonderful. I had thought there was a look about her of late . . .'

'She all but fainted, and I guessed.'

Diane nodded. Sly Catherine had tried to withhold the news. Diane laughed. Poor, humble little Queen. How much happier it was to be the sort of Queen she herself was! How pleasant to be able to be sorry for the real Queen of France!

Henry had no secrets from Diane. He said: 'She tried to plead for Anne d'Etampes.'

Diane was immediately alert.

'My dear, how foolish of her!'

Diane was smiling, but she was disturbed. She pictured the placid face of the Queen – the dark eyes were mild, but was the mouth inscrutable? Surely Catherine would never dare to intrigue with Diane's old enemy. Diane turned her face to the King and kissed him, but whilst he embraced her, her thoughts ran on. To rule a King needed more caution, more shrewdness, than to rule a Dauphin. Henry was sentimental and he had promised his father on the latter's death-bed to protect Anne d'Etampes. Diane recalled now with what fury she had heard the news that Henry had sent a kind message to Anne on her retirement to Limours when Francis died; in it he had hinted that she might return to court. He had promised his father, he insisted. He was a good man, though unsubtle; but he was also a grateful lover, a man to remember his friends. Anne de Montmorency was already back in favour, and there was a man Diane must watch lest he receive too much favour; but for the time Montmorency, who had his own score to settle with Anne d'Etampes, was Diane's ally.

Dear, simple Henry! It was but necessary to show him how Francis's mistress had plotted against Henry with his brother Charles for him to see that he was justified in releasing himself from any death-bed promise he had made to a man who was ignorant of the woman's duplicity. Anne's property was confiscated, her servants sent to prison; and her husband, who had been eager enough to profit from her relationship with King Francis, now accused her of fraud, and she was herself sent to prison.

Diane felt that Anne d'Etampes was paying in full for those insults she had directed against the Grande Sénéchale of Normandy. And now . . . this meek little Catherine must take it into her silly head to plead for the woman.

She would, of course, have to learn her lesson. She must realise that she could only be allowed to retain her position as long as she submitted to the uncrowned Queen.

'I trust,' said Diane later, 'that you informed the Queen of the perfidy of Madame d'Etampes in conspiring with your enemies against you?'

'I told her of this. I fancy she was distressed. She declared herself surprised.'

Well she might, thought Diane. She would have to be made to realise that it was solely through the clemency of the King's mistress that his wife was allowed to bear his children.

❖ ❖ ❖

Diane could not help feeling that it was again necessary to teach Catherine a lesson. She was beginning to think that the Queen's new standing had gone to her head. After all, reasoned Diane, the woman was but a Medici, descended from Italian tradesmen; Diane herself was a great lady of France, with royal blood in her veins. Yes, Catherine must understand that she owed her position to Diane; and, moreover, that her success in retaining it depended on Diane.

Catherine would learn a lesson more thoroughly, Diane was sure, if it were given in front of others. Therefore she chose a moment when there should be many august witnesses of the Queen's discomfiture.

It was the occasion of one of those gatherings which, as Queen, Catherine held from time to time. The King was not present; but among the distinguished company was Diane, Henry's sister Marguerite, Montmorency, and Francis de Guise.

Diane began by asking the Queen if she would at some time be kind and gracious enough to show her the plans she had made for the alterations to the castle of Chenonceaux.

'Why, Madame,' replied Catherine, 'I should be delighted

to show them to you. Of course, you understand that I have not the gifts of my gracious father-in-law, and my plans, I fear, leave much room for improvement.'

'Nevertheless, Madame, I should be glad to see them.'

Guy de Chabot, that stupid, reckless man who had once before shown himself to be Diane's enemy during the scandal concerning himself and his stepmother, said: 'Is Madame la Sénéchale thinking of improving on the plans of our gracious Queen?'

'That may be so, Monsieur de Chabot,' said Diane coldly, for the man's manner was insolent. He had shown himself a fool once before; she was sure that he was ready to do so again. He should realise that he was already in the King's bad graces; he could not help himself by showing a lack of respect towards the King's mistress.

Diane turned from him to Catherine.

Catherine said: 'I had thought of altering the southern façade and building the nine arches which Thomas Bohier projected . . . was it thirty years ago?'

Catherine glowed. She could not help it. Chenonceaux was one of her enthusiasms; it had given her so much pleasure to plan reconstructions when she had been smarting under humiliation. She was trapped, as she could be by her emotions, into speaking too glowingly.

Marguerite, who was very clever and able to talk interestingly on most subjects, joined in. There was something essentially kind about Marguerite, and she was glad to see the animation in the usually pale face of the Queen. Montmorency added his judgements; but artful de Guise guessed what was coming and remained silent.

Catherine said: 'One of these days I shall start work on

Chenonceaux; I shall invite all the greatest artists to help. I shall have the gardens laid out with flower borders; and I shall have ornamented grottoes and fountains.'

Diane answered coolly, since the moment could no longer be delayed: 'It is my sincerest hope that you will grace Chenonceaux with your presence whenever it is your desire to do so.'

Catherine stopped to look at Diane. Only by the faintest flicker of her eyelids did she betray her feelings. She smiled while she forced herself to hold her hands to her side and not rush forward to slap the serene and charming smile off the face of her enemy.

This was cruel, bitter humiliation. Diane had known of her love for Chenonceaux; deliberately she had trapped her into betraying her enthusiasm, her longing to claim the place as her own; then, before all these people, she had shown her that her desires were as nothing beside those of the woman who was the real Queen of France.

Never, thought Catherine, have I hated quite as much as I do now. Not even when I have watched her at Saint-Germain through the hole in the floor.

'So . . .?' began Catherine, and hated herself because she hesitated, aware as she was of the sly, laughing eyes of Francis de Guise, of the consternation in those of Marguerite, of the sympathy of de Chabot.

'The King has been good enough to bestow upon me the castle of Chenonceaux,' said Diane. 'The gift is in recognition of the valuable services rendered the State by my late husband.'

It was impossible not to admire the way in which Queen Catherine calmly went on discussing Chenonceaux after congratulating Queen Diane on the acquisition of what was, in

Catherine's mind, surely one of the most charming residences in France.

Indeed, thought Diane, the Italian woman learns her lessons with grace.

Catherine herself was thinking: one day, every score shall be settled. You shall escape nothing, Madame.

✦ ✦ ✦

'Monsieur, you are downcast today.'

Guy de Chabot found that, in this dance where one's partners changed continually, it was his turn briefly to dance with Queen Catherine.

He inclined his head. 'I am,' he answered, 'and I hope my condition does not give offence to Your Gracious Majesty.'

'We should prefer to see a smile upon your lips.'

He put one there.

'And not a forced one,' she said.

Now they must come closer in the dance and she took advantage of this to whisper to him: 'Do not be downcast. There is a way out, Monsieur.'

For a few seconds Guy de Chabot looked straight into the eyes of the Queen, and he felt that he had never really looked at Catherine before. Her lips were smiling, her eyes serene; and yet, he thought, there is something about her . . . something lurking there, something as yet not fully developed, something of the serpent . . . But what a fool I am. Anxiety, fear of death, is making me fanciful.

He did not understand her meaning and his blank expression told her so.

'You fear de Vivonne,' she whispered. 'Do not. There is a way out.'

Now they were not so close, and it was impossible to whisper. De Chabot's heart beat faster. It was true that he was afraid. He was not a coward, but he supposed that any man, seeing death staring him in the face, feared it. He must face de Vivonne in mortal combat, for he had been challenged, and King Henry had given the consent which King Francis, for the sake of Anne d'Etampes, had denied. De Vivonne was the best swordsman in France and to fight him was to fight with death.

There were times when one could swagger, pretend one did not know the meaning of fear; but this quiet Queen must have caught something in his face which he did not realise he had shown.

I am young, he thought; I do not wish to die.

What a gay adventure it had seemed, loving the King's mistress, as many had before him, and some after. And now she, so beautiful, completely desirable, was languishing in prison, and he was challenged to a duel which meant certain death.

And suddenly, unexpectedly, here was the Queen suggesting to him that she knew a way out. But what way out could meek little Catherine show him? It was the wish of the King and the King's powerful favourite that he should die. How could the Queen save him? The Queen had very little more power than he had. Why, only a short while ago he had seen Madame Diane humiliate her cruelly over this matter of Chenonceaux. And yet, suddenly, he had been made aware of the power of the Queen. He could not help it, but it made him shiver slightly, even while it filled him with hope. It was like being startled suddenly in a dark place by someone he had not known was near him. It was the Queen who had spoken to him; yet it was not the Queen's mild eyes that looked at him but the cold eyes of a serpent, calm, patiently waiting for the moment when poisonous fangs could be plunged into an enemy.

He had no opportunity of speaking to her for a while. He must continue in the dance, and now he had another partner, a saucy-eyed girl who regarded him with favour. He was very handsome, this de Chabot; and the fact that all believed he was not long for this world seemed to add to his purely physical charm. But just now he could think of nothing but the Queen.

He had wondered at her meekness over the affair of Chenonceaux. He remembered now how unnatural he had thought it, for a wife and a Queen, to accept insult so mildly. But was she so mild? He felt that for a moment she had lifted a veil and shown him some secret part of Queen Catherine. He understood it; it was perfectly clear. The King and Madame Diane had decided that he should die. He had been the lover of their old enemy; he had given the King, when he was Dauphin, some uneasy moments; he had swaggered about the court challenging him who had dared cast a slur on his honour and that of his stepmother, knowing full well that those who had done so were Dauphin Henry and his mistress. Now he was asked to pay for that folly. But what if, contrary to expectation, it were not de Vivonne who was victor in the combat, but de Chabot. What a surprise for the crowd who would come to see him die. What embarrassment for the King and his mistress. Diane had been the prime mover in this affair. Might it not be that the King would be so discomfited that he would feel resentment against her on whom he now doted? Yes, de Chabot could see how the Queen's mind worked. And if she could turn defeat into victory, death into life, what joy!

He did not see her in the dance again, but later that evening he had occasion to pass close to her. He looked at her pleadingly and he did not look in vain.

'Tomorrow evening. Masked. The house of the Ruggieri on the river.'

He inclined his head.

It was with apprehension and hope that he went to keep his appointment. It was difficult not to run through the streets of Paris. It was necessary to wrap himself in a sombre cloak that would cover his extravagant court garments; he would doubtless return after dark, and he had no wish to encounter a party of rogues. Moreover, she had said, 'Masked'. It would not do for any to discover that de Chabot was meeting the Queen at the house of her astrologers.

For the first time a new thought struck him. What if this meeting had nothing to do with the combat? He was attractive; he had been much sought after. Surely this could not mean just another love affair. With Catherine de' Medici! He felt cold suddenly, wishing himself back in the palace. Impossible, he thought. But was it? It was said that the Queen was neglected as soon as she became pregnant, that it was at Madame Diane's command that the King gave her children. People laughed. 'What a mild little thing is this Queen of ours. The Italian creature has no spirit.' And yet, for a moment at the dance when he had looked into her eyes, he believed he had seen a different woman from her whom the court knew. Could it be that she had no plan of helping him, that she desired him as a lover just as many had before her?

He stopped. He had come to the river; he saw the old house of the Italian magicians, and for some minutes he could not take the necessary steps which would lead him to the front door.

He thought he heard the whispering of a crowd. 'Remember Dauphin Francis . . .'

He did not know the Queen. No one knew the Queen. Yet for a moment he had thought those beautiful dark eyes were cold and implacable like the eyes of a serpent.

He understood why the King could not love his wife. Had de Chabot not been a man who knew he could, unless a miracle happened, shortly die, he would have turned and gone back hastily the way he had come.

Instead, he shrugged his shoulders and deliberately walked on to the house of the Ruggieri.

Paris sweltered in midsummer sunshine whilst its gothic towers and spires reached towards the bluest of skies. By the great walls of the Bastille and the Conciergerie the people trooped; they came along the south bank of the Seine, past the colleges and convents, while down the hill of St Genevieve students and artists, with rogues and vagabonds, came hurrying. They were intent on leaving behind them the walls of the capital, for quite close to the city at Saint-Germain-en-Laye, one of the grandest shows any of them had ever seen was being prepared for their enjoyment.

Tumblers and jugglers performed for the crowd; ballads – gay, sentimental and ribald – were sung; some of these songs were written in ridicule of the fallen favourite Madame d'Etampes, who, it was believed, was destined for execution; none dared sing now the songs that very lady had set in circulation concerning Diane de Poitiers. No! Diane had risen to a lofty eminence. Let us glorify her, said the people. Madame d'Etampes has fallen from grace; therefore let us

274

stamp upon her. If she had appeared among them, they would have tried to stone her to death.

Death was in the air. The people were going to see a man killed. They were going to see rich red blood stain the grass of the meadow, and looking on with them would be the King himself, the Italian woman, and that one who was the real Queen of France, although she did not possess the title – in short, Madame Diane de Poitiers; there would also be the great Anne de Montmorency and others of the King's ministers; in fact, all those people whose names were known throughout the land.

Small wonder that the people of Paris had turned out in their thousands to witness the mortal combat between two brave and gallant gentlemen.

De Chabot and de Vivonne were the two protagonists. Why did they fight? That was unimportant, but it was for some long-ago scandal. It was said that de Vivonne, whom everyone expected to win, was taking over the King's quarrel; and that de Chabot had been the lover of Madame d'Etampes before she had fallen into disgrace.

All that July night the crowds waited in the fields surrounding that one wherein the combat was to take place. Bets were taken; pockets were picked; men and women lay about on the grass amusing themselves in sundry ways whilst they waited.

And as the sun rose high, the gallants and brightly-clad ladies began to take their seats in the pavilion, which was decorated with cloth of gold and cloth of silver spattered with the lilies of France. There was Montmorency himself; the Guise brothers, the Cardinals, the Bishops, the Chamberlain – all the high officials of the court; and with them the ladies-in-waiting to the Queen.

On either side of the field were the tents of the combatants. In de Vivonne's tent – so confident was he of victory – had already been prepared a banquet to celebrate his triumph. He had borrowed the finest plate from the richest households of the court for this occasion; soups, venison, roast meats of all varieties, sweets and fruit, and great butts of wine, it was said, were in that tent; indeed the appetising odours were floating out to the crowd. Everyone's hope of victory went with de Vivonne. De Vivonne was the King's man; and it was believed that de Chabot had no stomach for the fight.

How delighted was the crowd with the glittering yet sinister sight which met its eyes. Just below the seat in which sat grim-faced Montmorency were five figures, all masked, all draped in black. These were the executioner and his assistants. When de Chabot was slain, it would be their lot to drag him to the gibbet as though he were a felon. It was a glorious and wonderful show – well worth waiting for. There was not a thief nor a pedlar, a prostitute nor a conjurer, a merchant nor a student in that vast crowd who would not have agreed to that.

Now the royal party was stepping out, so the show was all but due to begin. The heralds blew several fanfares on their trumpets, and now there appeared the royal group led by good King Henry. The crowd cheered itself hoarse. They loved their King – though, declared some, sighing for the magnificence of the most magnificent of kings, he was not such a one as his father had been. But others, who were too young to remember the charm of Francis, thought that none could be better than their good and virtuous King who was so faithful to his mistress. And here she was beside him, just as though she were his wife and Queen in name. And there again it showed the depth of his love for her, since in all other matters he would have the strictest etiquette observed. She, with him, acknowledged the cheers of the crowd, smiling graciously, beautiful in her black and white which made her look so pure and lovely that the coloured garments of those surrounding her seemed suddenly garish.

And then . . . the Queen. The crowd was silent. No cheers for the Italian woman. Perhaps they applauded the King and his mistress so heartily because of their dislike for the Italian woman.

'Dauphin Francis!' was hissed among the unforgetful crowd.

Catherine heard this. But one day, she thought, they will shout for me. One day they will know me for the true Queen of France in every respect.

It was the old hope of 'One Day'.

She could feel the child within her. Here I sit, she thought, pale-faced and quiet, with never a thought, some may imagine, but of the child soon to be born. Little do they know that I wait so patiently, not because I was born patient, but because I have learned patience. Little do they know that they would not be gathered here to witness this mortal combat but for the fact that, in the first place, *I* set the matter in motion.

She smiled graciously and laid her hands on her pearl-studded stomacher. Madalenna leaned towards her. 'Your Majesty is well?'

'Quite well, I thank you. A little faintness. It is to be expected.'

In the crowd they would have noticed the gesture, for there was little they missed; they would have seen Madalenna's anxious query. 'You see,' Catherine wished to say to her subjects, 'he has his mistress, but I shall bear his children. I alone can bear him kings and queens.'

The herald of Guinne, his silken tabard shimmering in the hot sun, stepped forward and blew a few notes on his trumpet. There was an immediate stillness in the air while the crowd waited for the announcement.

'This day, the tenth of July, our Sovereign Lord the King has ordered and granted free and fair field for mortal combat to Francis de Vivonne assailant and Guy de Chabot assailed to resolve by arms the question of honour which is at issue between them. Wherefore I make known to all, in the King's name, that none may turn aside the course of the present combat, neither aid nor hinder either of the combatants on pain of death.'

As soon as the herald ceased to speak, a great cheer went up. The excitement was intense, for the combat was about to begin.

De Vivonne came from the tent accompanied by his second – one of Diane's protégés – and friends numbering at least five hundred strong. They wore his colours – red and white – while before the hero of the day was carried his sword, shield, and banner on which was the image of St Francis. With this company, before which drummers and trumpeters marched, de Vivonne walked all round the field to the cheers of the people. When he had done this, he went into his tent while de Chabot with *his* second, but with far fewer supporters in black and white, did the same.

Next came the ceremony of testing the weapons to be used, which, as assailed, Guy de Chabot was to choose. This gave rise to a good deal of controversy, and arguments ensued while the afternoon wore on. The heat was intense, but Catherine scarcely felt the discomfort. This, she had determined, should be a day of triumph for her. Today, Henry was going to feel a little less pleased with his Diane than he had ever been before. Catherine did not expect to win her husband from his mistress on such an issue, but it would be such affairs as this, gradually piled one on top of the other, that would eventually, she was sure, turn him from his mistress to his waiting wife.

Diane was leaning forward in her seat, frowning at the delay. What was the trouble? Diane wished the affair done with, her enemy lying dead, a lesson to all those who dared flout the King's mistress.

Madame, thought Catherine, there is, I hope, a great surprise awaiting you.

This trouble over the weapons was the beginning. What joy it had been to wrap herself in a shabby and all-concealing cloak and keep the appointment she had made with Monsieur de Chabot at the home of the astrologers Ruggieri. It was not de Chabot who had chosen the weapons that would be used today; it was Catherine. De Chabot had spent hours taking lessons at that house from an Italian fencing-master. Ha! laughed Catherine to herself. There is much we Italians can do which these French cannot. We know better than they how to remove people who stand in our way!

How pleasant now to sit back languidly in her seat, and to know why there was this dispute about the weapons, while Diane leaned forward, not comprehending, wondering, as did the restive crowd, why the spectacle did not proceed.

De Chabot had declared that he wished to fight on foot, with armour, shields, and two-edged swords, and with short daggers of the old style – the heavy and hampering kind. De Vivonne was nonplussed by this choice, and for the first time was uneasy.

Diane's frown had deepened. It was for Montmorency, who

for the day was Master of the Ceremonies, to give judgement; and there he sat, the grim-faced old fool, determined to be just.

Catherine wanted to laugh outright. She saw further plans to be made. The King's mistress and the King's favourite adviser and best-loved counsellor could, in time, become enemies, jealous of the favour of the King. There would be an opportunity for exploiting her cunning.

In the meantime, to Diane's disgust, Montmorency had decided that, in spite of his strange choice, de Chabot must have his way.

From each of the four corners of the field a herald came, shouting: 'Nobles, Knights, Gentlemen, and all manner of people! On behalf of the King I expressly command all that, as soon as the combatants shall meet in combat, all present are to preserve silence, and not to speak, cough, spit, or make any sign with foot, hand, or eye which may aid, injure, or prejudice either of the said combatants. And, further, I expressly command all on behalf of the King, that during the combat they are not to enter the lists or assist either of the combatants in any circumstances whatsoever on peril of death.'

After this, first de Vivonne, then de Chabot, with their companies of supporters behind them, made one more progress round the field, whereupon each must kneel on a velvet cushion before a priest and swear that he had come to avenge his honour and that there was in his possession no charms nor incantations, and that his sole confidence was in God and the strength of his arms.

They were conducted to the middle of the field, their swords handed to them, and their daggers placed in their belts, while the Norman herald shouted at the top of his voice: '*Laissez aller les bons combatants!*'

The great moment had come. The two men slowly advanced towards one another.

Catherine, her hands lying in her lap, felt the mad racing of her heart. There was no colour in her face; otherwise she gave no sign of the intense excitement she was experiencing.

She knew that de Vivonne was not happy. The weapons were too cumbersome for a man accustomed to the swift rapier. He had been outwitted. If only de Chabot was as good now as he had been when facing the Italian fencing-master in the house of the Ruggieri, all would go as she wished.

She would have brought some charm with her that would have ensured de Chabot's victory, if she had dared; but that oath the men had taken before the priest, and which she had known must be taken before the combat began, had made her dismiss the idea. Some supernatural force, other than the one she would call upon with her charm, might be turned against her if she dabbled in such matters.

De Vivonne was springing on his opponent; the crowd caught its breath as he aimed a blow at de Chabot's head. But de Chabot remembered.

Ah, my beloved Italy, thought Catherine. You can show France how to fight.

De Chabot, while feigning to parry the blow with his sword, took it on his shield, and stooping to do so, thrust his sword into de Vivonne's knee.

Bravo! Bravo! thought Catherine, glancing towards Henry and Diane, and emulating their looks of consternation.

It was not serious, but to the braggart de Vivonne, the finest dueller in France, it came as a complete surprise, and as he staggered back, de Chabot was able to give him another blow on the same spot, and this time, a more violent one.

It is done, exulted Catherine.

And she was right.

His tendons had been severed, and de Vivonne, staggering back with an awful cry, let his sword fall from his hand as his blood spurted over the green grass.

The crowd roared. The combat was over. It was victory for de Chabot . . . and Catherine de' Medici. But my victory, thought Catherine, is the greater because none but myself and de Chabot know it is mine.

The breathless crowd waited. What now? Would de Chabot dispatch his victim, and hand him over to the executioner for the gibbet, or would he spare his life on receiving a confession that de Vivonne had lied and that de Chabot's cause was the just one?

De Chabot answered the question by shouting: 'De Vivonne, restore my honour; and ask mercy of God and the King for the wrong you have committed.'

The wretched de Vivonne, in direst pain, still was sufficiently aware of his surroundings to remember ambition. He tried to get up, but failing wretchedly, sank back on the grass.

Then came the moment for which Catherine had waited. De Chabot had left his victim and was kneeling before the King.

'Sire,' he said, 'I entreat you to esteem me a man of honour. I give de Vivonne to you. Let no imputation, Sire, rest either on his family or upon him on account of his offence; for I surrender him to you.'

Henry had never felt so embarrassed. Here he was, defeated before his court and the citizens of his capital; for de Vivonne's cause had been his, and it was Henry's honour that de Vivonne had been defending.

Catherine's elation was complete.

Now, my darling, she was thinking, who is to blame for bringing you to this unhappy pass? Whose action, in the first place, set the scandal abroad? Look into the face of her who sits beside you. She is the guilty one. Hate Diane for this; not de Chabot. Oh, my love, why waste time on one who bungles so, when here is your clever Queen who, with your power to help her, could outwit all the men and women of France.

How she loved him – even as he sat there, looking foolish and ashamed.

You've lost, Henry. Admit defeat. Oh, my dear foolish one, you must not hesitate. Have you forgotten that all Paris is watching you? Do you not know that mob hysteria can turn to adoration for a hero, and that hero, de Chabot, stands before you now? Do not betray yourself. Blame Diane. Hate Diane. But in the presence of your people do not forget your honour, your nobility.

But the King was silent.

There was a hissing whisper in the crowd. What meant this? The victor was there. It was a surprise, it was true, but who does not like to be surprised? Why did the King not speak? De Chabot, his head held high, had gone back to his foe, who tried to rise and throw himself in an access of hatred on the man who had ruined his future.

'Do not move, de Vivonne, or I shall kill you,' said de Chabot.

'Kill me and have done with it!' cried the wretched man.

And once again de Chabot presented himself to the King and asked that his honour be restored to him. But still Henry, bewildered and ashamed, did not speak.

Montmorency rose and knelt before the King. Diane's trembling hand was plucking at the King's sleeve. Henry *must* see reason. He could not so demean himself before those thousands of watching eyes. In a few moments the popularity of years could be lost.

Montmorency entreated. The victor must have his dues, Diane whispered.

'You have done your duty, de Chabot,' said Henry coldly, 'and your honour ought to be restored to you.'

Henry then rose abruptly. The trumpets rang out; and he with Diane and the Queen and his immediate followers walked out of the pavilion.

Catherine was delighted, for surely a King could rarely have felt so discomfited. If he would but remember who had led him to this!

She went to her apartments, and as she sat there she heard her women chattering.

What were they saying? What was the crowd saying . . . all those people who had lain about in the fields all night to see the combat? They had come to see a man killed and they had seen a King forget his honour.

But later she laughed to have thought it mattered what the people said; it was what they did that was of more moment. They broke into de Vivonne's tent, and had a good time with the victuals he had prepared to celebrate his conquest. They feasted and drank and made merry. They stole the rich plate which he had borrowed.

If there was no death for the crowd, there was plenty of fun instead. Perhaps Henry's feeble conduct was not so important as Catherine had thought it. Perhaps, for all her scheming, she had come no nearer to winning her husband from Diane.

I cannot endure it, she sobbed to herself during her lonely nights. If I cannot do it this way, I will find some other.

A few days later de Vivonne died. He might have lived if he had wished, but he had torn the bandages from his wounds and would not let the doctors attend him. Hardly anyone seemed to notice his passing.

The de Chabot and de Vivonne affair was finished. But the Queen developed a new interest in the study of poisons; and in her private bureau there were many locked drawers containing books and recipes as well as potions and powders.

✤ ✤ ✤

That November another girl was born. They called her Claude, after Henry's mother.

Henry was paying his nocturnal visits to Catherine again. They must get themselves more sons. Little Francis, at four years old, was a sickly child. Catherine watched over him anxiously whenever Diane allowed her to.

Henry had been crowned at Rheims that summer. Catherine had not been crowned Queen so far; but there was no fresh insult in this, since it was the custom of France that the Queen was not crowned at the King's impressive coronation. Her day was to follow.

During the *fêtes* which had accompanied the coronation of the King, Catherine had thought of how she could rid herself of Diane. There must be some slow and subtle poison, she told Cosmo and Lorenzo Ruggieri. She could not endure very much more of this humiliation which Diane imposed upon her. She *must* rid herself of her enemy. Did they not know that at Saint-Germain she had watched the woman and her own husband together?

The brothers shook their heads. Most respectfully and fervently, they advised her to have the hole in the floor sealed up, and to cease to think of the relationship between the King and Diane. They could not help her; they *dared* not help her. Why, even if Diane died from natural causes, the Queen would be suspected of poisoning her! Moreover, all those who had been known to advise the Queen would be imprisoned and tortured for confessions.

Catherine understood. Why, if Diane died, these two brothers would set about escaping from France with all speed!

She must not continue to think of removing Diane *that* way!

She listened to them and agreed she had no alternative but to take their advice because they were right; but all the same, she continued to consider the murder of Diane.

Diane did not spare the Queen. Often she entertained the royal party at Chenonceaux; then she would delight in showing Catherine how she was beautifying the place. It needed great strength of mind not to slip some quick poison into the woman's goblet.

Diane went from triumph to triumph. Chenonceaux was by no means the only gift the King bestowed on her. She was rich in jewels and estates; and her triumphs were mounting.

She now began to arrange the marriage of the heir to the throne.

The family of de Guise was linked to her by marriage, for her eldest daughter had married one of the de Guise brothers, so Diane sought to assist in the elevation of this dashing and ambitious family.

It was characteristic of Diane that, when she had made up her mind that something should be done, she would beg an audience of the King and Queen and discuss such matter with them, gaining that approval which the King would never deny her, and which Catherine had no power to give.

She did this when they were visiting Chenonceaux, as she wished to lay before them her plans for the little Dauphin's marriage.

She was received by the King and Queen, although, Catherine noted sardonically, it was as though *she* received *them*.

'Your Majesties are gracious to listen to me,' she said. 'It is this matter of the future of our beloved Dauphin. Who could be a better match for him than little Mary Stuart, the Queen of Scotland?'

Catherine said: 'The Queen of Scotland! Her mother was a Frenchwoman.'

'Your Gracious Majesty can have no objection to that?' asked Diane, her lips curling.

'A Frenchwoman,' continued Catherine quietly, 'a sister to the de Guise brothers. It may be that his Grace the King feels this family are a little too ambitious. A child of their house to come to France as its future Queen might make them feel of greater importance than they do already.'

'Queens come from strange places,' said Diane angrily.

Henry spoke. 'Let us consider this matter. It will be necessary to find a bride for the boy . . . sooner or later.'

'Francis is a baby yet,' said Catherine.

'The alliances of kings and queens are made while they are in their cradles,' said Diane.

Catherine bit her lip to keep back the flow of words. So this was a way of getting more power. Diane and the de Guises wished to rule France. Now they were beginning to do so through Diane, the King's mistress; later those ambitious de Guises would do so through their niece.

'The reports of the little girl,' said Diane, ignoring

Catherine and speaking to the King, 'are that she is both clever and charming. Think, Sire, what a fine thing that marriage would be for France. Think what she would bring to us!'

'Scotland!' said Catherine. 'A poor country, by all accounts!'

'Indeed, Your Majesty speaks truth there,' laughed Diane sweetly. 'It *is* a poor country. All the same it would not be an unpleasant thing to see it attached to the realm of France. But there is another matter which is of the greatest interest. Sire, have I your consent to speak of it?'

'My dear friend,' said the King, 'I beg you to speak. I know your wisdom of old and I readily give you all my attention.'

Catherine noticed how his eyes adored her. She felt an impulse to burst into weeping, to beg Diane to give him up, and to beg him to tell her what she herself could do to gain his love.

She hastily suppressed such folly.

'That little girl has a claim to the throne of England,' said Diane, 'and her claim is not a light one.'

'How so?' cried Catherine, longing to contradict her enemy. 'There is a young King on the throne of England.'

Diane laughed. 'That young King, Majesty, is a puny fellow. Small of stature, wan of complexion; I hear that he spits blood, and his hair is already falling out.'

Catherine knew it was useless to fight against them; Henry's eyes were shining; he was in favour of this Scottish marriage because Diane had suggested it, if for no other reason.

'And when he is dead,' continued Diane, 'who shall sit on England's throne? There are two women. Mary. Elizabeth. And both these women have been declared illegitimate at different times, *and* by their own father! Now little Mary Stuart, though not so close to the throne, was at least born in holy wedlock. You understand me?'

'I am inclined to think that it will be an excellent match for little Francis,' said Henry.

'Yes,' said Catherine slowly, 'an excellent match.'

Diane gave her that smile of condescending approval which Catherine loathed more than anything. But, thought Catherine, she is right. For France it will be good. For France there will be Scotland and possibly England. It is foolish to allow a personal grudge to spoil what would be good for France. France will be more important than ever; but so will the de Guises!

And so, negotiations for the Scottish marriage were started.

When Francis heard that he was to have a wife he was delighted. He could scarcely wait to see her. He put away many of his most precious possessions. 'I am keeping these for Mary,' he told Catherine.

Elisabeth was envious. '*Maman*,' she wanted to know, 'cannot I have a wife from Scotland?'

Catherine hugged her daughter. 'Nay, my love; but when the time is ripe a handsome husband will be found for you.'

Catherine spent as much time as she could manage in the nursery. This was possible because just at present there were other matters to occupy Diane. But while Catherine was with her children, superintending their education, working hard to win their affection, she was not insensible to what was happening throughout France.

The wars of religion had taken a new and bloodier turn. Jean Calvin was preaching Hell fire from Geneva, and crowds were flocking to his side; many in France were supporting him secretly. Even in the time of King Francis there had been men ready to risk their lives by tampering with the fine decorations of the church which to them seemed idolatrous. Now there was a fresh outburst of such desecrations; and Henry, supported by Diane, was a stauncher Catholic than Francis had been with Anne d'Etampes at his elbow to help the cause of the Reformers.

Catherine shrugged her shoulders over these differences; it seemed to her that life had taught her that there should be only one religion – self-advancement. She wanted power for herself as long as she lived; she wanted Valois-Medici Kings on the throne of France for ever. These religious factions – what were they? All very well for some to serve the Holy Church of Rome and some to swear by Calvin. But what was the difference? One believed in pomp and ceremony; the other in austerity. Who should say which would best please God? The Catholics persecuted the Protestants, but that was because the Catholics were the more powerful. Give Protestants the chance and they would be murdering and torturing Catholics. Take this man Calvin: he wished to usurp the place of the Pope – nothing less. What did he say? 'You shall obey my rules and mine only.' He was as strict and cruel as any Catholic.

Religion? thought Catherine, as she combed Elisabeth's hair. What is religion? Observe the rules of the church, yes! Just as one observes the rules of the court. It is a good thing. But right or wrong, good or bad? For me, it is good to rule France. For Diane and Henry, for the de Guises, it is also good to rule France. But if they rule, how can I? It is good in my eyes for me to rule, and bad in theirs. So much for good and bad!

No! Keep quiet. Take no sides – unless it is of benefit to take sides – for one side is as good, or as bad, as the other.

But straightforward Henry, fierce Montmorency, and

ardently Catholic Diane did not see the matter as did Catherine. To them the Catholic way was the only true way. They had not the gift which enabled them to look at a matter from the angle that was best suited to their own advantage; they could not say: 'This is good for us, therefore it is a good thing.'

If only Henry would listen to me! thought Catherine. How I would help him!

There was this tragedy of the salt tax rising which had done Henry no good. Why did he not consult his wife on State matters? Because he thought her colourless and unworthy of proffering advice. And how could she change that . . . while Diane lived? There must be a way of removing her enemy. She would read everything that had ever been written on the subject of subtle poisons; she would summon every seer, every magician to her presence, in the hope of finding some way in which it would be safe to rid herself of Diane. For it was *good* that she should do so. She was cleverer than Diane; and yet, unless she would suffer complete neglect, she must feign to possess a character which was not hers.

Once again, as she had done so many times before, she set about proving to herself that it would be no sin to rid herself of the woman she hated. If she herself could advise her husband instead of Diane, France, she assured herself, would be a happier country.

'Holy Mother of God,' she prayed. 'A miracle.'

This problem of the salt tax had arisen six years before, when Francis was on the throne, and Francis had dealt with it more cleverly than had his son.

Had I advised him, thought Catherine, I would have begged him to take a lesson from his father.

Under Francis, there had been an insurrection in the town of Rochelle against this tax – the *gabelle*. The citizens of Rochelle had refused to pay the tax and had even maltreated those men sent to collect it. Francis, wisely, had gone to Rochelle in person, and had, with that characteristic charm of his, won the citizens to his side. He had gone amongst them, smiling, charming, and begged them to have no fear. They had committed an offence, but he would dismiss that from his mind. They had his free pardon. The citizens of Rochelle had expected bloodshed and the pillaging and burning of their town by the King's men; instead, the charming Francis himself had visited them and smiled upon them. It was true that they were fined for their offence and the tax remained, but in Rochelle they talked warmly of the King long after he had gone, and they forgot the burden of the salt tax for a while.

Now that, Catherine thought, was the way in which to deal with the matter of the *gabelle*. But how differently from his father had Henry dealt with it.

There was a rising in the south, and one town joined another in its protest against the tax-collectors. When these collectors entered the towns they were seized and maltreated. Near Cognac, one was thrown into the river. 'Go, you rascal of a *gabelleur*!' cried the enraged citizens. 'Go and salt the fish of the Charente!'

Beggars and robbers swelled the ranks of the insurgents; the movement spread to the banks of the Gironde. This was like a minor civil war.

Oh, why would not the King listen to his wife! But he had no respect for her opinion. He preferred to listen to grim old Montmorency when he was not listening to Diane; and that old man's way of dealing with a rising was to march at the head of his soldiers; and whilst he said his prayers, he thought of what punishment he would deal out to these men of France who dared revolt against a tax which their Lord King had put upon them.

So down to Bordeaux marched Montmorency with ten companies behind him.

It was a different matter to face an army than to rob and pillage defenceless towns, so the vagabonds deserted and left the honest citizens to face the Constable's wrath.

What terror Montmorency had carried to the south! He was not content with hangings. He wished to show these men what happened to those who revolted against King Henry. He had the citizens of Bordeaux on their knees in the streets begging pardon; he imposed a heavy fine on the town while he selected one hundred and fifty of the leaders for execution.

Those insurgents who had thrown the collector into the river were themselves thrown into a fire which was prepared for the purpose.

'Go, rabid hounds!' cried the Constable. 'Go and grill the fish of the Charente which you salted with the body of an officer of your King and Sovereign.'

But death by fire was too easy a death, thought the Constable.

He would show these fools. Some were dismembered by four horses; some were broken on the wheel; others were attached to a scaffold, face down, their legs and arms being left free; thus they remained while the executioner smashed their limbs with an iron pestle without touching either their heads or bodies. All these things must rebellious citizens witness.

'King Henry's way is not the way of his father,' said the people of France.

Catherine knew this, because she wrapped her cloak about her and mingled with the gossiping crowds. None guessed that the quiet, plump woman who encouraged them to talk, was their Queen. Thus did she learn the sentiments of the people.

She enjoyed these excursions, for they gave her a sense of hidden power. She decided that whatever happened to her in the future she would adhere to this interesting habit.

She had convinced herself now that to murder Diane would be good, not evil. She continued to pray to the Virgin to show her the sort of miracle which could be made on Earth.

Death and horror at Bordeaux! Pageant and revelry in Lyons!

Catherine had looked forward to this visit to Lyons, for in this town she was sure she would be recognised as the Queen. The citizens of the provinces would not treat her as she had been treated in the capital.

The King had been in Piedmont and Turin, visiting his armies, and she and Diane, with an entourage, travelled to Lyons to meet Henry there. Catherine had enjoyed that journey, for during it she had been able to feel, briefly, that she was truly Queen. Moreover, she was once more pregnant and was expecting a child early in the new year.

Diane had been quiet and unobtrusive; the children were at Saint-Germain, where they were waiting to greet the little Queen of Scotland on her arrival; therefore Catherine had not to face the continual jealous irritation which seeing Diane with her children always brought her. As Henry was riding from Italy to Lyons, Catherine had not to watch him with Diane.

Thus would it always be, thought Catherine, if only I could

win to myself what is my just due. Holy Mother, show me that miracle.

It was September, and it seemed to Catherine that the autumn tints of the countryside had never been so glorious. Her spirits were high. The citizens of Lyons were preparing to greet their King and Queen – good, noble citizens, the backbone of France. They would do homage to their Queen, and the King's mistress would be forced to slip into the background. Did Diane know this? Did it account for her subdued manner?

Alas! when Henry joined them at Ainay, some miles from the town of Lyons, everything was back at normal. He had hardly a word to say to his Queen; his attention was all for Diane. It was long since those two had been together; there was much to talk of, love to be indulged in.

She could not see them together now, but Catherine's imagination was vivid. It tortured her; it maddened her. For what did the homage of the citizens of Lyons mean to her when Henry's love was denied her?

They thought her cold. If they but knew! To them she was just a machine . . . a machine for bearing children . . . because Fate had made her the King's wife. It was cruel. It was so coldly sordid and humiliating. 'The Queen is with child,' she seemed to hear Henry saying to Diane. 'Thank God. I am relieved of the necessity of visiting her.'

I will kill her, thought Catherine. There must be some slow poison that will make it seem like old age creeping on. Holy Mother, show it to me.

But even as she raged, calm common sense did not desert her. If anything happened to her, you would be blamed, she reminded herself. Remember Dauphin Francis, for he is not yet forgotten. Be careful. Rid yourself of any other who stands in your way, but not Diane . . . not yet, for you might find that in ridding yourself of your enemy you had also rid yourself of your husband.

They travelled in an immense and beautifully decorated gondola down the Rhone to Vaise; its seats were engraved with that device, the interlacing Ds and an H, which kind people pretended to believe was two Cs and an H.

Catherine reminded herself bitterly that this gondola would have been made to the King's instructions, and that was why it bore those letters.

At Vaise a pavilion had been made ready to receive them; and everywhere Catherine looked there were those significant letters. The whole country, then, was saying: 'It is not the Queen we must honour if we will please the King; it is his mistress.'

When they left the pavilion and entered the town they found themselves in an artificial forest which had been erected by the citizens for their reception. It was cleverly contrived, but it was spoiled for Catherine, for no sooner had they entered this man-made forest than through the artificial trees came a company of nymphs – all the most beautiful girls of the neighbourhood – and their leader, the loveliest of them all, carried a bow and a quiver. It was immediately apparent that she was meant to represent Diana, the goddess of the chase. She led a tame lion on a silver chain, and she asked the King to accept the animal from the citizens of Lyons.

And I, the Queen, Catherine thought, might be nothing but the attendant of Diane, for all the respect that is paid to me!

Yet there was worse to come. There followed the entry into Lyons itself, under triumphal arches, past the fluttering flags;

and, listening to the cries of the welcoming crowds, Catherine in her open litter, heavy with the weight of diamonds and wretchedness, knew that the acclamation was not for her, but for Diane, who rode behind her on her white palfrey dressed in her becoming garments of black and white.

The citizens of Lyons had no doubt of what was expected of them. When the burghers came forward to greet the ladies, they kissed the hand of Diane first, and that of the Queen second.

Between her lids, the Queen surveyed them.

Never, never had a Queen of France been so publicly humiliated.

After the triumphant journey through the cities of France, the royal party made its way to Saint-Germain.

Catherine was more unhappy at Saint-Germain than anywhere else; yet when she knew that they were bound for this palace, she could scarcely wait to reach her apartments. In them she could suffer more exquisite torture than in any other spot. Everywhere else she imagined; there she saw.

All were eager to see the little Queen of Scotland, who now living at Saint-Germain with the royal children, and the child was the chief topic of conversation as the cavalcade rode onwards.

On their arrival, the usual ceremonies which accompanied the King wherever he went were performed; and once again it was Diane who was treated with the homage and respect which should have been the Queen's.

Quietly, and as soon as she could do so unobserved, Catherine slipped away and went to the nurseries.

The nurses in attendance curtsied low.

'And how are the children? And how have they been in our absence?'

'Your Majesty, the baby is very well, and so is Mademoiselle Elisabeth.'

'And the young Prince?'

'He is not so well, Madame, but the coming of the little Queen has cheered him greatly.'

Catherine went into the first of the nurseries, where three children were playing together. Francis and Elisabeth smiled the queer, uncertain smiles they always gave her.

'Good day to you, my dears,' said Catherine.

'Good day to you, *Maman*,' said Francis. He was now five, and small for his years. Little Elisabeth was three and a half.

Now Catherine's eyes were on the newcomer. Mary Stuart was the loveliest little girl the Queen had ever seen; her hair was fair and softly curling, her eyes bright blue, her complexion delicately tinted, and her face a perfect heart shape. So this was little Mary Stuart! No wonder accounts of her charms had preceded her! She was enchanting; and Catherine was immediately aware that it was not merely enchantment of face and form.

The little girl's bow was graceful, and there was no sign of self-consciousness as she came forward to greet the Queen of France; her manner was completely dignified as though she had in mind that while she was now in the presence of the Queen of France, she herself was destined for that high rank.

She was six years old – a little older than Francis – and it was easy to see that in the short time she had known him she had made the boy her slave. Already he loved her. That was perhaps just as well, since he would have to marry her.

'Welcome to France, my dear.'

In perfect French the little girl thanked the Queen for her welcome.

'You had a comfortable journey, I trust,' said Catherine.

'Oh yes. Soon after we left the Clyde, though, an English squadron sighted us, but we escaped. That was most exciting.'

Her eyes sparkled. Could it be that she was only six? She seemed more than a year older than Francis. And even Elisabeth, Catherine noticed, was ready to follow her about and laugh when she laughed. She seemed to have been educated in advance of the little Valois. Well, they would all be educated together now, for the King had given orders that Mary Stuart was to be brought up as a French princess, although, in view of the exalted position she would one day hold, she would immediately take precedence of the little Valois girls.

The child chattered on in French. Yet she was a dignified little thing. She was, Catherine thought, a little too imperious. She seemed to be implying: You are the Queen, but I am the future Queen. I am the daughter of kings; and you come from a merchant family!

But that could not be. Catherine was a little over-sensitive on that point. She had suffered so much indignity that it might be that she was too ready to look for slights.

She sent for the child's governess who was a pretty red-headed widow, a natural daughter of James IV of Scotland. Her name was Lady Fleming; and she declared herself to be at the service of the Queen of France.

Catherine discussed the education of the children, and explained that she herself supervised, to a large extent, the children's education. She fancied Lady Fleming's smile was a trifle impertinent, as though she already knew that the Queen was only allowed to do what Madame Diane permitted. Truly, Catherine reminded herself, I am over-sensitive. It was the after-effects of the humiliation of Lyons.

'I shall be giving you instructions,' she told Lady Fleming and dismissed the woman.

'Now, children,' she said, 'tell me what you have been doing while you have been awaiting the coming of the King and myself.'

Francis was about to speak, but Mary spoke for him. They had played games which *she* had introduced; they had read books which *she* had brought with her. Francis' Latin was not very good, she feared; and Elisabeth scarcely knew anything at all.

'I can see you are a very learned young person,' said Catherine; at which the little Queen of Scotland was graciously pleased.

Catherine then asked questions about the court of Scotland, and Mary supplied the answers, while Francis and Elisabeth watched her in delight. Every now and then, Francis would say: '*Maman*, Mary says . . .' Or: 'Mary, tell my gracious mother of the way you ride in Scotland . . .' And Elisabeth kept murmuring Mary's name and clutching the elder child's gown with her fat little fingers.

An enchanting child, thought Catherine. But one to whom it would be necessary to teach a little humility.

And then Henry and Diane came into the room.

The attendants dropped to their knees and little Mary Stuart gave the most charming curtsy of all.

'Come here, little Mary, and let me look at you,' said Henry.

The lovely blue eyes were lifted to Henry's face with something like awe. She might be the future Queen of France, but here was the ruling King.

And how handsome is my Henry, thought Catherine, forgetting the new arrival at the sight of him in his black velvet garments. Her eyes went to the black velvet cap with the famous letters ornamenting it in flashing diamonds.

Henry was disturbed. He was comparing the lovely girl with poor delicate Francis. Poor boy! If he had looked sickly before, he looked ten times more so side by side with the dazzling Mary.

There was no doubt about it, Henry had a way with children. Their delight in him was spontaneous. Now he seemed to forget his dignity; he sank on to his knee and took the beautiful little face in his hands; he kissed first one smooth cheek and then the other.

'Methinks you and I shall love each other, Mary,' he said; and she blushed happily; already she loved him.

He signed for a chair and the attendants immediately brought him that one which was kept for him here in the nursery. Henry sat down and made the little girl aware of Diane.

The bow! The looks of respect! So Diane's fame had travelled to Scotland, and the bright little girl knew that if she would please the King of France, it was not the Queen to whom she must do homage, but Madame Diane.

'Welcome, Your Majesty,' said Diane. 'It makes me very happy to see you and to discover that you have already won the friendship of the Dauphin.'

'Oh yes,' said Mary lightly. 'He loves me. Do you not, dear Francis?'

'Oh yes, Mary.'

'And he would be so desolate if I went away. He has told me so.'

Francis nodded in agreement.

'Elisabeth too!' lisped Elisabeth; and Diane caught up the child in her arms and kissed her, while Francis climbed on to his father's knee, and patted the other, indicating that he wished Mary to use that.

Henry had an arm about each child.

'Now you must tell me what you have been doing, my dear little ones.'

They chattered, gay and laughing. Mary, her big eyes seeming to grow bigger, explained the perilous journey in detail, making the King laugh with her description of how they had foiled the English fleet. Diane, hugging Elisabeth, joined in their laughter; and Catherine suddenly realised that Mary Stuart was no longer a dignified little Queen; with the King and Diane she was just a six-year-old little girl.

There was no place for Catherine in that magic circle.

She crept away unnoticed, and went to the cradle in which lay little Claude. The baby at least seemed glad to see her. She clucked and laughed as her mother bent over her. Catherine held up a finger and the baby's eyes grew large as she stared at the jewel there. Then she reached for it, laughing.

'You love your mother then, Baby Claude,' murmured Catherine.

But she knew that Baby Claude would grow up soon; then she too would turn from her mother to Diane . . . unless a miracle happened.

The King grew more and more under the influence of Diane. He had created her Duchesse de Valentinois and bestowed greater and richer estates upon her. She was such a good Catholic that it was only right, thought the King, that the confiscated property of Protestants should be given to her, together with fines which the Jews were called upon to pay from time to time.

Brooding on her hatred, Catherine despised herself. Why did she not find some way of killing Diane? What folly it was to love, for it was only her love for Henry which stopped her again and again from trying one of the poisons she had in her possession. Sometimes she felt that it would be worth while risking the perpetual hatred of Henry if she could free herself from the continual humiliation of witnessing his love for Diane. But she knew her love for her husband was greater than her hatred for his mistress. That was the crux of her problem. While matters stood as they were, she had that period in between having children when she could share her husband with Diane; at other times she lived on her imagination. But Diane dead, and her death traced to Catherine, might mean banishment . . . anything, in which case she would be robbed of Henry's visits and those other intimacies which she enjoyed in her mind.

Sometimes she implored the Ruggieri to help her. They stood firm. No matter how subtle the poison, they dared not risk it. They begged her to cling to reason. It was difficult; it was only her desire for her husband that saved Diane's life.

Early the following year her son Louis was born, and in June of the same year she had her coronation. The crown of France was placed upon her head, but it was Diane who wore the Crown jewels; and it was Diane's head with that of the King which appeared on the medals.

Tired out by the celebrations which attended her coronation, she would lie in her bed and think yearningly of the King as she had seen him that day in his white armour covered by a tunic of cloth of silver, the scabbard of his sword encrusted with rubies and diamonds; with what dignity he had ridden his noble white charger, while over his head was held, by mounted men with frisky horses which pranced on each side of the King's, a canopy of blue velvet embroidered with golden *fleur-de-lys*.

He had looked so noble, so kingly. No wonder people cheered him.

Catherine clenched and unclenched her hands. If only . . . I will do it. I *will*. I do not care what happens. I will not see him doting on her, all the time giving her what belongs by right to me.

Many times during the darkness of night she poisoned Diane in her imagination; she saw herself sprinkling powdered white poison over the woman's food; she saw Diane turning the leaves of a book whose pages were smeared with some deadly solution that would seep into her skin; she saw her drawing on gloves that had been cunningly treated by Cosmo and Lorenzo.

But with morning, caution came hand in hand with common sense, and although she could not part with an idea which was an obsession and belonged to her life as much as did her love for her husband and her hatred for his mistress, she knew that the time was not yet ripe.

Contemplating the gaiety of the life at court, it seemed to Catherine that a colourfully embroidered cloth had been laid across something that was horrible, for the wars of religion were taking on a deep significance throughout the land. The *Chambre Ardente* – a special chamber to deal with Huguenots – had been created by Parliament. Henry was less cruel than many about him, and he did not wish to have his subjects tortured and burned at the stake, even though he was convinced that their misguided religious views might merit this punishment; but he was hemmed in by strong men and women who demanded punishment for the heretic. These were the wily de Guises, grown more powerful since their niece, Mary Stuart, had arrived in France, the cruel Montmorency, and Diane herself.

Calvin was flourishing, and Protestantism was growing everywhere; there were even some towns where the Reformers were in a majority; and where they were, as Diane did not hesitate to point out to the King, they did not refrain from persecuting Catholics. A firm hand was needed, said the Catholic party. Protestantism must be ruthlessly suppressed.

Catherine, concerned with her own obsession, felt aloof from the conflagration. She would state no opinions and favour none, unless it were beneficial to her to show favour. If the Protestants could help Catherine de' Medici in her fight against Diane, then they should have her help; but if the Catholics could prove advantageous in the same cause, then Catherine was all for the Catholics.

Watch and wait for an opportunity to defeat Diane. That should be her motto.

An opportunity did come her way, and she seized on it.

Henry was disturbed. It was all very well for his friends to tell him that the burning and torturing of heretics was a necessary duty. Even though Diane insisted on this, he could not feel happy about it. He would, he declared in an unguarded moment, be prepared to hear what an ambassador from the Reformed party had to tell him. The man could come to him and have no fear, on the King's honour, of being victimised for anything he might say on this occasion.

This announcement of the King's threw Diane and her friends into a state of uneasiness. There were men of great intelligence in the Reformed party; and the fact that the King had, without first consulting Diane, declared his willingness to hear their side of the case was in itself disconcerting.

Catherine was delighted. Could this mean a lessening of Diane's power, an inclination in the King to think for himself? She was alert, wondering if there was any small way in which she could turn this matter to her advantage.

There were several prisoners awaiting torture and execution, the King had said; and he was agreeable that one of them should be sent to him that he might state his case.

A prisoner, thought Catherine. She guessed that Diane had suggested that. Why, the King should have sent for Calvin or some such exalted member of the party. But a prisoner. There was no doubt that the King was as much under the influence of his Catholic mistress as ever.

So Diane, with her new relations, the de Guises, brought their man before the King. He was to be questioned in the presence of others besides Henry; indeed, there was a good gathering of ladies and gentlemen of the court seated about the King.

Catherine watched the wretched man who had been selected for cross-examination. He was a poor tailor, a man of no education; but as Catherine cunningly surveyed him it began to occur to her that Diane and her friends had not been so clever as they imagined.

She felt that mad racing of her heart that was the only indication of her excitement. This tailor was a man of ideals; there was no mistaking the burning zeal in his eyes; he stood before them unafraid, so sure that he was right and they were wrong. She was reminded at once of Montecuculi and how such men could be used by others whose zeal was not for a cause, an ideal, but for their own power and the fulfilment of their desires. Such men as Montecuculi and this poor tailor were made to be used by such as herself, the de Guises, Diane. But in this case she was cleverer than Diane and the de Guises. Had she been in their place, she would not have brought a fanatic and an idealist to speak against them.

The tailor looked wretched in his ragged clothes, the more so because of the brilliant colours and the jewel-studded garments of the court. How foolish to imagine such a man would be over-awed by splendid surroundings and costly jewels. To him there was no splendour but that of Heaven, to be attained only through what he believed to be the true religion.

He proved to be a man of some intelligence and he talked eloquently. It was easy to see that the King was not unimpressed. It was impossible, Henry was obviously thinking, not to admire spirit and courage, and these the man undoubtedly had, even though his religious views were to be regretted.

Catherine was trembling. She longed now to impose her will upon the man, as she could do easily enough with such as Madalenna. There was within Catherine a power which she did not fully understand. There were times when she would have a clear vision of something which had not at the time happened and which certainly would. It was a queer gift over which she had no control. But this other gift of concentration which enabled her to make others do as she wished in certain circumstances, she felt she was more able to guide.

How stimulating it was to endeavour to work her will on others! Now she wished the tailor to see her as the poor, neglected Queen of France, humiliated by the haughty harlot in black and white. No doubt he thought of her as that, but at this moment, his mind was far from the relationship of the King with his wife and mistress. Catherine would bring his thoughts to this matter, because she desired to will him to make an outburst, before all these people, against Diane.

She caught the man's eye and held it for several seconds. She forced herself to see herself through his eyes – the neglected wife, betrayed by a husband with an adulteress. She saw herself, if she had power, pleading for the Huguenots and Calvinists, helping those of the Protestant faith.

She felt the sweat in the palms of her hands; she was almost faint with the effort she had made.

Then Diane put a question to the tailor, and the moment had come.

'Madame,' he cried in ringing tones as he turned to the King's mistress, 'rest assured with having corrupted France, and do not mingle your filth with a thing so sacred as the truth of God.'

The silence which followed this outburst lasted only a few seconds, but it seemed longer to Catherine. The King had risen. His face was scarlet. Diane had been insulted. Henry, who had humiliated his Queen in a thousand ways, would not stand by and hear a word against his mistress.

Everyone was waiting for the King to speak. Diane was holding her head high and seemed haughtier than ever. Catherine, recovered from her mental strain, endeavoured to look as shocked as any present that a humble tailor could so speak of the Duchess of Valentinois. The tailor stood, defiant, unabashed, his eyes raised to the ceiling; he cared nothing, this man, because he believed that God and all the angels were on his side.

And while the King stood there, slow in his anger, struggling to find the words he needed to express his hatred of this man, two of the guards strode forward and seized the wretched tailor.

'Take him!' said Henry, through clenched teeth. 'He shall be burned alive in the Rue Saint-Antoine, and I myself will watch him burn.'

The tailor threw back his head and laughed.

He called to the saints to witness the puny revenge of a dishonourable King who had promised that he might be allowed to speak freely. Did they think to hurt him through what they could do to his miserable body? He welcomed death. He would die a hundred deaths for the true faith.

Catherine, as she watched the man carried out, knew that Henry was already ashamed of his conduct. This was the second time he had been publicly humiliated through Diane. Would he realise this? Would he not feel some resentment? Or was this just another of those petty victories which led nowhere?

Catherine watched her husband pace up and down his room. Through the open window they could hear the tramp of feet and the low chanting of many voices.

The wretched procession had almost completed its miserable journey through the streets.

Catherine took her place beside the King at the window. He

was already regretting that he had sworn to see the tailor burn. He had no stomach for this sort of thing.

Catherine, ever inclined to indiscretion in his presence, wondered whether she should whisper to him: 'It is through Diane that you suffer thus. You would not be standing at this window now to watch a wretched man perish in the flames by your orders, if it were not for her. She has brought you to this. Do you not see that if you would but listen to your Queen you need never suffer thus? I would never lead you to indiscretions such as this. I would never have let you humiliate yourself over the de Vivonne–de Chabot affair. Oh, my darling, why will you not be wise and love your wife so that she does not have to plot to humiliate you!'

But she would not again be trapped into betraying herself.

She said softly: 'They are tying up the tailor now.'

'Catherine,' said Henry, 'there is a strangeness about the man.'

'Yes,' she answered.

'A look of . . . what is it . . . do you know?'

'A look of martyrdom, Henry.'

Henry shivered.

'They are lighting his faggots now,' said Catherine. 'Soon he will take his arguments to the Judgement Seat. I wonder how he will fare there.'

'Methinks he sees us.'

Catherine drew back. From where he was placed that he might be seen from the palace windows, the tailor could command as good a view of the King as the King could of him.

The tailor's eyes found those of the King, and would not let them go. They stared at one another – the King in jewel-encrusted velvet, the tailor in his rough shirt.

Catherine watched the red flame as it crackled the wood about the martyr's feet; she saw the cruel fire run like a wild thing up the coarse shirt. She waited for the cry of agony, but none broke from the tailor's lips. Others groaned in their misery, but not the tailor.

The man's lips were moving; he was praying to God; and all the time he prayed, his eyes never left those of the King.

'Catherine!' said Henry in a hoarse whisper; and she felt his hand groping for hers; his palms were clammy and he was trembling. 'He will not take his eyes from me, Catherine.'

'Look away, Henry.'

'Catherine . . . I cannot.'

Nor could he.

Catherine crossed herself. It was as though the tailor had put a spell on the King, for Henry wanted to run from the window, to shut out the sight of the tailor's agony, but he could not; and he knew that, for the rest of his life, he would never forget the dying tailor.

But Catherine had almost forgotten the tailor, for Henry had turned to her for comfort; and it was her hand that he held. She was thinking, Out of small victories, large ones grow; a small miracle can be the forerunner of a great one.

Henry was praying silently, praying for the protection of the saints; and all the time, he stood there staring, until with a sudden crackling and roaring the faggots at the tailor's feet collapsed, and the flames roared up and the martyr's face was hidden by a wall of fire.

♣ Chapter X ♣

THE KING'S INDISCRETION

Catherine lay at Saint-Germain. Another boy had just been born. This was Charles Maximilian; and she had now three sons – Francis, Louis, who was more sickly than his elder brother, and Charles.

She should have been a happy woman, since that fertility for which she had once fervently prayed was hers; but her miserable jealousy persisted.

Only this morning, she had heard women talking beneath her window, and getting up from her bed, she had gone to the window and crouched there listening.

'The King has gone to Anet.'

'To Anet! At such a time! His place is here with his wife and new-born son.'

Catherine had imagined the lift of the shoulders, the sly smiles.

'Oh yes, my friend, it is the custom, is it not, for a King to be with his Queen at such a time? In all things our King is deeply sensible to what is right and what is wrong. But when Madame de Valentinois beckons . . . ah then, it is another matter!'

'Poor Queen Catherine! How sad she must be to find herself and her new son so neglected!'

'The Queen? . . .' The voice dropped so low that Catherine could not hear. And then: 'Something . . . strange about the Queen. I do not think she cares.'

Catherine laughed grimly. Not care indeed! And something strange? Perhaps they were right there. But what a cruel thing when a Queen must be pitied by her women!

Deliberately, then, the woman of Anet had lured Henry from Saint-Germain at such a time.

Catherine rose from her bed. Useless to remove the desk and rug and look into the room below. Instead she prayed; she wept; she cried out bitterly; and the subject of her prayers was: 'Holy Mother of God, show me a miracle.'

Was this the miracle?

It was Madalenna who brought the news to her. 'I have news, Gracious Majesty. The Duchesse de Valentinois lies sick at Anet.'

Sick at Anet! Catherine's heart began to beat more quickly. This was it. Her prayers were answered.

'The King is at Anet, Madalenna.'

'Yes, the King is with Madame la Duchesse, but it is said that she is very sick indeed.'

Catherine could not wait to summon the Ruggieri brothers to her. It was dusk, and, putting on her cloak, she went to see them. She was as active as ever after the birth of five children all following close upon one another. She hurried to the house by the river.

She knew as soon as she entered the house that Cosmo and

Lorenzo had heard the news. There was that stubborn look in their faces, that suspicion, as though they believed that in some way, although she had not long left her bed, she had contrived, in spite of their warnings and their care, to administer poison to the Duchess of Valentinois.

She was impatient with them, as they immediately closed all doors, drew the shutters and sent out their two servants, although they were Italians. They were afraid of the Queen's obsession.

'You have heard the news, I see,' she said, not without a touch of scorn.

'It is grave news,' said Cosmo.

'Grave news indeed! It is the best news I have heard for many years.'

'Beloved and Most Gracious Majesty,' begged Cosmo, 'we implore you to be calm. The Duchess is ill and none knows the nature of her sickness. Rumour spreads like fire on windy nights in this city.'

Catherine drummed her fingers on the table. 'Oh yes, yes. There will be some to say that I have had something slipped into her wine, sprinkled on her food, spread over the pages of a book . . . I know. They will accuse me of poisoning her.'

'It will be well for us all if the Duchess recovers.'

'It will not be well for me.' She stared first at one brother, then at the other. 'Lorenzo, Cosmo,' she said piteously, 'I would give all my worldly goods to hear that she was dead.'

'Madame, in the streets they talk,' said Cosmo.

'Talk! Talk! I know they talk. They will always talk. They accused me of having the Dauphin poisoned. I tell you I had no intention of having the Dauphin poisoned. Yet they accused me . . .'

'It is well that those whose death will bring advantage to us should not die,' said Lorenzo.

'Lorenzo, she will have to die one day. Why should it not be now?' She stood up and faced them. 'You have the means here. You have poisons . . . subtle poisons. Give me the key of your cabinet, Lorenzo.'

'Beloved Majesty, my brother and I will serve you in every way you wish . . . but we cannot let you destroy yourself.'

When she was with these men, she felt she had no need to hide her feelings; and now she was hysterical with grief, with unsatisfied desire, with humiliation and frustration.

'You mean you would destroy yourselves!' she cried angrily. 'That is it, Lorenzo! That is it, Cosmo! You fear The Boot and the Water Torture . . . and horrible death! You are not afraid for me . . . but for yourselves. What could I lose by her death? Nothing! I have everything to gain. I cannot be displaced. I am the mother of the future King of France. I command you to give me the key of your cabinet.'

The two brothers looked fearfully at each other.

'Madame,' began Lorenzo desperately, 'I implore you . . .'

'And I command *you*!'

Imperiously, Catherine held out her hand.

Cosmo nodded, and Lorenzo drew out the silver chain, from under his doublet, on which hung the key.

Catherine seized it, and strode towards the cabinet. The astrologers watched her, without moving.

She stood, looking at the array of bottles; each contained a substance which she knew could produce death. These brothers had taught her a little concerning their secrets; she had insisted on their doing so; therefore she was by no means ignorant on this matter of poisons.

'Give me something, Lorenzo.' She swung round and faced them. 'Something tasteless.'

Still the brothers did not move; they could only watch her with horrified eyes. Their thoughts flitted from this room to the sickening horror of the *salle de la question* in the Conciergerie.

Catherine stamped her foot. 'This!' she said, and laid her hand on a bottle.

Lorenzo took a step forward. 'Majesty, you could not do it. It would be necessary to take others into your confidence.'

'I have my friends.'

'The Boot makes havoc of the strongest ties of friendship, Madame.'

'You think of nothing but torture. Have I not suffered torture in my apartments at Saint-Germain?'

'Madame, allow us to have that hole filled in. It was a mistake that it should ever have been made.'

She felt tears in her eyes, and, looking from Lorenzo to Cosmo, she thought of them as two little boys whom she had known and who had been her friends in the Medici Palace when Alessandro was her enemy. They *were* her friends, true friends; and although they feared disaster for themselves, they also feared it for her. They were wise men.

They saw her hesitation, and she was aware of their relief. Perhaps she herself was also relieved. She felt that storm of passion passing. She was preparing to be calm Catherine who had learned the art of patience, the wisdom of waiting, the benefits of working in the dark.

'There is a ring the Duchess always wears,' said Cosmo. 'It is said that ring has strange properties.'

'I know the ring,' said Catherine. 'A large ruby. The King

gave it to Madame de Valentinois in the early days of their friendship.'

'Why is it that whatever else she wears, the Duchess is never without it?' said Lorenzo. 'The spell may well be in that ring. It is not natural for a man of the King's youth and vigour to remain faithful to an ageing woman. Only magic could do it. It may well be that the answer is in that ring.'

'If we could but lay our hands on the ring . . .' began Cosmo.

'It should not be impossible,' said Catherine, allowing her attention to be drawn from the poison cabinet.

'Gracious Madame, she never lets it off her finger.'

'But if she is sick it might not be impossible. If I might get one of my friends to help me . . . Yes, I begin to believe that there is something in this story of a ring.'

The brothers became excited. Lorenzo turned the key in the lock with shaking fingers; he hung the key on its chain and buttoned up his doublet. Both brothers breathed freely now.

Catherine stared at the closed doors of the cabinet and wondered why she allowed herself to be lured away from the sure method of poisoning.

The answer was simple. The stake was too high. Diane's death might not prove a stepping-stone to the King's love, but to his hatred.

There was no wisdom in loving as she did.

Diane was feeling very ill. It was the first time in her life that she had been ill, and she was alarmed. She had grown pale and thin, and had no idea what was the cause of her malady.

She was listless and had no great desire for company.

The King, like a devoted husband, insisted on being with her; he was very anxious.

Diane found it a great effort to continue with the strenuous routine she had set herself. She was no longer fit to ride in the morning; she felt herself incapable of entertaining the King and she wished he would curtail his visit.

Looking in her mirror, she scarcely recognised herself. She was sure of the King's devotion; he was the dearest and most honourable of men; but no one, she reasoned in her practical way, likes to be continually with the sick.

She decided that she would not keep him with her at Anet.

She said to him one day as he sat beside her bed: 'Henry, it is dull for you here.'

'My dearest, how could it be dull for me to be with you?'

'Oh, Henry, this is not the life we were wont to lead together.'

'We shall return to that.'

'I fear it is not good for you to remain.'

'I am happier with you than anywhere else. I trust that you will soon recover from this mysterious malady. I long to see you well again.'

She thought: I am too old to wear illness with grace. He must not see me wan and listless. Far better for him to leave me. I trust him. I shall recover the quicker for not being anxious as to how I seem to him.

She was determined he should go.

A woman entered with a drink of herbs which his best physician had prescribed for her.

'A thousand pardons, Sire,' said the woman, curtsying as she saw the King. 'It is time for Madame's dose. I crave your forgiveness for the interruption.'

'That is well enough, Marie,' said Diane. 'Give it to me and I will take the odious stuff.'

She drank off the liquid and handed the glass back to the woman with a smile.

'It is a great inducement to get well,' she said, 'that I may be expected to take more of that.'

The woman curtsied and went out.

'I have not seen her at Anet before,' said the King. 'Though she is not unfamiliar to me.'

'She is a nurse the Queen kindly sent to me. It was good of her. She has a high opinion of Marie. It is said that she is skilled in the mixing of medicines. Your physician thinks her a good and capable woman.'

'I am glad Catherine was sufficiently thoughtful as to send her.'

'Catherine is thoughtful, and my very good friend,' said Diane. 'I trust that she is managing the children well without me. I think that Fleming woman rather a silly creature. Much too foolish to be entrusted with the care of young Madame from Scotland.'

The King was silent; and Diane did not notice the slightly embarrassed look which had come into his eyes.

'Indeed,' went on Diane, 'little Mary is inclined to be pert, do you not think?'

The King still did not speak, and Diane smiled up at him.

'Do you not think she is inclined to pertness?'

'Who was that, my dear?'

'Mary Stuart.'

'Ah! Very high-spirited and lovely enough to be thoroughly spoiled, I fear.'

'Henry, my love.'

'Yes, my dearest?'

'You should not stay here. You should be at court. You forget, for my sake, I know, that you are King of this country.'

'I could not find it in my heart to leave you.'

'But you must. It worries me that you should neglect your duties for me. You have given me everything I could desire. Henry, I beg of you, go back to court. I cannot get well while you are here because I am anxious. I cannot forget that I keep you from your duties. Go to court. Write to me every day. I shall get well all the quicker in my desire to be with you again.'

He shook his head. Passionately he declared he could not leave her. Nothing, he assured her, could mean to him what she did. Gladly would he neglect everyone, everything, for her sake.

But as usual, eventually she got her way. And after he had gone she grew very ill indeed, but she would not have him told.

Marie, the Queen's nurse, continued most assiduously to care for her.

✦ ✦ ✦

Before the King returned to court little Louis died. It was saddening, but not heartbreaking, for he had been ailing since his birth, and the tragedy was not unexpected. His life had flickered like a candle in a draught, and it had seemed inevitable to all that the flame should be early extinguished.

Gloom hung over the court. The death of the little Prince, together with the sickness of his mistress, filled the King with melancholy. Catherine was filled with secret exultation. Louis' death had been expected, and the love she had for her children was a pale thing compared with this passion for her husband.

Louis was dead; but Henry was back; and in her possession

was the magic ruby ring. She had it carefully locked away; it would never do for the King to see it; and yet, when he was with her, she must wear it. She had forced herself to a pathetic belief in the ring, and this belief had been nourished by the Ruggieri brothers. In her heart she knew they thought: Let us keep her mind on the ring in order that it may not stray to our poison closet.

A week after Louis' death, Henry came to her. He was very gentle and courteous. Doubtless he thought: Poor Catherine! She has lost a child, and what has she but her children?

He sat on the chair which was kept for his use. She thought how handsome he was in his coat of black velvet with the diamonds which decorated it, flashing in the dim light from the candles. The greying hair and beard, while robbing him of youth, gave him dignity. His long white jewelled hands rested lightly on the rich fabric of the arms of the chair, while his head lay against the silver brocade that was embroidered with the golden *fleur-de-lys*. Looking round that room with its rich hangings, its costly bed, whose curtains were embroidered in red and purple, with its furnishings worth a fortune, Catherine thought yet again how happy she would be if Henry would but love her.

'You are filled with melancholy, Henry,' she said; and she went to him and, standing behind him, timidly laid a hand on his shoulder. She longed for him to take the hand, but he did not. She thought of the ring, lying ready in a drawer. The drawer was now unlocked; all she had to do was open it and slip the ring on her finger.

'My thoughts are with our son,' said Henry; he did not add: 'And at Anet.' But she knew that they were, and the knowledge filled her with bitterness.

'I know,' she said. 'It is sad indeed to lose a child, and that child a son.'

Her fingers pressed hard on his shoulder; she was now restraining that mad impulse, which his near presence always inspired in her, to throw her arms about his neck and speak to him of her wild love for him, of her burning desire.

'Poor little Louis,' murmured Henry. 'His coming into the world seemed so pointless, since so soon he has been taken from it.'

She must wear the ring. Now was the time. He would not notice that she wore it, for he hardly ever noticed what she wore. Yet if he became enamoured of her as he had been of Diane . . . She felt dizzy with joy at the thought, imagining his taking her hands, kissing each finger. But what would it matter then if he noticed the ring? The magic ornament would by that time have worked its spell.

'I have wept for him until I have no more tears left,' she said; and she sped to the drawer, and, taking out the ring, slipped it on her finger.

Her heart hammering, her eyes gleaming, she went back to the King's chair. He had not moved, but sat quite still staring blankly into space. The magic will take a little time to work, she thought.

'Henry, we must not grieve.' She stood behind his chair; she felt as if her excitement would choke her. She laid her hand on his greying hair and stroked it; the great ruby caught the light from the candle and winked back at her.

The King coughed in an embarrassed way and rose. He walked to the window and stood there uncertainly, his figure silhouetted against the hangings, infinitely desirable to her in all its virile manhood.

He had not changed at all. He did not wish her to touch him. Demonstrative affection on her part embarrassed him now as it ever did.

The magic was slow in working.

She twisted the ring on her finger.

'Francis is not as strong as I could wish,' she said. 'We must get ourselves more sons.'

He nodded, grimly, she thought, as if he was wondering when there might be an end to this unpleasant duty.

Nothing was changed. He sat and fiddled with the jars upon the table; she could see his face reflected in the mirror, gloomy, embarrassed.

She got into the magnificent bed, and waited, twisting the ring round and round on her finger, biting her lips to keep back her tears.

✢ ✢ ✢

One October day, a few weeks after the death of little Louis, Anne de Montmorency begged an audience of the Queen.

Catherine wondered what the harsh old man could want of her. She had never really liked him; she did not even admire him. He was too easy to understand, too straightforward to win her admiration; in her estimation, he was not even a good soldier. He had come to dishonour in the reign of the previous King; and if he were not careful the same thing might happen to him again. He was flouting Diane openly, which was absurd. He should have done what wise people did – work against her in the dark. Sooner or later there was going to be a battle between the King's mistress and the Constable. Silly old man! thought Catherine. It was sadly obvious who would win such a battle. If he wished to hold his place he should do as his betters did, and appear to be Diane's ally.

Still, she was interested to hear what he had to say. She was depressed and unhappy. The ruby ring had proved to have no magical qualities whatsoever. She had worn it for a week and the King's feeling for her had not changed one little bit. Her hopes had been raised and proved futile; and she had at first been furious with the Ruggieri brothers, who, she was sure, had deliberately misled her. They were right, of course; there was nothing she could do just yet. The destruction of Diane must wait awhile; she must continue to use less sure methods than poison . . . just for a while. She had wanted to fling the ring into the river, but even then her caution got the better of her passion. She sent it back to Anet so that Marie might find some way of returning it to Diane's finger.

There was one bright spot in the whole sorry affair. Diane's health was not improving, and she still forbade the King to visit her at Anet.

The suggested interview with Montmorency therefore promised to relieve the tedium, and she eagerly told her attendant to bring him to her.

The Constable bowed low over the Queen's hand. He had come, he said, to pay his respects to the new baby. As she took him to the nursery where Charles was sleeping peacefully, and watched him prod the baby's satiny cheek with a clumsy forefinger until he awoke and whimpered, she knew that Montmorency had not asked for an interview merely to do that.

She said: 'He is young yet, Constable, to realise the honour you do him. Come and see the other children. They will be delighted to see you.'

Francis and Elisabeth made the Constable pretty curtsies; and young Mary offered him an exhibition of her pert dignity.

After he had exchanged a few pleasantries with the children, the Constable said that the afternoon was mild, and he would deem it a great honour if the Queen would take a turn with him in the gardens, where they could chat undisturbed.

The last words excited Catherine, for she knew at once that Montmorency had something to say to her which he did not wish anyone to overhear; so, stimulated always by the very thought of intrigue, and guessing that this might have something to do with the absent Diane, Catherine readily consented to accompany him.

As they walked round the most private of the closed-in gardens, Montmorency said: 'Your Majesty will agree with me that it is peaceful here since some have been forced to leave it.'

Catherine, feeling her way cautiously, inquired: 'Whose absence has made the palace of Saint-Germain more peaceful to you, Constable?'

The Constable prided himself on being a blunt man. He was not one to prevaricate. 'I speak, Your Majesty, of the Duchess of Valentinois, now confined to her bed in the Château of Anet.'

'You are pleased that she is absent then, my Lord Constable?'

Montmorency frowned. Name of God, he thought. Was the Italian woman going to pretend she was surprised by that? The woman was a fool. Look at her meekness! She sat and smiled and bore no malice towards a woman who was as much her enemy as Spain was to France. What milk-and-water creature was this? Still, even such a one must have a spark of jealousy.

'I am pleased indeed, Madame,' he said gruffly. 'The lady has become overbearing of late.'

Catherine was delighted. It was pleasant to have the Constable of France on her side. But she must go carefully, and remember not to disclose her true feelings, even to those who professed to be her friends.

'Did it seem so to you?' she asked.

'It seems so to many, Madame. May I speak frankly to you?'

'I beg that you will.'

'Well, then, the King has been much enamoured of this lady, but the King is human. Madame la Duchesse de Valentinois is indisposed and cannot amuse the King. Why should there not be others to do so?'

Why not indeed! she thought. Why not his desirous and most jealous Queen! She said coolly: 'That seems sound sense, Constable.'

'The King is not one to move towards pleasure unless assisted, Madame.'

'Unless assisted!' repeated Catherine, with that sudden loud laughter which she usually managed to suppress because it belonged to the hidden Catherine rather than to the one she wished everyone to know.

'I repeat . . . unless assisted, Madame. There is a woman who attracts the King, and one I think who, were she given opportunities, might take the place of the absent Duchess.'

'Oh?' It was difficult now to hide her feelings; all the jealousy, all the bitterness was rising to the surface of her emotions. She said to herself: This man must not guess. No one must guess.

Montmorency was impatient. Enough of this side-stepping! he thought. If we decide to speak with bluntness, then let us speak with bluntness. 'I refer to the Scotswoman, Lady Fleming. The King has a fancy for her.'

'Lady Fleming! But . . . she is an old woman . . .'

'The King fancies old women. In any case, she is not as old as the Duchess.'

Catherine closed her eyes and looked away from the Constable. He must not see that she was almost in tears. She said uncertainly: 'The King has noticed her, I grant you. I thought it was because he interests himself in the education of the little Scot. It seems to me that if he has been seen talking to her, that is the reason.'

'Lady Fleming is an attractive woman, Madame. She is . . . different from our women because she is a foreigner. The King is human. Everyone at court is enamoured of the little Scots Queen. Why? She is pretty as a picture; she's full of witchery. But that is not all. She is . . . different. Half French; half Scot. It is the strangeness that attracts. His Gracious Majesty, with a little direction, could become enamoured of the Lady Fleming. It is to your own advantage as well as mine to unite him with a silly woman and separate him from the wily one of Anet.'

Catherine's eyes were shining now. A brief affair with the silly Scots widow . . . a break with Diane . . . and then? Waiting for him would be his true and loyal and most forgiving wife, who was, after all, the mother of his children. Here was a way to work a miracle which a silly ring could not give her.

She said, almost choking with the loud laughter, 'We could arrange a masque. The King could partner the widow . . . The wine . . . the music . . . and the absence of the Duchess . . .'

Montmorency nodded. 'The Fleming will do the rest. She only awaits the opportunity. The King may have been thinking of young Mary's education when he chatted in such friendly fashion with the governess, but the governess was thinking of the King.'

'I shall consider this, Monsieur de Montmorency,' said Catherine. 'And now, I beg of you, lead me back to my apartments.'

✤ ✤ ✤

The court was amused. The Constable had suggested a masque. What next? The grim old soldier planning gaiety! What could be behind that?

The Queen was taking upon herself the management of this affair – usurping the place of the absent Duchess of Valentinois. What sort of entertainment would harsh Montmorency and meek Catherine contrive between them?

Everyone had to admit that the idea was a novel one. The Queen would decide which characters were to be represented and, in secret, she would tell each person which of these characters had been allotted to him or her. Therefore the Queen alone would know, as she mingled with the guests, who it was beneath the mask and the elaborate costume. The Queen was to attend as herself; and she would give a jewel as a prize for what she considered the best costume. Each guest was in honour bound to keep his or her identity secret. It was a masque with a difference; there must be real surprise when masks were removed at midnight.

The Queen summoned the Lady Fleming to her presence.

The woman curtsied, while Catherine's keen eyes noticed that she was a little uneasy. Could it be that Henry had been a little more than friendly already? It seemed incredible.

Catherine dismissed her attendants.

She made the woman stand while she talked to her. Catherine's glittering eyes took in each detail of her appearance. The woman was pretty in a conventional way –

red hair, wide eyes, slightly parted lips that gave to the face a vacant air. She was plump; she was weak and helpless, appealing, Catherine supposed, in what Henry would see as her womanliness. Catherine could imagine her coquettish, eager, a willing partner in a romantic intrigue.

Did she imagine it, or was there now something insolent about the woman? She was older than Catherine. It was incredible and maddening. What had these women that the Queen had not?

'Your Majesty wished to see me?'

Catherine said: 'It concerns your costume for the ball. You know my plan.'

'Yes, Madame.'

'You are to come as Andromeda. You know the story of Andromeda? She was chained to a rock and given up to a monster. Perseus came to the rescue with the Medusa's head, the sight of which turned the dragon to stone. He freed Andromeda and married her.'

'Yes, Madame.'

'If you are in any doubt as to your costume you may consult me.'

'I am deeply grateful, Madame.'

'There is one other matter. For the purposes of the masque, you will need to be at the side of Perseus for the evening. You understand that. I wish to tell you this: who is who at the masque is to be a great secret, but in your case I am going to let you into the secret. You will understand the reason when I explain it to you. The part of Perseus is to be played by a very exalted person indeed; I would not wish you, Lady Fleming, to commit an indiscretion by . . . shall we say an over-familiarity.'

How the wanton creature's eyes sparkled! She knew what this meant. She was delighted. She was longing for the King even as the Queen longed. Catherine could have slapped her silly face.

'Your Most Gracious Majesty, you may rely upon me.'

Gracious I am indeed, thought Catherine grimly, to hand my husband over to such a ready wanton! And I know, Madame Fleming, that I may rely upon you to play the part Monsieur the Constable has chosen for you.

'You may go, Lady Fleming. Do not forget if there is any matter on which you wish to consult me concerning your costume, I shall be ready.'

'Your Gracious Majesty is very good to me.'

Catherine stared after the woman as she bowed herself out.

One could not hate such a simpering fool. She was all eagerness now, preparing herself to seduce the King,

Why should I let her do this? Catherine demanded of herself. Why should I myself not wear the costume of Andromeda? Why should it not be the Queen who must lure the King from his sick Duchess? Because the Queen could never do it. He knows her too well. No costume, no mask, could disguise the Queen in the King's eyes. Moreover, as Montmorency knows, as Lady Fleming herself knows, the King is attracted by the red-headed fool, and only needs the stimulation of wine, sensuous music, the inevitable romance of a lady in disguise – together with the prolonged absence of his mistress – to be tempted into committing an indiscretion.

❧ ❧ ❧

The King was adequately disguised in the armour of Perseus; the armour was of cloth of silver instead of mail. His greying hair was hidden and his eyes peered out through slits in his silken vizor.

He was enjoying the masque more than he had enjoyed anything since Diane had lain sick at Anet; and even his sorrow at his mistress's sickness was not so great, for the last few days had brought better news of her.

Andromeda pressed close to him. He was excited because he knew whose enticing form was beneath the costume of Andromeda; he had seen a red ringlet beneath her wig; moreover, that quaint and halting French of hers was unmistakable. The Scottish governess spoke the language of his country with some difficulty and great charm.

Catherine had chosen the music – Italian music. It was soft music, deeply sensuous; it was the sort of music to put ideas into a head that was usually a sober head.

Andromeda flirted gaily, pretending not to know who her partner was. He found himself responding – awkwardly, it was true – and enjoying it. After all, it was very enjoyable to be foolish, incognito.

'How happy I am that *I* was chosen to be Andromeda,' she murmured, 'since you are Perseus.'

She pressed against him as they danced. He felt younger than he had for a long time. He was reminded of a charming young girl in Piedmont; he was experiencing all he had experienced there . . . the same violent feelings, the same uncontrollable desire to kiss the woman and make love to her.

The image of Diane was fading, although it could never fade entirely. This was nothing, he hastened to explain to himself. Diane would understand. This was just a frivolous masque which the Queen had arranged because he was so melancholy, since his little son had died and his mistress was sick. It was nothing but an evening's frivolity.

Andromeda, warm and clinging, chattered on merrily. Her fingers clung to his, and she lifted her face, obviously expecting him to kiss her. He found himself doing so . . . while he explained to Diane:

This is nothing, Diane. Just a silly masque. The Queen arranged it because I was so wretched . . . anxious on your account.

Andromeda whispered: 'The wine I have taken would seem to have gone to my head. What of you . . . Perseus?'

'To mine also,' he answered.

That was true, he supposed. Catherine had most assiduously arranged that his cupbearer should keep his goblet continually replenished.

Andromeda called his attention to a laughing Daphne who went by with Apollo.

'Did it not seem to you that Apollo had a look of Monsieur de Guise?' whispered Andromeda.

'It did indeed.'

'There are some who cannot hide themselves whatever the disguise,' laughed Andromeda. She added quickly: 'And if we are right, and Apollo *is* Francis de Guise, I greatly doubt whether that Daphne will turn into a laurel before her Apollo has had his will.'

Henry laughed, and wondered what had happened to him tonight.

Diane's image was growing fainter. When he did think of her, he was sure that she would fully understand that this mild flirtation with the gay little Scot was not of the slightest importance. He was indulging in it merely because, missing

Diane, he wished to lighten the melancholy of one evening without her. He refused to remember that he had reasoned similarly during his infidelity at Piedmont.

'Let us dance no more,' said Andromeda. 'I am weary of dancing.'

She drew him from the throng, and it was comforting knowledge that no one would know that the King had left the dancers.

In the cool of an antechamber off the main hall, Lady Fleming turned to the King suddenly, and throwing her arms about him, kissed him passionately on the lips. The silk of his vizor was in her way and, laughing, she lifted it.

'That . . . was very forward of me, was it not?' she murmured coquettishly, waiting for his response.

'No . . . indeed not!' said the King haltingly; and he returned her kiss.

He realised now that he had always been attracted by the Scottish governess, not because of her interest in the education of his children, but because of her red hair, her white skin, and her pretty foreign ways. He knew too that she had been attracted by him, and the reverent glances she had sent his way had also been inviting.

Her small white hands stroked his face, and he felt his blood racing. This was Piedmont all over again.

She said: 'I know where we can be quite alone . . . for an hour or so . . .'

✦ ✦ ✦

In and out among the sweating dancers went the Queen, her alert eyes missing nothing. She saw them leave the ballroom, and, in spirit, she was with them, every passionate moment.

Her eyes were hard and angry. Hatred, jealousy, and cunning battled in her heart. Was she right to have done this thing? Did it not hurt her as much to picture him with the sly Scot as with Madame de Valentinois?

But patience! He will soon tire of that silly creature. One must be grateful for the small blessing. Remember, Diane cannot keep him faithful.

All these people were watching her, wondering at her. What a fool she was, they were thinking. She had organised the most amusing masque the reign had known, and she herself was taking no part in it. Why had she not played Psyche to the King's Cupid, or some such role? That was what Madame d'Etampes would have done in her day. Surely Queen Catherine did not enjoy being humiliated, and now that monster Valentinois was out of the way, here was her chance.

They did not know how little her husband cared for her, thought Catherine. Thank the Virgin that none but herself witnessed those embarrassing moments of his when he visited her.

Her head ached. She hated this masque. She longed for midnight.

What a fool she was to have put the love potion in his wine that he might become enamoured of the governess! But was it the love potion, or was it the governess's red hair and white skin? How many love potions had she used in a vain endeavour to win him for herself?

Again and again she asked herself why he should want this silly woman's love-making and turn from her own which would be given with her heart and soul instead of in a drunken frolic.

She could never find the answer to that question.

Midnight came.

She was glad that they had returned to the ballroom. It had happened already. That much she sensed from their demeanour. She felt bitterly humiliated, for with Diane, who was clever and beautiful, it was understandable; but with this red-haired slut with her parted lips and lascivious eyes . . .

But . . . it had happened; and Catherine guessed, by the look of them both, that it would happen again.

'Unmask!' She gave the order; she listened to the gasps of surprise. 'So it was *you*!' The giggles. 'I had no idea!'

Perseus and Andromeda were looking at each other as though they were intoxicated with something other than the wine they had both taken.

Montmorency's plan had succeeded admirably, thought the Queen. Moreover, tonight would not see the end of the King's indiscretion.

'I wish Lady Fleming to come here,' she announced.

The woman started; she blushed to the roots of her red hair, which was loose about her shoulders now that she had removed Andromeda's wig with her mask.

All eyes were on Lady Fleming. Catherine's glittered coldly. She knows, thought the guilty Lady Fleming. She is going to denounce me now . . . here . . . before them all. I shall be banished . . . I shall never be allowed to see him again. She looks so strange. She frightens me. Her eyes are like a serpent's eyes.

'Lady Fleming, you have given a very good performance this night.'

Lady Fleming could not speak. She felt her knees knocking together. The cold eyes continued to regard her.

'The most distinguished couple in the room is Andromeda and Perseus,' went on the Queen.

Everyone applauded, for now everyone knew who Perseus was.

'I could not take my eyes from you,' continued Catherine, and watched the colour rush into Lady Fleming's cheeks.

'Your Majesty . . . is gracious . . .' stammered the guilty creature.

'The prize is yours, Lady Fleming.'

Catherine took a ring from her finger and slipped it on to the trembling one of her husband's new mistress.

✤ ✤ ✤

The silly little governess was giving herself airs. It was noticed throughout the court.

It was already being whispered that the governess's elevation was due to the absence of Diane. What was going to happen, it was discreetly asked, when Madame la Duchesse returned? Would Madame Fleming be sent away, or would the King find the redhead more to his taste?

Little Mary Stuart, whose eyes were none the less sharp for being beautiful, had already whispered to young Francis that their governess was in love. Mary said they must trap her into an admission.

Catherine overheard them teasing the silly creature when she came into the nurseries one day.

'I declare,' said Mary, 'you do not listen to us. Your thoughts are far away. I think they were with your lover.'

'Hush. You must not say such things.'

'But I will. I will. You must confess, must she not, Francis, that she has a lover?'

'Indeed she must!' declared Francis.

'Now come. It is lesson time. You seem to forget.'

'It is you who forget to whom you speak. We ask a question and demand to be answered. Lady Fleming, please remember that one day Francis will be the King and I the Queen. When we ask questions we expect answers, and if you do not answer us . . . or treat us with the respect due to our rank . . . we shall . . . we shall . . .' The saucy creature paused for a while; then she added ominously: 'We shall not forget when we are on the throne.'

'I will not be treated thus . . .' said the stupid woman.

'Have you a lover? Have you a lover?' chanted Francis.

'Well . . . and what if I have?'

'Have you?' demanded Mary.

'Well . . . yes . . .'

Catherine turned away in disgust. It was time this folly was done with. Did not the silly creature understand that the only love affair she could enjoy with the King must be a secret one?

Then one day – as Catherine knew she would – Lady Fleming achieved her own dismissal.

She confided in Madalenna.

Catherine went off into loud laughter when Madalenna reported this to her. How like the woman to choose Madalenna!

'She asked me if I could keep a secret,' said Madalenna.

'And you said you could. Yes, Madalenna. Then she told you that the King visits her at night. And did you tell her that you knew; that you have been an unseen guest in their chamber, a witness to their lechery?'

'I . . . said nothing of that.'

'That was well. Come, Madalenna, waste no more time. What said she?'

'I carefully noted her words that I might give them exactly

as they were said. "God be thanked," she said. "I am with child."'

'With child!' cried Catherine. 'She said that?'

'She did, Madame. She said, "It is the King's child, and I feel honoured and happy about it. I am in such excellent health. I think there must be some magic in the royal blood to make me feel so well."'

Catherine stood by the window looking out on to the gardens below. A child. This was carrying that plan of Montmorency's too far.

Watching the King closely, she believed he was fast tiring of the silly creature. He was getting anxious; Catherine guessed that he was thinking of Diane. Never mind. He would hate having to confess his infidelity. Who knew, after her illness, Diane might not be quite so beautiful, quite so alert of mind. Perhaps Montmorency's plan had worked. Perhaps Lady Fleming had played the part allotted to her well, and now it was the Queen's turn to step in.

Diane was fast recovering, so came the news. Catherine must act quickly before she returned to court. She must remember the lesson which Diane had taught her at the time of the Piedmontese lapse. She must show the King that if he was in an embarrassing position his wife could help him as his mistress had often done.

She sought him immediately and found him with the children.

'Henry, I would speak with you. It is a matter of some importance.'

'I will join you in your apartment shortly,' he said.

'Oh please, Sire,' said Mary, 'do not leave us yet. You have been with us such a little while.'

338

Catherine looked sharply at Mary. She was not so enamoured of the little Queen as everyone else seemed to be. Beauty and grace were no compensation, in Catherine's eyes, for that pertness and insolent manner.

You are ill advised, my Queenlet, thought Catherine, if you think you may provoke me with impunity.

There was the insolent creature lifting her big beautiful eyes almost coquettishly to Henry, imploring him to ignore his wife's request.

Henry touched the golden hair lovingly. 'Well, a few moments more; then I must hear the Queen's business.'

Catherine swept out. Mary Stuart must be taught she could not always behave thus. Already she had taken Catherine's son and made him hers completely. There was no one in the world for Francis now but his beautiful and beloved Mary.

The King was not long in coming to her, and Catherine made sure that they were alone before she spoke.

'I have disquieting news, Henry.'

He raised his eyebrows.

'It is Lady Fleming,' she went on.

The King flushed. 'The Scottish woman?' he said.

Catherine nodded. She would not risk his displeasure by letting him think she was aware of his secret meetings with the governess. He was a man who liked to keep his weaknesses hidden from prying eyes. Did he not wish people to believe that his relationship with Diane was a platonic one? What Catherine wished to imply more than anything was: You may trust me. I wish you always to know that you may rely on your wife.

'She has whispered to one of my women that she is with child.'

Henry drew back as though she had struck him. It was obvious that he had heard nothing about this new development of his little love affair.

He sought refuge in hauteur. 'Catherine,' he said, 'the private affairs of a governess are no concern of ours.'

This was Henry at his least noble. He was in a position which he loathed, and because he could not rely on his wits to extricate him from a difficulty, he was an angry, rather petty Henry.

Yet thus Catherine loved him most tenderly.

'She should be no concern of ours, admittedly,' went on Catherine smoothly, 'but I gathered from my woman that the governess is with child by some personage of position in the court.'

'She was discreet enough to mention no names, then?' said the King with obvious relief.

'As yet,' said Catherine, 'I think the scandal has not travelled far. I cautioned my woman to silence and I think she will obey me.'

'I like it not,' said Henry, his mouth prim and tight, 'that such matters should be bruited about the court.'

Catherine went to him swiftly and impulsively laid a hand on his arm. 'My lord husband, you may rely upon me to keep this matter where it belongs.' Her eyes pleaded with him: can you not see that I would do everything you asked of me? Confide in me. Let me tell you of this overwhelming passionate love of mine. Let me have done with plots. Let me enjoy love with you.

But he was already turning away uncomfortably. 'Yes,' he said uneasily, 'see to that, please, Catherine.'

He went out, and she knew that the interview was a failure.

This time, was it that she had not said enough? The head of Catherine de' Medici was strong, but weak it became when her heart was involved.

A few days later Diane sent a message to the King telling him that she was ready to return to court; and he himself rode to Anet that he might accompany her.

The story of the Scotswoman was common knowledge now. While Diane was away, the King must play! it was whispered. But was it not rather foolish to have chosen such a silly woman for his indiscretion? Now it would be seen what Madame Diane had to say about the matter. Was it the end of the King's devotion to his ageing Duchess? Hardly! Since he rode to Anet to bring her back to court! But it must be remembered that the ravages of sickness could ruin an ageing woman's charms. What an interesting situation: Diane returning with her royal lover, while the Scottish governess grew in importance – in her own eyes at least – as she grew in size.

The King returned to Paris with Diane. Though she was paler and thinner, there were many who agreed she was as charming as ever; and moreover, the King's devotion was obvious. Wretchedly, Catherine, watching him more closely than any, detected in his demeanour a remorse – a secret remorse – and she knew that his infidelity worried him greatly and that he had not yet confessed it to Diane.

But what did that matter? Catherine had at last understood. She and Montmorency had wasted their time. Nothing could come between the King and the Duchess. No brief love affair with a red-headed governess, no scheming of a clever woman, could break up this surely most enduring love affair in the history of France.

Still, Diane would have some discomfiture to bear, and Catherine, since she could not break the King's devotion, must content herself with this.

Diane had lost none of her subtlety. It was to Catherine she came when she heard the news.

'I hear that the Lady Fleming is to become a mother,' said Diane.

'I have heard it also, Madame,' said Catherine meekly.

'The woman is a fool,' said Diane. 'She talks too much. Did Your Majesty know that the child is the King's?'

'I had heard that also. I fear it is a matter to grieve us both.'

'When a stupid woman's tongue begins to clack, it is a matter to grieve all concerned. I think you should insist on her banishment from court.'

'I see,' said Catherine. 'Have you spoken of this to the King?'

Diane shrugged her shoulders as though to say she did not consider the matter worth the King's attention. How clever she was! So she was going to let Henry see that she did not consider this infidelity – occurring while she herself was unavoidably kept from him – of the slightest importance. It was the same attitude that she had adopted over the Piedmont incident. How easy it was to manage a lover when you did not love with a fierce desire, a burning passion that robbed you, calm as you habitually were, of all good sense.

Catherine said slyly: 'The King loved this woman. Doubtless that was why she gave herself airs.'

'Madame, the brief attention of the King is no excuse for indiscretion.'

Oh, she was clever! *She* gave herself airs; but she had never been indiscreet.

'The King may not give his consent to her banishment,' said Catherine maliciously. 'It may be that he wishes to keep her at court.'

'He no longer wishes to keep her at court.'

The two women surveyed each other. Do as you are told! the uncrowned Queen of France was saying. The King amused himself because *I* was not here. Remember that. *You* could not prevent his straying. That is understandable. But now I have returned, and the governess who diverted him for a little while may be sent away.

Catherine used her lids as hoods to hide her glittering eyes; she feared they might betray her hatred of this woman.

'I doubt not, Madame,' she could not prevent herself saying, 'that you know the desires of the King's mind as well as you know those of his body.'

How foolish that was she realised at once. But I am the Queen! she thought weakly. Let her remember that.

Diane turned a shade paler, but gave no other sign of her anger.

She said calmly: 'As Your Gracious Majesty knows, it has been my constant care to devote myself to the King, yourself, and the children. That is why we are such excellent friends.'

That was like a queen talking to her woman. And yet, what could Catherine do? She must remember that every smile she received from her husband came by way of this woman; and now she believed herself to be once more with child, and this she owed to Diane. Her comparatively strong position at court had been given to her by Diane. However provoked, she must not forget that.

She lifted her eyes to Diane's face. 'Madame, as usual you are right. The woman's mistake was to talk too much. I will see that she leaves the court immediately.'

'That will be well,' smiled Diane. 'We must see that she lacks nothing, for we must not forget whose child it is she carries. Her indiscretion, though, makes her immediate banishment necessary.'

The interview was over. The little plot had failed. There might never have been a cleverly devised masque, a passionate Andromeda in pursuit of Perseus.

Henry was reassured that his mistress understood and forgave his brief lapse. She was even glad that he had found a temporary solace. Their love was not to be considered as merely on a physical plane. Did they not both know this? Henry was enchanted by this explanation of his folly; he seemed more devoted, more in love with Diane than ever.

But Diane was not so forgiving to others as she was to her royal lover. The walk together of the Queen and the Constable in the gardens had not gone unnoticed by Diane's spies; and out of that walk had grown the masque; and was it not at the masque that Henry had been given as partner the Scots governess? Diane felt she knew how to deal with the Queen; she knew equally well how to deal with the Constable.

To show how lightly she regarded this affair of the King's, she deliberately reminded the court of that other lapse of his by bringing into the royal nursery Henry's daughter by the Piedmont girl. She was a beautiful child, this daughter of Henry's, and more like her father than any of Catherine's children. Now fourteen, she was sweet-natured and charming. She was called Diane of France and was an example of what a girl could be when her education was supervised by the Duchess of Valentinois.

It was useless, Catherine realised, to fight for the King against such a one.

And there began again, when they were at Saint-Germain-en-Laye, the misery of watching the King and his mistress through the spy-hole in the floor.

In September of the following year a significant event took place. This was the birth of another boy to Catherine. There was nothing very special, one might have thought, in the birth of another child; Catherine had had five already, and four were left to her. This was a boy, it was true – but she had two boys already.

Yet, there was something about this child which moved her deeply. Was it a likeness to his father? For one thing, he was a bigger, healthier baby than Francis, Charles, and dead Louis had been. Catherine knew, with that curious prevision of hers, that this child was going to mean more to her than any of the others.

He was christened with pomp and ceremony such as had attended the christening of other members of the royal family. His names were Edward Alexander; but right from the first she called him Henry and he became known by that name.

'It is because he reminds me so of his father!' she said.

She tended him more than she had any of the others and he did much to soothe her. There was less watching through the floor, less spying generally, less mingling with the crowds in the city, than there had ever been before. Young Henry compensated her in some measure for the pain the older Henry caused her. She adored the child. It was to her he turned; he had cried when Diane took him into her arms. He did not stare wonderingly up into the King's face, but he clung to his mother.

At last there was a second love in her life, this child who comforted instead of tormented, and who gave something in return for what he took, love for love.

❧ Chapter XI ❧

THE DREAM OF NOSTRADAMUS

Twenty-three years of marriage – and her love for her husband had not abated. She was young yet – only thirty-seven – but she was beginning to grow fat; she had produced ten children in the last thirteen years; and she was still as passionately in love with Henry as she had been when a young girl.

Catherine knew – with that unerring instinct of hers – that there would be no more children. This year she had given birth to twins – little Jeanne, who had died a few hours after her birth, and Victoire, who had lived a few months before she followed her twin. But between the births of the twins and the beloved Henry had been born to Catherine two other children. One was Margot, now three years old and as enchanting a child as young Mary Stuart; the other was Hercule, born less than a year after Margot. Catherine could rest from child-bearing now. She had lost three children, but she had a goodly brood of seven, and four of them were boys.

She felt that she could congratulate herself on her children, though Francis, the Dauphin, caused both Henry and herself a good deal of anxiety. He had had a bad attack of smallpox, and on finally recovering was even more delicate than he had been before. Short in stature and not always very bright at his lessons, he was completely under the influence of the scheming little Scots Queen. He was thirteen, but looked no more than eleven; she was only fourteen, but she appeared to be quite seventeen. Young Charles, who was six, adored her, and was jealous because she was to marry his brother; Charles had turned out to be quite a little musician; he liked to play his lute to Mary, and to read verses to her. She was willing to listen, the little coquette, always ready for adulation; and Heaven knew there was plenty of that for Mary Stuart at the court of France. The child's airs and graces might have been intolerable but for her charm. They often *were* intolerable to Catherine – who was indifferent to charm, except in her two Henrys – but she bore with the girl, for she had decided that one day Mary Stuart should answer for her sins.

Catherine loved her daughters, Elisabeth and Claude, though mildly, for they were pretty, charming girls. Young Margot, even at three, showed signs of becoming a stronger personality. Lovely to look at, and imperious already, she had easily won the hearts of Diane and her father; she was bolder with her mother than any of the others – except Henry – dared be. Catherine admired her young daughter, but her great love was already given to young Henry.

He was five now, her beloved child – a Medici in every respect. He was entirely hers. She had one great regret regarding him, and that was that he was her third son, and not her first; she would have given much to have made him Dauphin of France. He was delightful; his beautifully shaped hands were *her* hands; his features were Italian; his eyes were the flashing Medici eyes. He was not, like his brothers, fond of the chase, though he rode well; Catherine had seen to that. An ardent horsewoman herself, she insisted that all her children should learn how to manage a horse. It was not lack of courage that made him less eager for the chase and outdoor games. He preferred to shine intellectually rather than by physical prowess. His manners were gracious and charming.

Everyone noticed how she loved this child, for, as it had been with her husband, where her love was concerned she threw caution away. 'The Queen loves the little Henry as she loves her right eye!' it was said. And it was true. When she embraced him, when she listened to his rather lisping, delightful way of speech, when he showed off in his fine new jacket – for he loved his clothes and was more interested in them than were any of the girls in theirs – when he brought his lap dogs for her to caress, she would think to herself: 'Oh, my beloved son, you are all Medici. Would I could put you on the throne of France.'

When she thought of the future, she would see him, in her mind's eye, mounting the throne. Is it truth I see? she would ask herself; and be unable to discover whether what she had seen was a vision of the future or a picture conjured up from her own powerful desires.

'If only he might be King!' she would sigh; and then: 'He *shall* be King!'

Her longing to see into the future increased, and when she heard reports of a certain prophet, she had him brought to court that she might question him.

This was a black-bearded Jew from Provence, a certain Michel de Nostredame, but he had Latinised his names, as did other scholars, and he was known as Nostradamus. He had been a doctor before he discovered his powers, and had studied at Montpellier at the same time as that quick-witted monk, Francis Rabelais.

Catherine told him that she wished him to foretell the future of her children, and for this purpose she had him brought to the royal nurseries; and as the court was at Blois at the time, he lived there in the household of the royal children.

Many were the conversations she had with him. She grew to admire him for his knowledge and to respect him for his goodness. He was a clever talker; she enjoyed his company.

He quickly realised that although she had engaged him to foretell the future of her children, it was the future of Henry in which she was most interested. He pointed this out to her, and she agreed.

'Leave the others and get to work on Henry's future,' she said.

He did this, and after some weeks he had news for her.

He pledged her to secrecy, for what he had to say he felt to be of great importance. He was a man who hated violence; as a doctor he had faced death many a time in poor towns where he had worked among plague-stricken victims, wrapped in a tarred cloak and wearing a mask to protect him from infection; he was ready to face danger to save life; he loathed having any part in that which might take life.

Catherine met him in his apartment where he did his work.

'It is of your son Henry I would wish to speak, if it pleases your Majesty.'

Catherine said nothing could please her more.

'I beg of you, Madame, keep this matter to yourself. I have seen into the future. Your son Henry will one day wear the crown.'

She was overcome with joy, and promised that she would

tell no one what she had heard. But when she was alone she began to think of the lives between. Henry – beloved husband, whom she adored – was one, and the thought of his being supplanted, even by young Henry, was agony to her. This love for her son was great, but it could not be compared with her love for her husband. Young Henry was but compensation for the loss of greater joys. But, she assured herself, the King is young yet; he is strong and healthy – far more so than any of his children – and he has many years before him. It is not of the King I must think. It is of the future of my darling Henry.

Yet there was Francis to come before Charles and Charles before Henry. What of them? They were young, only a few years older than their brother. And yet . . . Nostradamus had said that Henry should wear the crown.

She was obsessed with a desire to see into the future. She set the brothers Ruggieri working; they must find out if Nostradamus had really glimpsed the future or was merely telling her what he must guess she wished to hear. The brothers worked eagerly, delighted to find the Queen's thoughts diverted from her husband's mistress to the future of her favourite son.

They were able to tell her that they also believed young Henry would wear the crown of France.

Then, often her eyes would grow bright as they fell upon the pock-marked face of Francis; and eagerly she would watch Charles toying with his food. Both these boys ate sparingly and were quickly out of breath.

Catherine watched the children at their studies. They were growing up fast. In the last year or so young Francis, as

Dauphin, had had his own establishment; very soon now he would do what he wished to do more than anything else in the world, marry Mary Stuart.

How sick he looked. He could not last long. And yet . . . Nostradamus had hinted that he would wear the crown; and the brothers had supported Nostradamus. Perhaps he was not so sickly as he looked. He was not attending now; he was in that state of excitement which Mary always aroused in him. He was longing for his marriage; Mary was nothing loth, sickly as he was. She loved his adoration; it was so complete.

They were all in awe of Catherine – even Mary. She had but to turn her brilliant eyes upon them and they would obey her.

She said sharply now as Mary was turning to whisper to Francis: 'Now, Mary, you will translate for me.'

Mary translated the Latin prose in her quick and clever way. The child was so alert, so brilliant that it was not easy to find fault with her. Francis and Charles watched her with great admiration.

Need they both adore her so blatantly, wondered Catherine. Was that how it would be all through her life? Catherine believed so. The child herself believed it. Flushed and excited, she quickly reached the end of the passage Catherine had set her to translate.

'Bravo!' cried Francis.

'Silent, my son,' said Catherine sharply. 'There was a mistake.'

'But no!' cried Mary indignantly.

'But yes!' said Catherine, and she pointed it out.

Mary was angry; and Francis and Charles were angry with their mother. Even Elisabeth and Claude were on Mary's side, although more in awe of their mother than were the boys, so they did not show it.

'You did well, Mary,' said Catherine, 'but not quite so well as you thought. If you had gone more slowly, taken a little more care, you would have done better. It is well to remember that too much pride often brings disaster.'

The girl flushed and went through the passage again. This time she was word perfect. There was no denying that she was a clever little thing.

'Thank you. You elder ones may go now. I will hear Henry and Margot.'

But while she taught the younger children, she was aware of the older ones in a corner whispering together. Francis hung on Mary's words, kept hold of her hand; all his yearning for her was in his eyes. And Charles was hating his elder brother, because he would have the honour of marrying Mary, and had Charles been born first, that honour would have been his.

Poor little Princes! thought Catherine. They were born to envy, to fear, and to hate. As for Mary Stuart, she was born to make trouble for those about her . . . and mayhap for herself, for the child would have to learn that she was not quite so important to others as she was to herself.

Before Catherine now were her two best-loved children, for although she sometimes thought that young Henry, with the older Henry, had all the affection she had to give, she could not help but be fond of this bright and beautiful little daughter of hers. It was such a pleasure to listen to her three-year-old impudence, to contemplate her beauty and to remind herself that this little Margot was her daughter.

But her attention strayed again and again to the older children, and while she took Henry on to her lap and put her arm about Margot, and appeared to pay attention to them, she was really listening to the group at the window.

Mary was on the window-seat, while Francis sat on a stool, holding her hand, which she allowed to lie limply in his while he gazed up at her. Charles was stretched out on the floor also looking up at her with rapt attention; while Claude and Elisabeth sat on stools close by.

Mary was talking of religion, and Catherine frowned, for she considered the subject unsuitable.

During the last years the blood of many had stained the land of France. Henry had sworn, after the tailor's death, that he would never witness another burning, but that had not prevented many from being thrown to the flames. The *Chambre Ardente* had been busy during those years; heretics filled the damp and mouldy Conciergerie and the cruel Bastille; their groans had echoed through the hideous *Salle de la Question*: thousands had been left to fight the rats and die of starvation in the *oubliettes* of the Great and Little Chatelot. Many had met horrible deaths by the wheel and wild horses; some had their flesh torn with pincers and molten lead poured into their wounds; some were hung to roast over slow fires. The tongues of these victims were cut out so that the spectators could not be moved by their hymns and prayers. And all this had been done at the King's command in the name of Holy Church.

And now little Catholic Mary – primed by her uncles, the Guises – talked to the Princes and the Princesses of these things.

Catherine called them to her and they came defiantly.

'It is not meet to speak of such things,' she said severely.

'Is it not meet to speak of what *is*, then?' asked Mary.

'I would have you know that it is not good manners to speak of what is not pleasant.'

'Madame,' said Mary slyly, 'do you think it is not a good thing to rid our country of heretics?'

'I said that it was not a subject for the lips of children. That is all that concerns you. Go, and remember I forbid you to speak of such matters.'

So they went, and Mary Stuart, as impudent as she dared be, began to talk flippantly of the newest dance, in tones of contempt which she meant the Queen to hear. It was irritating, and worse still that the two boys and two girls should admire her for it.

Catherine had an impulse to take the insolent girl, throw her across a stool and whip the insolence out of her, and to do it before the others that they might witness her humiliation. Should she? No! It was not dignified for the reigning Queen of France to whip her successor.

✢ ✢ ✢

It was the hour which Catherine enjoyed more than any – that in which she held her *cercle*. During this, it seemed to her as though she were the Queen in truth.

It was graciously allowed her by the King and Diane – a reward for a meek and complaisant wife. She let it be known that she had instituted the *cercle* that she might receive men and women of the court and so become better acquainted with them; the talk must be of an enlivening and cultural nature, and it was considered an honour to attend and a slight to be shut out from the Queen's *cercle*.

The King often attended; he looked upon it as a courteous duty, and unless he was 'at home' at Anet, or there was a hunting party – in which case Catherine herself would usually be of it – he would come. Diane, of course, as first lady to the Queen, must be there. Montmorency made a point of occasional visits, although he declared that he was not at home in a lady's apartment and came because he liked to talk to the Queen about the royal children, for whom he professed great fondness. The Guises came, and Catherine was glad to have them there, although she greatly feared them, knowing them for the ruthlessly ambitious men they were, priming their niece, Mary Stuart, in all she did and said. It horrified Catherine to think of Francis as the slave of Mary, and Mary the tool of her scheming uncles. Pray the saints, there would be many years before Francis, with Mary, mounted the throne. The King was robust and not one of his sons equalled him in physique. Catherine often remembered that Francis the First and her own father had died of the same terrible disease. She and Henry were healthy people, but had they escaped the taint only to pass it on to their children? Young Francis and Charles were weaklings. She smiled suddenly. But her own darling Henry should not be. She was back at an old theme.

She could now look round the members of her *cercle* with pleasure and gratification. The poets Ronsard and Joachim du Bellay argued together; one of the three Coligny brothers was talking animatedly to Henry's sister Marguerite, for whom a husband had not yet been found, although she was advancing into her thirties; lovely Anne d'Este, the Italian woman whom Francis de Guise had married, was with the other two Colignys. All the most important personages of the court found it expedient to attend the Queen's *cercle*.

There was one thing she could not do, and that was exclude Diane. All her triumph turned to bitterness when she looked around and saw her enemy. As she received the homage of those about her, Catherine could not prevent pictures flashing in and out of her mind: little vignettes, scenes from the chamber below hers at Saint-Germain. Engraved on her memory were the tender gestures, the passionate love-making. There were many scores to be settled with Diane. Never would Catherine forget how, some years ago, when it had been necessary to appoint a Regent, Henry having gone in person to battle and tradition demanding that the Regent should be the Queen, Henry had, at Diane's instigation, so hemmed her in with counsellors that her power had been completely nullified. Catherine had accepted that state of affairs without protest, not wishing the people to know how, at his mistress's command, her husband would humiliate his wife. She did not forget it. She would never forget it; it was almost as bitter a memory as those that had come to her by way of the hole in the floor.

Montmorency was beside her now. He had brought a new medicine for little Hercule, as he had heard the child was ailing.

'Monsieur, you are too good!' said Catherine. 'The elephant's tooth you brought me proved beneficial to Charles.'

'You dissolved it well, I hope, Madame.'

'Indeed, yes.'

'This is a special herb. I have tested it on my servants.'

The Constable's eyes were on Diane, who was talking with the Duc de Guise and Mary Stuart, together with the Dauphin. He and Diane were enemies, in secret, though they did not distress the King by proclaiming their enmity; but Diane had never forgotten the part the Constable played in the affair of the Scottish governess,

Catherine turned to find Francis de Vendôme at her side. She smiled warmly, for this man had a special claim to her favour.

He was handsome – indeed, he was one of the handsomest men at court – and was of royal blood, having Bourbon connexions; he had always made a point of being very courteous to the Queen; but, most important of all, he had been cool to Diane. This had happened when she was looking for husbands for her daughters and had considered Francis de Vendôme, being of royal blood, a suitable *parti*. Francis de Vendôme, entitled Vidame of Chartres, had haughtily declined the alliance with the girl whom Diane afterwards succeeded in marrying to one of the Guises. Catherine had liked the young man for that; and in his turn he had made a habit of humbly seeking her out and giving her his respectful admiration. She was pleased to see him at her *cercle*.

Montmorency moved off, and she gave the Vidame permission to sit beside her.

The young man was amusing; he was always ready with the latest gossip, and she had found more than once that he soothed her wounded vanity. People glanced their way, and she knew they wondered whether this was the beginning of a love affair – although there had never been anything of this nature in the life of the Queen.

'Your Majesty is looking charming this evening.' The young man's handsome head moved closer to that of the Queen, who tried to show that the flattery did not interest her; she could not be blamed if it did, she reminded herself, since she had received so little in a lifetime of humiliations at the court of France.

'Poor old Montmorency seems troubled tonight,' she said.

'It is this affair of his son's. The old man is ambitious for the boy, and the boy, the saints preserve him, is ambitious for love.'

'I think the boy has spirit,' said Catherine.

'What we would call spirit, Madame, the old Constable calls folly.'

Catherine smiled. The whole court was talking of the Montmorency affair at the moment. The King had offered his natural daughter, Diane of France, to the Constable's son, and the Constable's son had already promised marriage to one of Catherine's ladies. Montmorency was furious to think that the young man had, by his impetuous act, spoiled his chances of linking his family with the King's. He had had the girl whom his son wished to marry shut up in a convent, and was endeavouring to get the Pope to annul the promise of marriage.

'Ah well,' went on the Vidame, 'it is a great temptation. The old Constable would rejoice to see his son make such a noble marriage. One understands.'

'One understands the Constable's feelings and those of his son. The latter is not the first to refuse a match that would bring him advantage.'

They exchanged smiles. Catherine was referring to the Vidame's declining the hand of Diane's daughter.

'Madame,' whispered the Vidame, 'there is one here who greatly enjoys the Constable's discomfiture.'

Again they could smile together, cosily, intimately. It was very pleasant to chat with someone who had proved that he had no wish to serve Diane.

'How well they hide their enmity from the King!' said the Vidame.

The Queen was silent, and he wondered if he had gone too far. He was ambitious; he had not thought ageing Diane could hold her influence at court as long as this; and even now, when he looked at her silver hair – though she was beautiful in spite

359

of it – and he felt, as all did, that she would hold the King's attention until she died, he was sure that he had done the right thing in winning the good graces of the quiet Queen instead of those of Diane. His was a waiting policy and the Queen was comparatively young. When he had looked into those dark eyes that could seem so mild, he had seen something which others had failed to see; he had discovered that Catherine was not the insignificant person many believed her to be. He remembered the death of Dauphin Francis which had made her Queen. Ah, Madame Serpent, he thought, could you solve that mystery? But sly she might be, subtle too, yet she was also a neglected wife; he was not rich, but his face, his breeding, his charming manners were his fortune, and he had always been a great success with women.

'How beautiful she looks,' said Catherine, 'in her black and white. I declare it becomes that silvery hair of hers more than it did the raven locks.'

'Beautiful, yes. What health she enjoys! There must be sorcery in it. But even sorcery cannot hold off the years indefinitely.'

'Yes; she has aged much since I first set eyes on her.' He had come close and she moved slightly.

'A thousand pardons, Madame,' he said. 'For one blessed moment I forgot you were the Queen.'

She looked away with a hint of impatience, but he knew that she was not displeased. The Vidame began to wonder seriously about the possibility of a love-affair with the Queen. He was sure it would be a most profitable love affair, and the poor Bourbons, with the King's four sons standing between them and the throne, could not afford to ignore any opportunity of advancement.

Catherine, too astute not to read his thoughts and to suspect his motive, was wondering how she might use the Vidame. Diane was ageing. The King was inclined to simplicity. He had never thought of his wife as an attractive woman. Would it be possible to gain his attention by letting him think that one of the handsomest men at court was interested in her?

It was a thought worth considering. Therefore she allowed the Vidame to stay at her side, and listened with apparent light-heartedness to his veiled compliments which he knew so well how to phrase.

She was watching the two lovers – Francis and Mary – on the window-seat. Francis de Guise and the Cardinal of Lorraine were still with them; the wily pair were talking merrily, and the children were going off into fits of laughter at their presumably witty conversation. Young Francis was staring up at the scarred face of Francis de Guise with adoration. Of what was the Duc de Guise speaking? Of Metz, where he had routed the Spaniards? Of his entry into Paris, where the people adored him even as young Francis was preparing to do? Even that terrible scar on his right cheek which had earned for him the name of *Le Balafré* – hideous though it was – he had turned to an advantage. The terrible Duc de Guise, the greatest soldier in France, the idol of Paris, the most scheming of a scheming family, the uncle of her who might one day be Queen! In that event it would be the Guise brothers who would become the power behind the throne. Now, as he talked, he was drawing others to him; and his brother, the Cardinal of Lorraine, was there to help him. The Cardinal was the cruellest of men, the most cunning, the most witty, the most ambitious and immoral man who ever strove for his own ends under the sanctifying robes of the Church. He was as ready with a quotation from the Bible or the classics as he was with a *risqué* story; he was completely unscrupulous. And this man, with Francis de Guise, stood behind the Scots Queen and the boy Francis awaiting the death of the King, that they, through these children, might rule France. And on whom did these men turn their flattery – on the pale-faced, delicate boy Dauphin or the lovely girl with that shining mass of hair and the most charming smile in France? The wily uncles would direct their niece, for she adored them, and the girl in turn would rule the Dauphin, since he was passionately in love with her.

Catherine stood up suddenly; she was determined to break up the conference by the window.

'Let us play a game,' she said. 'Let it be Pall-Mall.'

The ladies and gentlemen could all join in this, and it was better to have them playing than engaging in dangerous conversation.

Mary Stuart's eyes met those of the woman who was to be her mother-in-law, and the girl's mouth hardened. She knew that the merry conversation she was enjoying had been deliberately broken up.

So! thought Mary. She is jealous. I and the Dauphin surround ourselves with all the most important people in the land, and that makes her angry. The daughter of tradesmen is afraid that she will lose what little dignity she has!

Catherine noted the girl's pout, and laughed inwardly. Silly little Mary Stuart! She thought it was for her charm and her beauty that those uncles of hers flattered her. She did not realise that even to such rakes as the Guise brothers there were more important matters than beautiful women.

The King joined in the game of Pall-Mall, playing with that

enthusiasm which he gave to all games, and with that fine sportsmanship which made a game he played in as informal as any played without him.

How noble he looked at play! thought the Queen, and wondered when and if old age would ever ease her longing for him.

She passed among the players, and in doing so could not help but hear an ill-timed remark of Mary Stuart's:

'She likes not to see you gentlemen more interested in Francis and me than in herself. Is not that what one would expect from the daughter of tradesmen?'

Catherine's face was impassive. Let the insult pass for the moment; it would not be forgotten.

But, watching the King, she had little thought to spare for the girl. She could not live without the hope of one day luring him from Diane.

Would it be possible to kindle a spark of jealousy? And if so, might not slumbering passion be awakened?

Her speculative eyes sought the tall, handsome figure of the Vidame of Chartres.

In Catherine's apartments her women were robing her for the wedding of her eldest son. She could hear the bells ringing out all over the city and the people were already shouting in the streets.

As they slipped her jewel-studded gown over her head, she thought of the events which had befallen this land thick and fast in the last few months – events which had culminated in this marriage which neither she nor Diane and the King had wished to take place so soon. Francis and Mary were children yet – only fourteen and fifteen. They were madly in love – at least Francis was, and Mary was ready to pet him and love him because of the eagerness with which he did everything she asked of him.

In these last months those uncles of Mary Stuart had grown in importance. The idol of Paris had become almost the King of Paris. Even Diane, who had once worked steadily to advance them, was appalled by their rising power, and had even sunk her differences with Montmorency to work against their further rise.

Whatever happened at court, it seemed that wars must come and go, and this time the enemies of France had been both the Spaniards and the English – allies because the King of Spain was the husband of the Queen of England. The Spaniards had reached Saint-Quentin, surrounded it, besieged it, and the town had fallen to King Philip's men while Montmorency himself had been taken prisoner. Paris was threatened, and the country was in despair. The terrified Parisians were showing signs of panic, and there had been a few outbreaks of rioting.

Catherine could smile now as the jewels winked back at her, for out of this disaster had she achieved great triumph. She had been Regent in Henry's absence; and this time, sweeping aside all those who would hamper her, she gave the citizens of France a glimpse of the real woman behind that submissive façade. She had seen clearly that Paris must be lifted from its apathy and fear unless the whole of France was to be lost; and she had made her way to the Parliament and there demanded money for the armies, and had commanded that the people should not be told that the war was lost. So eloquently did she speak, so skilful were her arguments, so courageous her manner, and above all so calm was she, that she won the admiration of all those who had previously regarded her as a nonentity. Paris became hopeful. Funds were raised for the armies. Catherine was proved right. The war was not lost.

Then Francis de Guise – *Le Balafré* – saw an opportunity of saving his country and winning fresh honour for himself. He took Calais from the English. It was an unimportant little town, but the moral effect was tremendous, for the English, after two hundred years, were at last expelled from France, and the humiliation of having foreigners on French soil was at last removed. What mattered it that the Constable de Montmorency was a prisoner when there was Francis de Guise to fight the battles of France.

The Spaniards could not extend their lines of communication beyond Saint-Quentin; their armies were disbanded and withdrawn, and it became obvious that the Queen's bold action in demanding money to continue the fight had saved France from ignoble and unnecessary surrender.

Thinking back, Catherine could smile with more than elation, with hope of achieving her heart's desire. It was no longer possible to regard the Queen with indifference. The King showed in his manner a new respect for his wife. And there was the young Vidame de Chartres waiting to pay her his respectful admiration, which, at a sign from the Queen, could kindle into something deeper. Catherine thanked the saints nightly for the miracle of Saint-Quentin.

But the hero of the day was Francis de Guise, and to him must go great honour. Henry began by giving an Oriental masque for him in the Rue Saint-Antoine. It was lavish, colourful, expensive; worthy, said the Parisians, of their beloved *Le Balafré*. But the cunning Duke was after more glory than an Oriental masque could give him. He and his brother the Cardinal pressed for the marriage of their niece to the Dauphin; and, being well aware of the immense popularity – swollen now by the gain of Calais – of the impudent Guises, the King, with Diane, agreed that the marriage should take place at once.

'Bring me my pearls,' said Catherine; and they were brought and placed about her neck.

'Now send in my children, that I may inspect them,' she ordered.

They came – all except the bridegroom, who was being prepared for his wedding in his own establishment.

Catherine embraced first Elisabeth and Claude and complimented them on their charming appearance. 'My dears, you are excited, I can see, to witness your brother's marriage. Well, we shall soon be finding husbands for you, eh?'

'And for me also,' said saucy Margot, pushing forward out of her turn.

'If we can find someone who will put up with your wickedness, Mademoiselle Margot!' said her mother, trying to look severely at the brightest of all the faces before her.

'It is easy to find husbands for princesses,' said Margot, with wisdom beyond her five years. 'So one will be found for me, I doubt not.'

'I am not so sure,' said Elisabeth. 'Papa's sister, Aunt Marguerite, has no husband, and she is a princess.'

'Hush, my children, this is most unseemly talk,' said the Queen. 'The wedding has made you forget your manners.' Then her eyes went to her darling boy. He returned that special secret smile they kept for each other. 'And how is my little Henry today? Excited, wishing for a wedding of his own?'

He skipped towards her; his movements were graceful, more like a girl's than a boy's. The others noticed that he was not reprimanded for forgetting the respect owed to the Queen even though she was his mother.

Catherine stooped and kissed her beloved child, first on one cheek, then on the other.

Seven years old and growing in grace and beauty every day! Oh my darling, she thought, I would it were your wedding today and that you were the Dauphin! You would not care more for the flighty fair-haired beauty than for your own *Maman*.

'I would rather have a new clip for my coat, *Maman*, than a wedding,' said Henry seriously. 'I have seen a beautiful one in gold set with a sapphire.'

'So you wish for yet another ornament, my proud little popinjay?'

She would give an order for the clip. He should have it for his birthday.

He showed her his coat. Was it not magnificent? Did she not like it better than that of Hercule or even Charles? He, himself, had ordered the alterations to be made.

She pinched his cheek. 'So it is a little dressmaker you have become then?'

But she must remember the others waiting expectantly for notice.

She made Charles turn round that she might see the set of *his* coat. Silly, sullen little boy! He was angry and jealous because Mary was marrying his brother. His eyes were red with weeping. How stupid of a boy of eleven to think he had lost the love of his life!

Little Hercule, the baby, was four and very pretty indeed,

though Mademoiselle Margot outshone them all – except Henry, in Catherine's eyes – with her gay spirits and bright red cheeks and flashing eyes. She must pirouette and curtsy and take little Hercule by the arm and pretend that he was her bridegroom and that they were bowing to the crowds. The children were so comic that Catherine found herself bursting into loud laughter.

'We forget the time,' she declared at length. 'It will not do for us to be late.' She signed to the attendants. 'Take them now and see that they are ready when the time comes.'

The royal party had spent the night at the palace of the Bishop of Paris, and a gallery had been erected which ran from the palace to the west door of Notre Dame. This gallery was decorated with tapestries and cloth of silver and gold, wherever possible ornamented with the *fleur-de-lys*.

It was now time to join the party which was to make its way through the gallery to Notre Dame, and the King's gentlemen led the way, followed by princes, cardinals, archbishops, and abbots; then came the Papal Legate with the Dauphin and his brothers, the Bourbon princes following; and after that, the most enchanting sight of all – young Mary Stuart, dazzling all eyes in a white gown with a long train, while on her fair curling hair she wore a golden crown, decorated with pearls and coloured precious stones. The people gasped and could not take their eyes from her as the King himself led her into Notre Dame.

And after the King and the little Queen, came Catherine and her ladies.

Catherine's alert eyes missed nothing. Francis de Guise, she noted, was much in evidence – diabolically attractive with that hideous scar and his rich garments. He had taken Montmorency's place as Grand Master of the King's Household, and Catherine admired his cleverness in playing to the crowd. He had allowed the common people to use the scaffolding which had been erected for the occasion.

'*Vive Le Balafré!*' called the crowd. He knew well how to play to the humble people of Paris, he was their idol, determined to be their King.

Cardinal de Bourbon greeted the royal party as they entered the church. While he was delivering his oration, gold and silver coins were thrown to the crowds. Even in the church it was possible to hear the shouts of the people, shouts of delight from those who secured the money, shouts of protest and fear from those who were almost trampled to death in the struggle. All through the ceremony the shouting persisted, mingled with the screams of the injured.

Catherine was glad when they left the church, for by that time the weak had prevailed on the heralds to stop the scattering of money, crying out that unless they did, there would be many deaths to celebrate the wedding of their Dauphin.

Back at the Bishop's Palace a banquet awaited them, and after this the King led the bride in a dance; watching them, Catherine remembered her own wedding and magnificent Francis with the kind, debauched eyes holding her hand and telling her that she was Catherine of France now, not Caterina of Italy.

There was a lump in her throat; it was born of pity for that poor ignorant little girl from Italy. If only she could have been as wise as the present Catherine, what a lot of misery she would have saved herself!

But here was Francis, the hero of the occasion, bowing

before his mother, and begging for the honour of her hand in the dance.

She smiled at him.

'Come, my dear Dauphin, let us dance.'

All eyes were on the four of them now – the King and Mary; herself and Francis. On such occasions as this she felt that she took her rightful place in the land.

'You are looking well, my son,' she said, for indeed he was.

'It is the happiest day of my life,' said the bridegroom.

'You are fortunate, my son. You love your wife. It is a wonderful thing – providing, of course, that there is love on both sides.'

The boy looked at her with pity. He understood. She was thinking of her love for his father, and his father's for his mistress. Poor *Maman*! He had never thought of her as 'poor *Maman*' before.

But his own life was so wonderful that he could not brood on the sadness of others. Catherine saw how his eyes followed his dazzling young wife round the ballroom.

She laughed.

'It is with Mary that you should be dancing, my son.'

'*Maman*, tell me this: did you ever see anyone more beautiful?'

'No. I do not think I have. But I will tell you something, Monsieur le Dauphin. Your sister Margot may yet outshine her.'

'Nay, *Maman*, that would not be possible.'

She smiled, glad to see him happy, for he was her son. Let him enjoy his happiness, for she was convinced he could not live very long. He could not do so, for he had to make way for Charles and then for Henry. He *must* not do so!

Just after four o'clock in the afternoon that ball was over, for the party must now make its journey across the Seine to the Palais de Justice for the day's final festivities. The King and the Princes rode on beautiful prancing horses, the Queen and Mary Stuart in litters, while the Princesses rode in coaches, the ladies-in-waiting on white palfreys; and everywhere were decorations of rich cloth splashed lavishly with the golden lilies of France.

Supper was served in the Palais de Justice, and the civic authorities had decorated the place so fantastically, so magnificently, that people said it was comparable with the Elysian Fields. Each course was accompanied by the sweetest music, and, as the banquet progressed, merriment increased, and there was much lively conversation and gay laughter.

Yet another ball followed.

The Vidame de Chartres sought out the Queen. Catherine had caught the general excitement; the wine she had drunk made her flushed and excited; she seemed to see the world in more beautiful colours than ever before, and hope was high in her heart.

Her eyes never left the King, who too seemed excited and happier, so that he looked younger and reminded her of their earlier days together.

While he lives, thought the Queen, I shall continue to need him. Nothing else can seem important to me while his love is given elsewhere.

'What a lovely Queen the little Scot will make!' she said.

The Vidame answered. 'There is a lovely Queen now on the throne.'

His eyes were bright; he had drunk too freely.

Catherine laughed at the flattery, but she was not displeased.

371

She kept the Vidame at her side. She allowed him to hold her hand overlong in the dance, and she was sure that it was noticed.

Did Henry notice? She fancied so.

He respected her because of her prompt action over Saint-Quentin. Would he learn to desire her because the Vidame de Chartres was showing them all that he thought her an attractive woman?

She danced with the King; she danced with the Dauphin; and her only other partner was the Vidame.

When they returned to the Louvre after the ball, Catherine, looking into her mirror, saw that her eyes were brighter, her cheeks flushed. Hope had made her look ten years younger.

She wondered if the King would come to her. She imagined a little scene in which he upbraided her for her conduct with the Vidame. Happily, in her thoughts, she answered him: 'But Henry, can it mean that you are jealous?'

She scarcely slept that night; even in the early hours of the morning, she was still hoping that he would come.

But, as so many times before, he did not do so. Yet hope stayed with her.

✤ ✤ ✤

'One wedding begets another,' said Catherine to her eldest daughter.

Poor little Elisabeth! How small she looked. She was only fourteen – so young to be married.

Catherine had sent for the girl that she herself might break the news.

'My dearly beloved daughter, I wish to speak to you of your marriage.'

The girl's big dark eyes were fixed on her mother's face.

I grow soft, thought Catherine; for she was feeling uneasy, remembering a long-ago occasion when a girl of about this one's age was summoned to the presence of the Holy Pope who wished to talk to her about a marriage.

'Yes, my gracious mother?'

'You knew, did you not, that when Francis married, it would be your turn next?'

The poor child swallowed hard. 'Yes, gracious mother.'

'Why, you must not look sad, for this is great and wonderful news. Here is a fine marriage for you.'

The young girl waited. Who was it? She was thinking of the young men she knew. It might be one of the Bourbons, because they had royal blood. Or perhaps one of the Guises, who had lately become more than royal. There was the son of the Duc de Guise – young Henry. A rather frightening but entirely exciting prospect. Young Henry was going to be his father all over again.

'Oh, *Maman*,' she burst out suddenly, 'do not keep me in suspense. Who is it? *Who* . . .'

'You are going to Spain, my child. You are going to be the wife of his August Majesty, King Philip of Spain.'

The girl grew white, and looked as though she were about to faint. To Spain! Miles away from home! To the King of Spain. But he was an old man.

'You do not seem sensible of this great honour, my daughter.'

'But, *Maman*,' whispered Elisabeth, 'it is so far from home.'

'Nonsense!' said Catherine, forcing out her loud laugh. 'Think, my child, you will be a Queen . . . Queen of what many would say was the greatest country of all. Just think of that!'

'But I do not want to go.'

'Not want to be Queen of Spain?'

'No, *Maman*. I wish to stay a Princess of France.'

'What! And be an old maid like your Aunt Marguerite?'

'Well, she also is going to be married now. Why cannot I wait until I am as old as Aunt Marguerite?'

'Because, my dear, it is ordained that you should marry the King of Spain.'

'I hate the King of Spain.'

'Hush! Is this what you have to say after all my care in bringing you up, in guarding you, in teaching you what is expected of a princess?'

'He is an old man.'

'He is just past thirty.'

'But he is married to the Queen of England, *Maman*.'

'You surely knew that the Queen of England is dead?'

'But I heard he was to marry the new Queen of England.'

'Then you, who have listened to gossip, must now listen to good sense. You, my dear daughter, are to marry King Philip.'

'*Maman . . . when?*'

'Oh, it will be arranged soon, never fear.'

'But that is what I do fear. Will he come here . . . for me, or shall I be sent to him?'

'You will be married here in Notre Dame just as Francis was.'

'So . . . he will come for me?'

Catherine smoothed the hair back from her daughter's heated brow. 'Why, what airs you give yourself! Do you think the mighty King of Spain would make such a journey merely for a wife? No; you will be married by proxy. The Duke of

Alva will take the King's place. You enjoyed Francis's wedding, did you not? Well, now it is your turn.'

Elisabeth threw herself at her mother's feet. 'Oh, *Maman*, *Maman*, I do not want it. I cannot go. I do not want to leave my home for that old man.'

Catherine, softened, drew the girl up to her; she led her to a couch and sat with her arms about her; and, sitting thus, she talked to her as she had never before talked to any of her children, except Henry. She told her of her own childhood, of her ambitious, scheming relative, the Pope of Rome; she told of the Murate, and how the people had shouted for her to be thrown to the soldiery; and she told finally of her coming to France – how she had dreaded it, and how she had grown to love it.

The young girl listened, and was, in some small measure, comforted.

'But Spain is where my father went,' mourned Elisabeth. 'He was a prisoner there. There he spent his most unhappy years.'

'My dear,' said Catherine, 'it is not for us to choose, but to obey.'

'Yes, dear *Maman*.'

'We have all suffered as you think you do now. It may be that you will find the King of Spain such another as I found your father. There is not a better man in the whole world than your dear father, and yet I felt towards him once as you now feel towards King Philip.'

'I hope so, *Maman*, but I am filled with foreboding.'

Catherine embraced her daughter tenderly; she also was uneasy.

The King came into the Queen's private chamber, and she dismissed her attendants.

'I wish to speak to you, Henry.'

He turned towards her so that the sun shone full on his face. He had aged since the Siege of Saint-Quentin; he was passing beyond his prime. Catherine reminded herself that his splendid youth had been spent on Diane, and bitter resentment flared up within her,

'It is about Elisabeth,' she said.

He looked relieved. 'Elisabeth,' he repeated.

'She goes about tight-lipped and pale. I am afraid she will be ill. She has never been very strong.'

'It is an ordeal for a child to be told suddenly that she is to be married,' said Henry gently. 'It can be upsetting.'

He was thinking of the day, long ago, when he had been told he was to have an Italian bride.

She went to him, for she found herself unable to keep away from him; she slipped her arm through his. 'We understand that, Henry, do we not?'

'Indeed we do.'

She pressed his arm. 'And some of us learn that it is not so bad as we thought it might be.'

'That is so.'

She laughed, and laid her cheek against his sleeve. 'We have been fortunate, Henry.'

Now he was uneasy; was he reminded of those days when she had forsaken caution and begged that he return some of the fierce, demanding affection that she gave him?

He has not changed, she thought wretchedly.

But he must feel differently towards her. In the old days he had thought her a nonentity; now he was aware that she could be strong, could sway his ministers. Saint-Quentin was between the past and the present.

She stood stiffly beside him. 'There is no comfort we can offer our daughter then?'

He shook his head. 'Poor child!' he murmured.

'She will get over it. She is frightened because she is so young.'

'She will get over it,' he repeated.

'As others did . . . before her.'

He moved towards the door. She said desperately: 'Henry, I have heard whisperings.'

He stopped short, waiting, and she laughed lightly. 'You will be amused. Of whom do you think?'

'I have no idea. Not . . . not . . .' He turned to her and looked at her in horror, so that she felt her heart leap. He continued: 'Not . . . Elisabeth?'

She laughed again, this time bitterly. 'Oh no, not our daughter. The whisperings concerned none other than . . . myself.'

'You . . . Catherine! What do you mean?'

'You may have noticed that foolish young man – young Francis de Vendôme . . .'

Henry looked puzzled. 'What of him?' he asked.

'He has been dancing attendance on me rather much of late.'

Henry looked grave. 'Young Vendôme!' he said. 'It will be well to take care. Those Bourbons are a shiftless lot. Depend upon it, he is after something.'

How maddening he was! It had not occurred to him that the young man might be seeking a love affair with the Queen. Henry made it quite clear, when he said the young man was after something, that he meant an appointment at court.

377

Catherine felt it was foolish to persist, but she could not rid herself of the hope in her heart. 'There are some who think the young fool is . . . in love with me.'

Henry looked astonished. 'Oh, I shouldn't think so. You should take care. A shiftless, crafty lot these Bourbons . . . for ever seeking some advantage at court.'

'I wish I could be sure that you are right,' she said angrily.

But his thoughts were elsewhere and he did not perceive her anger.

When he left her she paced up and down her chamber. He was indifferent to her. The position had not changed as far as his love was concerned; he tolerated her now as he had tolerated her always. He respected her a little more, that was all; and she did not want his respect.

Very well, she would encourage Monsieur de Vendôme! She would indulge in a light flirtation. She would make people talk. Then perhaps Henry would take notice. There should be nothing more than a public flirtation; she had no desire for more; there was only one man she desired, and she knew there could be no other. But the only way she could endure her life was by hoping, by continuing to dream that one day he would turn to her.

She was interrupted by a knock on her door, and on bidding whoever was there to come in, a page entered with a letter for her.

She looked at it, and her heart beat faster, for she saw that it was in the handwriting of Nostradamus and had come from Provence, where he now was.

She dismissed the page and settled down to read what the astrologer had written.

She read and re-read the letter, and as she did so she was

conscious of a sense of foreboding. Nostradamus confessed that he had been hesitating about writing to her, but he had come to the conclusion that it was his duty to do so. He had been having very disturbing dreams lately and the central figures of these dreams were the King and Queen.

There was a dream he had had some years before, and he had been so impressed by it that, at the time, he had written it down. This dream now kept recurring. In the dream he saw two lions fighting; they fought twice. One of these lions was young and the other was older; the old lion was overcome, and the young lion gouged out the eye of the old lion, who suffered cruelly and died. That was the recurring dream.

Catherine, who believed fervently in the powers of her astrologers and their gift for seeing future events, pondered this deeply. Nostradamus hinted that the older of the two lions was the King, for the King's escutcheon bore the figure of a lion. Nostradamus was certain that the King was in some sort of danger. He begged the Queen to watch closely that no calamity might befall him.

Deep melancholy filled the Queen, for if Nostradamus had seen the old lion die, and the old lion represented Henry, and if this was a vision of the future, there was nothing on the earth that could save the King. If it was written in his destiny that the King must die, then would the King die.

Who was the young lion? Spain? Or England? Impossible. Neither could be called young. It might be that the lion was not Henry, but France. That was more likely. France was in danger. The first clash might be that disastrous outbreak of war which had resulted in the Siege of Saint-Quentin and had ended in the Treaty of Cateau-Cambrésis. There was no doubt that the signing of that treaty had been a great blow to France.

De Guise was against it, and he had said that in signing such a treaty the King had lost more in a day than he would have done in twenty years of reverses in the field. With a single stroke of the pen, the King had surrendered the Italian conquests of the last thirty years. This marriage of Elisabeth's and that of the King's sister Marguerite to the Duke of Savoy were the result. The King was weary of the Italian wars, and he was longing to get his good friend the Constable released from captivity. They had driven the English from French soil; let that satisfy France. Henry had declared that Italy was a snare which had entrapped French treasure and French lives since the days of his father and Charles V.

And yet . . . there was great mourning throughout France because of this treaty. It could be called the first clash, and from it the old lion had emerged licking his limbs.

What next, Catherine asked herself. Spain? Or England?

She said nothing of the dream of Nostradamus, but she felt gloom about her. Elisabeth was like a pale ghost going about the palace; she had lost her laughter, and her smile was a mockery of what it had once been.

Catherine saw a good deal of the Vidame de Chartres, allowed him special privileges, let him sit beside her during her *cercles*, listened with apparent pleasure to his gallantries.

But as preparations went on apace for the Spanish marriage, Catherine could not ward off the sense of impending doom.

From outlying districts people were coming into Paris. People were dancing in the streets and there were sounds of revelry all along the Seine. From the great buildings, flags and banners fluttered in the breeze – the flags of France and Spain.

It was a great day when Alva marched into the city, his five hundred men about him, clad in black, yellow, and red. The Parisians were disappointed in the Duke, though – a solemn man, all in black. On his right rode the Count Egmont, and on his left the Prince of Orange. These men were watched with suspicion. It was such a short time ago that they had led armies against Frenchmen. It was hard for bewildered men and women to understand the exigencies of government, the plots and plans of Kings.

A different wedding this from the last. Then it had been their own Dauphin and the loveliest girl they had ever seen; and the two were adorable, in love and so charming, having been brought up together, and having had eight years of happy companionship before they entered the married state. Now that was charming. That was romance. But this solemn Spaniard, all in black, to marry by proxy their little Princess! A man, whose hands were blood-stained with the blood of Frenchmen to repeat the marriage vows with a young girl because his master was too important to come to Paris and do so himself!

Philip of Spain! He was a bogey in the minds of many. Already twice married, it was said he had not been kind to the old Queen of England and had made her life wretched, had made her people hate her, and then had deserted her and left her lonely. The new Queen of England, a red-headed spitfire, had taken her revenge for her sister. She had plagued him, led him on, pretended to consider his advances, fooled him, snapped her fingers at him, and laughed, secure, she thought, in her island fortress. And so because Elizabeth of England would not have him, he would marry Elisabeth of France.

No, they could not feel that this was a happy wedding, as the Dauphin's had been.

And almost immediately after Elisabeth had her marriage by proxy, the King's sister Marguerite was to be married. The two weddings were to take place within the same month.

Well, for the people at least, any wedding was better than no wedding, for the revelries meant a release from tedium – a change from the monotonous business of getting a living.

There was a great cheering and throwing of hats in the air when the Princess appeared on the arm of her father. She was dressed in gleaming silver, and wore a large pear-shaped pearl on a fine gold chain, which was the gift of her husband-to-be. Catherine had not wished the girl to wear the pearl, for rumour had it that this pearl – which had its own grim history – brought grief to every possessor. But how could she defy etiquette by bidding the bride not to wear her bridegroom's gift?

The river sparkled gaily in the June sunshine; the bells began to ring, signifying to the crowds in the street that the marriage by proxy had taken place. Trumpets and bugles were blown as out of the Cathedral came the young girl, flushed now so that only those near her saw the wretchedness in her eyes.

'*Vive la Reine d'Espagne!*' shouted the crowds. Why, this meant peace with Spain. Peace . . . and no more war! It was easy therefore to forget the young girl who would have to leave her home and travel across the Pyrenees into Spain, to a strange land where she must live the rest of her life married to a man she had never seen, but of whose reputation for cold and calculating cruelty she had heard much.

But the bells were ringing; the people were shouting; and there was music in the streets.

Back to the Palais de Justice for the banquet; then on to the Louvre to dance and make merry.

Catherine watched the King dancing with his daughter. Shall I never grow away from this yearning? she asked herself. Shall I never overcome this passion and pain?

Henry seemed happier than he had for a long time. Peace ... for a time, he was thinking. An alliance with an old enemy – the best way of settling troubles. He was tired of the wars; to win Italy had been his father's dream; why should he have inherited that dream? In his reign it would be remembered that the English had been driven from the soil of France. That would wipe out the humiliation of Agincourt. He was happy. His little girl, Elisabeth? She was overawed. Who would not be at the prospect of marriage with the mighty Philip? He must try to make her understand how great was the honour done to her.

He spoke to her kindly and she lifted her leaden eyes to his face and tried to smile. She had always loved him dearly.

He had loved her also, as he loved all his children. He consoled himself: it was not for those of a royal house to choose their wives and husbands. Doubtless, Elisabeth would have wished to marry young de Guise. It was said that there was hardly a woman in France who would not. But she had to take Philip ... as he had had to take Catherine. One got over such tragedies.

They danced the solemn *passemento de España* in honour of the absent bridegroom. The Queen danced with the Duke of Alva.

But all the time Catherine danced, and later when she chatted gaily with the Vidame, she was conscious of evil near her.

It was not possible to forget the dream of Nostradamus.

The revelries continued. The Duke of Savoy had arrived in Paris for his marriage to the King's sister. He made a magnificent spectacle, surrounded by his men in their doublets of red satin, crimson shoes, and black velvet cloaks trimmed with gold lace.

There must be more lavish entertainments; the Duke of Savoy must not feel that his wedding was of less importance than that which had just taken place.

In the Rue Saint-Antoine, close to Les Tournelles, an arena had been set up for a tournament, and in her apartments in the palace Catherine sat listening to the hammering as the pavilion was erected; and as she listened her uneasiness was intensified. The thought came to her that these men were preparing a scaffold or stands for men and women to witness an execution rather than a tournament.

I have allowed this fellow Nostradamus to unnerve me, she thought.

It is nothing. Why, I only felt the gloom when I heard from him.

＊　＊　＊

It was the thirteenth of June and a day of glorious sunshine. Henry came to the Queen's apartment to conduct her to the tournament. He looked wonderfully handsome, she thought; he was glowing with the pleasure he expected this day to bring him. He was boyish in his love of sport, and there was little he enjoyed as much as a tournament.

He was impatient to be gone, but she had an overwhelming desire to detain him. Everything seemed more vivid to her today than it usually was. As he stood at the window looking down at the crowds, pictures of the past kept flashing in and out of her mind and she was filled with conflicting emotions. She was angry and jealous, tender and passionate in turns. She had to suppress an impulse to rush to him, to fling her arms about him, to beg him to kiss her, to make love to her as he never had, with that fervour and passion which she had seen him bestow on someone else. Tears were in her eyes. She thought of his standing at a window watching the agonising death of a tailor; then he had held her hand, and in comforting him, she felt she had been closer to him than ever before.

'Come,' he said, 'let us go down to the arena. They are impatient to start the tournament. Listen to the shouting. They are shouting for us.'

She went to him quickly and, taking his hand, clung to it. He looked at her in surprise.

'Henry,' she said, passionately, 'do not go . . . Stay here with me . . .'

He thought she was crazy. She laughed suddenly and dropped her hands.

'Catherine, I do not understand. Stay here? . . .'

'No!' she cried fiercely. 'You do not understand. When have you ever understood?'

He drew back. She was frightened suddenly. What a fool she was! Had she not at her age learned to control her passion?

'How foolish,' she said. 'I . . . I am not myself. I am worried . . . Henry, desperately worried.'

He looked shocked, but no longer bewildered. She was worried. This then was not one of those alarming demonstrations he had learned to dread in the old days.

She hesitated. But this was not the moment to tell him of the dream. She said: 'Our daughter . . . she looks so tragic. It worries me, Henry. It frightens me.'

There was real fear in her eyes, but it was not for Elisabeth. He believed it was, though, and he sought to soothe her.

'It will pass, Catherine. It is because she is such a child.'

'She looks so tragic.'

'But we know these things pass. They are not so bad as they seem.'

She was talking desperately; her one desire being to keep him with her. 'What do we know of Philip?'

'That he is King of Spain, that he is the most powerful man in Europe . . . that his match with our daughter is one of which we may be justly proud.'

She threw herself at him and clung to him. 'You do me so much good, Henry. You are so sound, so full of good sense.'

Her trembling hands stroked his coat, and, looking up at him, she saw that he was smiling benignly. He did not know that it was a passionate wife who clung to him. He thought it was an anxious mother.

'There, Catherine. Your anxiety is natural,' he said. 'But we must delay no longer. Let us go down to the arena. Can you not hear how impatient they are to start the tournament?'

He took her hand and led her from the room.

When they left the palace and the trumpets heralded their approach, the crowd cheered wildly.

'*Vive le Roi! Vive la Reine!*' shouted the people.

Yes, thought Catherine. Long live the King! Long live the Queen! And for the love of the Virgin let us get on with the tournament!

All through that day Catherine's uneasiness was with her. The sun shone hotly on the gallery in which she sat with the Duke

386

of Savoy and the ladies of the court, but not more hotly than her hatred of Diane, sitting close to her, white-haired and regal, as certain now of the King's affection as she ever was.

Henry was the hero of that day. That was right, thought Catherine, right and fitting. He had given a wonderful display, riding a spirited horse which had been a gift from the Duke of Savoy.

He had chosen for his opponent a young captain of the Scottish guard, a certain Montgomery, a noble-looking youth and a clever combatant.

Watching, there was one moment of terror for Catherine, for the young Scotsman all but threw the King from his horse. A ripple of horror ran through the crowd. Catherine leaned forward, holding her breath, praying. But the King had righted himself.

'Hurrah!' shouted the loyal crowd, for the King was now thrusting boldly at the young man. And then: 'Hurrah! *Vive le Roi!*' For the King had thrown the young Scotsman and victory was his.

Catherine felt that the palms of her hands were wet. How nervous she was! Why, it was nothing but sport. She listened to the joyous shouting of the crowd. It was fitting that the King of France should win in the fight with a foreigner.

Henry came to the gallery, and it was near Diane that he sat. While they took refreshments, he discussed the fight with the Duke of Savoy and the ladies, and, wishing to compliment young Montgomery on his fight, the King had him brought to the gallery.

'You did well,' said the King. 'You were indeed a worthy opponent.'

Montgomery bowed.

'Come,' said the King, 'take refreshment with us.'

Montgomery was honoured, he said, to take advantage of such a gracious suggestion.

Watching the young man, Henry said suddenly: 'Methinks that, had you been fighting with another, you might have thrown him.'

Montgomery flushed slightly. 'Nay, Sire, yours was the greater skill.'

This remark was applauded by the Duke and the ladies, but, watching the King and knowing him so well, Catherine was aware of the niggling doubt in his mind. It was very likely true. Young Montgomery was a splendid specimen of manhood; Henry was strong, but he had seen forty years.

Henry said: 'There should be no handicaps in true sport. The laurels that come by way of kingship cannot be worn with dignity.'

Montgomery did not know what to answer to this, and the King immediately announced that he wished to break another lance before sunset and that Captain Montgomery should be his opponent.

'Sire,' said the Duke of Savoy, 'the day is hot and you have acquitted yourself with honour. Why not put off the breaking of this lance until tomorrow?'

'I am impatient,' smiled Henry, 'to face this young man once more. I cannot wait until tomorrow. My people will be delighted to see me in action again today. They are a good and loyal crowd and it is my duty to serve them.'

The young Scotsman was anxious. He was desperately afraid that he might make himself unpopular by proving himself the victor. He was young; the King was ageing; it was a delicate matter.

He made an attempt to excuse himself, but this attempt made the King more sure than ever, that, had the young man wished, he could have unseated him.

'Come,' said Henry, with some impatience, 'and do your best.'

There was no gainsaying the King's command. The two rode out together.

The delighted crowd cheered anew; and then, in that sudden breathless silence when the two men faced each other, lances raised, a young boy in one of the lower galleries pushed himself forward and, white of face and strained of eye, shouted in a loud, ringing voice: 'Sire, do not fight!'

There was a hush over the vast assembly. Then someone seized the boy and hustled him away. But Catherine, sensing now that disaster was upon her, rose in her seat. She swayed dizzily. Diane was beside her, supporting her.

'*Madame la Reine* is feeling ill,' she heard Diane say. 'Pray help me . . .'

Catherine was helped back to her seat. It was too late to do anything now, she knew. The combat had started, and in a few seconds it was all over.

Montgomery had struck the King on the gorget a little below his visor; the Scotsman's lance was shattered, the stump slid upwards raising the King's visor, and the splinter entered the King's right eye.

Henry, striving to suppress his groans, tried to lift his lance and failed. There was a shocked stillness everywhere while he fell forward.

In a second, his gentlemen had reached him and seized his swaying body; they were stripping him of his armour.

Catherine, standing now, straining to see the face that she

loved, caught a glimpse of it covered in blood, while Henry fell fainting into the arms of his men.

Beside Catherine stood Diane, her fingers clutching the black-and-white satin of her skirt, and the white of her gown was not whiter than her face.

The King was dying, for the steel had entered his eye, and there was nothing that could be done. All the great doctors, surgeons and apothecaries, all the learned men of France were at his bedside. Philip of Spain sent his celebrated surgeon, André Vésale. But nothing could save the King.

He lay tossing in agony while violent fever overtook him. He spoke of one thing only. No blame for this should be attached to Montgomery. That was his urgent wish. Already people were saying that the young man was a Protestant and that he had been primed to do this; but the King, in his agony, was determined that all should remember how the boy had had no wish to fight, and that he must be told not to grieve, as he had but obeyed the King.

Consciousness eluded Henry. He lay silent and could not be revived with rose-water and vinegar.

Paris had changed from a city of joy to one of mourning whilst its people stood about near Les Tournelles waiting for news. But though the doctors dressed the wound and were even able to remove some splinters, though they purged the King with rhubarb and camomile, and bled him, still they could not save his life.

The days passed and with them passed the King's agony; for he remained in a stupor from which none could rouse him.

The Queen was desolate, pacing up and down her apartments, having the children brought to her, embracing them all in turn, sending them away that she might weep alone.

Oh my darling, she thought. I have lost you all these years to her; now am I to lose you to death?

How cruel was life! She had watched Diane grow older, and she had believed her own day must come; but now death was threatening to take him, and she knew it would succeed, for such things were revealed to her. She lay on her bed and thought of him as she had first seen him, a shy and sullen boy, preparing to hate her; she thought of his coming to her, at Diane's command, of the years of suppressed passion, of the hope that had waxed and waned through the long tormented years.

And what of Diane?

Catherine laughed suddenly and bitterly as she clenched and unclenched her long white fingers.

Ah, Madame, she thought, you were everything to him. Now you have lost everything.

Reports were constantly brought to her by people who thought to cheer her. 'The King is a little better. He seems to have fallen into a quietness.' Better? She knew, with that curious instinct of hers, that he could not recover.

She sent an imperious message to Diane. The crown jewels were to be returned to her at once; and with them all the presents that Henry had given her. 'Hold nothing back,' ran the Queen's revealing message, 'for I have noted well each one.'

When this message was taken to Diane, she lifted her grief-stricken face to the messenger and smiled bitterly. She was realising now that she had never really known the Queen.

There were a few at court who secretly spoke of Catherine as Madame Serpent; Diane could now believe that those people understood Henry's widow better than she had done.

'Is the King dead, then, that I am treated thus?' she asked.

'No, Madame,' she was told, 'but it is believed he can only linger a little longer.'

Diane stood up and answered imperiously: 'So long as an inch of life remains to him I desire my enemies to know that I fear them not, and that, as long as he is alive, I shall not obey them. But, when he is dead, I do not wish to survive him, and all the bitternesses which they may be able to inflict upon me will be only sweets in comparison with my loss. And so, whether my King be alive or dead, I do not fear my enemies.'

When these words were repeated to her, Catherine knew that once more her enemy had the better of her. In love, she had acted carelessly again.

She rocked herself to and fro in her misery. Never to see him again. Never to watch him jealously as he bent his head to listen to Diane. There could never be another man for Catherine. Love was dead with Henry, and her passion would be buried in the tomb with him.

Mary Stuart, weeping for her father-in-law, could not keep the shine of expectancy out of her eyes. In a few days she would be the Queen of France. Young Francis, who had loved his father dearly, was being so courted now by the de Guises, was being so prepared for kingship by his clever little Mary, that he too felt excitement mingling with his sorrow.

It will be the de Guises who will rule France now, not the Queen-Mother! thought Catherine in the midst of her grief, and the realisation was brought home to her that she desired power almost as much as she had desired her husband. I do not forget that this I owe to Mary Stuart!

She fell to fresh weeping.

Henry, come back to me. Give me a chance. Diane grows old, and I am not so old. I have never known the true love of a man, and if you leave me now I never shall.

Word went through the palace: 'The Queen is prostrate in her grief.'

The body of the King was embalmed and laid in a leaden coffin. With great solemnity and lamentation, it was borne to Notre Dame, and from there to Saint-Denis, with a great company of all the highest in the land.

The Cardinal of Lorraine officiated; he it was who pronounced the funeral oration as the coffin was lowered into the vault.

Montmorency broke his baton and threw its fragments over the coffin, whereupon the four officials did likewise. It was a touching scene.

And when it was done, the ceremonial cry rang out: *'Le Roi est mort. Vive le Roi François!'*

Then the trumpets sounded. The ceremony was over. King Henry was in his grave, and sickly, pock-marked Francis was the King of France.

The walls and floors of Catherine's apartments were covered in black. Her bed and her altar were also in the same sombre covering. Only two wax tapers burned, and she herself was wrapped from head to foot in a black veil which covered her plain black gown.

She was truly prostrate with grief. It had come upon her so suddenly. She had had some premonition of evil, it was true, but she had not believed it could be the death of Henry.

She had loved him completely; and now there was nothing left to her but revenge.

Diane! *Lex talionis!* An eye for an eye; a tooth for a tooth.

For nearly thirty years, Madame, I have suffered humiliation. I have watched you through a hole in the floor with a man for whom I longed. I have seen the citizens of Lyons kiss your hand before mine. I have heard you called the Queen of France when that title was mine. Madame, that is now changed. Your day is done, and out of misery and sorrow is mine born.

She started up from her black-covered bed and went to her bureau; she unlocked the secret drawer.

Let her death be long and lingering. Let there be much pain, for there must be long agony to compensate for the years of misery.

'He was beginning to like me,' she whispered. 'I had pleased him at the time of Saint-Quentin. He appeared at my *cercle*. In time I would have won him from the ageing widow. And now I have lost all . . . and nothing is left to me but revenge.'

Diane had said that she did not fear her enemies, that any bitterness that might be inflicted on her would be sweet compared with her loss. Perhaps the greater punishment would be to let her live, for if she died suddenly and of poison, people would say: 'The Queen-Mother has done this.'

Ah, had she planned cautiously in those early days of her passion, she might have won her husband long ere this. But her love had weakened her. Now that she had lost her love, she could plan with caution.

She flung herself on to her bed and wept. Her women thought her grief would drive her mad, so they sent in one who they thought could comfort her.

Little Henry stared at her with wondering eyes; she held out her arms and he ran into them. She took his face in her hands and kissed him. Then she smiled slowly, reminding herself that she had someone left to love.

She had this boy – this other Henry – and she had France. She had the hope of gaining power, as once she had had the hope of gaining Henry's love.

Diane had ruled France through Catherine's husband. Why should not Catherine rule France through her sons?

Tears began to flow down her pallid cheeks, and the little boy took a perfumed handkerchief from his belt and kneeled on her lap to wipe them away.

❈ ❈ ❈

The Vidame de Chartres had an arrogant air; yet he was tender in his manner to the Queen-Mother.

Catherine went about the court in her deep mourning – sad, yet sly, seeming wrapped in melancholy, yet missing nothing.

She had restrained herself over this matter of Diane. She had turned from her poison-closet, realising that the woman who had been the shining light of the court for so long could be more wretched in exile than in death. Let her return her gifts and jewels; let her make a present of the Château de Chenonceaux to the Queen, in exchange for which the Queen would magnanimously give her the Château de Chaumont, which she had always considered to be unlucky, and then exile her to Anet. The Queen-Mother must not forget that Diane was related to the Guises and that, although through the death of the King she could no longer be of great use to them, they would not wish to see her poisoned. Moreover, this family which feigned to show great respect for Catherine, who, on account of Francis' age, was practically Regent, would not hesitate to accuse her if their once-powerful relative died suddenly and mysteriously.

Catherine found solace in her grief by making plans for a glorious future. She looked about her, wondering how she could use people for her own advancement; she was working now for power, not for love; and thus she could work more calmly.

Her greatest enemies were the Guises, for they were preparing now to rule the country through the young King and Queen.

She smiled on the gallant Vidame; she had thought that, since she had used him in an attempt to provoke Henry's jealousy, he would no longer be of use to her; but this was not so. The young man was ambitious; he was a Bourbon, and the Bourbons were the natural enemies of the Guises.

Why should not the Queen-Mother secretly make plans with the House of Bourbon to outwit the House of Guise? Once the Guises were removed from power, nothing stood between the young King and Queen and the Queen-Mother. As for Mary Stuart, she was a child; she could be managed to Catherine's satisfaction if her scheming uncles were removed.

She permitted the Vidame to visit her secretly, and told him something of her plans.

'I wish you,' she said, 'to take letters from me to the Prince of Condé.'

The Vidame's eyes were full of speculation then, for Condé was the head of the House of Bourbon, and he knew what this meant.

'I will serve you with my life,' he declared, kissing Catherine's hand, 'and, serving you, shall hope for some reward.'

Catherine answered: 'Queens are not asked for rewards, Monsieur.'

'Madame,' he said, 'I do not ask you as a Queen, but as a woman.'

She smiled and her smile held some promise. She eagerly awaited his return with the answers to her letters.

But it was not the Vidame who came to her.

A page was brought into her presence to tell her that the Duc de Guise was asking to be admitted immediately; she gave permission that he should be sent to her.

The candles in their sconces flickered as the door opened and shut behind the man. There he stood – arrogant, virile, with a smile on his hideously scarred face.

'I crave your Majesty's pardon for the intrusion,' he said. 'But . . . there is treason abroad.'

She studied him calmly, her face blank.

'The Vidame de Chartres has been arrested.'

'Is that so? Why is this?'

'Treasonable documents have been found on his person, Madame.'

'What documents?'

'Letters to the Prince of Condé.'

'A plot?' said Catherine.

'It is feared so, Madame. He is to be sent to the Bastille.'

'I gave no orders that this should be done,' she answered haughtily.

Le Balafré bowed low. 'Madame, it was thought to save you trouble. I have the order for his arrest here. It is signed by the King.'

She nodded.

She was defeated. She knew that her battle with the Guises would be as long and as arduous as her battle with Diane. Power was no easier to win than love.

Heavily cloaked, cunningly disguised, Catherine hurried through the streets of Paris to the sombre building of the Bastille.

It was dusk, and she had chosen this hour; for it was imperative that she be not recognised. She shuddered as she looked up at the dark towers and the ramparts with their cannon.

A cloaked figure that had seemed part of the thick wall moved towards her, and she knew she was recognised, by the reverent tone of the man's voice.

'Madame, all is ready.'

He led the way through a small door into a dark corridor, up a flight of stairs, along more corridors. Catherine smelt the odour indigenous to prisons – damp, age, slime, sweat, blood, death.

Below her were hideous dungeons where men fought for their lives with the rats that shared their cells; close to her were the *oubliettes* where men and women lay forgotten, and the *calottes* where human beings were incarcerated to endure extreme cold in winter and suffocating heat in summer, and where it was not possible to stand upright; somewhere in this terrible place was the *Salle de la Question* where men and women suffered the water torture or the horrors of the Boot. But the Vidame de Chartres was not housed in *oubliette* nor *calotte*; his sojourn in the Bastille had been a comparatively comfortable one, for he had powerful friends; moreover, he had not hesitated to point out that the Queen-Mother herself was a particularly dear friend.

Tomorrow the Vidame was to be released; it was for this reason that Catherine had arranged to visit him.

Her guide had halted before a heavy door; this he unlocked; beyond it was another door which he also unlocked.

'Enter, Madame,' he said. 'I will wait outside. It will be well if you do not stay more than fifteen minutes. There may be a jailor here after that, and your presence would be difficult to explain.'

'I understand,' said Catherine.

The Vidame rose as she entered his cell. He came swiftly towards her and, taking her hand, kissed it fervently.

She studied his face in the faint light that came through the barred window. The window was small and it was growing dark outside so that it was not easy to see him, yet she fancied that three months in prison had left their mark upon him.

'It was good of you to come . . . Catherine,' he said.

She flinched a little at the use of her Christian name, but he did not notice that.

'You are to be released tomorrow,' she told him.

'Tomorrow!' His voice was hysterical with joy. 'And you . . . my Queen . . . have done this for me.' He was on his knees; he took her hand again and she felt his tears fall on it.

How arrogant he was! He had had great success with

women; he believed himself to be irresistible to all women; he did not know that Catherine de' Medici was no ordinary woman. He could not guess that she had but used him in the hope of arousing jealousy in her husband, that when he had bungled the simple matter of carrying letters to his powerful relative she had no further use for him; that this release of his was yet another move of the Guises, to set him free that they might watch him and catch him again and perhaps others with him; he did not guess that the last thing the Queen-Mother wanted was his release.

She stood back, pressed against the cold stone wall.

He said in a whisper: 'How did you get in?'

She answered: 'There are many who serve me.'

'Yes,' he whispered slowly. 'Yes. I see.'

'You will be watched when you come out,' she said rapidly. 'It will be well for you to leave France.'

He came close to her so that she could feel his breath on her cheek. 'Leave France! Leave . . . you! Though you asked me to do that, I could not.'

'It is the wise thing to do,' she said.

She heard his quick intake of breath. 'Can it be that you would wish to be rid of me?' There was in his voice a desperate note; she understood; he was determined not to be banished. He was prepared to run risks. Why not? He was an ambitious man. One thing he was not prepared for, and that was exile.

'They will be suspicious of you,' she said. 'They will have you watched.'

'You cannot think that I am afraid of danger?'

'I think you would be wise to get away. Go to Italy.'

'I feel my life is here . . . beside you . . . serving you . . .'

She drew closer to the wall, but he came closer too.

'There is much to be done,' he said. 'The King is young, and is your son. The little Queen . . . she is but a child. You and I . . . with others to help us, could get the Protestants to rise against these upstart Guises. I have news. I have not been idle in here. I have laid deep plans. The Protestants are straining at the leash. They but await a leader.'

'And you will be that leader?' she said, her voice expressionless.

'You, Catherine, are the Regent of France. It is for you to rule this country.'

'And you . . . would work for me . . . serve me . . . no matter how dangerous the work?'

'To serve you is the only course I would follow. You dare not send me from you. The court has seen our deep and tender friendship. Why, Catherine, our names have been linked. I could tell many secrets . . .'

She laughed. 'We have been nothing but friends.'

'Who would believe that? Ah, you see how devoted I am. You must, for the sake of honour, keep me at your side, for I declare, so deep in love am I, that I would let nothing stand in the way of keeping at your side.'

'Listen to me now,' she said, 'for I dare stay no longer. Tomorrow you will be released. We will meet, but secretly. Depend upon it, the spies of the de Guises will be watching you. Come, if you can, at this hour to the house of the brothers Ruggieri. You know it? It is close to the river.'

'At this hour,' he repeated. And then: 'Yes, I know the house.'

'I will be waiting, and we will talk of the future over a goblet of good Italian wine.'

He would have kissed her lips, but haughtily she held out her hand.

He bowed low, and, turning, she hurried out of the cell.

* ✢ *

Catherine sat in her room. She had asked that she might be quite alone. Looking in her mirror, she saw a woman, fattening, coarsening, who had never been really beautiful even in her youth; thick, pallid skin, sly mouth, and those flashing dark eyes.

This was an important day in her life. It was three months since she had lost her love, but that tragedy was behind her now. She must look to the future. Last evening, at dusk, she had gone to the house near the river, and there she had met that ambitious young man who wished to become her lover. He had great plans for himself, this Vidame de Chartres.

She had talked to him calmly, kindly, and affectionately over a goblet of wine.

Together they had planned to put down the mighty Guises. They had arranged to meet again, this night.

The sly mouth smiled, for Catherine realised that the ache in her heart was growing less acute. There was so much work to be done. Her eyes went to the cabinet in the corner of the room. None but herself knew the secrets of that cabinet. In it lurked death, to be administered to the enemies of Catherine de' Medici.

For years she had planned the murder of Diane; but now that she was calm, she could see that it would be pointless to murder Diane. Yet, all those years when she had added secret after secret to her cabinet, she had thought of murder; and now murder was a part of her life, a servant, ready at her command, waiting for that moment when it could work for her.

She was not happy as she could have been with the love of Henry, but she was stimulated. She knew that a bitter battle was before her, but she also knew the strength of her armour.

She was going to fight the seemingly all-powerful de Guises. Sickly Francis was on the throne. How long could he live? Then it would be the turn of Charles. He was but a boy yet, and his upbringing was in the hands of his mother. She would get an Italian tutor for him. A face leaped to her mind. Yes, she knew the tutor she would get; and Charles should be taught a way of life that some might call unnatural. He was not strong; he was peevish . . . but pliable. She did not wish Charles to marry – but if he did, he must not have children. While Charles was on the throne, his mother would rule; and after Charles would come beloved Henry, whose pleasure it would be to serve his mother, as it would be hers to serve him.

Power was beckoning her, and she would have to fight for it with all her craft and cunning, in all the devious ways she had learned in a lifetime of humiliation. She would deeply relish such a fight.

Madalenna was knocking at the door.

'Come in.'

Madalenna's eyes were wide, her face pale.

'You have something to tell me, Madalenna?'

'Terrible news, Madame.'

'Of whom?'

'Madame, the Vidame de Chartres was released from the Bastille yesterday . . .'

'Is that such terrible news?'

'Oh, Madame . . . you have not heard. He died . . . last night.

He had been out in the city . . . and when he returned, he was ill . . . violently ill. He died at midnight.'

Madalenna looked fearfully at her mistress, who was holding a kerchief to her eyes.

'Madame,' stammered Madalenna, 'I wish to offer . . . my . . . my deep sympathy.'

Catherine answered from the depth of the kerchief: 'You may go, Madalenna. Leave me . . . leave me . . .'

As the door shut on Madalenna, Catherine thrust the kerchief into her mouth to stifle the gusty laughter which was shaking her.

Madalenna's sympathy! Perhaps others in this palace would be sorry for a woman whom they believed to have lost her lover?

Poor Vidame, she thought. This is the end of your flirtation with a Queen; it is also the end of the brilliant career you planned for yourself. You have been the first to learn that it is unwise to ignore the wishes of Catherine de' Medici.

She was exultant. Thoughts of murder had haunted her for so long; now she would be their master. She understood much now. The future, brilliant and powerful, stretched out before her; and she was free to take what she wanted. She had been the victim of her emotions – hot-blooded, impetuous, making so many mistakes. She had been Catherine de' Medici in love.

But now she was free. It was the end of Catherine de' Medici in love.

�֎ Acknowledgements ✣

In the work of research which was necessary when writing this book, I have been led from one source to another, old and new; and I wish to acknowledge, with grateful thanks, the guidance I have received from the undermentioned works:

Guizot's *History of France*
Louis Battifol's *Century of the Renaissance*
Hudson's *France*
Tighe Hopkin's *Dungeons of Old Paris*
Francis Watson's *Life and Times of Catherine de' Medici*
Colonel F. Young's *The Medici*
T. A. Trollope's *Girlhood of Catherine de' Medici*
Edith Sichel's *Catherine de' Medici*
H. Noel Williams' *Henri*

**Order further Jean Plaidy titles
from your local bookshop, or have them delivered
direct to your door by Bookpost**

☐	**Uneasy Lies the Head**	0 09 949248 2	£6.99
☐	**Katharine, the Virgin Widow**	0 09 949314 4	£6.99
☐	**The Shadow of the Pomegranate**	0 09 949315 2	£6.99
☐	**The King's Secret Matter**	0 09 949316 0	£6.99
☐	**The Italian Woman**	0 09 949318 7	£6.99
☐	**Queen Jezebel**	0 09 949319 5	£6.99

Free post and packing

Overseas customers allow £2 per paperback

Phone: 01624 677237

Post: Random House Books
c/o Bookpost, PO Box 29, Douglas, Isle of Man IM99 1BQ

Fax: 01624 670923

email: bookshop@enterprise.net

Cheques (payable to Bookpost) and credit cards accepted

Prices and availability subject to change without notice.
Allow 28 days for delivery.
When placing your order, please state if you do not wish to receive any
additional information.

www.randomhouse.co.uk/arrowbooks

CIRCULATING STOCK ███████ PUBLIC LIBRARIES
BLOCK LOAN
WD 31-3-14